THE COMPLETE ACTION STORIES

ALSO BY ROBERT E. HOWARD

Graveyard Rats and Other Stories
Waterfront Fists

THE COMPLETE ACTION STORIES

ROBERT E. HOWARD

EDITED BY AND WITH
AN INTRODUCTION BY PAUL HERMAN

WILDSIDE PRESS

To Dena, Brandon and Connor, who tolerate my "little projects."

"The TNT Punch" appeared in the January 1931 issue. "The Sign of the Snake" appeared in the June 1931 issue. "Blow the Chinks Down!" appeared in the October 1931 issue. "Breed of Battle" appeared in the November 1931 issue. "Dark Shanghai" appeared in the January 1932 issue. "Mountain Man" appeared in the March-April 1934 issue. "Guns of the Mountains" appeared in the May-June 1934 issue. "The Scalp Hunter" appeared in the August 1934 issue. "A Gent from Bear Creek" appeared in the October 1934 issue. "The Road to Bear Creek" appeared in the December 1934 issue. "The Haunted Mountain" appeared in the February 1935 issue. "War on Bear Creek" appeared in the April 1935 issue. "The Feud Buster" appeared in the June 1935 issue. "Cupid from Bear Creek" appeared in the August 1935 issue. "The Riot at Cougar Paw" appeared in the October 1935 issue. "The Apache Mountain War" appeared in the December 1935 issue. "Pilgrims to the Pecos" appeared in the February 1936 issue. "Pistol Politics" appeared in the April 1936 issue. "Evil Deeds at Red Cougar" appeared in the June 1936 issue. "High Horse Rampage" appeared in the August 1936 issue. "No Cowherders Wanted" appeared in the September 1936 issue. "The Conquerin' Hero of the Humbolts" appeared in the October 1936 issue. "Sharp's Gun Serenade" appeared in the January 1937 issue.

Published by:

Wildside Press
P.O. Box 301
Holicong, PA 18928-0301 USA
www.wildsidepress.com

CONTENTS

INTRODUCTION

CONAN IS THE most famous character ever created by Texas author Robert E. Howard. Through the last few years of his life, REH wrote 21 complete Conan stories, and five partial stories. Seventeen of these were successfully sold to *Weird Tales*. Conan was genre-busting, and while some may consider REH's "The Shadow Kingdom" as the first true sword-and-sorcery story, it was the Conan stories that changed the literary world. While REH may have experimented with Kull, he hit his natural stride with Conan.

One truism of REH, he was not a one-trick pony. He wrote for a number of different pulps, in all sorts of genres. Being a big fan of boxing, and indeed being an accomplished boxer himself down at the local ice house, it was natural for REH to begin writing for Fiction House's *Fight Magazine* in 1929. The editor for Fiction House, Jack Byrne, liked REH's material, and kept asking for more. And unlike *Weird Tales*, Fiction House was much more timely about payment. So when Jack Byrne asked for more stories to publish in another Fiction House magazine, *Action Stories*, REH was more than happy to comply.

In January 1931, REH debuted in *Action Stories* with another boxing yarn. These were more in the line of Sailor Steve Costigan stories, about a not-very-bright tramp sailor going from port to port, prize-fighting and getting fooled constantly. It also allowed REH to try some similar boxing stories with different characters, though Jack Byrne apparently turned at least a couple of them back into Sailor Steve Costigan stories. None of the *Action Stories* boxing tales have ever seen mainstream reprinting. "Blow the Chinks Down!" and "Dark Shanghai" and are being presented here in English for the first time since their original pulp appearance. The remaining three boxing stories have generally only been available in small run chapbook or fanzine publications, and are being presented in this format here for the first time.

A couple years after REH created Conan, he created another genre-busting character and story type for *Action Stories*. The character is Breckinridge Elkins, and the story type, is, well, different. It still amazes me that no one has ever come up with a good title for the genre that REH created with this character. It has elements of humor, tall tales, and westerns (REH himself referred to these stories as "Westerns"), but still uses a character of superior violence. These stories have much in common with the Conan stories. Breck Elkins is a superior physical fighter, master of all weapons he works with, incredibly fast and strong, master of fighting multiple foes at once, using whatever he can lay his hands on. Breck's strength and knack for destroying property and waves of foes surpasses all other REH heroes. Indeed, having Conan or Breck simply fighting another human one-on-one is just not a fight. The opponents must be beasts, monsters, waves of enemies, or other superior humans. They are both barbarians in the civilizations they wander through. And as Conan had developed from Kull, so Breck Elkins had developed from Sailor Steve Costigan. Indeed, REH liked to use transition stories to shift from one character to the next. From Kull to Conan, it was "The Phoenix on the Sword," in which Conan is a barbarian king like Kull. For Breck Elkins, it is "Mountain Man," a story that involves our Not-Too-Bright Super-Hillbilly getting into a boxing match. As with Conan, REH truly hit his stride with the creation of Breck Elkins. And as with Conan, REH wrote over 20 Breck Elkins stories. He also wrote a Breck Elkins novel for a British publisher by combining the first nine Breck Elkins stories from *Action Stories*, reordering and rewriting them slightly to add a common thread, and adding some additional material. Eighteen Breck Elkins stories first appeared in *Action Stories*. The later nine have been reprinted in the Grant hardback editions of *Pride of Bear Creek* and *Mayhem on Bear Creek*, as well as the subsequent rare Ace paperback *Heroes of Bear Creek* (though *all* italics were removed from these publications, per Don Grant's choice). The first nine Breck Elkins stories in this volume have never been reprinted except in one newspaper and one chapbook.

Breck Elkins stories are a very different type of story in many respects, and allowed REH to explore a number of personal topics that he could not address elsewhere. Most REH barbaric heroes have no family to speak of, at most vaguely referenced in a sentence. But the Breck Elkins stories are all about family and friends, and Breck interacting with them. So here you get to see Breck dealing with his father, aunts, uncles, cousins, sisters, and brothers (though *never* his mother, hmmm). Breck trying to help out friends constantly gets him in trouble. You also get to see REH deal with topics more direct to his life. Two of the most interesting topics are falling in love, especially with a schoolteacher (REH's One True Love was Novalyne Price Ellis, a schoolteacher he dated but then later broke up with), and suicide. Indeed, the last story, Sharp's Gun Serenade, is chilling to read, and makes one wander if the secondary character of Jack Sprague is suppose to be REH himself, waiting to be saved from suicide by the schoolteacher's love, as Jack was in the story.

All stories in this book are being presented in their original order as published. They include all 23 stories that appeared in *Action Stories* from 1931 to 1937. The artwork is that which originally appeared with each story in *Action Stories*. Certainly some interesting interpretations of Breckinridge Elkins.

As is typical of writings of this era, some word usage and attitudes are not PC, fair warning.

I have tried to minimize the editing, and leave the works as much as possible as they first appeared. I have cleaned up obvious typos, of which there were few, and tried to create some consistency from inconsistent usages and words. The biggest change may be the consistent italicizing of the sound effect words, such as *bam, crack, smash*, etc., something that was not handled consistently in the original publications.

REH also had a real problem with compound words. Though I think the average person would never notice in reading the stories, REH quite often got the structure wrong (one word, two words, or hyphenated). I saw the same types of errors in *The Yellow Jacket* pieces, and do not know if it was intentional or not, but I doubt it was. More likely he considered himself a good speller, and didn't bother to look up every word, he was paid by the word and had to get stories done and out, and then later no one else caught it in the editing. I have only changed those that are most readily apparent, or that he changed from one story to the next, to create consistency in this volume.

I hope you enjoy this book. I think there is a wealth of insight into REH to be gained by reading these stories. Any comments, corrections or suggestions for later printings are welcome, at paul.herman@halliburton.com.

—Paul Herman

COMMENTS ON THE WILDSIDE PRESS EDITION

Finally, all these stories are now available in hardback and readily obtainable from the usual sources, as all REH should be. We can only hope the trend will continue.

THE TNT PUNCH

THE FIRST THING THAT happened in Cape Town, my white bulldog Mike bit a policeman and I had to come across with a fine of ten dollars, to pay for the cop's britches. That left me busted, not more'n an hour after the *Sea Girl* docked.

The next thing who should I come on to but Shifty Kerren, manager of Kid Delrano, and the crookedest leather-pilot which ever swiped the gate receipts. I favored this worthy with a hearty scowl, but he had the everlasting nerve to smile welcomingly and hold out the glad hand.

"Well, well! If it ain't Steve Costigan! Howdy, Steve!" said the infamous hypocrite. "Glad to see you. Boy, you're lookin' fine! Got good old Mike with you, I see. Nice dawg."

He leaned over to pat him.

"Grrrrrr!" said good old Mike, fixing for to chaw his hand. I pushed Mike away with my foot and said to Shifty, I said: "A big nerve you got, tryin' to fraternize with me, after the way you squawked and whooped the last time I seen you, and called me a dub and all."

"Now, now, Steve!" said Shifty. "Don't be foolish and go holdin' no grudge. It's all in the way of business, you know. I allus did like you, Steve."

"Gaaahh!" I responded ungraciously. I didn't have no wish to hobnob none with him, though I figgered I was safe enough, being as I was broke anyway.

I've fought that palooka of his twice. The first time he outpointed me in a ten-round bout in Seattle, but didn't hurt me none, him being a classy boxer but kinda shy on the punch.

Next time we met in a Frisco ring, scheduled for fifteen frames. Kid Delrano give me a proper shellacking for ten rounds, then punched hisself out in a vain attempt to stop me, and blowed up. I had him on the canvas in the eleventh and again in the twelfth and with the fourteenth a minute to go, I rammed a right to the wrist in his solar plexus that put him down again. He had sense enough left to grab his groin and writhe around.

And Shifty jumped up and down and yelled: "Foul!" so loud the referee got scared and rattled and disqualified me. I swear it wasn't no foul. I landed solid above the belt line. But I officially lost the decision and it kinda rankled.

SO NOW I GLOWERED at Shifty and said: "What you want of me?"

"Steve," said Shifty, putting his hand on my shoulder in the old comradely way his kind has when they figger on putting the skids under you, "I know you got a heart of gold! You wouldn't leave no feller countryman in the toils, would you? Naw! Of course you wouldn't! Not good old Steve. Well, listen, me and the Kid is in a jam. We're broke—and the Kid's in jail.

"We got a raw deal when we come here. These Britishers went and disqualified the Kid for merely bitin' one of their ham-and-eggers. The Kid didn't mean nothin' by it. He's just kinda excitable thataway."

"Yeah, I know," I growled. "I got a scar on my neck now from the rat's fangs. He got excitable with me, too."

"Well," said Shifty hurriedly, "they won't let us fight here now, and we figgered on movin' upcountry into Johannesburg. Young Hilan is tourin' South Africa and we can get a fight with him there. His manager—er, I mean a promoter there—sent us tickets, but the Kid's in jail. They won't let him out unless we pay a fine of six pounds. That's thirty dollars, you know. And we're broke.

"Steve," went on Shifty, waxing eloquent, "I appeals to your national pride! Here's the Kid, a American like yourself, pent up in durance vile, and for no more reason than for just takin' up for his own country—"

"Huh!" I perked up my ears. "How's that?"

"Well, he blows into a pub where three British sailors makes slanderous remarks about American ships and seamen. Well, you know the Kid—just a big, free-hearted, impulsive boy, and terrible proud of his country, like a man should be. He ain't no sailor, of course, but them remarks was a insult to his countrymen and he wades in. He gives them limeys a proper drubbin' but here comes a host of cops which hauls him before the local magistrate which hands him a fine we can't pay.

"Think, Steve!" orated Shifty. "There's the Kid, with thousands of admirin' fans back in the States waitin' and watchin' for his triumphal return to the land of the free and the home of the brave. And here's him, wastin' his young manhood in a stone dungeon, bein' fed on bread and water and maybe beat up by the jailers, merely for standin' up for his own flag and nation. For defendin' the honor of American sailors, mind you, of which you is one. I'm askin' you, Steve, be you goin' to stand by and let a feller countryman languish in the 'thrallin' chains of British tyranny?"

"Not by a long ways!" said I, all my patriotism roused and roaring. "Let bygones be bygones!" I said.

It's a kind of unwritten law among sailors ashore that they should stand by their own kind. A kind of waterfront law, I might say.

"I ain't fought limeys all over the world to let an American be given the works by 'em now," I said. "I ain't got a cent, Shifty, but I'm goin' to get some dough.

"Meet me at the American Seamen's Bar in three hours. I'll have the dough for the Kid's fine or I'll know the reason why.

"You understand, I ain't doin' this altogether for the Kid. I still intends to punch his block off some day. But he's an American and so am I, and I reckon I ain't so small that I'll let personal grudges stand in the way of helpin' a countryman in a foreign land."

"Spoken like a man, Steve!" applauded Shifty, and me and Mike hustled away.

A short, fast walk brung us to a building on the waterfront which had a sign saying: "The South African Sports Arena." This was all lit up and yells was coming forth by which I knowed fights was going on inside.

The ticket shark told me the main bout had just begun. I told him to send me the promoter, "Bulawayo" Hurley, which I'd fought for of yore, and he told me that Bulawayo was in his office, which was a small room next to the ticket booth. So I went in and seen Bulawayo talking to a tall, lean gent the sight of which made my neck hair bristle.

"Hey, Bulawayo," said I, ignoring the other mutt and coming direct to the point, "I want a fight. I want to fight tonight—right now. Have you got anybody you'll throw in with me, or if not willya let me get up in your ring and challenge the house for a purse to be made up by the crowd?"

"By a strange coincidence," said Bulawayo, pulling his big mustache, "here's Bucko Brent askin' me the same blightin' thing."

Me and Bucko gazed at each other with hearty disapproval. I'd had dealings with this thug before. In fact, I built a good part of my reputation as a bucko-breaker on his lanky frame. A bucko, as you likely know, is a hard-case mate, who punches his crew around. Brent was all that and more. Ashore he was a prize-fighter, same as me.

Quite a few years ago I was fool enough to ship as A.B. on the *Elinor,* which he was mate of then. He's an Australian and the *Elinor* was an Australian ship. Australian ships is usually good crafts to sign up with, but this here *Elinor* was a exception. Her cap'n was a relic of the old hellship days, and her mates was natural-born bullies. Brent especially, as his nickname of "Bucko" shows. But I was broke and wanted to get to Makassar to meet the *Sea Girl* there, so I shipped aboard the *Elinor* at Bristol.

Brent started ragging me before we weighed anchor.

Well, I stood his hazing for a few days and then I got plenty and we went together. We fought the biggest part of one watch, all over the ship from the mizzen cross trees to the bowsprit. Yet it wasn't what I wouldst call a square test of manhood because marlin spikes and belaying pins was used free and generous on both sides and the entire tactics smacked of rough house.

In fact, I finally won the fight by throwing him bodily offa the poop. He hit on his head on the after deck and wasn't much good the rest of the cruise, what with a broken arm, three cracked ribs and a busted nose. And the cap'n wouldn't even order me to scrape the anchor chain less'n he had a gun in each hand, though I wasn't figgering on socking the old rum-soaked antique.

Well, in Bulawayo's office me and Bucko now set and glared at each other, and what we was thinking probably wasn't printable.

"Tell you what, boys," said Bulawayo, "I'll let you fight ten rounds as soon as the main event's over with. I'll put up five pounds and the winner gets it all."

"Good enough for me," growled Bucko.

"Make it six pounds and it's a go," said I.

"Done!" said Bulawayo, who realized what a break he was getting, having me fight for him for thirty dollars.

Bucko give me a nasty grin.

"At last, you blasted Yank," said he, "I got you where I want you. They'll be no poop deck for me to slip and fall off this time. And you can't hit me with no hand spike."

"A fine bird you are, talkin' about hand spikes," I snarled, "after tryin' to tear off a section of the main-rail to sock me with."

"Belay!" hastily interrupted Bulawayo. "Preserve your ire for the ring."

"Is they any *Sea Girl* men out front?" I asked. "I want a handler to see that none of this thug's henchmen don't dope my water bottle."

"Strangely enough, Steve," said Bulawayo, "I ain't seen a *Sea Girl* bloke tonight. But I'll get a handler for you."

WELL, THE MAIN EVENT went the limit. It seemed like it never would get over with and I cussed to myself at the idea of a couple of dubs like them was delaying the performance of a man like me. At last, however, the referee called it a draw and kicked the both of them outa the ring.

Bulawayo hopped through the ropes and stopped the folks who'd started to go, by telling them he was offering a free and added attraction—Sailor Costigan and Bucko Brent in a impromptu grudge bout. This was good business for Bulawayo. It tickled the crowd who'd seen both of us fight, though not ag'in each other, of course. They cheered Bulawayo to the echo and settled back with whoops of delight.

Bulawayo was right—not a *Sea Girl* man in the house. All drunk or in jail or something, I suppose. They was quite a number of thugs there from the *Nagpur*—Brent's present ship—and they all rose as one and gimme the razz. Sailors is funny. I know that Brent hazed the liver outa them, yet they was rooting for him like he was their brother or something.

I made no reply to their jeers, maintaining a dignified and aloof silence only except to tell them that I was going to tear their pet mate apart and strew the fragments to the four winds, and also to warn them not to try no monkey-shines behind my back, otherwise I wouldst let Mike chaw their legs off. They greeted my brief observations with loud, raucous bellerings, but looked at Mike with considerable awe.

The referee was an Englishman whose name I forget, but he hadn't been outa the old country very long, and had evidently got his experience in the polite athletic clubs of London. He says: "Now understand this, you blighters, w'en H'I says break, H'I wants no bally nonsense. Remember as long as H'I'm in 'ere, this is a blinkin' gentleman's gyme."

But he got in the ring with us, American style.

Bucko is one of these long, rangy, lean fellers, kinda pale and rawboned. He's got a thin hatchet face and mean light eyes. He's a bad actor and that ain't no lie. I'm six feet and weigh one ninety. He's a inch and three-quarters taller'n me, and he weighed then, maybe, a pound less'n me.

BUCKO COME OUT STABBING with his left, but I was watching his right. I knowed he packed his T.N.T. there and he was pretty classy with it.

In about ten seconds he nailed me with that right and I seen stars. I went back on my heels and he was on top of me in a second, hammering hard with both hands, wild for a knockout. He battered me back across the ring. I wasn't really hurt, though he thought I was. Friends of his which had seen me perform before was yelling for him to be careful, but he paid no heed.

With my back against the ropes I failed to block his right to the body and he rocked my head back with a hard left hook.

"You're not so tough, you lousy mick—" he sneered, shooting for my jaw. *Wham!* I ripped a slungshot right uppercut up inside his left and tagged him flush on the button. It lifted him clean offa his feet and dropped him on the seat of his trunks, where he set looking up at the referee with a goofy and glassy-eyed stare, whilst his friends jumped up and down and cussed and howled: "We told you to be careful with that gorilla, you conceited jassack!"

But Bucko was tough. He kind of assembled hisself and was up at the count of "Nine," groggy but full of fight and plenty mad. I come in wide open to finish him, and run square into that deadly right. I thought for a instant the top of my head was tore off, but rallied and shook Bucko from stem to stern with a left hook under the heart. He tin-canned in a hurry, covering his retreat with his sharp-shooting left. The gong found me vainly follering him around the ring.

The next round started with the fans which was betting on Bucko urging him to keep away from me and box me. Them that had put money on me was yelling for him to take a chance and mix it with me.

But he was plenty cagey. He kept his right bent across his midriff, his chin tucked behind his shoulder and his left out to fend me off. He landed repeatedly with that left and brung a trickle of blood from my lips, but I paid no attention. The left ain't made that can keep me off forever. Toward the end of the round he suddenly let go with that right again and I took it square in the face to get in a right to his ribs.

Blood spattered when his right landed. The crowd leaped up, yelling, not noticing the short-armed smash I ripped in under his heart. But he noticed it, you bet, and broke ground in a hurry, gasping, much to the astonishment of the crowd, which yelled for him to go in and finish the blawsted Yankee.

Crowds don't see much of what's going on in the ring before their eyes, after all. They see the wild swings and haymakers but they miss most of the real punishing blows—the short, quick smashes landed in close.

Well, I went right after Brent, concentrating on his body. He was too kind of long and rangy to take much there. I hunched my shoulders, sunk my head on my hairy chest and bulled in, letting him pound my ears and the top of my head, while I slugged away with both hands for his heart and belly.

A left hook square under the liver made him gasp and sway like a mast in a high wind, but he desperately ripped in a right uppercut that caught me on the chin and kinda dizzied me for a instant. The gong found us fighting out of a clinch along the ropes.

My handler was highly enthusiastic, having bet a pound on me to win by a knockout. He nearly flattened a innocent ringsider showing me how to put over what he called "The Fitzsimmons Smoker." I never heered of the punch.

Well, Bucko was good and mad and musta decided he couldn't keep me away anyhow, so he come out of his corner like a bounding kangaroo, and swarmed all over me before I realized he'd changed his tactics. In a wild mix-up a fast, clever boxer can make a slugger look bad at his own game for a few seconds, being as the cleverer man can land quicker and oftener, but the catch is, he can't keep up the pace. And the smashes the slugger lands are the ones which really counts.

THE CROWD WENT CLEAN crazy when Bucko tore into me, ripping both hands to head and body as fast as he couldst heave one after the other. It looked like I was clean swamped, but them that knowed me tripled their bets. Brent wasn't hurting me none—cutting me up a little, but he was hitting too fast to be putting much weight behind his smacks.

Purty soon I drove a glove through the flurry of his punches. His grunt was plainly heered all over the house. He shot both hands to my head and I come back with a looping left to the body which sunk in nearly up to the wrist.

It was kinda like a bull fighting a tiger, I reckon. He swarmed all over me, hitting fast as a cat claws, whilst I kept my head down and gored him in the belly occasionally. Them body punches was rapidly taking the steam outa him, together with the pace he was setting for hisself. His punches was getting more like slaps and when I seen his knees suddenly tremble, I shifted and crashed my right to his jaw with everything I had behind it. It was a bit high or he'd been out till yet.

Anyway, he done a nose dive and hadn't scarcely quivered at "Nine," when the gong sounded. Most of the crowd was howling lunatics. It looked to them like a chance blow, swung by a desperate, losing man, hadst dropped Bucko just when he was winning in a walk.

But the old-timers knowed better. I couldst see 'em lean back and wink at each other and nod like they was saying: "See, what did I tell you, huh?"

Bucko's merry men worked over him and brung him up in time for the fourth round. In fact, they done a lot of work over him. They clustered around him till you couldn't see what they was doing.

Well, he come out fairly fresh. He had good recuperating powers. He come out cautious, with his left hand stuck out. I noticed that they'd evidently spilt a lot of water on his glove; it was wet.

I glided in fast and he pawed at my face with that left. I didn't pay no attention to it. Then when it was a inch from my eyes I smelt a peculiar, pungent kind of smell! I ducked wildly, but not quick enough. The next instant my eyes felt like somebody'd throwed fire into 'em. Turpentine! His left glove was soaked with it!

I'd caught at his wrist when I ducked. And now with a roar of rage, whilst I could still see a little, I grabbed his elbow with the other hand and, ignoring the smash he gimme on the ear with his right, I bent his arm back and rubbed his own glove in his own face.

He give a most ear-splitting shriek. The crowd bellered with bewilderment and astonishment and the referee rushed in to find out what was happening.

"I say!" he squawked, grabbing hold of us, as we was all tangled up by then. "Wot's going on 'ere? I say, it's disgryceful—*OW!*"

By some mischance or other, Bucko, thinking it was me, or swinging blind, hit the referee right smack between the eyes with that turpentine-soaked glove.

Losing touch with my enemy, I got scared that he'd creep up on me and sock me from behind. I was clean blind by now and I didn't know whether he was or not. So I put my head down and started swinging wild and reckless with both hands, on a chance I'd connect.

Meanwhile, as I heered afterward, Bucko, being as blind as I was, was doing the same identical thing. And the referee was going around the ring like a race horse, yelling for the cops, the army, the navy or what have you!

THE CROWD WAS CLEAN off its nut, having no idee as to what it all meant.

"That blawsted blighter Brent!" howled the cavorting referee in response to the inquiring screams of the maniacal crowd. "'E threw vitriol in me blawsted h'eyes!"

"Cheer up, cull!" bawled some thug. "Both of 'em's blind too!"

"'Ow can H'I h'officiate in this condition?" howled the referee, jumping up and down. "Wot's tyking plyce in the bally ring?"

"Bucko's just flattened one of his handlers which was climbin' into the ring, with a blind swing!" the crowd whooped hilariously. "The Sailor's gone into a clinch with a ring post!"

Hearing this, I released what I had thought was Brent, with some annoyance. Some object bumping into me at this instant, I took it to be Bucko and knocked it head over heels. The delirious howls of the multitude informed me of my mistake. Maddened, I plunged forward, swinging, and felt my left hook around a human neck. As the referee was on the canvas this must be Bucko, I thought, dragging him toward me, and he proved it by sinking a glove to the wrist in my belly.

I ignored this discourteous gesture, and, maintaining my grip on his neck, I hooked over a right with all I had. Having hold of his neck, I knowed about where his jaw oughta be, and I figgered right. I knocked Bucko clean outa my grasp and from the noise he made hitting the canvas I knowed that in the ordinary course of events, he was through for the night.

I groped into a corner and clawed some of the turpentine outa my eyes. The referee had staggered up and was yelling: "'Ow in the blinkin' 'Ades can a man referee in such a mad-'ouse? Wot's 'ere, wot's 'ere?"

"Bucko's down!" the crowd screamed. "Count him out!"

"W'ere is 'e?" bawled the referee, blundering around the ring.

"Three p'ints off yer port bow!" they yelled and he tacked and fell over the vaguely writhing figger of Bucko. He scrambled up with a howl of triumph and begun to count with the most vindictive voice I ever heered. With each count he'd kick Bucko in the ribs.

"—H'eight! Nine! Ten! H'and you're h'out, you blawsted, blinkin' blightin', bally h'assassinatin' pirate!" whooped the referee, with one last tremendjous kick.

I climb over the ropes and my handler showed me which way was my dressing-room. Ever have turpentine rubbed in your eyes? Jerusha! I don't know of nothing more painful. You can easy go blind for good.

But after my handler hadst washed my eyes out good, I was all right. Collecting my earnings from Bulawayo, I set sail for the American Seamen's Bar, where I was to meet Shifty Kerren and give him the money to pay Delrano's fine with.

IT WAS QUITE A BIT past the time I'd set to meet Shifty, and he wasn't nowhere to be seen. I asked the barkeep if he'd been there and the barkeep, who knowed Shifty, said he'd waited about half an hour and then hoisted anchor. I ast the barkeep if he knowed where he lived and he said he did and told me. So I ast him would he keep Mike till I got back and he said he would. Mike despises Delrano so utterly I was afraid I couldn't keep him away from the Kid's throat, if we saw him, and I figgered on going down to the jail with Shifty.

Well, I went to the place the bartender told me and went upstairs to the room the landlady said Shifty had, and started to knock when I heard men talking inside. Sounded like the Kid's voice, but I couldn't tell what he was saying so I knocked and somebody said: "Come in."

I opened the door. Three men was sitting there playing pinochle. They was Shifty, Bill Slane, the Kid's sparring partner, and the Kid hisself.

"Howdy, Steve," said Shifty with a smirk, kinda furtive eyed, "whatcha doin'
away up here?"

"Why," said I, kinda took aback, "I brung the dough for the Kid's fine, but I
see he don't need it, bein' as he's out."

Delrano hadst been craning his neck to see if Mike was with me, and now he
says, with a nasty sneer: "What's the matter with your face, Costigan? Some street
kid poke you on the nose?"

"If you wanta know," I growled, "I got these marks on your account. Shifty
told me you was in stir, and I was broke, so I fought down at The South African to
get fine-money."

At that the Kid and Slane bust out into loud and jeering laughter—not the
kind you like to hear. Shifty joined in, kinda nervous-like.

"Whatcha laughin' at?" I snarled. "Think I'm lyin'?"

"Naw, you ain't lyin'," mocked the Kid. "You ain't got sense enough to.
You're just the kind of a dub that would do somethin' like that."

"You see, Steve," said Shifty, "the Kid—"

"Aw shut up, Shifty!" snapped Delrano. "Let the big sap know he's been took
for a ride. I'm goin' to tell him what a sucker he's been. He ain't got his blasted
bulldog with him. He can't do nothin' to the three of us."

DELRANO GOT UP AND stuck his sneering, pasty white face up close to mine.

"Of all the dumb, soft, boneheaded boobs I ever knew," said he, and his tone
cut like a whip lash, "you're the limit. Get this, Costigan, I ain't broke and I ain't
been in jail! You want to know why Shifty spilt you that line? Because I bet him ten
dollars that much as you hate me and him, we could hand you a hard luck tale and
gyp you outa your last cent.

"Well, it worked! And to think that you been fightin' for the dough to give
me! Ha-ha-ha-ha-ha! You big chump! You're a natural born sucker! You fall for
anything anybody tells you. You'll never get nowheres. Look at me—I wouldn't give
a blind man a penny if he was starvin' and my brother besides. But you—oh, what a
sap!

"If Shifty hadn't been so anxious to win that ten bucks that he wouldn't wait
down at the bar, we'd had your dough, too. But this is good enough. I'm plenty
satisfied just to know how hard you fell for our graft, and to see how you got beat
up gettin' money to pay *my* fine! Ha-ha-ha!"

By this time I was seeing them through a red mist. My huge fists was clenched
till the knuckles was white, and when I spoke it didn't hardly sound like my voice
at all, it was so strangled with rage.

"They's rats in every country," I ground out. "If you'd of picked my pockets or slugged me for my dough, I coulda understood it. If you'd worked a cold deck or crooked dice on me, I wouldn'ta kicked. But you appealed to my better nature, 'stead of my worst.

"You brung up a plea of patriotism and national fellership which no decent man woulda refused. You appealed to my natural pride of blood and nationality. It wasn't for you I done it—it wasn't for you I spilt my blood and risked my eyesight. It was for the principles and ideals you've mocked and tromped into the muck— the honor of our country and the fellership of Americans the world over.

"You dirty swine! You ain't fitten to be called Americans. Thank gosh, for everyone like you, they's ten thousand decent men like me. And if it's bein' a sucker to help out a countryman when he's in a jam in a foreign land, then I thanks the Lord I am a sucker. But I ain't all softness and mush—feel this here for a change!"

And I closed the Kid's eye with a smashing left hander. He give a howl of surprise and rage and come back with a left to the jaw. But he didn't have a chance. He'd licked me in the ring, but he couldn't lick me bare-handed, in a small room where he couldn't keep away from my hooks, not even with two men to help him. I was blind mad and I just kind of gored and tossed him like a charging bull.

If he hit at all after that first punch I don't remember it. I know I crashed him clean across the room with a regular whirlwind of smashes, and left him sprawled out in the ruins of three or four chairs with both eyes punched shut and his arm broke. I then turned on his cohorts and hit Bill Slane on the jaw, knocking him stiff as a wedge. Shifty broke for the door, but I pounced on him and spilled him on his neck in a corner with a open-handed slap.

I THEN STALKED FORTH in silent majesty and gained the street. As I went I was filled with bitterness. Of all the dirty, contemptible tricks I ever heered of, that took the cake. And I got to thinking maybe they was right when they said I was a sucker. Looking back, it seemed to me like I'd fell for every slick trick under the sun. I got mad. I got mighty mad.

I shook my fist at the world in general, much to the astonishment and apprehension of the innocent by-passers.

"From now on," I raged, "I'm harder'n the plate on a battleship! I ain't goin' to fall for *nothin'*! Nobody's goin' to get a blasted cent outa me, not for no reason what-the-some-ever—"

At that moment I heered a commotion going on nearby. I looked. Spite of the fact that it was late, a pretty good-sized crowd hadst gathered in front of a kinda third-class boarding-house. A mighty purty blonde-headed girl was standing there, tears running down her cheeks as she pleaded with a tough-looking old sister who stood with her hands on her hips, grim and stern.

"Oh, please don't turn me out!" wailed the girl. "I have no place to go! No job—oh, please. Please!"

I can't stand to hear a hurt animal cry out or a woman beg. I shouldered through the crowd and said: "What's goin' on here?"

"This hussy owes me ten pounds," snarled the woman. "I got to have the money or her room. I'm turnin' her out."

"Where's her baggage?" I asked.

"I'm keepin' it for the rent she owes," she snapped. "Any of your business?"

The girl kind of slumped down in the street. I thought if she's turned out on the street tonight they'll be hauling another carcass outa the bay tomorrer. I said to the landlady, "Take six pounds and call it even."

"Ain't you got no more?" said she.

"Naw, I ain't," I said truthfully.

"All right, it's a go," she snarled, and grabbed the dough like a sea-gull grabs a fish.

"All right," she said very harshly to the girl, "you can stay another week. Maybe you'll find a job by that time—or some other sap of a Yank sailor will come along and pay your board."

She went into the house and the crowd give a kind of cheer which inflated my chest about half a foot. Then the girl come up close to me and said shyly, "Thank you. I—I—I can't begin to tell you how much I appreciate what you've done for me."

Then all to a sudden she threw her arms around my neck and kissed me and then run up the steps into the boarding-house. The crowd cheered some more like British crowds does and I felt plenty uplifted as I swaggered down the street. Things like that, I reflected, is worthy causes. A worthy cause can have my dough any time, but I reckon I'm too blame smart to get fooled by no shysters.

I COME INTO THE AMERICAN Seamen's Bar where Mike was getting anxious about me. He wagged his stump of a tail and grinned all over his big wide face and I found two American nickels in my pocket which I didn't know I had. I give one of 'em to the barkeep to buy a pan of beer for Mike. And whilst he was lapping it, the barkeep, he said: "I see Boardin'-house Kate is in town."

"Whatcha mean?" I ast him.

"Well," said he, combing his mustache, "Kate's worked her racket all over Australia and the West Coast of America, but this is the first time I ever seen her in South Africa. She lets some landlady of a cheap boardin'-house in on the scheme and this dame pretends to throw her out. Kate puts up a wail and somebody—

usually some free-hearted sailor about like you—happens along and pays the landlady the money Kate's supposed to owe for rent so she won't kick the girl out onto the street. Then they split the dough."

"Uh huh!" said I, grinding my teeth slightly. "Does this here Boardin'-house Kate happen to be a blonde?"

"Sure thing," said the barkeep. "And purty as hell. What did you say?"

"Nothin'," I said. "Here. Give me a schooner of beer and take this nickel, quick, before somebody comes along and gets it away from me."

THE SIGN OF THE SNAKE

I WAS READY FOR TROUBLE. Canton's narrow waterfront streets were still and shadowy in that hour before dawn when I left the docks. The guttering street lamps gave little light. My bulldog, Bill, bristled suddenly and began to rumble in his throat. There was a rattle of feet on the cobblestones down an alley to the right. Then the sound of a heavy fall, scuffling, a strangled scream.

Plainly it was none of my business. But I quickened my pace and dashing around the corner, nearly fell over a writhing, struggling mass on the cobblestones. The dim light of a street lamp showed me what was going on. Two men fought there in deadly silence. One was a slim young Chinese in European clothes. Down on his back in the muck, he was. Kneeling on his chest was a slant-eyed devil in native riggings. He was big and lean, with a face like a Taoist devil-mask. With one talon-like hand, he clutched the throat of the smaller man. A knife flashed in his other hand.

I recognized him for what he was—one of the bloody hatchet-men the big tongs and secret societies use for their dirty work. I followed my natural instinct and knocked him senseless with a smashing right hook behind the ear. He stretched out without a twitch and the young Chinese sprang up, gasping and wild eyed.

"Thank you, my friend," he gurgled in perfect English. "I owe my life to you. Here, take this . . ." And he tried to stuff a wad of banknotes into my hand.

I drew back. "You owe me nothing," I growled. "I'd have done as much for any man."

"Then please accept my humble and sincere thanks," he exclaimed, seizing my hand. "You are an American, are you not? What is your name?"

"I'm Steve Costigan, first mate of the trading vessel *Panther*," I answered.

"I will not forget," he said. "I will repay you some day, as my name is Yotai T'sao. But now I must not linger. This is my one chance of escape. If I can get aboard the English ship that is anchored in the bay, I am safe. But I must go before this beast comes to. Best that you go too. May fortune attend you. But beware of the Yo Thans."

The next instant he was racing down the street at full speed. Watching him in amazement, I saw him sprint onto the docks and dive off, without the slightest pause. I heard the splash as he hit and a little later I saw, in the growing gray light, a widening ripple aiming toward the British *S.S. Marquis,* which lay out in the bay. I left off wondering what it could mean, when the hatchet-man scrambled uncertainly to his feet. More or less ironically, I said: "Well, my bully boy, give me the low-down on this business, will you?"

His answer was a look of such diabolic hatred as to almost send cold shivers down my spine. He limped away into the shadows. I dismissed the whole affair from my mind and went on down the street.

About sun-up I decided I would get a little sleep in preparation for the day. It was my first shore leave in weeks, and I was determined to make the most of it. I turned into a seamen's boarding house kept by a Eurasian called Diego, got a room and turned in.

I WAS WAKENED BY BILL'S growling. He was clawing at the locked door and looking up at the transom, which was open. Then I saw something lying on my chest—a piece of stiff paper, rolled into a dart-shaped wad. I unrolled it, but there were no words on it, either English or Chinese, just a picture portraying a coiled snake, somewhat resembling a cobra. That was all.

Somewhat puzzled, I rose and dressed and shouted for Diego. When he came I said: "Look, Diego. Someone threw this through the transom onto my chest. Do you know what the meaning of it is."

He took a single look. Then he leaped back with a shriek: "Yo Than. Death.

It's the murder sign of the Yo Thans."

"What do you mean?" I growled. "Who are these Yo Thans?"

"A Chinese secret society," gasped Diego, white and shaking like a leaf. "International criminals—murderers. Three times have I seen men receive the sign of the snake. Each time he who received it dies before the sun rose again. Get back to your ship. Hide, stay aboard until she sails. Maybe you can escape."

"Skulk aboard my ship like a cringing rat?" I growled. "I, who am known as a fighting man in every Asiatic port? I've never run or hidden from any man yet. Tell me, who is Yotai T'sao?"

But Diego was gripped by the yellow hand of fear.

"I'll tell you nothing," he screamed. "I'm risking my life talking to you. Get out, quick. You mustn't stay here. I can't have another murder in my house. Go, please, Steve."

"All right," I snapped. "Don't burst a blood-vessel, Diego. I'm going."

In disgust, I stalked forth in quest of food. While I ate and Bill had his scoffings from a panikin on the floor, I reviewed the situation and had the uncomfortable feeling that I had somehow blundered into the affairs of some mysterious gang of Oriental cut-throats. Under the bland outer surface of the Orient run dark and mysterious currents of plot and intrigue, unknown to white men—unless one unluckily goes beyond his depth in native affairs and is caught by some such deadly undertow.

In that case. . . . Well, it is no uncommon thing for a white man to disappear, to simply vanish as into thin air. Perhaps he is never heard of again. Perhaps his knife-riddled body is found floating in the river, or cast up on the beach. In either event, only silence rewards investigations. China never speaks. Like a vast, sleeping yellow giant she preserves her ancient and mysterious silence inviolate.

Finishing my meal, I sauntered out into the streets again, with their filth and glamor, sordidity and allure going hand in hand; throngs of Orientals buying and selling, bargaining in their monotonous sing-song, sailors of all nations rolling through the crowds. . . .

I began to have a queer feeling that I was being followed. Again and again I wheeled quickly and scanned the crowd, but in that teeming swarm of yellow slant-eyed faces it was impossible to tell whether anyone was trailing me. Yet the sensation persisted.

AS THE DAY WORE ON I found myself in Froggy Ladeau's American Bar, at the edge of the waterfront district. There I spied a man I knew—an Englishman named Wells, who had some sort of a government job. I sat down at his table. "Wells," I said, "did you ever hear of a man named Yotai T'sao?"

"That I have," he answered. "But I fear the blighter's been potted off. He's been working with the government trying to get evidence against a certain gang of dangerous criminals and last night he disappeared."

"He's all right," I replied. "I saw him swim out to an English ship which weighed anchor shortly after sun-up. But who are these criminals?"

"Bad blokes," said Wells, taking a long swig of ale. "An organized society. It's rumored their chief is a coral button mandarin. They specialize in murder and blackmail, to say nothing of smuggling, gun-running and jewel-stealing. Of late they've been tampering with bigger things—governmental secrets. The Yo Thans, they're called. The government would jolly well like to lay hands on them. But you've no idea what snaky customers they are. They're here, there and everywhere. We know they exist, but we can't nab the beggars. If the natives would talk—but they won't, and there's China for you. Even victims of the society won't blab. So what can we do?

"But the government has gotten a promise of assistance from the most Honorable and Eminent Yun Lai Kao. You've heard of him?"

"Sure," I nodded. "Sort of a wealthy Oriental recluse and philanthropist, isn't he?"

"That and more. The natives look on him as a sort of god. He has almost unbelievable power in Canton, though he's never bothered to wield it very much. He's a philosopher—too busy considering abstract ideals and principles to bother with material things. He seldom ever appears in public. It was the very deuce to get him interested enough in sordid reality to promise to help the government scotch a gang of thugs. That shows, too, how helpless the government really is in this matter, when it has to call on private individuals. The only argument that moved him was the assurance that the Yo Thans are swiftly assuming a political importance, and were likely to start a civil war in China."

"Is it that important?" I asked, startled.

"Believe me, it is. These things grow fast. The unknown power, the nameless man, directing the activities of these thugs, is ruthless and clever as the devil, quite capable of raising the red flag of anarchy if he gets a little more power. China is a powder keg, ready for some unscrupulous rogue to set it off. No conservative Chinese wants that to happen. That's why Yun Lai Kao agreed to help. And with his power over the natives, I believe the government will lay the Yo Thans by the heels."

"What sort of a man is this mandarin, Yun Lai Kao?" I asked. "A venerable, white bearded patriarch, with ten-inch finger nails encased in gold and a load of Confucian epigrams?"

"Not by a long shot," answered Wells. "He doesn't look the type of a mystic at all. A clean-cut chap in middle life, he is, with a firm jaw and gimlet eyes—a graduate from Oxford too, by the way. Should have been a scientist or a soldier. Some queer quirk in his Oriental mind turned him to philosophy."

A COMMOTION BURST out in the bar. Ladeau was having some kind of a row with a big sailor. Suddenly the sailor hauled off and hit Froggy between the eyes. Ladeau crashed down on a table, with beer mugs and seltzer water bottles spilling all over him, and began yelling for Big John Clancy, his American bouncer. Hearing this, the sailor took to his heels. But Ladeau, floundering around in the ruins of the table with his eyes still full of stars, didn't see that. Big John came barging in and Froggy yelled: "Throw him out! Beat him up! Give him the bum's rush! Out with him, John!"

"Out with who?" roared Clancy, glaring around and doubling up his huge fists.

"That blasted sailor," bawled Froggy. Clancy then made a natural mistake. As it happened, I was the only sailor in the bar. I had just turned back to speak to Wells, when to my outraged amazement, I felt myself gripped by what appeared to be a gorilla.

"Out with you, my bully," growled Big John, hauling me out of my chair and trying to twist me around and get a hammerlock on my right arm.

I might have explained the situation, but my nerves were on edge already. And being mate on a tough tramp trader makes a man handier with his fists than with his tongue. I acted without conscious thought and jolted him loose from me with a left hook under the heart that nearly upset him. It would have finished an ordinary man, but Big John was built like a battleship. He gave a deafening roar and plunged headlong on me, locking both of his mighty arms around me. We went to the floor together, smashing a few chairs in our fall. As we cursed and wrestled, his superior weight enabled him to get on top of me.

At that instant my bulldog Bill landed square between Clancy's shoulders. By some chance his jaws missed Big John's bull neck, but ripped out the whole back of his coat. Big John gave a yell of fright and with a desperate heave of his enormous shoulders, shook Bill off and jumped up. I arose, too, and caught Bill just as he was soaring for Clancy's throat. I pushed him back, ordering him to keep out of it, and then turned toward Big John, who was snorting and blowing like a grampus in his wrath.

I was seeing red myself.

"Come on, you son-of-a-seahorse," I snarled. "If it's fighting you want, I'll give you a belly-full."

At that he gave a terrible howl and came for me, crazy-eyed. Ladeau ran between us, dancing and howling like a burnt cat.

"Git away, Froggy," bellowed Big John, swinging his huge arms like windmills. "Git outa the way! I'm goin' to smear this salt-water tramp all over the joint."

"Wait a minute, please, John," screamed Ladeau, pushing against Clancy's broad chest with both hands. "This here is Steve Costigan of the *Panther*."

"What do I care who he is?" roared Big John. "Git outa the way!"

"You can't fight in here," Froggy howled desperately. "If you two tangles here, you'll tear the joint down. I can't afford it. Anyway, he ain't the man that hit me."

"Well, he's the swine that hit me," rumbled Big John.

"Get aside, Froggy," I snapped. "Let us have it out. It's the only way."

"No, no!" shrieked Ladeau. "It cost me five hundred dollars to repair the place after you throwed Red McCoy out, John, and I seen Costigan lick Bully Dawson in a saloon in Hong Kong. They had to rebuild the joint. Come down on the beach, back of the Kago Tong warehouses and fight it out where you can't bust nothin' but each others' noses."

"A jolly good idea," put in Wells. "You fellows don't want to make a spectacle of yourselves here, in a respectable district, and have the police on you. If you must fight, why don't you do as Ladeau says?"

Big John folded his mighty arms and glared at me, as he growled: "Fair enough. I ain't the man to do useless damage. I'll be at the beach as quick as I can get there. Get some of your crew, Costigan, so as to have fair play all around. And get there as soon as you can."

"Good enough," I snapped. Turning on my heel, I left the bar. Oh, it seems foolish, no doubt, grown men fighting like school boys. But reputations grow. A man in the ordinary course of duty acquires the name of a fighter and before he knows it, his pride is forcing him into fights to maintain it.

HOPING TO FIND SOME of the *Panther's* crew, I went down the narrow waterfront streets. My efforts met with no success. As a last resort, I thought of a shop down a little side street in the native quarter, run by a Chinese named Yuen Lao, who sells trinkets such as sailors buy in foreign ports to give to their sweethearts.

With the thought that I might find some of my friends there, I turned into the obscure, winding street. I noticed that there were even fewer people traversing it than usual. An old man with a cage full of canary birds, a coolie pulling a cart, a fish peddler or so—that was all.

I saw the shop just ahead of me. Then?with a vicious *zing*—something came humming through the air. It hissed by my neck as I instinctively ducked. It thudded into the wall at my shoulder—a long thin bladed knife, stuck a good three inches into the hard boards and quivering from the force of the throw. Had it hit me, it would have gone clear through me.

I looked across the street, but all I could see was the blank fronts of a row of vacant shops. The windows all seemed to be boarded up, but I knew that the knife had come from one of them. The Chinese on the street paid no attention to me at all. They went about their affairs as if they seen nothing, not even me. Little use to ask them if they saw the knife-thrower. China never speaks.

And the thought of the Yo Thans came back to me with a shudder. It had been no idle threat, that cryptic sign of the snake. They had struck and missed, but they would strike again and again until they opened the Doors of Doom for Steve Costigan. Cold sweat broke out on me. This was like fighting a cobra in the dark.

I turned into Yuen Lao's shop, with its shelves of jade idols, coral jewelry and tiny ivory elephants. A bronze Buddha squatted on a raised dais, its inscrutable face veiled by the smoke of burning joss sticks. Only Yuen Lao, tall and lean, with a mask-like face, stood in the shop.

I turned to leave, when he came quickly from behind his counter.

"You are Costigan, mate of the *Panther*?" said he in good English. I nodded, and he continued in a lowered voice. "You are in danger. Do not ask me how I know. These things have a way of getting about among the Chinese. Listen to me. I would be your friend. And you need friends. Without my aid, you will be dead before dawn."

"Oh, I don't know," I growled, involuntarily tensing my biceps. "I've never been in a jamb yet that I couldn't slug my way out of."

"Your strength will not help you." He shook his head. "Your shipmates cannot aid you. Your enemies will strike secretly and subtly. Their sign is the cobra. And, like the cobra, they kill swiftly, silently, giving their victim no chance to defend himself."

I began to feel wild and desperate, like a wolf in a trap, as the truth of his words came home to me.

"How am I going to fight men who won't come into the open?" I snarled, helplessly, knotting my fists until the knuckles showed white. "Get them in front of me and I'll battle the whole gang. But I can't smoke them out of their hives."

"You must listen to me," said Yuen Lao. "I will save you. I have no cause to love the Yo Thans."

"But why have they turned on me?" I asked in perplexity.

"You prevented their chief hatchet-man from slaying Yotai T'sao," said he. "Yotai T'sao was doomed, tried and sentenced by their most dread tribunal. He had intrigued his way into their secret meeting places and councils, to get evidence to use against them in the court. For he was a spy of the government. His life was forfeit and not even the government could save him from the vengeance of the Yo

Thans. Last night he sought to escape and was trapped by Yaga, the hatchet-man who hunted him down and caught him almost on the wharves. There had Yotai T'sao died but for you. Today he is far at sea and safe. But the vengeance of the Yo Thans is turned upon you. And you are doomed."

"A nice mess," I muttered.

"But I am your friend," continued Yuen Lao. "And I hate the Yo Thans. I am more than I seem."

"Are you a government spy too?" I asked.

"Shh!" He laid his long finger to his lips and glanced around quickly and warily. "The very walls have ears in Canton. But I will tell you this. There is but one man in Canton who can save you, who will, if I ask him, speak the word that will make even the Yo Thans stay their hands."

"Yun Lai Kao," I muttered.

Yuen Lao started and peered at me intensely for an instant. Then he seemed to nod, almost imperceptibly.

"Tonight I will take you to—this—this man. Let him remain nameless, for the present. You must come alone, hinting your errand to no one. Trust me!"

"It's not many hours till sundown," I muttered. "When and where shall I meet you?"

"Come to me alone, in the Alley of Bats, as soon as it is well dark. And go now, quickly. We must not be seen too much together. And be wary, lest the Yo Thans strike again before we meet."

AS I LEFT THE SHOP I HAD a distinct feeling of relief. I had not been inclined to trust Yuen Lao's mere word, but his evident connection with the mighty and mysterious mandarin, Yun Lai Kao, together with what Wells had said of the mandarin, reassured me. If I could evade the hatred of the unknown murderers until dark. . . .

Suddenly, with a curse of annoyance, I remembered that at this very moment I was supposed to be on my way to the beach to fight Big John Clancy with my naked fists. Well, it must be done. Even if I died that night, I must keep that appointment. I could not go out with men thinking I dared not meet Big John in open fight. Besides, the thought came to me, that was the safest place in Canton for me—on the open beach, surrounded by men of my own race. The problem lay in getting there alive. I made no further attempts to find the crew, but set off at a rapid walk, keeping my eye alert and passing alleyways very warily. Bill sensed my caution and kept close to me, walking stiff-legged, rumbling deep and ominously in his throat.

But I arrived unharmed at the strip of open beach behind the big warehouses.

Big John was already there, stripped to the waist, growling his impatience and flexing his mighty arms. Froggy Ladeau was there and half a dozen others, all friends of Clancy. Wells was not there. I couldn't help wondering about that.

"I couldn't find any of my friends, Clancy," I said abruptly. "But I'm not afraid of not getting fair play. I've always heard of you as a square shooter. My dog won't interfere. I'll make him understand that. But Froggy can hold him if you'd rather."

"You've kept me waitin'," growled Big John. "Let's get goin'."

It's like a dream now, that fight on the Kago Tong beach. Men still talk about it, from Vladivostok to Sumatra, wherever the roving brotherhood gathers to spin old yarns over their glasses.

"No kickin', gougin', or bitin'," Big John growled. "Let it be a white man's fight."

And a white man's fight it was, there on the naked beach, both of us stripped to the waist, with no weapons but our naked fists. What a man John Clancy was! I was six feet tall and weighed 190 pounds. He stood six feet one and three quarter inches and he weighed 230 pounds—all bone and muscle it was, with never an ounce of fat on him. His legs were like tree trunks, his arms looked as if they had been molded out of iron, and his chest was arching and broad as a door. A massive, corded neck upheld a lion-like head and a face like a Roman senator's.

I weighed my chances as we approached each other, I and this giant who had never known defeat. In sheer strength and bulk he had the edge. But I was strong, too, in those days, and I knew that I was the faster man and the more scientific boxer.

He came at me like a charging bull and I met him half-way. Mine was the skill or fortune to get in the first punch, a smashing left hook square to the jaw. It stopped him dead in his tracks. But he roared and came on again, shaking his lion-like head. I went under his gigantic swings to rip both hands to his body. I was fast enough and skilled enough to avoid his mightiest blows for a time, but let it not be thought that I back-pedalled and ran, or fought a merely defensive fight. Men do not fight that way on the beach—or anywhere in the raw edges of the world.

I stood up to him and he stood up to me. My head was singing with his blows and the blood trickled from my mouth. Blue welts showed on his ribs and one of his eyes was closing.

He loomed like a giant over me as I ducked his terrible swing. It whistled over my head and my glancing return tore the skin on his ribs. Gad, his right hand whistled past my face like a white hot brick, and when he landed he shook me from head to heel. But my battles with men and with the Seven Seas had toughened me into steel and whale-bone endurance. I stood up to it.

I was landing the more and cleaner blows. Again and again I had him floundering, but always he came back with a crashing, bone-crushing attack I could not altogether avoid. I bulled in close, ducking inside his wide looping smashes, and ripped both hands to body and head. I had the better at the infighting. But, staggering under a machine-gun fire of short hooks and uppercuts, he suddenly ripped up an uppercut of his own. Gad, my head snapped back as if my neck was broken. Only blind instinct made me fall into Big John and clinch before he could strike again. And I held on with a grizzly grip not even he could break, until my head cleared.

The onlookers had formed a tense ring about us. Their nails bit into their clenching palms and their breaths came in swift gasps. There was no other sound save the scruff of our feet on the beach, the thud and smash of savagely driven blows, an occasional grunt, and Bill's low, incessant growling.

CLANCY'S HUGE FIST banged against my eye, half closing it. My right crashed full into his mouth and he spit out a shattered tooth.

My left hook was doing most of the damage. Big John was too fond of using his right. He drew it back too far before he let it go. Again and again I beat him to the punch with my left, and I made raw beef out of the right side of his jaw. Sometimes he would duck clumsily and my hook would smash on his ear, which was a beautiful cauliflower before the fight was over. But I was not unmarked.

Things floated in a red mist. I saw Big John's face before me, with the lips smashed and pulped, one eye closed and blood streaming from his nose. My arms were growing heavy, my feet slow. I stumbled as I side-stepped. The taste of blood was in my mouth. How long we had stood toe to toe, exchanging terrific smashes, I did not know. It seemed like ages. In chaotic, flashing glances, I saw the strained, white, tense faces of the onlookers.

From somewhere smashed Big John's thundering right hand. Square on the jaw it crashed. I felt myself falling into an abyss of blackness, shot with a million gleams and darts of light. I struck the beach hard, and the jolt of the fall jarred me back into my senses. I looked up, shaking the blood and sweat out of my eyes, and saw Big John looming above me. He was swaying, wide-braced on his mighty legs. His great, hairy chest was heaving as his breath came in panting gasps. I dragged myself to my feet. The knowledge that he was in as bad a way as I, nerved my weary muscles.

"You must be made outa iron," he croaked, lurching toward me. I took a deep breath and braced myself to meet his right. The blow was a glancing one and I blasted both hands under his heart. He reeled like a ship in rough weather, but came back with a left swing that staggered me. Again he swung his right, like a club.

I ducked and straightened with a left hook that cracked on the side of his head. But it was high. I felt my knuckles crumple. His knees buckled and I put all I had behind my right. Like a swinging maul, it smashed on Big John Clancy's jaw. And he swayed and fell.

I felt men about me, heard their awed congratulations, felt Bill's cold wet nose shoved into my hand. Froggy was staring down at the senseless form of Big John in a sort of unbelieving horror.

Then came memory of Yuen Lao and the Yo Thans. I shook the blood and sweat from my eyes, pulling away from the men who were pawing over me. The sun was setting. If I expected to see that sun rise again, I must meet Yuen Lao and go with him to Yun Lai Kao.

Snatching up my clothes, I tore away from the amazed men and reeled drunkenly up the beach. Out of sight of the group, I dropped from sheer exhaustion. It was minutes before I could rise and go on.

My mind cleared as I walked, and my head ceased to sing from Big John's smashes. I was fiercely weary, sore and bruised. It seemed impossible for me to get my wind back. My left hand was swollen and sore, and the skin was torn on my right knuckles. One of my eyes was partly closed, my lips were smashed and cut, my ribs battered black and blue. But the cool wind from the sea helped me, and with the recuperative powers of youth and an iron frame, I regained my wind, shook off some of my weariness and felt fairly fit as I neared the Alley of Bats, in the growing darkness.

I FOUND TIME TO WONDER why the Yo Thans had not struck again. There was something unnatural about the whole business, it seemed to me. Since that knife had been flung at me earlier in the day, I had had no sign at all of the existence of that murderous gang.

I came unharmed to the narrow, stinking rat-den in the heart of the native quarter which the Chinese call, for some unknown reason, the Alley of Bats. It was pitch-dark there. I felt cold shivers creep up and down my spine. Suddenly a figure loomed up beside me and Bill snarled. In my nervousness I almost struck out at the figure, when Yuen Lao's voice halted me. He was like a ghost in the deep shadows. Bill growled savagely.

"Come with me," whispered Yuen Lao. And I groped after him. Down that alley he led me. Across another even darker and nastier. Through a wide shadowy courtyard. Down a narrow side street, deep in the heart of what I knew must be a mysterious native quarter seldom seen by white men. Down another alley and into a dimly lighted courtyard. He stopped before a heavy arched doorway.

As he rapped upon it, I realized the utter silence, eeriness and brooding mystery of the place. Truly, I was in the very heart of ancient and enigmatic China, as surely as if I had been five hundred miles in the interior. The very shadows seemed lurking perils. I shuddered involuntarily.

Three times Yuen Lao rapped. Then the door swung silently inward, to disclose a veritable well of darkness. I could not even see who had opened the door. Yuen Lao entered first, motioning me to follow. I stepped in, Bill crowding close after me. The door slammed between us, leaving the dog on the outside. I heard the click of a heavy lock. Bill was clawing and whining outside the door. And then the lights came on. While I blinked like a blinded owl, I heard a low throaty chuckle that sent involuntary shivers up and down my spine. My eyes became accustomed to the light. I saw that I was in a big room, furnished in true Oriental style. The walls were covered with velvet and silken hangings, ornamented with silver dragons worked into the fabric. A faint scent of some Eastern incense or perfume pervaded the atmosphere.

Ranged about me were ten big, dark, wicked-faced men, naked except for loin-cloths. Malays they were, tougher and stronger than any Chinese. On a kind of tiger-skin covered dais across the room an unmistakable Chinaman sat on a lacquer-worked chair. He was clad in robes worked in dragons like those on the hangings, and his keen piercing eyes gleamed through holes in the mask which hid his features. But it was the figure which stood image-like beside the lacquered chair which drew and held my gaze. It was the hatchet-man from whom I had rescued Yotai T'sao on the wharfs that morning.

In a sickening instant I realized that I was trapped. Blind fool that I was, to walk into the snare. A child might have suspected that mask-faced snake of a Yuen Lao. He too was a Yo Than, I realized. And he had not brought me to the Honorable and Benevolent Yun Lai Kao. He had brought me before the nameless and mysterious chief of the Yo Thans, to die like a butchered sheep.

And there he stood before me, Yuen Lao, smiling evilly. I acted instinctively. Square into his mouth I crashed my right before he could move. His teeth caved in and he dropped like a log.

The masked man on the dais laughed. And in his laughter sounded all the ancient and heartless cruelty of the Orient.

"The white barbarian is strong and fierce," he mocked. "But this night, my bold savage, you shall learn what it is to interfere with the plans of Kang Kian of the Yo Thans. Fool, to pit your paltry powers against mine. You, with the striding arrogance of your breed.

"Know, fool, before you die, that the ancient dragon that is China is waking slowly beneath the feet of the foreign dogs, and their doom is not far off. Soon I, Kang Kian, master of the Yo Thans, will come from the shadows, raise the dragon banner of revolution and mount again the ancient throne of my ancestors. Your fate will be the fate of all your race who oppose me. I laugh at you. Do you deem yourself important because the future emperor of China deigns to see personally to your removal? Bah! I merely crush you as I crush the gnat that annoys me."

Then he spoke shortly to the Malays: "Kill him."

THEY CLOSED IN ON me silently, drawing knives, strangling cords and loaded cudgels. It looked like trail's end for Steve Costigan. I, with two black eyes, ribs pounded black and blue, one hand broken, from one fierce fight, pitted against these trained killers. They approached warily. Bill, outside, sensing my peril, began to roar and hurl himself against the bolted door. I tensed myself for one last rush. The thought flashed through me that perhaps Bill would escape my fate. I hoped that it might be so.

I drew back, tensed and watchful as a hawk. The ring was closing in on me. The nearest Malay edged within reach. He raised his knife for the death leap. I smashed my heel to his knee and distinctly heard the bone snap. He went down. I leaped across him and hit that closing ring as a plunging fullback hits a line.

Cudgels swished past my head. I felt a knife lick along my ribs. Then I was through, bounding across the room and onto the dais.

Kang Kian screamed. He jerked a pistol from his robes. How he missed me at that range, I cannot say. The powder flash burned my face, but before he could fire again I knocked him head over heels with a blow that was backed with the power of desperation. The pistol flew out of reach.

The hatchet-man was on me like a clawing cat. He drove a long knife deep into my chest muscles. Then I got in a solid smash. His jaw was brittle. It crunched like an egg-shell. I swung his limp form up bodily above my head and hurled him into the clump of Malays who came leaping up on the dais, bowling over the front line like ten-pins. The rest came at me.

Carried beyond myself on a red wave of desperate battle fury, I caught up the lacquered chair and swung it with all my strength. Squarely it landed and I felt my victim's shoulder bone give way. But the chair flew into splinters. Then a whistling cudgel stroke laid my scalp open and knocked me to my knees. The whole pack piled on me, hacking and slashing. But their very numbers hindered them. Somehow, I managed to shake them off momentarily and stagger up.

A big Chinaman I had not seen before bobbed up from nowhere and got a bone-breaking wrestling hold on my right arm. A giant Malay was thrusting for my life. I could not wrench my right free. So, setting my teeth, I slugged him with my broken left. I went sick and dizzy from the pain of it, but the Malay dropped like a sack.

But they downed me again, as my berserk fighting frenzy waned. They swarmed over me and forced me down by sheer weight of man-power. I heard Kang Kian yelling to them with the rage of a fiend in his voice, and a big dark-skinned devil raised his knife and drove it down for my heart. Somehow, I managed to throw up my left arm and take the blade through it. That arm felt like I'd bathed in molten lead.

Then I heard the door crash and splinter. A familiar voice roared like a high sea. And something like a white cannon-ball hit the clump of natives on top of me.

The press slackened as the group flew apart. I reeled up, sick, dizzy and weak from loss of the blood that was spurting from me in half a dozen places. As in a daze, I saw Bill leaping and tearing at dark, howling figures which fell over each other trying to get away. And I saw a white giant ploughing through them as a battleship goes through breakers.

Big John Clancy!

I saw him seize a Malay in each hand, by the neck, crack their heads together and throw them into a corner. A dusky giant ran in, lunging upward with a stroke meant to disembowel, only to be stretched senseless by one blow of Big John's mighty fist. The big Chinaman—a wrestler, by his looks—got a headlock on Clancy. But Big John broke the hold, wheeled and threw the wrestler clear over his shoulders, head over heels. The Chinaman hit on his head and he didn't get up.

That was enough for the Yo Thans. They scattered like a flock of birds, all except Kang Kian, the masked lord. He sprang for the fallen pistol. Before he could reach it, Bill, jaws already streaming red, dragged him down. One fearful scream broke from the Yo Than's yellow lips and then Bill's iron jaws tore out his throat.

BIG JOHN CAME QUICKLY toward me. "By golly, Costigan," he rumbled, "you look like you been through a sawmill. Here, lemme tie up some of them stabs before you bleed to death. You've lost a gallon of blood already. We got to git you where you can git dressed right. But for the time bein' we'll see can we stop the bleedin'."

He ripped strips from his shirt and began to bandage me. Bill climbed all over me, wagging his stump of a tail and licking my hand.

I gazed at Big John in amazement. I had thought my own vitality unusual, but Big John's endurance was beyond belief. He looked as if he'd been mauled by a gorilla. I was astounded to realize the extent to which I had punished him in our battle. Yet he seemed almost as fresh and fit as ever. My smashes which had blackened his eyes, smashed his lips, ripped his ears, shattered some of his teeth and laid open his jaw, had battered him down and out, but had not sapped the vast reservoir of his vitality. I had merely weakened him momentarily and knocked him out, that was all, and accomplishing that feat had taken more of my strength than it had his.

"I supposed you'd be laid up for a week after our fight," I said bluntly.

He snorted. "You must think I'm effeminate. I wasn't out but a few minutes. And when I'd got back my breath, I was ready to go on with the fight. Of course I'm kinda stiff and sore and tired-like, right now, but that amounts to nothing.

"When I'd got my bearin's I looked around for you. Froggy and them had a hard time convincin' me that I'd been licked, for the first time in my life. I'll swear, I still don't see how it could of happened. Anyway, I started right out to find you and take you apart, because I was mighty near blind mad. A coolie had seen you go into the Alley of Bats and I followed, not long behind you. I know Canton better'n most white men, but I got clean tangled up in all them alley-ways and courtyards.

"Then I heard your dog makin' a big racket. I knowed it was yours, because they ain't but one dog in China with a voice like his. So I come and found him roarin' and plungin' at the door and I heard the noise inside. So knowin' you must be in some kind of a jamb, I just up and busted in. Who was them thugs, anyhow?"

I told him quickly about Yotai T'sao and the Yo Thans. He growled: "I mighta knowed it. I've heard of 'em. I bet they won't put no snake sign on no more Americans very soon. Come on, let's get outa here."

"I don't know how to thank you, Clancy," I said. "You certainly saved my hide. . . ."

"Aw, don't thank me," he grunted. "I couldn't see them mutts bump off a white man. And you'd sure give 'em a tussle by yourself. Naw, don't thank me. Remember I was lookin' for you to beat you up."

"Well," said I, "I hate to fight a man whose saved my life, but if you're set on it . . ."

He laughed gustily and slapped me on the back. "Thunderation, Steve, I wouldn't hit a man which has just stopped as many knives as you have. Anyway, I'm beginnin' to like you. Who's this?"

A tall man in European clothes stepped suddenly into the doorway, with a revolver in one hand.

"Wells!" I exclaimed. "What are you doing here?"

"Following a tip-off I got earlier in the evening," he said crisply. "I got wind of a secret session of the Yo Thans to be held here."

"So you are a Secret Service man after all," I said slowly. "If I'd known that, I might not have all these knife-stabs in my hide."

"I've been trailing the Yo Thans for some time," he answered. "Working with special powers invested in me by British and Chinese authorities. Whose this dead man?"

"He called himself Kang Kian and boasted that he was the mysterious lord of the Yo Thans and the next emperor of China," I answered, with an involuntary shudder, as I glanced at the grisly havoc Bill's ripping fangs had wrought. Wells' eyes blazed. He stepped forward and tore away the blood stained mask, revealing the smooth yellow face and clean-cut aristocrat features of a middle-aged China-man.

Wells recoiled with an exclamation.

"My word! Can it be possible! No wonder he delayed the aid he promised the government?and only promised, I can see now, to avert suspicion. And no wonder he was able to keep his true identity a secret. Clancy, Costigan, this is the Honor-able and Eminent Yun Lai Kao."

"What, the philosopher and philanthropist?" Clancy, who knew Canton, was even more amazed than I.

Wells nodded slowly. "What strange quirk in his nature led him along this path?" he said half to himself. "What a mind he had. What heights he might have risen to, but for that one twist in his soul. Who can explain it?"

Clancy, who knew the Orient, seemed to be groping for words to frame a thought.

"China," he said, "is China. And there's no use in a white man tryin' to figger her out."

Aye, China is China—vast, aloof, inscrutable, the Sphynx of the nations.

BLOW THE CHINKS DOWN!

A FAMILIAR STOCKY SHAPE, stood with a foot on the brass rail, as I entered the American Bar, in Hong-kong. I glared at the shape disapprovingly, recognizing it as Bill McGlory of the *Dutchman.* That is one ship I enthusiastically detest, this dislike being shared by all the bold lads aboard the *Sea Girl,* from the cap'n to the cook.

I shouldered up along the bar. Ignoring Bill, I called for a whisky straight.

"You know, John," said Bill, addressing hisself to the bartender, "you got no idee the rotten tubs which calls theirselves ships that's tied up to the wharfs right now. Now then, the *Sea Girl* for instance. An' there's a guy named Steve Costigan—"

"You know, John," I broke in, addressing myself to the bartender, "it's clean surprisin' what goes around on their hind laigs callin' theirselves sailor-men, these days. A baboon got outa the zoo at Brisbane and they just now spotted it on the wharfs here in Hong-kong."

"You don't say," said John the bar-keep. "Where'd it been?"

"To sea," I said. "It'd shipped as A.B. mariner on the *Dutchman* and was their best hand."

With which caustic repartee, I stalked out in gloating triumph, leaving Bill McGlory gasping and strangling as he tried to think of something to say in return. To celebrate my crushing victory over the enemy I swaggered into the La Belle Cabaret and soon seen a good looking girl setting alone at a table. She was toying with her cigaret and drink like she was bored, so I went over and set down.

"Evenin', Miss," I says, doffing my cap. "I'm just in from sea and cravin' to toss my money around. Do you dance?"

She eyed me amusedly from under her long, drooping lashes and said: "Yes, I do, on occasion. But I don't work here, sailor."

"Oh, excuse me, Miss," I said, getting up. "I sure beg your pardon."

"That's all right," she said. "Don't run away. Let's sit here and talk."

"That's fine," I said, setting back down again, when to my annoyance a sea-going figger bulked up to the table.

Even', Miss," said Bill McGlory, fixing me with a accusing stare. "Is this walrus annoyin' you?"

"Listen here, you flat-headed mutt—" I begun with some heat, but the girl said: "Now, now, don't fight, boys. Sit down and let's all talk sociably. I like to meet people from the States in this heathen land. My name is Kit Worley and I work for Tung Yin, the big Chinese merchant."

"Private secretary or somethin'?" says Bill.

"Governess to his nieces," said she. "But don't let's talk about me. Tell me something about yourselves. You boys are sailors, aren't you?"

"I am," I replied meaningly. Bill glared at me.

"Do tell me about some of your voyages," said she hurriedly. "I just adore ships."

"Then you'd sure like the *Dutchman,* Miss Worley," beamed Bill. "I don't like to brag, but for trim lines, smooth rig, a fine figger and speed, they ain't a sailin' craft in the China trade can hold a candle to her. She's a dream. A child could steer her."

"Or anybody with a child's mind," I says. "And does—when you're at the wheel."

"Listen here, you scum of the Seven Seas," said Bill turning brick color. "You layoff the *Dutchman.* I'd never have the nerve to insult a sweet ship like her if I sailed in a wormy, rotten-timbered, warped-decked, crank-ruddered, crooked-keeled, crazy-rigged tub like the *Sea Girl.*"

"You'll eat them words with a sauce of your own blood," I howled.

"Boys!" said Miss Worley. "Now, boys."

"Miss Worley," I said, getting up and shedding my coat, "I'm a law-abidin'
and peaceful man, gentle and generous to a fault. But they's times when patience
becomes a vice and human kindness is a stumblin' block on the road of progress.
This baboon in human form don't understand no kind of moral suasion but a
bust on the jaw."

"Come out in the alley," squalled Bill, bounding up like a jumping-jack.

"Come on," I said. "Let's settle this here feud once and for all. Miss Worley,"
I said, "wait here for the victor. I won't be gone long."

Out in the alley, surrounded by a gang of curious coolies, we squared off
without no more ado. We was well matched, about the same height and weighing
about 190 pounds each. But as we approached each other with our fists up, a form
stepped between. We stopped and glared in outraged surprise. It was a tall, slender
Englishman with a kind of tired, half humorous expression.

"Come, come, my good men," he said. "We can't have this sort of thing, you
know. Bad example to the natives and all that sort of thing. Can't have white men
fighting in the alleys these days. Times too unsettled, you know. Must uphold the
white man's standard."

"Well, by golly," I said. "I've had a hundred fights in Hong-kong and nobody
yet never told me before I was settin' a bad example to nobody."

"Bad tactics, just the same," he said. "And quite too much unrest now. If the
discontented Oriental sees white men bashing each other's bally jaws, the white
race loses just that much prestige, you see."

"But what right you got buttin' into a private row?" I complained.

"Rights vested in me by the Chinese government, working with the British
authorities, old topper," said the Englishman. "Brent is the name."

"Sir Peter Brent of the Secret Service, hey?" I grunted. "I've heard tell of you.
But I dunno what you could do if we was to tell you to go chase yourself."

"I could summon the bally police and throw you in jail, old thing," he said
apologetically. "But I don't want to do that."

"Say," I said, "You got any idee how many Chinee cops it'd take to lug Steve
Costigan and Bill McGlory to the hoosegow?"

"A goodly number, I should judge," said he. "Still if you lads persist in this
silly feud, I shall have to take the chance. I judge fifty would be about the right
number."

"Aw, hell," snorted Bill, hitching up his britches. "Let's rock him to sleep and
go on with the fray. He can't do nothin'."

But I balked. Something about the slim Britisher made me feel mad and
ashamed too. He was so frail looking alongside us sluggers.

"Aw, let it slide for the time bein'," I muttered. "We'd have to lay him out first before he'd let us go on, and he's too thin to hit. We might bust him in half. Let it go, if he's so plumb set on it. We got the whole world to fight in."

"You're gettin' soft and sentimental," snorted Bill. And with that he swaggered off in high disgust.

I eyed him morosely.

"Now he'll probably think I was afraid to fight him," I said gloomily. "And it's all your fault."

"Sorry, old man," said Sir Peter. "I'd have liked to have seen the mill myself, by jove. But public duty comes first, you know. Come, forget about it and have a drink."

"I ain't a-goin' to drink with you," I said bitterly. "You done spoilt my fun and made me look like a coward."

And disregarding his efforts to conciliate me, I shoved past him and wandered gloomily down the alley. I didn't go back to the La Belle. I was ashamed to admit to Miss Worley that they wasn't no fight. But later on I got to thinking about it and wondering what Bill told her in case he went back to her. It would be just like him to tell her I run out on him and refused to fight, I thought, or that he flattened me without getting his hair ruffled. He wasn't above punching a wall or something and telling her he skinned them knuckles on my jaw.

So I decided to look Miss Worley up and explain the whole thing to her—also take her to a theater or something if she'd go. She was a very pretty girl, refined and educated—anybody could tell that—yet not too proud to talk with a ordinary sailorman. Them kind is few and far betweenst.

I asked a bar-keep where Tung Yin lived and he told me. "But," he added, "you better keep away from Tung Yin. He's a shady customer and he don't like whites."

"You're nuts," I said. "Any man which Miss Kit Worley works for is bound to be okay."

"Be that as it may," said the bar-keep. "The cops think that Tung Yin was some way mixed up in the big diamond theft."

"What big diamond theft?" I said.

"Gee whiz," he said. "Didn't you hear about the big diamond theft last month?"

"Last month I was in Australia," I said impatiently.

"Well," he said, "somebody stole the Royal Crystal—that's what they called the diamond account of a emperor of China once usin' it to tell fortunes, like the gypsies use a crystal ball, y'know. Somebody stole it right outa the government museum. Doped the guards, hooked the stone and got clean away. Slickest thing I ever heard of in my life. That diamond's worth a fortune. And some think that

Tung Yin had a hand in it. Regular international ruckus. They got Sir Peter Brent, the big English detective, workin' on the case now."

"Well," I said, "I ain't interested. Only I know Tung Yin never stole it, because Miss Worley wouldn't work for nobody but a gent."

SO I WENT TO TUNG YIN'S place. It was a whopping big house, kinda like a palace, off some distance from the main part of the city. I went in a 'ricksha and got there just before sundown. The big house was set out by itself amongst groves of orange trees and cherry trees and the like, and I seen a airplane out in a open space that was fixed up like a landing field. I remembered that I'd heard tell that Tung Yin had a young Australian aviator named Clanry in his employ. I figgered likely that was his plane.

I started for the house and then got cold feet. I hadn't never been in a rich Chinee's dump before and I didn't know how to go about it. I didn't know whether you was supposed to go up and knock on the door and ask for Miss Kit Worley, or what. So I decided I'd cruise around a little and maybe I'd see her walking in the garden. I come up to the garden, which had a high wall around it, and I climbed up on the wall and looked over. They was lots of flowers and cherry trees and a fountain with a bronze dragon, and over near the back of the big house they was another low wall, kind of separating the house from the garden. And I seen a feminine figger pass through a small gate in this wall.

Taking a chance it was Miss Worley, I dropped into the garden, hastened forward amongst the cherry trees and flowers, and blundered through the gate into a kind of small court. Nobody was there, but I seen a door just closing in the house so I went right on through and come into a room furnished in the usual Chinese style, with tapestries and screens and silk cushions and them funny Chinese tea tables and things. A chorus of startled feminine squeals brung me up standing and I gawped about in confusion. Miss Worley wasn't nowhere in sight. All I seen was three or four Chinese girls which looked at me like I was a sea serpent.

"What you do here?" asked one of them.

"I'm lookin' for the governess," I said, thinking that maybe these was Tung Yin's nieces. Though, by golly, I never seen no girls which had less of the schoolgirl look about 'em.

"Governor?" she said. "You crazee? Governor him live along Nanking."

"Naw, naw," I said. "Gover-*ness*, see? The young lady which governesses the big boy's nieces—Tung Yin's nieces."

"You crazee," she said decisively. "Tung Yin him got no fool nieces."

"Say, listen," I said. "We ain't gettin' nowhere. I can't speak Chinee and you evidently can't understand English. I'm lookin' for Miss Kit Worley, see?"

"Ooooh!" she understood all right and looked at me with her slant eyes widened. They all got together and whispered while I got nervouser and nervouser. I didn't like the look of things, somehow. Purty soon she said: "Mees Worley she not live along here no more. She gone."

"Well," I said vaguely, "I reckon I better be goin'." I started for the door, but she grabbed me. "Wait," she said. "You lose your head, suppose you go that way."

"Huh?" I grunted, slightly shocked and most unpleasantly surprised. "What? I ain't done nothin'."

She made a warning gesture and turning to one of the other girls said: "Go fetch Yuen Tang."

The other girl looked surprised: "Yuen Tang?" she said kind of dumb-like, like she didn't understand. The first girl snapped something at her in Chinee and give her a disgusted push through the door. Then she turned to me.

"Tung Yin no like white devils snooping around," she said with a shake of her head. "Suppose he find you here, he cut your head off—snick," she said dramatically, jerking her finger acrost her throat.

I will admit cold sweat bust out on me.

"Great cats," I said plaintively. "I thought this Tung Yin was a respectable merchant. I ain't never heard he was a mysterious mandarin or a brigand or somethin'. Stand away from that door, sister. I'm makin' tracks."

Again she shook her head and laying a finger to her lips cautiously, she beckoned me to look through the door by which I'd entered. The gate opening into the garden from the courtyard was partly open.

What I seen made my hair stand up. It was nearly dark. The garden looked shadowy and mysterious, but it was still light enough for me to make out the figgers of five big coolies sneaking along with long curved knives in their hands.

"They look for you," whispered the girl. "Tung Yin fear spies. They know somebody climb the wall. Wait, we hide you."

THEY GRABBED ME AND pushed me into a kind of closet and shut the door, leaving me in total darkness. How long I stood there sweating with fear and nervousness, I never knowed. I couldn't hear much in there and what I did hear was muffled, but it seemed like they was a lot of whispering and muttering going on through the house. Once I heard a kind of galloping like a lot of men running, then they was some howls and what sounded like a voice swearing in English.

Then at last the door opened. A Chinaman in the garb of a servant looked in and I was about to bust him one, when I seen the Chinese girl looking over his shoulder.

"Come out cautiously," he said, in his hissing English. "I am your friend and would aid you to escape, but if you do not follow my directions exactly, you will not live to see the sunrise. Tung Yin will butcher you."

"Holy cats," I said vaguely. "What's he got it in for me for? I ain't done nothin'."

"He mistrusts all men," said the Chinaman. "I am Yuen Tang and I hate his evil ways, though circumstances have forced me to do his bidding. Come."

That was a nice mess for a honest seaman to get into, hey? I followed Yuen Tang and the girl, sweating profusely, and they led me through long, deserted corridors and finally stopped before a heavy barred door.

"Through this door lies freedom," hissed Yuen Tang. "To escape from the house of Tung Yin you must cross the chamber which lies beyond this portal. Once through, you will come to an outer door and liberty. Here." He shoved a small but wicked looking pistol into my hand.

"What's that for?" I asked nervously, recoiling. "I don't like them things."

"You may have to shoot your way through," he whispered. "No man knows the guile of Tung Yin. In the darkness of the chamber he may come upon you with murder in his hand."

"Oh gosh," I gasped wildly. "Ain't they no other way out?"

"None other," said Yuen Tang. "You must take your chance."

I felt like my legs was plumb turning to taller. And then I got mad. Here was me, a peaceful, law-abiding sailorman, being hounded and threatened by a blame yellow-belly I hadn't never even seen.

"Gimme that gat," I growled. "I ain't never used nothin' but my fists in a fray, but I ain't goin' to let no Chinee carve me up if I can help it."

"Good," purred Yuen Tang. "Take the gun and go swiftly. If you hear a sound in the darkness, shoot quick and straight."

So, shoving the gun into my sweaty fingers, him and the girl opened the door, pushed me through and shut the door behind me. I turned quick and pushed at it. They'd barred it on the other side and I could of swore I heard a sort of low snicker.

I strained my eyes trying to see something. It was as dark as anything. I couldn't see nothing nor hear nothing. I started groping my way forward, then stopped short. Somewhere I heard a door open stealthily. I started sweating. I couldn't see nothing at all, but I heard the door close again, a bolt slid softly into place and I had the uncanny sensation that they was somebody in that dark room with me.

CUSSING FIERCELY TO myself because my hand shook so, I poked the gun out ahead of me and waited. A stealthy sound came to me from the other side of the chamber and I pulled the trigger wildly. A flash of fire stabbed back at me and I heard the lead sing past my ear as I ducked wildly. I was firing blindly, as fast as I could jerk the trigger, figgering on kind of swamping him with the amount of lead I was throwing his way. And he was shooting back just as fast. I seen the flash spitting in a continual stream of fire and the air was full of lead, from the sound. I heard the bullets sing past my ears so close they nearly combed my hair, and spat on the wall behind me. My hair stood straight up, but I kept on jerking the trigger till the gun was empty and no answering shots came.

Aha, I thought, straightening up. I've got him. And at that instant, to my rage and amazement, there sounded a metallic click from the darkness. It was incredible I should miss all them shots, even in the dark. But it must be so, I thought wrathfully. He wasn't laying on the floor full of lead; his gun was empty too. I knowed that sound was the hammer snapping on a empty shell.

And I got real mad. I seen red. I throwed away the gun and, cussing silently, got on my all-fours and begun to crawl stealthily but rapidly acrost the floor. If he had a knife, this mode of attack would give me some advantage.

That was a blame big chamber. I judge I'd traversed maybe half the distance across it when my head come into violent contact with what I instinctively realized was a human skull. My opponent had got the same idee I had. Instantly we throwed ourselves ferociously on each other and there begun a most desperate battle in the dark. My unseen foe didn't seem to have no knife, but he was a bearcat in action. I was doing my best, slugging, kicking, rassling and ever and anon sinking my fangs into his hide, but I never see the Chinaman that could fight like this 'un fought. I never seen one which could use his fists, but this 'un could.

I heard 'em swish past my head in the dark and purty soon I stopped one of them fists with my nose. Whilst I was trying to shake the blood and stars outa my eyes, my raging opponent clamped his teeth in my ear and set back. With a maddened roar, I hooked him in the belly with such heartiness that he let go with a gasp and curled up like a angle-worm. I then climbed atop of him and set to work punching him into a pulp, but he come to hisself under my very fists, as it were, pitched me off and got a scissors hold that nearly caved my ribs in.

Gasping for breath, I groped around and having found one of his feet, got a toe-hold and started twisting it off. He give a ear-piercing and bloodthirsty yell and jarred me loose with a terrific kick in the neck.

We arose and fanned the air with wild swings, trying to find each other in the dark. After nearly throwing our arms out of place missing haymakers, we abandoned this futile and aimless mode of combat and having stumbled into each other, we got each other by the neck with our lefts and hammered away with our rights.

A minute or so of this satisfied my antagonist, who, after a vain attempt to find my right and tie it up, throwed hisself blindly and bodily at me. We went to the floor together. I got a strangle hold on him and soon had him gurgling spasmodically. A chance swat on the jaw jarred me loose, but I come back with a blind swing that by pure chance crunched solidly into his mouth. Again we locked horns and tumbled about on the floor.

"DERN YOUR YELLER hide," said the Chinaman between gasps. "You're the toughest Chinee I ever fit in my life, but I'll get you yet!"

"Bill McGlory," I said in disgust. "What you doin' here?"

"By golly," said he. "If I didn't know you was Tung Yin, I'd swear you was Steve Costigan."

"I am Steve Costigan, you numb-skull," I said impatiently, hauling him to his feet.

"Well, gee whiz," he said. "Them girls told me I might have to shoot Tung Yin to make my getaway, but they didn't say nothin' about you. Where is the big shot?"

"How should I know?" I snapped. "Yuen Tang and a girl told me Tung Yin was goin' to chop my head off. And they gimme a gun and pushed me in here. What you doin' anyway?"

"I come here to see Miss Worley," he said. "She'd done left when I went back to the La Belle. I looked around the streets for her, then I decided I'd come out to Tung Yin's and see her."

"And who told you you could come callin' on her?" I snarled.

"Well," he said smugly, "anybody could see that girl had fell for me. As far as that goes, who told you to come chasin' after her?"

"That's entirely different," I growled. "Go ahead with your story."

"Well," he said, "I come and knocked on the door and a Chinaman opened it and I asked for Miss Worley and he slammed the door in my face. That made me mad, so I prowled around and found a gate unlocked in the garden wall and come in, hopin' to find her in the garden. But a gang of tough lookin' coolies spotted me and though I tried to explain my peaceful intentions, they got hard and started wavin' knives around.

"Well, Steve, you know me. I'm a peaceful man but I ain't goin' be tromped on. I got rights, by golly. I hauled off and knocked the biggest one as cold as a wedge. Then I lit out and they run me clean through the garden. Every time I made for the wall, they headed me off, so I run through the courtyard into the house and smack into Tung Yin hisself. I knowed him by sight, you see. He had a golden pipe-case which he was lookin' at like he thought it was a million dollars or somethin'. When he seen me, he quick stuck it in his shirt and give a yelp like he was stabbed.

"I tried to explain, but he started yelling to the coolies in Chinese and they bust in after me. I run through a door ahead of 'em and slammed it in their faces and bolted it, and whilst I was holding it on one side and they was tryin' to kick it down on the other side, up come a Chinagirl which told me in broken English that she'd help me, and she hid me in a closet. Purty soon her and a coolie come and said that Tung Yin was huntin' me in another part of the house, and that they'd help me escape. So they took me to a door and gimme a gun and said if I could get through the room I'd be safe. Then they shoved me in here and bolted the door behind me. The next thing I knowed, bullets was singin' past my ears like a swarm of bees. You sure are a rotten shot, Steve."

"You ain't so blamed hot yourself," I sniffed. "Anyway, it looks to me like we been took plenty, and you sure are lucky to be alive. For some reason or other Tung Yin wanted to get rid of us and he seen a good way to do it without no risk to his own hide, by gyppin' us into bumpin' each other off. Wait, though—looks to me like that mutt Yuen Tang engineered this deal. Maybe Tung Yin didn't know nothin' about it."

"Well, anyway," said Bill, "they's somethin' crooked goin' on here that these Chinese don't want known. They think we're government spies, I betcha."

"Well, let's get outa here," I said.

"I bet they think we're both dead," said Bill. "They told me these walls was sound-proof. I bet they use this for a regular murder room. I been hearin' a lot of dark tales about Tung Yin. I'm surprised a nice girl like Miss Worley would work for him."

"Aw," I said, "we musta misunderstood her. She don't work here. The Chinagirls told me so. He ain't got no nieces. It musta been somebody else."

Well let's get out and argy later," Bill said. "Come on, let's feel around and find a door."

"Well," I said, "what good'll that do? The doors is bolted, ain't they?"

"Well, my gosh," he said, "can't we bust 'em down? Gee whiz, you'd stop to argy if they was goin' to shoot you."

We felt around and located the walls and we hadn't been groping long before I found what I knowed was bound to be a door. I told Bill and he come feeling his way along the wall. Then I heard something else.

"Easy, Bill," I whispered. "Somebody's unboltin' this door from the other side."

STANDING THERE SILENTLY, we plainly heard the sound of bolts being drawn. Then the door began opening and a crack of light showed. We flattened ourselves on either side of the door and waited, nerves tense and jumping.

Right then my white bulldog, Mike, could 'a' been able to help, if he hadn't been laid up with distemper.

The door opened. A Chinaman stuck his head in, grinning nastily. He had a electric torch in his hand and he was flashing it around over the floor—to locate the corpses, I reckon.

Before he had time to realize they wasn't no corpses, I grabbed him by the neck and jerked him headlong into the room. Bill connected a heavy right swing with his jaw. The Chinee stiffened, out cold. I let him fall careless-like to the floor. He'd dropped the light when Bill socked him. It went out when it hit the floor, but Bill groped around, and found it and flashed it on.

"Let's go," said Bill, so we went into the dark corridor outside and shut the door and bolted it. Bill flashed his light around, for it was dark in the corridor. We went along it and come through a door. Lights was on in that chamber, and in them adjoining it, but everything was still and deserted. We stole very warily through the rooms but we seen nobody, neither coolies, servants nor girls.

The house was kind of disheveled and tumbled about. Some of the hangings and things was gone. Things was kind of jerked around like the people had left all of a sudden, taking part of their belongings with 'em.

"By golly," said Bill. "This here's uncanny. They've moved out and left it with us."

I was opening a door and started to answer, then stopped short. In the room beyond, almost within arm's length, as I seen through the half open door, was Yuen Tang. But he wasn't dressed in servant's clothes no more. He looked like a regular mandarin. He had a golden pipe case in his hands and he was gloating over it like a miser over his gold.

"There's Yuen Tang," I whispered.

"Yuen Tang my pet pig's knuckle," snorted Bill. "That's Tung Yin hisself."

The Chinaman heard us and his head jerked up. His eyes flared and then narrowed wickedly. He stuck the case back in his blouse, quick but fumbling, like anybody does when they're in a desperate hurry to keep somebody from seeing something.

His other hand went inside his waist-sash and come out with a snub-nosed pistol. But before he could use it, me and Bill hit him simultaneous, one on the jaw and one behind the ear. Either punch woulda settled his hash. The both of 'em together dropped him like a pole-axed steer. The gun flew outa his hand and he hit the floor so hard the golden pipe case dropped outa his blouse and fell open on the floor.

"Let's get going before he comes to," said I impatiently, but Bill had stopped and was stooping with his hands on his knees, eying the pipe case covetously.

"Boy, oh boy," he said. "Ain't that some outfit? I betcha it cost three or four hundred bucks. I wisht I was rich. Them Chinee merchant princes sure spread theirselves when it comes to elegance."

I looked into the case which laid open on the floor. They was a small pipe with a slender amber stem and a ivory bowl, finely carved and yellow with age, some extra stems, a small silver box of them funny looking Chinese matches, and a golden rod for cleaning the pipe.

"By golly," said Bill, "I always wanted one of them ivory pipes."

"Hey," I said, "You can't hook Tung Yin's pipe. He ain't a-goin' to like it."

"Aw, it won't be stealin'," said Bill. "I'll leave him mine. 'Course it's made outa bone instead of ivory, but it cost me a dollar'n a half. Wonder you didn't bust it while ago when we was fightin'. I'll change pipes with him and he won't notice it till we're outa his reach."

"Well, hustle, then," I said impatiently. "I don't hold with no such graft, but what can you expect of a mutt from the *Dutchman?* Hurry up, before Tung Yin comes to and cuts our heads off."

So Bill took the ivory pipe and put his pipe in the case and shut the case up and stuck it back in Tung Yin's blouse. And we hustled. We come out into the courtyard. They wasn't no lanterns hanging there, or if they was they wasn't lighted, but the moon had come up and it was bright as day.

AND WE RAN RIGHT SMACK into Miss Kit Worley. There she was, dressed in flying togs and carrying a helmet in her hand. She gasped when she seen us.

"Good heavens," she said. "What are you doing here?"

"I come here to see you, Miss Worley," I said. "And Tung Yin made out like he was a servant tryin' to save me from his master, and gimme a gun and sent me into a dark room and, meanwhile, Bill had come buttin' in where he hadn't no business and they worked the same gag on him and we purty near kilt each other before we found out who we was."

She nodded, kind of bewildered, and then her eyes gleamed.

"I see," she said. "I see." She stood there twirling her helmet a minute, kind of studying, then she laid her hands on our shoulders and smiled very kindly and said: "Boys, I wish you'd do me a favor. I'm leaving in a few minutes by plane and I have a package that must be delivered. Will you boys deliver it?"

"Sure," we said. So she took out a small square package and said: "Take this to the Red Dragon. You know where that is? Sure you would. Well, go in and give it to the proprietor, Kang Woon. Don't give it to anyone else. And when you hand it to him, say, 'Tung Yin salutes you.' Got that straight?"

"Yeah," said Bill. "But gee whiz, Miss Worley, we can't leave you here to the mercy of them yellow-skinned cut-throats."

"Don't worry." She smiled. "I can handle Tung Yin. Go now, please. And thank you."

Well, she turned and went on in the house. We listened a minute and heard somebody howling and cussing in Chinese, and knowed Tung Yin had come to. We was fixing to go in and rescue Miss Worley, when we heard her talking to him, sharp and hard-like. He quieted down purty quick, so we looked at each other plumb mystified, and went on out in the garden and found the gate Bill come in at and went through it. We hadn't gone but a few yards when Bill says: "Dern it, Steve, I've lost that pipe I took offa Tung Yin."

"Well, gee whiz," I said disgustedly. "You ain't goin' back to look for it."

"I had it just before we come outa the garden," he insisted. So I went back with him, though highly disgusted, and he opened the gate and said: "Yeah, here it is. I musta dropped it as I started through the gate. Got a hole in my pocket."

About that time we seen three figgers in the moonlight crossing the garden—Miss Worley, Tung Yin and a slim, dark young fellow I knowed must be Clanry, the Australian aviator. All of 'em was dressed for flying, though Tung Yin looked like he'd just dragged on his togs recent. He looked kind of disrupted generally. As we looked we seen Miss Worley grab his arm and point and as Tung Yin turned his head, Clanry hit him from behind, hard, with a blackjack. For the second time that night the merchant prince took the count.

Miss Worley bent over him, tore his jacket open and jerked out that same golden pipe case. Then her and Clanry ran for a gate on the opposite side of the garden. They went through, leaving it open in their haste and then we saw 'em running through the moonlight to the plane, which lay amongst the orange groves. They reached it and right away we heard the roar of the propeller. They took off perfect and soared away towards the stars and outa sight.

As we watched, we heard the sound of fast driving autos. They pulled up in front of the place. We heard voices shouting commands in English and Chinese. Then Tung Yin stirred and staggered up, holding his head. From inside the house come the sound of doors being busted open and a general ruckus. Tung Yin felt groggily inside his blouse, then tore his hair, shook his fists at the sky, and run staggeringly across the garden to vanish through the other gate.

"What you reckon this is all about?" wondered Bill. "How come Miss Worley wanted Tung Yin's pipe, you reckon?"

"How should I know?" I replied. "Come on. This ain't any of our business. We got to deliver this package to Kang Woon."

So we faded away. And as we done so a backward look showed men in uniform ransacking the house and estate of Tung Yin.

No 'rickshas being available, we was purty tired when we come to the Red Dragon, in the early hours of morning. It was a low class dive on the waterfront which stayed open all night. Just then, unusual activity was going on. A bunch of natives was buzzing around the entrance and some Chinese police was shoving them back.

"Looks like Kang Woon's been raided," I grunted.

"That's it," said Bill. "Well, I been expectin' it, the dirty rat. I know he sells opium and I got a good suspicion he's a fence, too."

WE WENT UP TO THE DOOR and the Chinese cops wasn't going to let us in. We was about to haul off and sock 'em, when some autos drove up and stopped and a gang of soldiers with a Chinese officer and a English officer got out. They had a battered looking Chinaman with 'em in handcuffs. He was the one me and Bill socked and locked up in the murder room. They all went in and we fell in behind 'em and was in the dive before the cops knew what we was doing.

It was a raid all right. The place was full of men in the uniform of the Federal army and the Chinese constabulary. Some of 'em—officers, I reckon—was questioning the drunks and beggars they'd found in the place. Over on one side was a cluster of Chinamen in irons, amongst them Kang Woon, looking like a big sullen spider. He was being questioned, but his little beady black eyes glinted dull with murder and he kept his mouth shut.

"There's the mutt which butted in, on our fight," grunted Bill in disgust.

One of the men questioning Kang Woon was Sir Peter Brent; the others was a high rank Chinese officer and a plain clothes official of some sort.

The British officer we'd followed in saluted and said: "I regret to report, Sir Peter, that the birds have flown the bally coop. We found the house deserted and showing signs of a recent and hurried evacuation. We found this Chinaman lying unconscious in an inner chamber which was locked from the outside, but we've gotten nothing out of him. We heard a plane just as we entered the house and I greatly fear that the criminals have escaped by air. Of Tung Yin and the others we found no trace at all, and though we made a careful search of the premises, we did not discover the gem."

"We did not spring the trap quick enough," said Sir Peter. "I should have suspected that they would be warned."

Well, while they was talking, me and Bill went up to Kang Woon and handed him the package. He shrunk back and glared like we was trying to hand him a snake, but we'd been told to give it to him, so we dropped it into his lap and said: "Tung Yin salutes you," just like Miss Worley had told us. The next minute we was grabbed by a horde of cops and soldiers.

"Hey," yelled Bill wrathfully. "What kinda game is this?" And he stood one of 'em on the back of his neck with a beautiful left hook.

I'm a man of few words and quick action. I hit one of 'em in the solar plexus and he curled up like a snake. We was fixing to wade through them deluded heathens like a whirlwind through a cornfield when Sir Peter sprang forward.

"Hold hard a bit, lads," he ordered. "Let those men go."

They fell away from us and me and Bill faced the whole gang belligerently, snorting fire and defiance.

"I know these men." he said. "They're honest American sailors."

"But they gave this to the prisoner," said the Chinese official, holding up the package.

"I know," said Sir Peter. "But if they're mixed up in this affair, I'm certain it's through ignorance rather than intent. They're rather dumb, you know."

Me and Bill was speechless with rage. The official said: "I'm not so sure."

THE OFFICIAL OPENED the package and said: "Ah, just as I suspected. The very case in which the gem was stolen."

He held it up and it was a jewel case with the arms of the old Chinese empire worked on it in gold. Kang Woon glowered at it and his eyes was Hell's fire itself.

"Now look." The official opened it and we all gasped. Inside was a large white gem which sparkled and glittered like ice on fire. The handcuffed Chinaman gave a howl and kind of collapsed.

"The Royal Crystal," cried the official in delight. "The stolen gem itself. Who gave you men this package?"

"None of your blamed business," I growled and Bill snarled agreement.

"Arrest them," exclaimed the official, but Sir Peter interposed again. "Wait." And he said to us: "Now, lads, I believe you're straight, but you'd best come clean, you know."

We didn't say nothing and he said: "Perhaps you don't know the facts of the case. This stone—which is of immense value—was stolen from the governmental museum. We know that it was stolen by a gang of international thieves who have been masquerading as honest merchants and traders. This gang consisted of Tung Yin, Clanry the aviator, a number of lesser crooks who pretended to be in Tung Yin's employ, and a girl called Clever Kit Worley."

"Hey, you," said Bill. "You lay offa Miss Worley."

"Aha," said Sir Peter, "I fancied I'd strike fire there. Now come, lads, didn't Clever Kit give you that stone?"

We still didn't say nothing. About that time the Chinaman the soldiers had brung with them hollered: "I'll tell. I'll tell it all. They've betrayed me and left me to go to prison alone, have they? Curse them all!"

He was kind of hysterical, but talked perfect English—was educated at Oxford, I learned later. Everybody looked at him and he spilled the beans so fast his words tripped over each other: "Tung Yin, Clanry and the Worley woman stole the Royal Crystal. They were equal partners in all the crimes they committed. We—the coolies, the dancing girls and I—were but servants, doing their bidding, getting no share of the loot, but being paid higher salaries than we could have earned honestly. Oh, it was a business proposition, I tell you.

"Tonight we got the tip that the place was to be raided—Tung Yin has plenty of spies. No sooner had we received this information than these sailors came blundering in, hunting Kit Worley, who had charmed them as she has so many men. The woman and Clanry were not in the house. They were preparing the plane for a hurried flight. Tung Yin supposed these men to be spies of the government, so he sent some of his servants to beguile the one, while he donned a disguise of menial garments and befooled the other. We sent them into a dark chamber to slay each other. And, meanwhile, we hurried our plans for escape.

"Clanry, the Worley woman and Tung Yin were planning to escape in the plane, and they promised to take me with them. Tung Yin told the coolies and dancing girls to save themselves as best they could. They scattered, looting the house as they fled. Then Tung Yin told me to look into the death chamber and see if the two foreign devils had killed each other. I did so—and was knocked senseless. What happened then I can only guess, but that Tung Yin, Clanry and Kit Worley escaped in the plane, I am certain, though how these men came to have the gem is more than I can say."

"I believe I can answer that," said Sir Peter. "I happen to know that Kang Woon here has been handling stolen goods for the Tung Yin gang. That's why we raided him tonight at the same time we sent a squad to nab the others at Tung Yin's place. But as you've seen, we were a bit too late. Kang Woon had advanced them quite a bit of money already for the privilege of handling the stone for them—the amount to be added to his commission when the gem was sold. The sale would have made them all rich, even though they found it necessary to cut it up and sell it in smaller pieces. They dared not skip without sending this stone to Kang Woon, for he knew too much. But watch."

He laid the gem on a table and hit it with his pistol butt and smashed it into bits. Everybody gawped. Kang Woon gnashed his teeth with fury.

"A fake, you see," said Sir Peter. "I doubt if any but an expert could have told the difference. I happen to have had quite a bit of experience in that line, don't you know. Yes, Tung Yin and Kit Worley and Clanry planned to double-cross Kang Woon. They sent him this fake, knowing that they would be out of his reach before he learned of the fraud. He's an expert crook, but not a jewel expert, you know. And now I suppose Tung Yin and his pals are safely out of our reach with the Royal Crystal."

WHILE WE WAS LISTENING Bill took out the pipe he'd stole from Tung Yin and began to cram tobaccer in it. He cussed disgustedly.

"Hey, Steve," said he. "What you think? Somebody's gone and crammed a big piece of glass into this pipe bowl." He was trying to work it loose.

"Gimme that pipe," I hollered and jerked it outa his hands. Disregarding his wrathful protests, I opened my knife and pried and gouged at the pipe bowl until the piece of glass rolled into my hand. I held it up and it caught the candle lights with a thousand gleams and glittering sparkles.

"The Royal Crystal," howled the Chinese. And Sir Peter grabbed it.

"By Jove," he exclaimed. "It's the real gem, right enough. Where did you get it?"

"Well," I said, "I'll tell you. Seein' as how Miss Worley is done got away and you can't catch her and put her in jail—and I don't mind tellin' you I'm glad of it, 'cause she mighta been a crook but she was nice to me. I see now why she and Clanry wanted that pipe case. It was a slick place to hide the gem in, but nothin's safe from one of them thieves offa the *Dutchman.* Tung Yin was goin' to double-cross Kang Woon and Clanry and Miss Worley double-crossed Tung Yin, but I betcha they look funny when they open that golden pipe case and find nothin' in it but Bill's old pipe."

"Aw," said Bill, "I betcha she keeps it to remember me by. I betcha she'll treasure it amongst her dearest soovernears."

Sir Peter kind of tore his hair and moaned: "Will you blighters tell us what it's all about and how you came by that gem?"

"Well," I said, "Tung Yin evidently had the gem in his pipe and Bill stole his pipe. And . . .Well, it's a long story."

"Well, I'll be damned," said Sir Peter. "The keenest minds in the secret service fail and a pair of blundering bone-headed sailors succeed without knowing what it's all about."

"Well," said Bill impatiently, "if you mutts are through with me and Steve, we aims for to go forth and seek some excitement. Up to now this here's been about the tiresomest shore leave I've had yet."

BREED OF BATTLE

ME AND MY WHITE BULLDOG Mike was peaceably taking our beer in a joint on the waterfront when Porkey Straus come piling in, plumb puffing with excitement.

"Hey, Steve!" he yelped. "What you think? Joe Ritchie's in port with Terror."

"Well?" I said.

"Well, gee whiz," he said, "you mean to set there and let on like you don't know nothin' about Terror, Ritchie's fightin' brindle bull? Why, he's the pit champeen of the Asiatics. He's killed more fightin' dogs than—"

"Yeah, yeah," I said impatiently. "I know all about him. I been listenin' to what a bear-cat he is for the last year, in every Asiatic port I've touched."

"Well," said Porkey, "I'm afraid we ain't goin' to git to see him perform."

"Why not?" asked Johnnie Blinn, a shifty-eyed bar-keep.

"Well," said Porkey, "they ain't a dog in Singapore to match ag'in' him. Fritz Steinmann, which owns the pit and runs the dog fights, has scoured the port and they just ain't no canine which their owners'll risk ag'in' Terror. Just my luck. The

- 57 -

chance of a lifetime to see the fightin'est dog of 'em all perform. And they's no first-class mutt to toss in with him. Say, Steve, why don't you let Mike fight him?"

"Not a chance," I growled. "Mike gets plenty of scrappin' on the streets. Besides, I'll tell you straight, I think dog fightin' for money is a dirty low-down game. Take a couple of fine, upstandin' dogs, full of ginger and fightin' heart, and throw 'em in a concrete pit to tear each other's throats out, just so a bunch of four-flushin' tin-horns like you, which couldn't take a punch or give one either, can make a few lousy dollars bettin' on 'em."

"But they likes to fight," argued Porkey. "It's their nature."

"It's the nature of any red-blooded critter to fight. Man or dog!" I said. "Let 'em fight on the streets, for bones or for fun, or just to see which is the best dog. But pit-fightin' to the death is just too dirty for me to fool with, and I ain't goin' to get Mike into no such mess."

"Aw, let him alone, Porkey," sneered Johnnie Blinn nastily. "He's too chicken-hearted to mix in them rough games. Ain't you, Sailor?"

"Belay that," I roared. "You keep a civil tongue in your head, you wharfside rat. I never did like you nohow, and one more crack like that gets you this." I brandished my huge fist at him and he turned pale and started scrubbing the bar like he was trying for a record.

"I wantcha to know that Mike can lick this Terror mutt," I said, glaring at Porkey. "I'm fed up hearin' fellers braggin' on that brindle murderer. Mike can lick him. He can lick any dog in this lousy port, just like I can lick any man here. If Terror meets Mike on the street and gets fresh, he'll get his belly-full. But Mike ain't goin' to get mixed up in no dirty racket like Fritz Steinmann runs and you can lay to that." I made the last statement in a voice like a irritated bull, and smashed my fist down on the table so hard I splintered the wood, and made the decanters bounce on the bar.

"Sure, sure, Steve," soothed Porkey, pouring hisself a drink with a shaky hand. "No offense. No offense. Well, I gotta be goin'."

"So long," I growled, and Porkey cruised off.

UP STROLLED A MAN WHICH had been standing by the bar. I knowed him—Philip D'Arcy, a man whose name is well known in all parts of the world. He was a tall, slim, athletic fellow, well dressed, with bold gray eyes and a steel-trap jaw. He was one of them gentleman adventurers, as they call 'em, and he'd did everything from running a revolution in South America and flying a war plane in a Balkan brawl, to exploring in the Congo. He was deadly with a six-gun, and as dangerous as a rattler when somebody crossed him.

"That's a fine dog you have, Costigan," he said. "Clean white. Not a speck of any other color about him. That means good luck for his owner."

I knowed that D'Arcy had some pet superstitions of his own, like lots of men which live by their hands and wits like him.

"Well," I said, "anyway, he's about the fightin'est dog you ever seen."

"I can tell that," he said, stooping and eying Mike close. "Powerful jaws—not too undershot—good teeth—broad between the eyes—deep chest—legs that brace like iron. Costigan, I'll give you a hundred dollars for him, just as he stands."

"You mean you want me to sell you Mike?" I asked kinda incredulous.

"Sure. Why not?"

"Why not!" I repeatedly indignantly. "Well, gee whiz, why not ask a man to sell his brother for a hundred dollars? Mike wouldn't stand for it. Anyway, I wouldn't do it."

"I need him," persisted D'Arcy. "A white dog with a dark man—it means luck. White dogs have always been lucky for me. And my luck's been running against me lately. I'll give you a hundred and fifty."

"D'Arcy," I said, "you couldst stand there and offer me money all day long and raise the ante every hand, but it wouldn't be no good. Mike ain't for sale. Him and me has knocked around the world together too long. They ain't no use talkin'."

His eyes flashed for a second. He didn't like to be crossed in any way. Then he shrugged his shoulders.

"All right. We'll forget it. I don't blame you for thinking a lot of him. Let's have a drink."

So we did and he left.

I WENT AND GOT ME A shave, because I was matched to fight some tramp at Ace Larnigan's Arena and I wanted to be in shape for the brawl. Well, afterwards I was walking down along the docks when I heard somebody go: "Hssst!"

I looked around and saw a yellow hand beckon me from behind a stack of crates. I sauntered over, wondering what it was all about, and there was a Chinese boy hiding there. He put his finger to his lips. Then quick he handed me a folded piece of paper, and beat it, before I couldst ask him anything.

I opened the paper and it was a note in a woman's handwriting which read:

> Dear Steve,
>
> I have admired you for a long time at a distance, but have been too timid to make myself known to you. Would it be too much to ask you to give me an opportunity to tell you my emotions by word of mouth? If you care at all, I will meet you by the old Manchu House on the Tungen Road, just after dark.

An affectionate admirer.

P .S. Please, oh please be there! You have stole my heart away!

"Mike," I said pensively, "ain't it plumb peculiar the strange power I got over wimmen, even them I ain't never seen? Here is a girl I don't even know the name of, even, and she has been eatin' her poor little heart out in solitude because of me. Well—" I hove a gentle sigh—"it's a fatal gift, I'm afeared."

Mike yawned. Sometimes it looks like he ain't got no romance at all about him. I went back to the barber shop and had the barber to put some ile on my hair and douse me with perfume. I always like to look genteel when I meet a feminine admirer.

Then, as the evening was waxing away, as the poets say, I set forth for the narrow winding back street just off the waterfront proper. The natives call it the Tungen Road, for no particular reason as I can see. The lamps there is few and far between and generally dirty and dim. The street's lined on both sides by lousy looking native shops and hovels. You'll come to stretches which looks clean deserted and falling to ruins.

Well, me and Mike was passing through just such a district when I heard sounds of some kind of a fracas in a dark alley-way we was passing. Feet scruffed. They was the sound of a blow and a voice yelled in English: "Halp! Halp! These Chinese is killin' me!"

"Hold everything," I roared, jerking up my sleeves and plunging for the alley, with Mike at my heels. "Steve Costigan is on the job."

It was as dark as a stack of black cats in that alley. Plunging blind, I bumped into somebody and sunk a fist to the wrist in him. He gasped and fell away. I heard Mike roar suddenly and somebody howled bloody murder. Then *wham!* A blackjack or something like it smashed on my skull and I went to my knees.

"That's done yer, yer blawsted Yank," said a nasty voice in the dark.

"You're a liar," I gasped, coming up blind and groggy but hitting out wild and ferocious. One of my blind licks musta connected because I heard somebody cuss bitterly. And then *wham*, again come that blackjack on my dome. What little light they was, was behind me, and whoever it was slugging me, couldst see me better'n I could see him. That last smash put me down for the count, and he musta hit me again as I fell.

I COULDN'T OF BEEN OUT but a few minutes. I come to myself lying in the darkness and filth of the alley and I had a most splitting headache and dried blood was clotted on a cut in my scalp. I groped around and found a match in my pocket and struck it.

The alley was empty. The ground was all tore up and they was some blood scattered around, but neither the thugs nor Mike was nowhere to be seen. I run down the alley, but it ended in a blank stone wall. So I come back onto the Tungen Road and looked up and down but seen nobody. I went mad.

"Philip D'Arcy!" I yelled all of a sudden. "He done it. He stole Mike. He writ me that note. Unknown admirer, my eye. I been played for a sucker again. He thinks Mike'll bring him luck. I'll bring him luck, the double-crossin' son-of-a-seacook. I'll sock him so hard he'll bite hisself in the ankle. I'll bust him into so many pieces he'll go through a sieve—"

With these meditations, I was running down the street at full speed, and when I busted into a crowded thoroughfare, folks turned and looked at me in amazement. But I didn't pay no heed. I was steering my course for the European Club, a kind of ritzy place where D'Arcy generally hung out. I was still going at top-speed when I run up the broad stone steps and was stopped by a pompous looking doorman which sniffed scornfully at my appearance, with my clothes torn and dirty from laying in the alley, and my hair all touseled and dried blood on my hair and face.

"Lemme by," I gritted, "I gotta see a mutt."

"Gorblime," said the doorman. "You cawn't go in there. This is a very exclusive club, don't you know. Only gentlemen are allowed here. Cawn't have a blawsted gorilla like you bursting in on the gentlemen. My word! Get along now before I call the police."

There wasn't time to argue.

With a howl of irritation I grabbed him by the neck and heaved him into a nearby goldfish pond. Leaving him floundering and howling, I kicked the door open and rushed in. I dashed through a wide hallway and found myself in a wide room with big French winders. That seemed to be the main club room, because it was very scrumptiously furnished and had all kinds of animal heads on the walls, alongside of crossed swords and rifles in racks.

They was a number of Americans and Europeans setting around drinking whiskey-and-sodas, and playing cards. I seen Philip D'Arcy setting amongst a bunch of his club-members, evidently spinning yards about his adventures. And I seen red.

"D'Arcy!" I yelled, striding toward him regardless of the card tables I upset. "Where's my dog?"

PHILIP D'ARCY SPRANG UP with a kind of gasp and all the club men jumped up too, looking amazed.

"My word!" said a Englishman in a army officer's uniform. "Who let this boundah in? Come, come, my man, you'll have to get out of this."

"You keep your nose clear of this or I'll bend it clean outa shape," I howled, shaking my right mauler under the aforesaid nose. "This ain't none of your business. D'Arcy, what you done with my dog?"

"You're drunk, Costigan," he snapped. "I don't know what you're talking about."

"That's a lie," I screamed, crazy with rage. "You tried to buy Mike and then you had me slugged and him stole. I'm on to you, D'Arcy. You think because you're a big shot and I'm just a common sailorman, you can take what you want. But you ain't gettin' away with it. You got Mike and you're goin' to give him back or I'll tear your guts out. Where is he? Tell me before I choke it outa you."

"Costigan, you're mad," snarled D'Arcy, kind of white. "Do you know whom you're threatening? I've killed men for less than that."

"You stole my dog!" I howled, so wild I hardly knowed what I was doing.

"You're a liar," he rasped. Blind mad, I roared and crashed my right to his jaw before he could move. He went down like a slaughtered ox and laid still, blood trickling from the corner of his mouth. I went for him to strangle him with my bare hands, but all the club men closed in between us.

"Grab him," they yelled. "He's killed D'Arcy. He's drunk or crazy. Hold him until we can get the police."

"Belay there," I roared, backing away with both fists cocked. "Lemme see the man that'll grab me. I'll knock his brains down his throat. When that rat comes to, tell him I ain't through with him, not by a dam' sight. I'll get him if it's the last thing I do."

And I stepped through one of them French winders and strode away cursing between my teeth. I walked for some time in a kind of red mist, forgetting all about the fight at Ace's Arena, where I was already due. Then I got a idee. I was fully intending to get ahold of D'Arcy and choke the truth outa him, but they was no use trying that now. I'd catch him outside his club some time that night. Meanwhile, I thought of something else. I went into a saloon and got a big piece of white paper and a pencil, and with much labor, I printed out what I wanted to say. Then I went out and stuck it up on a wooden lamp-post where folks couldst read it. It said:

> I WILL PAY ANY MAN FIFTY DOLLARS ($50) THAT CAN FIND MY BULDOG MIKE WHICH WAS STOLE BY A LO-DOWN SCUNK.
> STEVE COSTIGAN.

I was standing there reading it to see that the words was spelled right when a loafer said: "Mike stole? Too bad, Sailor. But where you goin' to git the fifty to pay the reward? Everybody knows you ain't got no money."

"That's right," I said. So I wrote down underneath the rest:

P. S. I AM GOING TO GET FIFTY DOLLARS FOR LICKING SOME MUTT AT ACE'S AREENER THAT IS WHERE THE REWARD MONEY IS COMING FROM.
       S. C.

I then went morosely along the street wondering where Mike was and if he was being mistreated or anything. I moped into the Arena and found Ace walking the floor and pulling his hair.

"Where you been?" he howled. "You realize you been keepin' the crowd waitin' a hour? Get into them ring togs."

"Let 'em wait," I said sourly, setting down and pulling off my shoes. "Ace, a yellow-livered son-of-a-skunk stole my dog."

"Yeah?" said Ace, pulling out his watch and looking at it. "That's tough, Steve. Hustle up and get into the ring, willya? The crowd's about ready to tear the joint down."

I CLIMBED INTO MY trunks and bathrobe and mosied up the aisle, paying very little attention either to the hisses or cheers which greeted my appearance. I clumb into the ring and looked around for my opponent.

"Where's Grieson?" I asked Ace.

"'E 'asn't showed up yet," said the referee.

"Ye gods and little fishes!" howled Ace, tearing his hair. "These bone-headed leather-pushers will drive me to a early doom. Do they think a pummoter's got nothin' else to do but set around all night and pacify a ragin' mob whilst they play around? These thugs is goin' to lynch us all if we don't start some action right away."

"Here he comes," said the referee as a bath-robed figger come hurrying down the aisle. Ace scowled bitterly and held up his hands to the frothing crowd.

"The long delayed main event," he said sourly. "Over in that corner, Sailor Costigan of the *Sea Girl*, weight 190 pounds. The mutt crawlin' through the ropes is 'Limey' Grieson, weight 189. Get goin'—and I hope you both get knocked loop-legged."

The referee called us to the center of the ring for instructions and Grieson glared at me, trying to scare me before the scrap started—the conceited jassack. But

I had other things on my mind. I merely mechanically noted that he was about my height—six feet—had a nasty sneering mouth and mean black eyes, and had been in a street fight recent. He had a bruise under one ear.

We went back to our corners and I said to the second Ace had give me: "Bonehead, you ain't seen nothin' of nobody with my bulldog, have you?"

"Naw, I ain't," he said, crawling through the ropes. "And beside . . . Hey, look out."

I hadn't noticed the gong sounding and Grieson was in my corner before I knowed what was happening. I ducked a slungshot right as I turned and clinched, pushing him outa the corner before I broke. He nailed me with a hard left hook to the head and I retaliated with a left to the body, but it didn't have much enthusiasm behind it. I had something else on my mind and my heart wasn't in the fight. I kept unconsciously glancing over to my corner where Mike always set, and when he wasn't there, I felt kinda lost and sick and empty.

Limey soon seen I wasn't up to par and began forcing the fight, shooting both hands to my head. I blocked and countered very slouchily and the crowd, missing my rip-roaring attack, began to murmur. Limey got too cocky and missed a looping right that had everything he had behind it. He was wide open for a instant and I mechanically ripped a left hook under his heart that made his knees buckle, and he covered up and walked away from me in a hurry, with me following in a sluggish kind of manner.

After that he was careful, not taking many chances. He jabbed me plenty, but kept his right guard high and close in. I ignores left jabs at all times, so though he was outpointing me plenty, he wasn't hurting me none. But he finally let go his right again and started the claret from my nose. That irritated me and I woke up and doubled him over with a left hook to the guts which wowed the crowd. But they yelled with rage and amazement when I failed to foller up. To tell the truth, I was fighting very absent-mindedly.

AS I WALKED BACK TO my corner at the end of the first round, the crowd was growling and muttering restlessly, and the referee said: "Fight, you blasted Yank, or I'll throw you h'out of the ring." That was the first time I ever got a warning like that.

"What's the matter with you, Sailor?" said Bonehead, waving the towel industriously. "I ain't never seen you fight this way before."

"I'm worried about Mike," I said. "Bonehead, where-all does Philip D'Arcy hang out besides the European Club?"

"How should I know?" he said. "Why?"

"I wanta catch him alone some place," I growled. "I betcha—"

"There's the gong, you mutt," yelled Bonehead, pushing me out of my corner. "For cat's cake, get in there and FIGHT. I got five bucks bet on you."

I wandered out into the middle of the ring and absent-mindedly wiped Limey's chin with a right that dropped him on his all-fours. He bounced up without a count, clearly addled, but just as I was fixing to polish him off, I heard a racket at the door.

"Lemme in," somebody was squalling. "I gotta see Meest Costigan. I got one fellow dog belong along him."

"Wait a minute," I growled to Limey, and run over to the ropes, to the astounded fury of the fans, who rose and roared.

"Let him in, Bat," I yelled and the feller at the door hollered back: "Alright, Steve, here he comes."

And a Chinese kid come running up the aisle grinning like all get-out, holding up a scrawny brindle bull-pup.

"Here that one fellow dog, Mees Costigan," he yelled.

"Aw heck," I said. "That ain't Mike. Mike's white. I thought everybody in Singapore knowed Mike—"

At this moment I realized that the still groggy Grieson was harassing me from the rear, so I turned around and give him my full attention for a minute. I had him backed up ag'in' the ropes, bombarding him with lefts and rights to the head and body, when I heard Bat yell: "Here comes another'n, Steve."

"Pardon me a minute," I snapped to the reeling Limey, and run over to the ropes just as a grinning coolie come running up the aisle with a white dog which might of had three or four drops of bulldog blood in him.

"Me catchum, boss," he chortled. "Heap fine white dawg. Me catchum fifty dolla?"

"You catchum a kick in the pants," I roared with irritation. "Blame it all, that ain't Mike."

At this moment Grieson, which had snuck up behind me, banged me behind the ear with a right hander that made me see about a million stars. This infuriated me so I turned and hit him in the belly so hard I bent his back-bone. He curled up like a worm somebody'd stepped on and while the referee was counting over him, the gong ended the round.

They dragged Limey to his corner and started working on him. Bonehead, he said to me: "What kind of a game is this, Sailor? Gee whiz, that mutt can't stand up to you a minute if you was tryin'. You shoulda stopped him in the first round. Hey, lookit there."

I glanced absent-mindedly over at the opposite corner and seen that Limey's seconds had found it necessary to take off his right glove in the process of reviving him. They was fumbling over his bare hand.

"They're up to somethin' crooked," howled Bonehead. "I'm goin' to appeal to the referee."

"HERE COMES SOME MORE mutts, Steve," bawled Bat and down the aisle come a Chinese coolie, a Jap sailor, and a Hindoo, each with a barking dog. The crowd had been seething with bewildered rage, but this seemed to somehow hit 'em in the funny bone and they begunst to whoop and yell and laugh like a passel of hyenas. The referee was roaming around the ring cussing to hisself and Ace was jumping up and down and tearing his hair.

"Is this a prize-fight or a dog-show," he howled. "You've rooint my business. I'll be the laughin' stock of the town. I'll sue you, Costigan."

"Catchum fine dawg, Meest' Costigan," shouted the Chinese, holding up a squirming, yowling mutt which done its best to bite me.

"You deluded heathen," I roared, "that ain't even a bull dog. That's a chow."

"You clazee," he hollered. "Him fine blull dawg."

"Don't listen," said the Jap. "Him bull dog." And he held up one of them pint-sized Boston bull-terriers.

"Not so," squalled the Hindoo. "Here is thee dog for you, sahib. A pure blood Rampur hound. No dog can overtake him in thee race—"

"Ye gods!" I howled. "Is everybody crazy? I oughta knowed these heathens couldn't understand my reward poster, but I thought—"

"*Look out, sailor,*" roared the crowd.

I hadn't heard the gong. Grieson had slipped up on me from behind again, and I turned just in time to get nailed on the jaw by a sweeping right-hander he started from the canvas. *Wham!* The lights went out and I hit the canvas so hard it jolted some of my senses back into me again.

I knowed, even then, that no ordinary gloved fist had slammed me down that way. Limey's men hadst slipped a iron knuckle-duster on his hand when they had his glove off. The referee sprung forward with a gratified yelp and begun counting over me. I writhed around, trying to get up and kill Limey, but I felt like I was done. My head was swimming, my jaw felt dead, and all the starch was gone outa my legs. They felt like they was made outa taller.

My head reeled. And I could see stars over the horizon of dogs.

"... Four ..." said the referee above the yells of the crowd and the despairing howls of Bonehead, who seen his five dollars fading away. "... Five ... Six ... Seven ..."

"There," said Limey, stepping back with a leer. "That's done yer, yer blawsted Yank."

Snap! went something in my head. That voice. Them same words. Where'd I heard 'em before? In the black alley offa the Tungen Road. A wave of red fury washed all the grogginess outa me.

I FORGOT ALL ABOUT MY taller legs. I come off the floor with a roar which made the ring lights dance, and lunged at the horrified Limey like a mad bull. He caught me with a straight left coming in, but I didn't even check a instant. His arm bent and I was on top of him and sunk my right mauler so deep into his ribs I felt his heart throb under my fist. He turned green all over and crumbled to the canvas like all his bones hadst turned to butter. The dazed referee started to count, but I ripped off my gloves and pouncing on the gasping warrior, I sunk my iron fingers into his throat.

"Where's Mike, you gutter rat?" I roared. "What'd you do with him? Tell me, or I'll tear your windpipe out."

"'Ere, 'ere," squawked the referee. "You cawn't do that. Let go of him, I say. Let go, you fiend."

He got me by the shoulders and tried to pull me off. Then, seeing I wasn't even noticing his efforts, he started kicking me in the ribs. With a wrathful beller, I rose up and caught him by the nape of the neck and the seat of the britches and throwed him clean through the ropes. Then I turned back on Limey.

"You Limehouse spawn," I bellered. "I'll choke the life outa you."

"Easy, mate, easy," he gasped, green-tinted and sick. "I'll tell yer. We stole the mutt?Fritz Steinmann wanted him—"

"Steinmann?" I howled in amazement.

"He warnted a dorg to fight Ritchie's Terror," gasped Limey. "Johnnie Blinn suggested he should 'ook your Mike. Johnnie hired me and some strong-arms to turn the trick—Johnnie's gel wrote you that note—but how'd you know I was into it—"

"I oughta thought about Blinn," I raged. "The dirty rat. He heard me and Porkey talkin' and got the idee. Where is Blinn?"

"Somewheres gettin' sewed up," gasped Grieson. "The dorg like to tore him to ribbons afore we could get the brute into the bamboo cage we had fixed."

"Where is Mike?" I roared, shaking him till his teeth rattled.

"At Steinmann's, fightin' Terror," groaned Limey. "Ow, lor'—I'm sick. I'm dyin'."

I riz up with a maddened beller and made for my corner. The referee rose up outa the tangle of busted seats and cussing fans and shook his fist at me with fire in his eye.

"Steve Costigan," he yelled. "You lose the blawsted fight on a foul."

"So's your old man," I roared, grabbing my bathrobe from the limp and gibbering Bonehead. And just at that instant a regular bedlam bust loose at the ticket-door and Bat come down the aisle like the devil was chasing him. And in behind him come a mob of natives—coolies, 'ricksha boys, beggars, shopkeepers, boatmen and I don't know what all—and every one of 'em had at least one dog and some had as many as three or four. Such a horde of chows, Pekineses, terriers, hounds and mongrels I never seen and they was all barking and howling and fighting.

"Meest' Costigan," the heathens howled, charging down the aisles: "You payum flifty dolla for dogs. We catchum."

The crowd rose and stampeded, trompling each other in their flight and I jumped outa the ring and raced down the aisle to the back exit with the whole mob about a jump behind me. I slammed the door in their faces and rushed out onto the sidewalk, where the passers-by screeched and scattered at the sight of what I reckon they thought was a huge and much battered maniac running at large in a red bathrobe. I paid no heed to 'em.

Somebody yelled at me in a familiar voice, but I rushed out into the street and made a flying leap onto the running board of a passing taxi. I ripped the door open and yelled to the horrified driver: "Fritz Steinmann's place on Kang Street— and if you ain't there within three minutes I'll break your neck."

WE WENT CAREENING through the streets and purty soon the driver said: "Say, are you an escaped criminal? There's a car followin' us."

"You drive," I yelled. "I don't care if they's a thousand cars follerin' us. Likely it's a Chinaman with a pink Pomeranian he wants to sell me for a white bull dog."

The driver stepped on it and when we pulled up in front of the innocent-looking building which was Steinmann's secret arena, we'd left the mysterious pursuer clean outa sight. I jumped out and raced down a short flight of stairs which led from the street down to a side entrance, clearing my decks for action by shedding my bathrobe as I went. The door was shut and a burly black-jowled thug was lounging outside. His eyes narrowed with surprise as he noted my costume, but he bulged in front of me and growled: "Wait a minute, you. Where do you think you're goin'?"

"In!" I gritted, ripping a terrible right to his unshaven jaw.

Over his prostrate carcass I launched myself bodily against the door, being in too much of a hurry to stop and see if it was unlocked. It crashed in and through its ruins I catapulted into the room.

It was a big basement. A crowd of men—the scrapings of the waterfront—was ganged about a deep pit sunk in the concrete floor from which come a low, terrible, worrying sound like dogs growling through a mask of torn flesh and bloody hair—like fighting dogs growl when they have their fangs sunk deep.

The fat Dutchman which owned the dive was just inside the door and he whirled and went white as I crashed through. He threw up his hands and screamed, just as I caught him with a clout that smashed his nose and knocked six front teeth down his throat. Somebody yelled: "Look out, boys! Here comes Costigan! He's on the kill!"

The crowd yelled and scattered like chaff before a high wind as I come ploughing through 'em like a typhoon, slugging right and left and dropping a man at each blow. I was so crazy mad I didn't care if I killed all of 'em. In a instant the brink of the pit was deserted as the crowd stormed through the exits, and I jumped down into the pit. Two dogs was there, a white one and a big brindle one, though they was both so bloody you couldn't hardly tell their original color. Both had been savagely punished, but Mike's jaws had locked in the death-hold on Terror's throat and the brindle dog's eyes was glazing.

Joe Ritchie was down on his knees working hard over them and his face was the color of paste. They's only two ways you can break a bull dog's death-grip; one is by deluging him with water till he's half drowned and opens his mouth to breathe. The other'n is by choking him off. Ritchie was trying that, but Mike had such a bull's neck, Joe was only hurting his fingers.

"For gosh sake, Costigan," he gasped. "Get this white devil off. He's killin' Terror."

"Sure I will," I grunted, stooping over the dogs. "Not for your sake, but for the sake of a good game dog." And I slapped Mike on the back and said: "Belay there, Mike; haul in your grapplin' irons."

Mike let go and grinned up at me with his bloody mouth, wagging his stump of a tail like all get-out and pricking up one ear. Terror had clawed the other'n to rags. Ritchie picked up the brindle bull and clumb outa the pit and I follered him with Mike.

"You take that dog to where he can get medical attention and you do it pronto," I growled. "He's a better man than you, any day in the week, and more fittin' to live. Get outa my sight."

He slunk off and Steinmann come to on the floor and seen me and crawled to the door on his all-fours before he dast to get up and run, bleeding like a stuck hawg. I was looking over Mike's cuts and gashes, when I realized that a man was standing nearby, watching me.

I wheeled. It was Philip D'Arcy, with a blue bruise on his jaw where I'd socked him, and his right hand inside his coat.

"D'ARCY," I SAID, WALKING up to him. "I reckon I done made a mess of things. I just ain't got no sense when I lose my temper, and I honestly thought you'd stole Mike. I ain't much on fancy words and apologizin' won't do no good. But I always try to do what seems right in my blunderin' blame-fool way, and if you wanta, you can knock my head off and I won't raise a hand ag'in' you." And I stuck out my jaw for him to sock.

He took his hand outa his coat and in it was a cocked six-shooter.

"Costigan," he said, "no man ever struck me before and got away with it. I came to Larnigan's Arena tonight to kill you. I was waiting for you outside and when I saw you run out of the place and jump into a taxi, I followed you to do the job wherever I caught up with you. But I like you. You're a square-shooter. And a man who thinks as much of his dog as you do is my idea of the right sort. I'm putting this gun back where it belongs—and I'm willing to shake hands and call it quits, if you are."

"More'n willin'," I said heartily. "You're a real gent." And we shook. Then all at once he started laughing.

"I saw your poster," he said. "When I passed by, an Indian babu was translating it to a crowd of natives and he was certainly making a weird mess of it. The best he got out of it was that Steve Costigan was buying dogs at fifty dollars apiece. You'll be hounded by canine-peddlers as long as you're in port."

"The *Sea Girl's* due tomorrer, thank gosh," I replied. "But right now I got to sew up some cuts on Mike."

"My car's outside," said D'Arcy. "Let's take him up to my rooms. I've had quite a bit of practice at such things and we'll fix him up ship-shape."

"It's a dirty deal he's had," I growled. And when I catch Johnnie Blinn I'm goin' kick his ears off. But," I added, swelling out my chest seven or eight inches, "I don't reckon I'll have to lick no more saps for sayin' that Ritchie's Terror is the champeen of all fightin' dogs in the Asiatics. Mike and me is the fightin'est pair of scrappers in the world."

DARK SHANGHAI

THE FIRST MAN I MET, when I stepped offa my ship onto the wharfs of Shanghai, was Bill McGlory of the *Dutchman,* and I should of took this as a bad omen because that gorilla can get a man into more jams than a Chinese puzzle. He says: "Well, Steve, what do we do for entertainment—beat up some cops or start a free-for-all in a saloon?"

I says: "Them amusements is low. The first thing I am goin' to do is to go and sock Ace Barlow on the nose. When I was in port six months ago somebody drugged my grog and lifted my wad, and I since found out it was him."

"Good," said Bill. "I don't like Ace neither and I'll go along and see it's well done."

So we went down to the Three Dragons Saloon and Ace come out from behind the bar grinning like a crocodile, and stuck out his hand and says: "Well, well, if it ain't Steve Costigan and Bill McGlory! Glad to see you, Costigan."

"And I'm glad to see you, you double-crossin' polecat," I says, and socked him on the nose with a peach of a right. He crashed into the bar so hard he shook the walls and a demijohn fell off a shelf onto his head and knocked him stiff, and I thought Bill McGlory would bust laughing.

Big Bess, Ace's girl, give a howl like a steamboat whistle.

"You vilyun!" she squalled. "You've killed Ace. Get out of here, you murderin' son of a skunk!" I don't know what kind of knife it was she flashed, but me and Bill left anyway. We wandered around on the waterfront most of the day and just about forgot about Ace, when all of a sudden he hove in view again, most unexpectedly. We was bucking a roulette wheel in Yin Song's Temple of Chance, and naturally was losing everything we had, including our shirts, when somebody tapped me on the shoulder. I turned around and it was Ace. I drawed back my right mauler but he said: "Nix, you numb-skull—I wanta talk business with you."

His nose was skinned and both his eyes was black, which made him look very funny, and I said: "I bet you went and blowed your nose—you shouldn't never do that after bein' socked."

"I ain't here to discuss my appearance," he said annoyedly. "Come on out where we can talk without bein' overheard."

"Foller you out into the alley?" I asked. "How many thugs you got out there with blackjacks?"

At this moment Bill lost his last dime and turned around and seen Ace and he said: "Wasn't one bust on the snoot enough?"

"Listen, you mugs," said Ace, waving his arms around like he does when excited, "here I got a scheme for makin' us all a lot of dough and you boneheads stand around makin' smart cracks."

"You're goin' to fix it so we make dough, hey?" I snorted. "I may be dumb, Ace Barlow, but I ain't that dumb. You ain't no pal of our'n."

"No, I ain't!" he howled. "I despises you! I wisht you was both in Davy Jones's locker! But I never lets sentiment interfere with business, and you two saps are the only men in Shanghai which has got guts enough for the job I got in mind."

I LOOKED AT BILL AND Bill looked at me, and Bill says: "Ace, I trusts you like I trusts a rattlesnake—but lead on. Them was the honestest words I ever heard you utter."

Ace motioned us to foller him, and he led us out of the Temple of Chance into the back of his grog-shop, which wasn't very far away. When we had set down and he had poured us some licker, taking some hisself, to show us it was on the level, he said: "Did you mutts ever hear of a man by the name of John Bain?"

"Naw," I said, but Bill scowled: "Seems like I have—naw—I can't place the name—"

"Well," said Ace, "he's a eccentric milyunaire, and he's here in Shanghai. He's got a kid sister, Catherine, which he's very fond of—"

"I see the point," I snapped, getting up and sticking the bottle of licker in my hip pocket. "That's out, we don't kidnap no dame for you. C'mon, Bill."

"That's a dirty insult!" hollered Ace. "You insinyouatin' I'd stoop so low as to kidnap a white woman?"

"It wouldn't be stoopin' for you," sneered Bill. "It would be a step upwards."

"Set down, Costigan," said Ace, "and put back that bottle, les'n you got money to pay for it. . . . Boys, you got me all wrong. The gal's already been kidnapped, and Bain's just about nuts."

"Why don't he go to the police?" I says.

"He has," said Ace, "but when could the police find a gal the Chineeses has stole? They'd did their best but they ain't found nothin'. Now listen—this is where you fellers come in. I *know* where the gal is!"

"Yeah?" we said, interested, but only half believing him.

"I guess likely I'm the only white man in Shanghai what does," he said. "Now I ask you—are you thugs ready to take a chance?"

"On what?" we said.

"On the three-thousand-dollar reward John Bain is offerin' for the return of his sister," said Ace. "Now listen—I know a certain big Chinee had her kidnapped outa her 'rickshaw out at the edge of the city one evenin'. He's been keepin' her prisoner in his house, waitin' a chance to send her up-country to some bandit friends of his'n; then they'll be in position to twist a big ransome outa John Bain, see? But he ain't had a chance to slip her through yet. She's still in his house. But if I was to tell the police, they'd raid the place and get the reward theirselves. So all you boys got to do is go get her and we split the reward three ways."

"Yeah," said Bill bitterly, "and git our throats cut while doin' it. What you goin' to do?"

"I give you the information where she is," he said. "Ain't that somethin'? And I'll do more—I'll manage to lure the big Chinee away from his house while you go after the gal. I'll fake a invitation from a big merchant to meet him somewheres—I know how to work it. An hour before midnight I'll have him away from that house. Then it'll be pie for you."

ME AND BILL MEDITATED.

"After all," wheedled Ace, "she's a white gal in the grip of the yeller devils."

"That settles it," I decided. "We ain't goin' to leave no white woman at the mercy of no Chinks."

"Good," said Ace. "The gal's at Yut Lao's house—you know where that is? I'll contrive to git him outa the house. All you gotta do is walk in and grab the gal. I dunno just where in the house she'll be, of course; you'll have to find that out for yourselves. When you git her, bring her to the old deserted warehouse on the Yen Tao wharf. I'll be there with John Bain. And listen—the pore gal has likely been mistreated so she don't trust nobody. She may not wanta come with you, thinkin' you've come to take her up-country to them hill-bandits. So don't stop to argy— just bring her along anyhow."

"All right," we says and Ace says, "Well, weigh anchor then, that's all."

"That ain't all, neither," said Bill. "If I start on this here expedition I gotta have a bracer. Gimme that bottle."

"Licker costs money," complained Ace as Bill filled his pocket flask.

"Settin' a busted nose costs money, too," snapped Bill, "so shut up before I adds to your expenses. We're in this together for the money, and I want you to know I don't like you any better'n I ever did."

Ace gnashed his teeth slightly at this, and me and Bill set out for Yut Lao's house. About half a hour to midnight we got there. It was a big house, set amongst a regular rat-den of narrow twisty alleys and native hovels. But they was a high wall around it, kinda setting it off from the rest.

"Now we got to use strategy," I said, and Bill says, "Heck, there you go makin' a tough job outa this. All we gotta do is walk up to the door and when the Chinks open it, we knock 'em stiff and grab the skirt and go."

"Simple!" I said sourcastically. "Do you realize this is the very heart of the native quarters, and these yeller-bellies would as soon stick a knife in a white man as look at him?"

"Well," he said, "if you're so smart, you figger it out."

"Come on," I said, "we'll sneak over the wall first. I seen a Chinee cop snoopin' around back there a ways and he give us a very suspicious look. I bet he thinks you're a burglar or somethin'."

Bill shoved out his jaw. "Does he come stickin' his nose into our business, I bends it into a true-lover's knot."

"This takes strategy," I says annoyedly. "If he comes up and sees us goin' over the wall, I'll tell him we're boardin' with Yut Lao and he forgot and locked us out, and we lost our key."

"That don't sound right, somehow," Bill criticized, but he's always jealous, because he ain't smart like me, so I paid no heed to him, but told him to foller me.

WELL, WE WENT DOWN a narrow back-alley which run right along by the wall, and just as we started climbing over, up bobbed the very Chinese cop I'd mentioned. He musta been follering us.

"Stop!" he said, poking at me with his night-stick. "What fella monkey-business catchee along you?"

And dawgoned if I didn't clean forget what I was going to tell him!

"Well," said Bill impatiently, "speak up, Steve, before he runs us in."

"Gimme time," I said snappishly, "don't rush me—lemme see now—Yut Lao boards with us and he lost his key—no, that don't sound right—"

"Aw, nuts!" snorted Bill and before I could stop him he hit the Chinee cop on the jaw and knocked him stiff.

"Now you done it!" said I. "This will get us six months in the jug."

"Aw, shut up and git over that wall," growled Bill. "We'll git the gal and be gone before he comes to. Then with that reward dough, I'd like to see him catch us. It's too dark here for him to have seen us good."

So we climbed into the garden, which was dark and full of them funny-looking shrubs the Chineeses grows and trims into all kinds of shapes like ships and dragons and ducks and stuff. Yut Lao's house looked even bigger from inside the wall and they was only a few lights in it. Well, we went stealthily through the garden and come to a arched door which led into the house. It was locked but we jimmied it pretty easy with some tools Ace had give us—he had a regular burglar's kit, the crook. We didn't hear a sound; the house seemed to be deserted.

We groped around and Bill hissed, "Steve, here's a stair. Let's go up."

"Well," I said, "I don't hardly believe we'll find her upstairs or nothin'. They proberly got her *in* a underground dunjun or somethin'."

"Well," said Bill, "this here stair don't go no ways but up and we can't stand here all night."

So we groped up in the dark and come into a faintly lighted corridor. This twisted around and didn't seem like to me went nowheres, but finally come onto a flight of stairs going down. By this time we was clean bewildered—the way them heathens builds their houses would run a white man nuts. So we went down the stair and found ourselves in another twisting corridor on the ground floor. Up to that time we'd met nobody. Ace had evidently did his job well, and drawed most everybody outa the house.

All but one big coolie with a meat cleaver.

WE WAS JUST CONGRATULATING ourselves when *swish! crack!* A shadow falling acrost me as we snuck past a dark nook was all that saved my scalp. I ducked just as something hummed past my head and sunk three inches deep into the wall. It was a meat cleaver in the hand of a big Chinee, and before he could wrench it loose, I tackled him around the legs like a fullback bucking the line and we went to the floor together so hard it knocked the breath outa him. He started flopping and kicking, but I would of had him right if it hadn't of been for Bill's carelessness. Bill grabbed a lacquered chair and swung for the Chinee's head, but we was revolving on the floor so fast his aim wasn't good. *Wham!* I seen a million stars. I rolled offa my victim and lay, kicking feebly, and Bill used what was left of the chair to knock the Chinaman cold.

"You dumb bonehead," I groaned, holding my abused head on which was a bump as big as a goose-egg. "You nearly knocked my brains out."

"You flatters yourself, Steve," snickered Bill. "I was swingin' at the Chinee—and there he lays. I always gits my man."

"Yeah, after maimin' all the innocent bystanders within reach," I snarled. "Gimme a shot outa that flask."

We both had a nip and then tied and gagged the Chinee with strips tore from his shirt, and then we continued our explorations. We hadn't made as much noise as it might seem; if they was any people in the house they was all sound asleep. We wandered around for a while amongst them dark or dim lighted corridors, till we seen a light shining under a crack of a door, and peeking through the keyhole, we seen what we was looking for.

On a divan was reclining a mighty nice-looking white girl, reading a book. I was plumb surprised; I'd expected to find her chained up in a dunjun with rats running around. The room she was in was fixed up very nice indeed, and she didn't look like her captivity was weighing very heavy on her; and though I looked close, I seen no sign of no chain whatever. The door wasn't even locked.

I opened the door and we stepped in quick. She jumped up and stared at us.

"Who are you?" she exclaimed. "What are you doing here?"

"Shhhhh!" I said warningly. "We has come to rescue you from the heathen!"

To my shocked surprise, she opened her mouth and yelled, "Yut Lao!" at the top of her voice.

I GRABBED HER AND CLAPPED my hand over her mouth, whilst goose-flesh riz up and down my spine.

"Belay there!" I said in much annoyance. "You wanta get all our throats cut? We're your friends, don't you understand?"

Her reply was to bite me so viciously that her teeth met in my thumb. I yelped involuntarily and let her go, and Bill caught hold of her and said soothingly, "Wait, Miss—they's no need to be scared—*ow!*" She hauled off and smacked him in the eye with a right that nearly floored him, and made a dart for the door. I pounced on her and she yanked out my hair in reckless handfuls.

"Grab her feet, Bill," I growled. "I come here to rescue this dame and I'm goin' to do it if we have to tie her hand and foot."

Well, Bill come to my aid and in the end we had to do just that—tie her up, I mean. It was about like tying a buzz-saw. We tore strips offa the bed-sheets and bound her wrists and ankles, as gentle as we could, and gagged her likewise, because when she wasn't chawing large chunks out of us, she would screech like a steamboat whistle. If they'd been anybody at large in the house they'd of sure heard. Honest to gosh, I never seen anybody so hard to rescue in my life. But we finally got it done and laid her on the divan.

"Why Yut Lao or anybody else wants this wildcat is more'n I can see," I growled, setting down and wiping the sweat off and trying to get my wind back. "This here's gratitude—here we risks our lives to save this girl from the clutches of the Yeller Peril and she goes and bites and kicks like we was kidnappin' her ourselves."

"Aw, wimmen is all crazy," snarled Bill, rubbing his shins where she had planted her French heels. "Dawgone it, Steve, the cork is come outa my flask in the fray and alt my licker is spillin' out."

"Stick the cork back in," I urged. And he said, "You blame fool, what you think I'd do? But I can't find the cork."

"Make a stopper outa some paper," I advised, and he looked around and seen a shelf of books. So he took down a book at random, tore out the fly-leaf and wadded it up and stuck it in the flask and put the book back. At this moment I noticed that I'd carelessly laid the girl down on her face and she was kicking and squirming, so I picked her up and said, "You go ahead and see if the way's clear; only you gotta help me pack her up and down them stairs."

"No need of that," he said. "This room's on the ground floor, see? Well, I bet this here other door opens into the garden." He unbolted it and sure enough it did.

"I bet that cop's layin' for us," I grunted.

"I bet he ain't," said Bill, and for once he was right. I reckon the Chinee thought the neighborhood was too tough for him. We never seen him again.

WE TOOK THE OPPOSITE side from where we come in at, and maybe you think we had a nice time getting that squirming frail over the wall. But we finally done it and started for the old deserted warehouse with her. Once I started to untie her and explain we was her friends, but the instant I started taking off the gag, she sunk her teeth into my neck. So I got mad and disgusted and gagged her again.

I thought we wouldn't never get to the warehouse. Tied as she was, she managed to wriggle and squirm and bounce till I had as soon try to carry a boa-constrictor, and I wisht she was a man so I could sock her on the jaw. We kept to back alleys and it ain't no uncommon sight to see men carrying a bound and gagged girl through them twisty dens at night, in that part of the native quarters, so if anybody seen us, they didn't give no hint. Probably thought we was a couple of strong-arm gorillas stealing a girl for some big mandarin or something.

Well, we finally come to the warehouse, looming all silent and deserted on the rotting old wharf. We come up into the shadder of it and somebody went, "Shhhh!"

"Is that you, Ace?" I said, straining my eyes—because they wasn't any lamps or lights of any kind anywheres near and everything was black and eery, with the water sucking and lapping at the piles under our feet.

"Yeah," came the whisper, "right here in this doorway. Come on—this way—I got the door open."

We groped our way to the door and blundered in, and he shut the door and lit a candle. We was in a small room which must have been a kind of counting or checking room once when the warehouse was in use. Ace looked at the girl and didn't seem a bit surprised because she was tied up.

"That's her, all right," he says. "Good work. Well, boys, your part's did. You better scram. I'll meet you tomorrer and split the reward."

"We'll split it tonight," I growled. "I been kicked in the shins and scratched and bit till I got tooth-marks all over me, and if you think I'm goin' to leave here without my share of the dough, you're nuts."

"You bet," said Bill. "We delivers her to John Bain, personal."

ACE LOOKED INCLINED to argy the matter, but changed his mind and said, "All right, he's in here—bring her in."

So I carried her through the door Ace opened, and we come into a big inner room, well lighted with candles and fixed up with tables and benches and things. It was Ace's secret hangout. There was Big Bess and a tall, lean feller with a pale poker-face and hard eyes. And I felt the girl stiffen in my arms and kind of turn cold.

"Well, Bain," says Ace jovially, "here she is!"

"Good enough," he said in a voice like a steel rasp. "You men can go now."

"We can like hell," I snapped. "Not till you pay us."

"How much did you promise them?" said Bain to Ace.

"A grand apiece," muttered Ace, glancing at us kind of uneasy, "but I'll tend to that."

"All right," snapped Bain, "don't bother me with the details. Take off her gag."

I done so, and untied her, watching her nervously so I could duck if she started swinging on me. But it looked like the sight of her brother wrought a change in her. She was white and trembling.

"Well, my dear," said John Bain, "we meet again."

"Oh, don't stall!" she flamed out. "What are you going to do to me?"

Me and Bill gawped at her and at each other, but nobody paid no attention to us.

"You know why I had you brought here," said Bain in a tone far from brotherly. "I want what you stole from me."

"And you stole it from old Yuen Kiang," she snapped. "He's dead—it belongs to me as much as it does to you!"

"You've hidden from me for a long time," he said, getting whiter than ever, "but it's the end of the trail Catherine, and you might as well come through. Where's that formula?"

"Where you'll never see it!" she said, very defiant.

"No?" he sneered. "Well, there are ways of making people talk—"

"Give her to me," urged Big Bess with a nasty glint in her eyes.

"I'll tell you nothing!" the girl raged, white to the lips. "You'll pay for persecuting an honest woman this way—"

John Bain laughed like a jackal barking. "Fine talk from you, you snake-in-the-grass! Honest? Why, the police of half a dozen countries are looking for you right now!"

John Bain jumped up and grabbed her by the wrist, but I throwed him away from her with such force he knocked over a table and fell across it.

"Hold everything!" I roared. "What kind of a game is this?"

JOHN BAIN PULLED HISSELF up and his eyes was dangerous as a snake's.

"Get out of here and get quick!" he snarled. "Ace can settle with you for this job out of the ten thousand I'm paying him. Now get out, before you get hurt!"

"Ten thousand!" howled Bill. "Ace is gettin' ten thousand? And us only a measly grand apiece?"

"Belay everything!" I roared. "This is too blame complicated for me. Ace sends us to rescue Bain's sister from the Chinks, us to split a three-thousand-dollar reward—now it comes out that Ace gets ten thousand—and Bain talks about his sister robbin' him—"

"Oh, go to the devil!" snapped Bain. "Barlow, when I told you to get a couple of gorillas for this job, I didn't tell you to get lunatics."

"Don't you call us looneyticks," roared Bill wrathfully. "We're as good as you be. We're better'n you, by golly! I remember you now—you ain't no more a milyunaire than I am! You're a adventurer—that's what old Cap'n Hurley called you—you're a gambler and a smuggler and a crook in general. And I don't believe this gal is your sister, neither."

"Sister to that swine?" the girl yelped like a wasp had stung her. "He's persecuting me, trying to get a valuable formula which is mine by rights, in case you don't know it—"

"That's a lie!" snarled Bain. "You stole it from me—Yuen Kiang gave it to me before he got blown up in that experiment in his laboratory—"

"Hold on," I ordered, slightly dizzy, "lemme get this straight—"

"Aw, it's too mixed up," growled Bill. "Let's take the gal back where we got her, and bust Ace on the snoot."

"Shut up, Bill," I commanded. "Leave this to me—this here's a matter which requires brains. I gotta get this straight. This girl ain't Bain's brother—I mean, he ain't her sister. Well, they ain't no kin. She's got a formula—whatever that is—and he wants it. Say, was you hidin' at Yut Lao's, instead of him havin' you kidnapped?"

"Wonderful," she sneered. "Right, Sherlock!"

"Well," I said, "we been gypped into doin' a kidnappin' when we thought we was rescuin' her; that's why she fit so hard. But why did Ace pick us?"

"I'll tell you, you flat-headed gorilla!" howled Big Bess. "It was to get even with you for that poke on the nose. And what you goin' to do about it, hey?"

"I'll tell you what we're goin' to do!" I roared. "We don't want your dirty dough! You're all a gang of thieves! This girl may be a crook, too, but we're goin' to take her back to Yut Lao's! An' right off."

Catherine caught her breath and whirled on us.

"Do you mean that?" she cried.

"You bet," I said angrily. "We may look like gorillas but we're gents. They gypped us, but they ain't goin' to harm you none, kid."

"But it's my formula," snarled John Bain. "She stole it from me."

"I don't care what she stole!" I roared. "She's better'n you, if she stole the harbor buoys! Get away from that door! We're leavin'!"

THE REST WAS KIND OF like a explosion—happened so quick you didn't have much time to think. Bain snatched up a shotgun from somewhere but before he could bring it down I kicked it outa his hands and closed with him. I heard Bill's yelp of joy as he lit into Ace, and Catherine and Big Bess went together like a couple of wildcats.

Bain was all wire and spring-steel. He butted me in the face and started the claret in streams from my nose, he gouged at my eye and he drove his knee into my belly all before I could get started. But I finally lifted him bodily and slammed him head-first onto the floor, though, and that finished Mr. John Bain for the evening. He kind of spread out and didn't even twitch.

Well, I looked around and seen Bill jumping up and down on Ace with both feet, and I seen Catherine was winning her scrap, too. Big Bess had the advantage of weight but she was yeller. Catherine sailed into her, fist and tooth and nail, and inside of a minute Big Bess was howling for mercy.

"What I want to know," gritted Catherine, sinking both hands into her hair and setting back, "is why you and that mutt Barlow are helping Bain!"

"Ow, leggo!" squalled Big Bess. "Ace heard that Bain was lookin' for you, and Ace had found out you was hidin' at Yut Lao's. Bain promised us ten grand to get you into his hands—Bain stood to make a fortune outa the formula—and we figgered on gyppin' Costigan and McGlory into doin' the dirty work and then we was goin' to skip on the early mornin' boat and leave 'em holdin' the bag!"

"So!" gasped Catherine, getting up and shaking back her disheveled locks, "I guess that settles *that!*"

I looked at Bain and Ace and Big Bess, all kind of strewn around on the floor, and I said I reckon it did.

"You men have been very kind to me," she said. "I understand it all now."

"Yeah," I said, "they told us Yut Lao had you kidnapped."

"The skunks!" she said. "Will you do me just one more favor and keep these thugs here until I get a good start? If I can catch that boat that sails just at dawn, I'll be safe."

"You bet," I said, "but you can't go through them back-alleys alone. I'll go back with you to Yut Lao's and Bill can stay here and guard these saps."

"Good," she said. "Let me peek outside and see that no one's spying."

So she slipped outside and Bill picked up the shotgun and said, "Hot dawg, will I guard these babies! I hope Ace will try to jump me so I can blow his fool head off!"

"Hey!" I hollered, "be careful with that gun, you sap!"

"Shucks," he says, very scornful, "I cut my teeth on a gun—"

Bang! Again I ducked complete extinction by such a brief hair's breadth that that charge of buckshot combed my hair.

"You outrageous idjit!" I says, considerably shooken. "I believe you're tryin' to murder me. That's twice tonight you've nearly kilt me."

"Aw don't be onreasonable, Steve," he urged. "I didn't know it had a hair-trigger—I was just tryin' the lock, like this, see—"

I took the death-trap away from him and threw it into the corner.

"Gimme a nip outa the flask," I said. "I'll be a rooin before this night's over."

I took a nip which just about emptied the flask, and Bill got to looking at the wadded-up fly-leaf which was serving as a stopper.

"Lookit, Mike," he said, "this leaf has got funny marks on it, ain't it?"

I glanced at it, still nervous from my narrer escape; it had a lot of figgers and letters and words which didn't mean nothing to me.

"That's Chinese writin'," I said peevishly. "Put up that licker; here comes Miss Deal."

She run in kind of breathless. "What was that shot?" she gasped.

"Ace tried to escape and I fired to warn him," says Bill barefacedly.

I told Bill I'd be back in a hour or so and me and the girl went out into those nasty alleys. I said, "It ain't none of my business, but would you mind tellin' me what this formula-thing is?"

"It's a new way to make perfume," she said.

"Perfume?" I snift. "Is that all?"

"Do you realize millions of dollars are spent each year on perfume?" she said. "Some of it costs hundreds of dollars an ounce. The most expensive kind is made from ambergris. Well, old Yuen Kiang, a Chinese chemist, discovered a process by which a certain chemical could be substituted for ambergris, producing the same result at a fraction of the cost. The perfume company that gets this formula will save millions. So they'll bid high.

"Outside of old Yuen Kiang, the only people who knew of its existence were John Bain, myself, and old Tung Chin, the apothecary who has that little shop down by the docks. Old Yuen Kiang got blown up in some kind of an experiment, he didn't have any people, and Bain stole the formula. Then I lifted it off of Bain, and have been hiding ever since, afraid to venture out and try to sell it. I've been paying Yut Lao plenty to let me stay in his house, and keep his mouth shut. But now it's all rosy! I don't know how much I can twist out of the perfume companies for the formula, but I know it'll run up into the hundred thousands!"

We'd reached Yut Lao's house and I went in through a side-gate—she had a key—and went into her room the same I way me and Bill had brung her out.

"I'm going to pack and make that boat," she said. "I haven't much time. Steve—I trust you—I'm going to show you the formula. Yut Lao knows nothing about it—I wouldn't have trusted him if he'd known why I was hiding—he thinks I've murdered somebody.

"The simplest place to hide anything is the best place. I destroyed the original formula after copying it on the flyleaf of a book, and put the book on this shelf, in plain sight. No one would ever think to look there—they'd tear up the floor and the walls first—"

And blamed if she didn't pull down the very book Bill got to make his stopper! She opened it and let out a howl like a lost soul.

"It's gone!" she screeched. "The leaf's been torn out! I'm robbed!"

At this moment a portly Chinee appeared at the door, some flustered.

"What catchee?" he squalled. "Too much monkey-business!"

"You yellow-bellied thief!" she screamed. "You stole my formula!"

And she went for him like a cat after a sparrow. She made a flying leap and landed right in his stummick with both hands locked in his pig-tail. He squalled like a fire-engine as he hit the floor, and she began grabbing his hair by the handfuls.

A BIG CLAMOR RIZ in some other part of the house. Evidently all Yut Lao's servants had returned too. They was jabbering like a zoo-full of monkeys and the clash of their knives turned me cold.

I grabbed Catherine by the slack of her dress and lifted her bodily offa the howling Yut Lao which was a ruin by this time. And a whole passel of coolies come swarming in with knives flashing like the sun on the sea-spray. Catherine showed some inclination of going to the mat with the entire gang—I never see such a scrapping dame in my life—but I grabbed her up and racing across the room, plunged through the outer door and slammed it in their faces.

"Beat it for the wall while I hold the door!" I yelled, and Catherine after one earful of the racket inside, done so with no more argument. She raced acrost the garden and begun to climb the wall. I braced myself to hold the door and *crash!* a hatchet blade ripped through the wood a inch from my nose.

"Hustle!" I yelled in a panic and she dropped on the other side of the wall. I let go and jumped back; the door crashed outwards and a swarm of Chineeses fell over it and piled up in a heap of squirming yeller figgers and gleaming knives. The sight of them knives lent wings to my feet, as the saying is, and I wish somebody had been timing me when I went acrost that garden and over that wall, because I bet I busted some world's speed records.

Catherine was waiting for me and she grabbed my hand and shook it.

"So long, sailor," she said. "I've got to make that boat now, formula or not. I've lost a fortune, but it's been lots of fun. I'll see you some day, maybe."

"Not if I see you first, you won't," I said to myself, as she scurried away into the dark, then I turned and run like all get-out for the deserted warehouse.

I was thinking of the fly-leaf Bill McGlory tore out to use for a stopper. Them wasn't Chinese letters—them was figgers—technical symbols and things! The lost formula! A hundred thousand dollars! Maybe more! And since Bain stole it from Yuen Kiang which was dead and had no heirs, and since Catherine stole it from Bain, then it was as much mine and Bill's as it was anybody's. Catherine hadn't seen Bill tear out the sheet; she was lying face down on the divan.

I gasped as I run and the sweat poured off me. A fortune! Me and Bill was going to sell that formula to some perfume company and be rich men!

I didn't keep to the back-alleys this time, but took the most direct route; it was just getting daylight. I crossed a section of the waterfront and I seen a stocky figger careening down the street, bellering, "Abel Brown the sailor." It was Bill.

"Bill McGlory." I said sternly, "you're drunk!"

"If I wasn't I'd be a wonder!" he whooped hilariously. "Steve, you old seahorse, this here's been a great night for us!"

"Where's Ace and them?" I demanded.

"I let 'em go half an hour after you left," he said. "I got tired settin' there doin' nothin'."

"Well, listen, Bill," I said, "where abouts is that—"

"Haw! Haw! Haw!" he roared, bending over and slapping his thighs. "Lemme tell you somethin'! Steve, you'll die laughin'! You knew old Tung Chin which runs a shop down on the waterfront, and stays open all night? Well, I stopped there to fill my flask and he got to lookin' at that Chineese writin' on that paper I had stuffed in it. He got all excited and what you think? He gimme ten bucks for it!"

"Ten bucks!" I howled. "You sold that paper to Tung Chin?"

"For ten big round dollars!" he whooped. "And boy, did I licker up! Can you imagine a mutt payin' good money for somethin' like that? What you reckon that sap wanted with that fool piece of paper? Boy, when I think how crazy them Chineese is—"

And he's wondering to this day why I hauled off and knocked him stiffer than a red-brick pagoda.

MOUNTAIN MAN

I WAS ROBBING A BEE TREE, when I heard my old man calling: "Breckinridge! Oh, Breckinridge! Where air you? I see you now. You don't need to climb that tree. I ain't goin' to larrup you."

He come up, and said: "Breckinridge, ain't that a bee settin' on yore ear?"

I reached up, and sure enough, it was. Come to think about it, I had felt kind of like something was stinging me somewhere.

"I swar, Breckinridge," said pap, "I never seen a hide like your'n. Listen to me: old Buffalo Rogers is back from Tomahawk, and the postmaster there said they was a letter for me, from Mississippi. He wouldn't give it to nobody but me or some of my folks. I dunno who'd be writin' me from Mississippi; last time I was there, was when I was fightin' the Yankees. But anyway, that letter is got to be got. Me and yore maw has decided you're to go git it. Yuh hear me, Breckinridge?"

"Clean to Tomahawk?" I said. "Gee whiz, pap!"

"Well," he said, combing his beard with his fingers, "yo're growed in size, if not in years. It's time you seen somethin' of the world. You ain't never been more'n thirty miles away from the cabin you was born in. Yore brother John ain't able to go on account of that ba'r he tangled with, and Bill is busy skinnin' the ba'r. You been to whar the trail passes, goin' to Tomahawk. All you got to do is foller it and turn to the right where it forks. The left goes on to Perdition."

Well, I was all eager to see the world, and the next morning I was off, dressed in new buckskins and riding my mule Alexander. Pap rode with me a few miles and give me advice.

"Be keerful how you spend that dollar I give you," he said. "Don't gamble. Drink in reason; half a gallon of corn juice is enough for any man. Don't be techy—but don't forgit that yore pap was once the rough-and-tumble champeen of Gonzales County, Texas. And whilst yo're feelin' for the other feller's eye, don't be keerless and let him chaw yore ear off. And don't resist no officer."

"What's them, pap?" I inquired.

"Down in the settlements," he explained, "they has men which their job is to keep the peace. I don't take no stock in law myself, but them city folks is different from us. You do what they says, and if they says give up yore gun, why, you up and do it!"

I was shocked, and meditated awhile, and then says: "How can I tell which is them?"

"They'll have a silver star on their shirt," he says, so I said I'd do like he told me. He reined around and went back up the mountains, and I rode on down the path.

WELL, I CAMPED THAT NIGHT where the path come out on to the main trail, and the next morning I rode on down the trail, feeling like I was a long way from home. I hadn't went far till I passed a stream, and decided I'd take a bath. So I tied Alexander to a tree, and hung my buckskins near by, but I took my gun belt with my old cap-and-ball .44 and hung it on a limb reaching out over the water. There was thick bushes all around the hole.

Well, I div deep, and as I come up, I had a feeling like somebody had hit me over the head with a club. I looked up, and there was a feller holding on to a limb with one hand and leaning out over the water with a club in the other hand.

He yelled and swung at me again, but I div, and he missed, and I come up right under the limb where my gun hung. I reached up and grabbed it and let *bam* at him just as he dived into the bushes, and he let out a squall and grabbed the seat of his pants. Next minute I heard a horse running, and glimpsed him tearing away through the brush on a pinto mustang, setting his horse like it was a red-hot stove, and dern him, he had my clothes in one hand! I was so upsot by this that I missed him clean, and jumping out, I charged through the bushes and saplings, but he was already out of sight. I knowed it was one of them derned renegades which hid up in the hills and snuck down to steal, and I wasn't afraid none. But what a fix I was in! He'd even stole my moccasins.

I couldn't go home, in that shape, without the letter, and admit I missed a robber twice. Pap would larrup the tar out of me. And if I went on, what if I met some women, in the valley settlements? I don't reckon they was ever a youngster half as bashful as what I was in them days. Cold sweat bust out all over me. At last, in desperation, I buckled my belt on and started down the trail toward Tomahawk. I was desperate enough to commit murder to get me some pants.

I was glad the Indian didn't steal Alexander, but the going was so rough I had to walk and lead him, because I kept to the brush alongside the trail. He had a tough time getting through the bushes, and the thorns scratched him so he hollered, and ever' now and then I had to lift him over jagged rocks. It was tough on Alexander, but I was too bashful to travel in the open trail without no clothes on.

AFTER I'D GONE MAYBE a mile I heard somebody in the trail ahead of me, and peeking through the bushes, I seen a most peculiar sight. It was a man on foot, going the same direction as me, and he had on what I instinctively guessed was city clothes. They wasn't buckskin, and was very beautiful, with big checks and stripes all over them. He had on a round hat with a narrow brim, and shoes like I hadn't never seen before, being neither boots nor moccasins. He was dusty, and he cussed as he limped along. Ahead of him I seen the trail made a horseshoe bend, so I cut straight across and got ahead of him, and as he come along, I stepped out of the brush and threw down on him with my cap-and-ball.

He threw up his hands and hollered: "Don't shoot!"

"I don't want to, mister," I said, "but I got to have clothes!"

He shook his head like he couldn't believe I was so, and he said: "You ain't the color of a Injun, but—what kind of people live in these hills, anyway?"

"Most of 'em's Democrats," I said, "but I got no time to talk politics. You climb out of them clothes."

"My God!" he wailed. "My horse threw me off and ran away, and I've been walkin' for hours, expecting to get scalped by Injuns any minute, and now a naked lunatic on a mule demands my clothes! It's too much!"

"I can't argy, mister," I said; "somebody may come up the trail any minute. Hustle!" So saying I shot his hat off to encourage him.

He give a howl and shucked his duds in a hurry.

"My underclothes, too?" he demanded, shivering though it was very hot.

"Is that what them things is?" I demanded, shocked. "I never heard of a man wearin' such womanish things. The country is goin' to the dogs, just like pap says. You better get goin'. Take my mule. When I get to where I can get some regular clothes, we'll swap back."

He clumb on to Alexander kind of dubious, and says to me, despairful: "Will you tell me one thing—how do I get to Tomahawk?"

"Take the next turn to the right," I said, "and—"

Just then Alexander turned his head and seen them underclothes on his back, and he give a loud and ringing bray and sot sail down the trail at full speed, with the stranger hanging on with both hands. Before they was out of sight they come to where the trail forked, and Alexander took the left instead of the right, and vanished amongst the ridges.

I put on the clothes, and they scratched my hide something fierce. I hadn't never wore nothing but buckskin. The coat split down the back, and the pants was too short, but the shoes was the worst; they pinched all over. I throwed away the socks, having never wore none, but put on what was left of the hat.

I went on down the trail, and took the right-hand fork, and in a mile or so I come out on a flat, and heard horses running. The next thing a mob of horsemen bust into view. One of 'em yelled: "There he is!" and they all come for me, full tilt. Instantly I decided that the stranger had got to Tomahawk, after all, and set a posse on to me for stealing his clothes.

SO I LEFT THE TRAIL AND took out across the sage grass and they all charged after me, yelling for me to stop. Well, them dern shoes pinched my feet so bad I couldn't hardly run, so after I had run five or six hundred yards, I perceived that the horses were beginning to gain on me. So I wheeled with my cap-and-ball in my hand, but I was going so fast, when I turned, them dern shoes slipped and I went over backwards into some cactus just as I pulled the trigger. So I only knocked the hat off of the first horseman. He yelled and pulled up his horse, right over me nearly, and as I drawed another bead on him, I seen he had a bright shiny star on his shirt. I dropped my gun and stuck up my hands.

They swarmed around me—cowboys, from their looks. The man with the star dismounted and picked up my gun and cussed.

"What did you lead us this chase through this heat and shoot at me for?" he demanded.

"I didn't know you was a officer," I said.

"Hell, McVey," said one of 'em, "you know how jumpy tenderfeet is. Likely he thought we was Santry's outlaws. Where's yore horse?"

"I ain't got none," I said.

"Got away from you, hey?" said McVey. "Well, climb up behind Kirby here, and let's get goin'."

To my astonishment, the sheriff stuck my gun back in the scabbard, and I clumb up behind Kirby, and away we went. Kirby kept telling me not to fall off, and it made me mad, but I said nothing. After a hour or so we come to a bunch of houses they said was Tomahawk. I got panicky when I seen all them houses, and would have jumped down and run for the mountains, only I knowed they'd catch me, with them dern pinchy shoes on.

I hadn't never seen such houses before. They was made out of boards, mostly, and some was two stories high. To the northwest and west the hills riz up a few hundred yards from the backs of the houses, and on the other sides there was plains, with brush and timber on them.

"You boys ride into town and tell the folks that the shebangs starts soon," said McVey. "Me and Kirby and Richards will take him to the ring."

I COULD SEE PEOPLE milling around in the streets, and I never had no idee there was that many folks in the world. The sheriff and the other two fellows rode around the north end of the town and stopped at a old barn and told me to get off. So I did, and we went in and they had a kind of room fixed up in there with benches and a lot of towels and water buckets, and the sheriff said: "This ain't much of a dressin'-room, but it'll have to do. Us boys don't know much about this game, but we'll second as good as we can. One thing—the other fellow ain't got no manager or seconds neither. How do you feel?"

"Fine," I said, "but I'm kind of hungry."

"Go get him somethin', Richards," said the sheriff.

"I didn't think they ate just before a bout," said Richards.

"Aw, I reckon he knows what he's doin'," said McVey. "Gwan."

So Richards left, and the sheriff and Kirby walked around me like I was a prize bull, and felt my muscles, and the sheriff said: "By golly, if size means anything, our dough is as good as in our britches right now!"

My dollar was in my belt. I said I would pay for my keep, and they haw-hawed and slapped me on the back and said I was a great joker. Then Richards come back with a platter of grub, with a lot of men wearing boots and guns, and they stomped in and gawped at me, and McVey said, "Look him over, boys! Toma-hawk stands or falls with him today!"

They started walking around me like him and Kirby done, and I was embarrassed and et three or four pounds of beef and a quart of mashed potaters, and a big hunk of white bread, and drunk about a gallon of water, because I was pretty thirsty. Then they all gaped like they was surprised about something, and one of 'em said: "How come he didn't arrive on the stagecoach yesterday?"

"Well," the sheriff said, "the driver told me he was so drunk they left him at Bisney, and come on with his luggage, which is over there in the corner. They got a horse and left it there with instructions for him to ride to Tomahawk as soon as he sobered up. Me and the boys got nervous today when he didn't show up, so we went out lookin' for him, and met him hoofin' it down the trail."

"I bet them Perdition hombres starts somethin'," said Kirby. "Ain't a one of 'em showed up yet. They're settin' over at Perdition soakin' up bad licker and broodin' on their wrongs. They shore wanted this show staged over there. They claimed that since Tomahawk was furnishin' one-half of the attraction, and Gunstock the other half, the razee ought to be throwed at Perdition."

"Nothin' to it," said McVey. "It laid between Tomahawk and Gunstock, and we throwed a coin and won it. If Perdition wants trouble, she can get it. Is the boys r'arin' to go?"

"Is they!" said Richards, "Every bar in Tomahawk is crowded with hombres full of licker and civic pride. They're bettin' their shirts, and they has been nine fights already. Everybody in Gunstock's here."

"Well, let's get goin'," said McVey, getting nervous. "The quicker it's over, the less blood there's likely to be spilt."

The first thing I knowed, they had laid hold of me and was pulling my clothes off, so it dawned on me that I must be under arrest for stealing the stranger's clothes. Kirby dug into the baggage which was in one corner of the stall, and dragged out a funny looking pair of pants; I know now they was white silk. I put 'em on because I hadn't nothing else to put on, and they fit me like my skin. Richards tied a American flag around my waist, and they put some spiked shoes on my feet.

I LET 'EM DO LIKE THEY wanted to, remembering what pap said about not resisting an officer. Whilst so employed, I began to hear a noise outside, like a lot of people whooping and cheering. Pretty soon in come a skinny old gink with whiskers and two guns on, and he hollered: "Listen, Mac, dern it, a big shipment of gold is down there waitin' to be took off by the evenin' stage, and the whole blame town is deserted on account of this foolishness. Suppose Comanche Santry and his gang gets wind of it?"

"Well," said McVey, "I'll send Kirby here to help you guard it."

"You will like hell," said Kirby; "I'll resign as deputy first. I got every cent of my dough on this scrap, and I aim to see it."

"Well, send somebody!" said the old codger. "I got enough to do runnin' my store, and the stage stand, and the post office, without—"

He left, mumbling in his whiskers, and I said: "Who's that?"

"Aw," said Kirby, "that's old man Braxton that runs that store down at the other end of town, on the east side of the street. The post office is in there, too."

"I got to see him," I said, "there's a letter—"

Just then another man come surging in and hollered: "Hey, is your man ready? Everybody's gettin' impatient."

"All right," said McVey, throwing over me a thing he called a bathrobe. Him and Kirby and Richards picked up towels and buckets and we went out the opposite door from what we come in, and there was a big crowd of people there, and they whooped and shot off their pistols. I would have bolted back into the barn, only they grabbed me and said it was all right. We went through the crowd and I never seen so many boots and pistols in my life, and we come to a square pen made out of four posts set in the ground, and ropes stretched between. They called this a ring, and told me to get in it. I done so, and they had turf packed down so the ground was level as a floor and hard and solid. They told me to set down on a stool in one corner, and I did, and wrapped my robe around me like a Injun.

Then everybody yelled, and some men, from Gunstock, they said, clumb through the ropes on the other side. One of them was dressed like I was, and I never seen such a human. His ears looked like cabbages, his nose was flat, and his head was shaved. He set down in a opposite corner.

Then a fellow got up and waved his arms, and hollered: "Gents, you all know the occasion of this here suspicious event. Mr. Bat O'Tool, happenin' to pass through Gunstock, consented to fight anybody which would meet him. Tomahawk 'lowed to furnish that opposition, by sendin' all the way to Denver to procure the services of Mr. Bruiser McGoorty, formerly of San Francisco."

He pointed at me. Everybody cheered and shot off their pistols and I was embarrassed and bust out in a cold sweat.

"This fight," said the fellow, "will be fit accordin' to London Prize Ring Rules, same as in a champeenship go. Bare fists, round ends when one of 'em's knocked down or throwed down. Fight lasts till one or t'other ain't able to come up to the scratch at the call of time. I, Yucca Blaine, have been selected referee because, bein' from Chawed Ear, I got no prejudices either way. Are you all ready? Time!"

MCVEY HAULED ME OFF my stool and pulled off my bathrobe and pushed me out into the ring. I nearly died with embarrassment, but I seen the fellow they called O'Tool didn't have on more clothes than me. He approached and held out his hand, so I held out mine. We shook hands and then without no warning, he hit me an awful lick on the jaw with his left. It was like being kicked by a mule. The first part of me which hit the turf was the back of my head. O'Tool stalked back to

his corner, and the Gunstock boys was dancing and hugging each other, and the
Tomahawk fellows was growling in their whiskers and fumbling for guns and
bowie knives.

McVey and his men rushed into the ring before I could get up and dragged
me to my corner and began pouring water on me.

"Are you hurt much?" yelled McVey.

"How can a man's fist hurt anybody?" I asked. "I wouldn't have fell down,
only it was so unexpected. I didn't know he was goin' to hit me. I never played no
game like this before."

McVey dropped the towel he was beating me in the face with, and turned
pale. "Ain't you Bruiser McGoorty of San Francisco?" he hollered.

"Naw," I said; "I'm Breckinridge Elkins, from up in the Humbolt mountains. I come here to get a letter for pap."

"But the stage driver described them clothes—" he begun wildly.

"A feller stole my clothes," I explained, "so I took some off'n a stranger.
Maybe he was Mr. McGoorty."

"What's the matter?" asked Kirby, coming up with another bucket of water.
"Time's about ready to be called."

"We're sunk!" bawled McVey. "This ain't McGoorty! This is a derned hill-
billy which murdered McGoorty and stole his clothes."

"We're rooint!" exclaimed Richards, aghast. "Everybody's bet their dough
without even seein' our man, they was that full of trust and civic pride. We can't
call it off now. Tomahawk is rooint! What'll we do?"

"He's goin' to get in there and fight his derndest," said McVey, pulling his
gun and jamming it into my back. "We'll hang him after the fight."

"But he can't box!" wailed Richards.

"No matter," said McVey; "the fair name of our town is at stake; Tomahawk
promised to furnish a fighter to fight this fellow O'Tool, and—"

"Oh," I said, suddenly seeing light. "This here is a fight, ain't it?"

McVey give a low moan, and Kirby reached for his gun, but just then the
referee hollered time, and I jumped up and run at O'Tool. If a fight was all they
wanted, I was satisfied. All that talk about rules, and the yelling of the crowd had
had me so confused I hadn't knowed what it was all about. I hit at O'Tool and he
ducked and hit me in the belly and on the nose and in the eye and on the ear. The
blood spurted, and the crowd yelled, and he looked dumbfounded and gritted
between his teeth: "Are you human? Why don't you fall?"

I spit out a mouthful of blood and got my hands on him and started chewing
his ear, and he squalled like a catamount. Yucca run in and tried to pull me loose,
and I give him a slap under the ear and he turned a somersault into the ropes.

"Your man's fightin' foul!" he squalled, and Kirby said: "You're crazy! Do you see this gun? You holler 'foul' once more, and it'll go off!"

MEANWHILE O'TOOL HAD broke loose from me, and caved in his knuckles on my jaw, and I come for him again, because I was mad by this time. He gasped: "If you want to make an alley-fight out of it, all right! I wasn't raised in Five Points for nothing!" He then rammed his knee into my groin, and groped for my eye, but I got his thumb in my teeth and begun masticating it, and the way he howled was a caution.

By this time the crowd was crazy, and I throwed O'Tool and begun to stomp him, when somebody let bang at me from the crowd and the bullet cut my silk belt and my pants started to fall down.

I grabbed 'em with both hands, and O'Tool riz and rushed at me, bloody and bellering, and I didn't dare let go my pants to defend myself. So I whirled and bent over and lashed out backwards with my right heel like a mule, and I caught him under the chin. He done a cartwheel in the air, his head hit the turf, and he bounced on over and landed on his back with his knees hooked over the lower rope. There wasn't no question about him being out. The only question was, was he dead?

A great roar of "Foul" went up from the Gunstock men, and guns bristled all around the ring.

The Tomahawk men was cheering and yelling that I had won fair and square, and the Gunstock men was cussing and threatening me, when somebody hollered: "Leave it to the referee!"

"Sure," said Kirby, "He knows our man won fair, and if he don't say so, I'll blow his head off!"

"That's a lie!" bellered a man from Gunstock. "He knows it was a foul, and if he says it wasn't, I'll carve his liver with this here bowie knife!"

At these words Yucca keeled over in a dead faint, and then a clatter of hoofs sounded above the din, and out of the timber that hid the trail from the east, a gang of horsemen rode at a run. Everybody whirled and yelled: "Look out, here comes them Perdition illegitimates!"

Instantly a hundred guns covered them, and McVey demanded: "Come ye in peace or in war?"

"We come to unmask a fraud!" roared a big man with a red bandanner around his neck. "McGoorty, come forth!"

A familiar figger, now dressed in cowboy togs, pushed forward on my mule. "There he is!" this figger yelled, pointing at me. "That's the desperado which robbed me! Them's my tights he's got on!"

"What's this?" roared the crowd.

"A dern fake!" bellered the man with the red bandanner. "This here is Bruiser McGoorty!"

"Then who's he?" somebody bawled, pointing at me.

"My name's Breckinridge Elkins and I can lick any man here!" I roared, getting mad. I brandished my fists in defiance, but my britches started sliding down again, so I had to shut up and grab 'em.

"Aha!" the man with the red bandanner howled like a hyener. "He admits it! I dunno what the idee is, but these Tomahawk polecats has double-crossed somebody! I trusts that you jackasses from Gunstock realizes the blackness and hellishness of their hearts! This man McGoorty rode into Perdition a few hours ago in his unmentionables, astraddle of that there mule, and told us how he'd been held up and robbed and put on the wrong road. You skunks was too proud to stage this fight in Perdition, but we ain't the men to see justice scorned with impunity! We brought McGoorty here to show you you was bein' gypped by Tomahawk! That man ain't no prize fighter; he's a highway robber!"

"These Tomahawk coyotes has framed us!" squalled a Gunstock man, going for his gun.

"You're a liar!" roared Richards, bending a .45 barrel over his head.

THE NEXT INSTANT GUNS was crashing, knives was gleaming, and men was yelling blue murder. The Gunstock braves turned frothing on the Tomahawk warriors, and the men from Perdition, yelping with glee, pulled their guns and begun fanning the crowd indiscriminately, which give back their fire. McGoorty give a howl and fell down on Alexander's neck, gripping around it with both arms, and Alexander departed in a cloud of dust and smoke.

I grabbed my gunbelt, which McVey had hung over the post in my corner, and I headed for cover, holding on to my britches whilst the bullets hummed around me as thick as bees. I wanted to take to the brush, but I remembered that blamed letter, so I headed for town. Behind me there rose a roar of banging guns and yelling men. Just as I got to the backs of the row of buildings which lined the street, I run into something soft head on. It was McGoorty, trying to escape on Alexander. He had hold of only one rein, and Alexander, evidently having circled one end of the town, was traveling in a circle and heading back where he started from.

I was going so fast I couldn't stop, and I run right over Alexander and all three of us went down in a heap. I jumped up, afraid Alexander was killed, but he scrambled up snorting and trembling, and then McGoorty weaved up, making funny noises. I poked my cap-and-ball into his belly.

"Off with them pants!" I yelped.

"My God!" he screamed. *"Again?* This is getting to be a habit!"

"Hustle!" I bellered. "You can have these scandals I got on now."

He shucked his britches, grabbed them tights and run like he was afeard I'd want his underwear too. I jerked on the pants, forked Alexander and headed for the south end of town. I kept behind the buildings, though the town seemed to be deserted, and purty soon I come to the store where Kirby had told me old man Braxton kept the post office. Guns was barking there, and across the street I seen men ducking in and out behind a old shack, and shooting.

I tied Alexander to a corner of the store and went in the back door. Up in the front part I seen old man Braxton kneeling behind some barrels with a .45-90, and he was shooting at the fellows in the shack across the street. Every now and then a slug would hum through the door and comb his whiskers, and he would cuss worse'n pap did that time he sot down in a bear trap.

I went up to him and tapped him on the shoulder and he give a squall and flopped over and let go *bam!* right in my face and singed off my eyebrows. And the fellows across the street hollered and started shooting at both of us.

I'd grabbed the barrel of his Winchester, and he was cussing and jerking at it with one hand and feeling in his boot for a knife with the other'n, and I said: "Mr. Braxton, if you ain't too busy, I wish you'd gimme that there letter which come for pap."

"Don't never come up behind me that way again!" he squalled. "I thought you was one of them dern outlaws! Look out! Duck, you fool!"

I let go his gun, and he took a shot at a head which was aiming around the shack, and the head let out a squall and disappeared.

"Who are them fellows?" I asked.

"Comanche Santry and his bunch, from up in the hills," snarled old man Braxton, jerking the lever of his Winchester. "They come after that gold. A hell of a sheriff McVey is; never sent me nobody. And them fools over at the ring are makin' so much noise, they'll never hear the shootin' over here. Look out, here they come!"

SIX OR SEVEN MEN RUSHED out from behind the shack and ran across the street, shooting as they come. I seen I'd never get my letter as long as all this fighting was going on, so I unslung my old cap-and-ball and let *bam!* at them three times, and three of them outlaws fell across each other in the street, and the rest turned around and run back behind the shack.

"Good work, boy!" yelled old man Braxton. "If I ever—oh, Judas Iscariot, we're blowed up now!"

Something was pushed around the corner of the shack and come rolling down toward us, the shack being on higher ground than the store was. It was a keg, with a burning fuse which whirled as the keg revolved and looked like a wheel of fire.

"What's in that keg?" I asked.

"Blastin' powder!" screamed old man Braxton, scrambling up. "Run, you dern fool! It's comin' right into the door!"

He was so scared he forgot all about the fellows across the street, and one of 'em caught him in the thigh with a buffalo rifle, and he plunked down again, howling blue murder. I stepped over him to the door—that's when I got that slug in my hip—and the keg hit my legs and stopped, so I picked it up and heaved it back across the street. It hadn't no more'n hit the shack when *bam!* it exploded and the shack went up in smoke. When it stopped raining pieces of wood and metal, they wasn't any sign to show any outlaws had ever hid behind where that shack had been.

"I wouldn't believe it if I hadn't saw it," old man Braxton moaned faintly.

"Are you hurt bad, Mr. Braxton?" I asked.

"I'm dyin'," he groaned. "Plumb dyin'!"

"Well, before you die, Mr. Braxton," I said, "would you mind givin' me that there letter for pap?"

"What's yore pap's name?" he asked.

"Roarin' Bill Elkins," I said.

He wasn't hurt as bad as he thought. He reached up and got hold of a leather bag and fumbled in it and pulled out a envelope. "I remember tellin' old Buffalo Rogers I had a letter for Bill Elkins," he said, fingering it over. Then he said: "Hey, wait! This ain't for yore pap. My sight is gettin' bad. I read it wrong the first time. This is for Bill *Elston* that lives between here and Perdition."

I want to spike a rumor which says I tried to murder old man Braxton and tore his store down for spite. I've done told how he got his leg broke, and the rest was accidental. When I realized that I had went through all that embarrassment for nothing, I was so mad and disgusted I turned and run out of the back door, and I forgot to open the door and that's how it got tore off the hinges.

I then jumped on to Alexander and forgot to untie him from the store. I kicked him in the ribs, and he bolted and tore loose that corner of the building, and that's how come the roof to fall in. Old man Braxton inside was scared and started yelling bloody murder, and about that time a lot of men come up to investigate the explosion which had stopped the three-cornered battle between Perdition, Tomahawk and Gunstock, and they thought I was the cause of everything, and they all started shooting at me as I rode off.

Then was when I got that charge of buckshot in my back.

I went out of Tomahawk and up the hill trail so fast I bet me and Alexander looked like a streak. And I says to myself the next time pap gets a letter in the post office, he can come after it hisself, because it's evident that civilization ain't no place for a boy which ain't reached his full growth and strength.

GUNS OF THE MOUNTAINS

THIS BUSINESS BEGUN with Uncle Garfield Elkins coming up from Texas to visit us. Between Grizzly Run and Chawed Ear the stage got held up by some masked bandits, and Uncle Garfield, never being able to forget that he was a gun-fighting fool thirty or forty years ago, pulled his old cap-and-ball instead of putting up his hands like he was advised to. For some reason, instead of blowing out his light, they merely busted him over the head with a .45 barrel, and when he come to he was rattling on his way toward Chawed Ear with the other passengers, minus his money and watch.

It was his watch what caused the trouble. That there timepiece had been his grandpap's, and Uncle Garfield sot more store by it than he did all his kin folks.

When he arriv up in the Humbolt mountains where our cabin was, he imejitly let in to howling his woes to the stars like a wolf with the belly-ache. And from then on we heered nothing but that watch. I'd saw it and thunk very little of it. It was big as my fist, and wound up with a key which Uncle Garfield was always losing and looking for. But it was solid gold, and he called it a hairloom, whatever them things is. And he nigh driv the family crazy.

"A passle of big hulks like you-all settin' around and lettin' a old man get robbed of all his property," he would say bitterly. "When *I* was a young buck, if'n *my* uncle had been abused that way, I'd of took the trail and never slept nor et till I brung back his watch and the scalp of the skunk which stole it. Men now days—" And so on and so on, till I felt like drownding the old jassack in a barrel of corn licker.

Finally pap says to me, combing his beard with his fingers: "Breckinridge," says he, "I've endured Uncle Garfield's belly-achin' all I aim to. I want you to go look for his cussed watch, and don't come back without it."

"How'm I goin' to know where to look?" I protested, aghast. "The feller which got it may be in Californy or Mexico by now."

"I realizes the difficulties," says pap. "But if Uncle Garfield knows somebody is out lookin' for his dern timepiece, maybe he'll give the rest of us some peace. You git goin', and if you can't find that watch, don't come back till after Uncle Garfield has went home."

"How long is he goin' to stay?" I demanded.

"Well," said pap, "Uncle Garfield's visits allus lasts a year, at least."

At this I bust into profanity.

I said: "I got to stay away from home a year? Dang it, pap, Jim Braxton'll steal Ellen Reynolds away from me whilst I'm gone. I been courtin' that girl till I'm ready to fall dead. I done licked her old man three times, and now, just when I got her lookin' my way, you tells me I got to up and leave her for a year for that dern Jim Braxton to have no competition with."

"You got to choose between Ellen Reynolds, and yore own flesh and blood," said pap. "I'm darned if I'll listen to Uncle Garfield's squawks any longer. You make yore own choice—but, if you don't choose to do what I asks you to, I'll fill yore hide with buckshot every time I see you from now on."

Well, the result was that I was presently riding morosely away from home and Ellen Reynolds, and in the general direction of where Uncle Garfield's blasted watch might possibly be.

I passed by the Braxton cabin with the intention of dropping Jim a warning about his actions whilst I was gone, but he wasn't there. So I issued a general defiance to the family by slinging a .45 slug through the winder which knocked a cob pipe outa old man Braxton's mouth. That soothed me a little, but I knowed very well that Jim would make a bee-line for the Reynolds' cabin the second I was out of sight. I could just see him gorging on Ellen's bear meat and honey, and bragging on hisself. I hoped Ellen would notice the difference between a loud mouthed boaster like him, and a quiet, modest young man like me, which never bragged, though admittedly the biggest man and the best fighter in the Humbolts.

I hoped to meet Jim somewhere in the woods as I rode down the trail, for I was intending to do something to kinda impede his courting while I was gone, like breaking his leg, or something, but luck wasn't with me.

I headed in the general direction of Chawed Ear, and the next day seen me riding in gloomy grandeur through a country quite some distance from Ellen Reynolds.

PAP ALWAYS SAID MY curiosity would be the ruination of me some day, but I never could listen to guns popping up in the mountains without wanting to find out who was killing who. So that morning, when I heard the rifles talking off amongst the trees, I turned Cap'n Kidd aside and left the trail and rode in the direction of the noise.

A dim path wound up through the big boulders and bushes, and the shooting kept getting louder. Purty soon I come out into a glade, and just as I did, *bam!* somebody let go at me from the bushes and a .45-70 slug cut both my bridle reins nearly in half. I instantly returned the shot with my .45, getting just a glimpse of something in the brush, and a man let out a squall and jumped out into the open, wringing his hands. My bullet had hit the lock of his Winchester and mighty nigh jarred his hands off him.

"Cease that ungodly noise," I said sternly, p'inting my .45 at his bay-winder, "and tell me how come you waylays innercent travelers."

He quit working his fingers and moaning, and he said: "I thought you was Joel Cairn, the outlaw. You're about his size."

"Well, I ain't," I said. "I'm Breckinridge Elkins, from the Humbolts. I was just ridin' over to learn what all the shootin' was about."

The guns was firing in the trees behind the fellow, and somebody yelled what was the matter.

"Ain't nothin' the matter," he hollered back. "Just a misunderstandin'." And he said to me: "I'm glad to see you, Elkins. We need a man like you. I'm Sheriff Dick Hopkins, from Grizzly Run."

"Where at's your star?" I inquired.

"I lost it in the bresh." he said. "Me and my deputies have been chasin' Tarantula Bixby and his gang for a day and a night, and we got 'em cornered over there in a old deserted cabin in a holler. The boys is shootin' at 'em now. I heard you comin' up the trail and snuck over to see who it is. Just as I said, I thought you was Cairn. Come on with me. You can help us."

"I ain't no deputy," I said. "I got nothin' against Tranchler Bixby."

"Well, you want to uphold the law, don't you?" he said.

"Naw," I said.

"Well, gee whiz!" he wailed. "If you ain't a hell of a citizen! The country's goin' to the dogs. What chance has a honest man got?"

"Aw, shut up," I said. "I'll go over and see the fun, anyhow."

So he picked up his gun, and I tied Cap'n Kidd, and follered the sheriff through the trees till we come to some rocks, and there was four men laying behind them rocks and shooting down into a hollow. The hill sloped away mighty steep into a small basin that was just like a bowl, with a rim of slopes all around. In the middle of this bowl there was a cabin and puffs of smoke was coming from the cracks between the logs.

The men behind the rocks looked at me in surprize, and one of them said, "What the hell—?"

But the sheriff scowled at them and said, "Boys, this here is Breck Elkins. I done told him already about us bein' a posse from Grizzly Run, and about how we got Tarantula Bixby and two of his cutthroats trapped in that there cabin."

One of the deputies bust into a guffaw and Hopkins glared at him and said: "What *you* laughin' about, you spotted hyener?"

"I swallered my tobaccer and that allus gives me the hystericals," mumbled the deputy, looking the other way.

"Hold up your right hand, Elkins," requested Hopkins, so I done so, wondering what for, and he said: "Does you swear to tell the truth, the whole truth and nothing but the truth, e pluribus unum, anno dominecker, to wit in status quo?"

"What the hell are you talkin' about?" I demanded.

"Them which God has j'ined asunder let no man put together," said Hopkins. "Whatever you say will be used against you and the Lord have mercy on yore soul. That means you're a deputy. I just swore you in."

"Go set on a tack," I snorted disgustedly. "Go catch your own thieves. And don't look at me like that. I might bend a gun over your skull."

"But Elkins," pleaded Hopkins, "with yore help we can catch them rats easy. All you got to do is lay up here behind this big rock and shoot at the cabin and keep 'em occupied till we can sneak around and rush 'em from the rear. See, the bresh comes down purty close to the foot of the slope on the other side, and gives us cover. We can do it easy, with somebody keepin' their attention over here. I'll give you part of the reward."

"I don't want no derned blood-money," I said, backing away. "And besides— *ow!*"

I'd absent-mindedly backed out from behind the big rock where I'd been standing, and a .30-30 slug burned its way acrost the seat of my britches.

"Dern them murderers!" I bellered, seeing red. "Gimme a rifle! I'll learn 'em to shoot a man behind his back. Gwan, take 'em in the rear. I'll keep 'em busy."

"Good boy!" said Hopkins. "You'll get plenty for this!"

IT SOUNDED LIKE SOMEBODY was snickering to theirselves as they snuck away, but I give no heed. I squinted cautiously around the big boulder, and begun sniping at the cabin. All I could see to shoot at was the puffs of smoke which marked the cracks they was shooting through, but from the cussing and yelling which begun to float up from the shack, I must have throwed some lead mighty close to them.

They kept shooting back, and the bullets splashed and buzzed on the rocks, and I kept looking at the further slope for some sign of Sheriff Hopkins and the posse. But all I heard was a sound of horses galloping away toward the west. I wondered who it could be, and I kept expecting the posse to rush down the opposite slope and take them desperadoes in the rear, and whilst I was craning my neck around a corner of the boulder—*whang!* A bullet smashed into the rock a few inches from my face and a sliver of stone took a notch out of my ear. I don't know of nothing that makes me madder'n to get shot in the ear.

I seen red and didn't even shoot back. A mere rifle was too paltry to satisfy me. Suddenly I realized that the big boulder in front of me was just poised on the slope, its underside partly embedded in the earth. I throwed down my rifle and bent my knees and spread my arms and gripped it.

I shook the sweat and blood outa my eyes, and bellered so them in the hollow could hear me: "I'm givin' you-all a chance to surrender! Come out, your hands up!"

They give loud and sarcastic jeers, and I yelled: "All right, you ring-tailed jackasses! If you gets squashed like a pancake, it's your own fault. *Here she comes!*"

And I heaved with all I had. The veins stood out on my temples, my feet sunk into the ground, but the earth bulged and cracked all around the big rock, rivelets of dirt begun to trickle down, and the big boulder groaned, give way and lurched over.

A dumfounded yell riz from the cabin. I leaped behind a bush, but the outlaws was too surprized to shoot at me. That enormous boulder was tumbling down the hill, crushing bushes flat and gathering speed as it rolled. And the cabin was right in its path.

Wild yells bust the air, the door was throwed violently open, and a man hove into view. Just as he started out of the door I let *bam* at him and he howled and ducked back just like anybody will when a .45-90 slug knocks their hat off. The next instant that thundering boulder hit the cabin. *Smash!* It knocked it sidewise like a ten pin and caved in the wall, and the whole structure collapsed in a cloud of dust and bark and splinters.

I run down the slope, and from the yells which issued from under the ruins, I knowed they hadn't all been killed.

"Does you-all surrender?" I roared.

"Yes, dern it!" they squalled. "Get us out from under this landslide!"

"Throw out yore guns," I ordered.

"How in hell can we throw anything?" they hollered wrathfully. "We're pinned down by a ton of rocks and boards and we're bein' squoze to death. Help, murder!"

"Aw, shut up," I said. "You don't hear *me* carryin' on in no such hysterical way, does you?"

Well, they moaned and complained, and I sot to work dragging the ruins off them, which wasn't no great task. Purty soon I seen a booted leg and I laid hold of it and dragged out the critter it was fastened to, and he looked more done up than what my brother Bill did that time he rassled a mountain lion for a bet. I took his pistol out of his belt, and laid him down on the ground and got the others out. There was three, altogether, and I disarm 'em and laid 'em out in a row.

Their clothes was nearly tore off, and they was bruised and scratched, and had splinters in their hair, but they wasn't hurt permanent. They sot up and felt of theirselves, and one of 'em said: "This here is the first earthquake I ever seen in this country."

"T'warn't no earthquake," said another'n. "It was a avalanche."

"Listen here, Joe Partland," said the first 'un, grinding his teeth, "I says it was a earthquake, and I ain't the man to be called a liar—"

"Oh, you ain't?" said the other'n, bristling up. "Well, lemme tell you somethin', Frank Jackson—"

"This ain't no time for such argyments," I admonished 'em sternly. "As for that there rock, I rolled that at you myself."

They gaped at me. "Who are you?" said one of 'em, mopping the blood offa his ear.

"Never mind," I said. "You see this here Winchester? Well, you-all set still and rest yourselves. Soon as the sheriff gets here, I'm goin' to hand you over to him."

His mouth fell open. "Sheriff?" he said, dumb-like. "What sheriff?"

"Dick Hopkins, from Grizzly Run," I said.

"Why, you derned fool!" he screamed, scrambling up.

"Set down!" I roared, shoving my rifle barrel at him, and he sank back, all white and shaking. He could hardly talk.

"Listen to me!" he gasped. *"I'm Dick Hopkins! I'm sheriff of Grizzly Run!*

These men are my deputies."

"Yeah?" I said sarcastically. "And who was the fellows shootin' at you from the brush?"

"Tarantula Bixby and his gang," he said. "We was follerin' 'em when they jumped us, and bein' outnumbered and surprized, we took cover in that old hut. They robbed the Grizzly Run bank day before yesterday. And now they'll be gettin' further away every minute! Oh, Judas J. Iscariot! Of all the dumb, bone-headed jackasses—"

"Heh! heh! heh!" I said cynically. "You must think I ain't got no sense. If you're the sheriff, where at's your star?"

"It was on my suspenders," he said despairingly. "When you hauled me out by the laig my suspenders caught on somethin' and tore off. If you'll lemme look amongst them ruins—"

"You set still," I commanded. "You can't fool me. You're Tranchler Bixby yourself. Sheriff Hopkins told me so. Him and the posse will be here in a little while. Set still and shut up."

WE STAYED THERE, AND the fellow which claimed to be the sheriff moaned and pulled his hair and shed a few tears, and the other fellows tried to convince me they was deputies till I got tired of their gab and told 'em to shut up or I'd bend my Winchester over their heads. I wondered why Hopkins and them didn't come, and I begun to get nervous, and all to once the fellow which said he was the sheriff give a yell that startled me so I jumped and nearly shot him. He had something in his hand and was waving it around.

"See here?" His voice cracked he hollered so loud. "I found it! It must have fell down into my shirt when my suspenders busted! Look at it, you dern mountain grizzly!"

I looked and my flesh crawled. It was a shiny silver star.

"Hopkins said he lost his'n," I said weakly. "Maybe you found it in the brush."

"You know better!" he bellered. "You're one of Bixby's men. You was sent to hold us here while Tarantula and the rest made their getaway. You'll get ninety years for this!"

I turned cold all over as I remembered them horses I heard galloping. I'd been fooled! This *was* the sheriff! That pot-bellied thug which shot at me had been Bixby hisself! And whilst I held up the real sheriff and his posse, them outlaws was riding out of the country.

Now wasn't that a caution?

"You better gimme that gun and surrender," opined Hopkins. "Maybe if you do they won't hang you."

"Set still!" I snarled. "I'm the biggest sap that ever straddled a mustang, but even saps has their feelin's. You ain't goin' to put me behind no bars. I'm goin' up this slope, but I'll be watchin' you. I've throwed your guns over there in the brush. If any of you makes a move toward 'em, I'll put a harp in his hand."

Nobody craved a harp.

They set up a chant of hate as I backed away, but they sot still. I went up the slope backwards till I hit the rim, and then I turned and ducked into the brush and run. I heard 'em cussing somethin' awful down in the hollow, but I didn't pause. I come to where I'd left Cap'n Kidd, and a-forked him and rode, thankful them outlaws had been in too big a hurry to steal him. I throwed away the rifle they give me, and headed west.

I aimed to cross Wild River at Ghost Canyon, and head into the uninhabited mountain region beyond there. I figgered I could dodge a posse indefinite once I got there. I pushed Cap'n Kidd hard, cussing my reins which had been notched by Bixby's bullet. I didn't have time to fix 'em, and Cap'n Kidd was a iron-jawed outlaw.

He was sweating plenty when I finally hove in sight of the place I was heading for. As I topped the canyon's crest before I dipped down to the crossing, I glanced back. They was a high notch in the hills a mile or so behind me. And as I looked three horsemen was etched in that notch, against the sky behind 'em. I cussed fervently. Why hadn't I had sense enough to know Hopkins and his men was bound to have horses tied somewheres near? They'd got their mounts and follered me, figgering I'd aim for the country beyond Wild River. It was about the only place I could go.

Not wanting no running fight with no sheriff's posse, I raced recklessly down the sloping canyon wall, busted out of the bushes—and stopped short. Wild River was on the rampage—bank full in the narrow channel and boiling and foaming. Been a big rain somewhere away up on the head, and the horse wasn't never foaled which could swum it.

They wasn't but one thing to do, and I done it. I wheeled Cap'n Kidd and headed up the canyon. Five miles up the river there was another crossing, with a bridge—if it hadn't been washed away.

CAP'N KIDD HAD HIS SECOND wind and we was going lickety-split, when suddenly I heard a noise ahead of us, above the roar of the river and the thunder of his hoofs on the rocky canyon floor. We was approaching a bend in the gorge where a low ridge run out from the canyon wall, and beyond that ridge I heard guns banging. I heaved back on the reins—and both of 'em snapped in two!

Cap'n Kidd instantly clamped his teeth on the bit and bolted, like he always done when anything out of the ordinary happened. He headed straight for the bushes at the end of the ridge, and I leaned forward and tried to get hold of the bit rings with my fingers. But all I done was swerve him from his course. Instead of following the canyon bed on around the end of the ridge, he went right over the rise, which sloped on that side. It didn't slope on t'other side; it fell away abrupt. I had a fleeting glimpse of five men crouching amongst the bushes on the canyon floor with guns in their hands. They looked up—and Cap'n Kidd braced his legs and slid to a halt at the lip of the low bluff and simultaneously bogged his head and threw me heels over head down amongst 'em.

My boot heel landed on somebody's head, and the spur knocked him cold and blame near scalped him. That partly bust my fall, and it was further cushioned by another fellow which I landed on in a sitting position, and which took no further interest in the proceedings. The other three fell on me with loud brutal yells, and I reached for my .45 and found to my humiliation that it had fell out of my scabbard when I was throwed.

So I riz with a rock in my hand and bounced it offa the head of a fellow which was fixing to shoot me, and he dropped his pistol and fell on top of it. At this juncture one of the survivors put a buffalo gun to his shoulder and sighted, then evidently fearing he would hit his companion which was carving at me on the other side with a bowie knife, he reversed it and run in swinging it like a club.

The man with the knife got in a slash across my ribs and I then hit him on the chin which was how his jaw-bone got broke in four places. Meanwhile the other'n swung at me with his rifle, but missed my head and broke the stock off across my shoulder. Irritated at his persistency in trying to brain me with the barrel, I laid hands on him and threwed him head-on against the bluff, which is when he got his fractured skull and concussion of the brain, I reckon.

I then shook the sweat from my eyes, and glaring down, rekernized the remains as Bixby and his gang. I might have knew they'd head for the wild Country across the river, same as me. Only place they could go.

Just then, however, a clump of bushes parted, near the river bank, and a big black-bearded man riz up from behind a dead horse. He had a six-shooter in his hand and he approached me cautiously.

"Who're you?" he demanded. "Where'd you come from?"

"I'm Breckinridge Elkins," I answered, mopping the blood offa my shirt. "What is this here business, anyway?"

"I was settin' here peaceable waitin' for the river to go down so I could cross," he said, "when up rode these yeggs and started shootin'. I'm a honest citizen—"

"You're a liar," I said with my usual diplomacy. "You're Joel Cairn, the wust outlaw in the hills. I seen your pitcher in the post office at Chawed Ear."

With that he p'inted his .45 at me and his beard bristled like the whiskers of a old timber wolf.

"So you know me, hey?" he said. "Well, what you goin' to do about it, hey? Want to colleck the reward money, hey?"

"Naw, I don't," I said. "I'm a outlaw myself, now. I just run foul of the law account of these skunks. They's a posse right behind me."

"They is?" he snarled. "Why'nt you say so? Here, le's catch these fellers' horses and light out. Cheap skates! They claims I double-crossed 'em in the matter of a stagecoach hold-up we pulled together recently. I been avoidin' 'em 'cause I'm a peaceful man by nater, but they rode onto me onexpected today. They shot my horse first crack; we been tradin' lead for more'n a hour without doin' much damage, but they'd got me eventually, I reckon. Come on. We'll pull out together."

"No, we won't," I said. "I'm a outlaw by force of circumstances, but I ain't no murderin' bandit."

"Purty particular of yore comperny, ain'tcha?" he sneered. "Well, anyways, help me catch me a horse. Yore's is still up there on that bluff. The day's still young—"

He pulled out a big gold watch and looked at it; it was one which wound with a key.

I JUMPED LIKE I WAS SHOT. "Where'd you get that watch?" I hollered.

He jerked up his head kinda startled, and said: "My grandpap gimme it. Why?"

"You're a liar!" I bellered. "You took that off'n my Uncle Garfield. *Gimme that watch!*"

"Are you crazy?" he yelled, going white under his whiskers. I plunged for him, seeing red, and he let *bang!* and I got it in the left thigh. Before he could shoot again I was on top of him, and knocked the gun up. It banged but the bullet went singing up over the bluff and Cap'n Kidd squealed and started changing ends. The pistol flew outa Cairn's hand and he hit me vi'lently on the nose which made me see stars. So I hit him in the belly and he grunted and doubled up; and come up with a knife out of his boot which he cut me across the boozum with, also in the arm and shoulder and kicked me in the groin. So I swung him clear of the ground and throwed him headfirst and jumped on him with both feet. And that settled him.

I picked up the watch where it had fell, and staggered over to the cliff, spurting blood at every step like a stuck hawg.

"At last my search is at a end!" I panted. "I can go back to Ellen Reynolds who patiently awaits the return of her hero—"

It was at this instant that Cap'n Kidd, which had been stung by Cairn's wild shot and was trying to buck off his saddle, bucked hisself off the bluff. He fell on me. . . .

The first thing I heard was bells ringing, and then they turned to horses galloping. I set up and wiped off the blood which was running into my eyes from where Cap'n Kidd's left hind hoof had split my scalp. And I seen Sheriff Hopkins, Jackson and Partland come tearing around the ridge. I tried to get up and run, but my right leg wouldn't work. I reached for my gun and it still wasn't there. I was trapped.

"Look there!" yelled Hopkins, wild-eyed. "That's Bixby on the ground—and all his gang. And ye gods, there's Joel Cairn! What is this, anyhow? It looks like a battlefield! What's that settin' there? He's so bloody I can't recognize him!"

"It's the hill-billy!" yelped Jackson. "Don't move or I'll shoot 'cha!"

"I already been shot," I snarled. "Gwan—do yore wust. Fate is against me."

They dismounted and stared in awe.

"Count the dead, boys," said Hopkins in a still, small voice.

"Aw," said Partland, "ain't none of 'em dead, but they'll never be the same men again. Look! Bixby's comin' to! Who done this, Bixby?"

Bixby cast a wabbly eye about till he spied me, and then he moaned and shriveled up.

"He done it!" he waited. "He trailed us down like a bloodhound and jumped on us from behind! He tried to scalp me! He ain't human!" And he bust into tears.

They looked at me, and all took off their hats.

"Elkins," said Hopkins in a tone of reverence, "I see it all now. They fooled you into thinkin' they was the posse and us the outlaws, didn't they? And when you realized the truth, you hunted 'em down, didn't you? And cleaned 'em out single handed, and Joel Cairn, too, didn't you?"

"Well," I said groggily, "the truth is—"

"We understand," Hopkins soothed. "You mountain men is all modest. Hey, boys, tie up them outlaws whilst I look at Elkins' wounds."

"If you'll catch my horse," I said, "I got to be ridin' back—"

"Gee whiz, man!" he said, "you ain't in no shape to ride a horse! Do you know you got four busted ribs and a broke arm, and one leg broke and a bullet in the other'n, to say nothin' of bein' slashed to ribbons? We'll rig up a litter for you. What's that you got in your good hand?"

I suddenly remembered Uncle Garfield's watch which I'd kept clutched in a death grip. I stared at what I held in my hand; and I fell back with a low moan. All I had in my hand was a bunch of busted metal and broken wheels and springs, bent and smashed plumb beyond recognition.

"Grab him!" yelled Hopkins. "He's fainted!"

"Plant me under a pine tree, boys," I murmured weakly; "just carve on my tombstone: 'He fit a good fight but Fate dealt him the joker.'"

A FEW DAYS LATER A melancholy procession wound its way up the trail into the Humbolts. I was packed on a litter. I told 'em I wanted to see Ellen Reynolds before I died, and to show Uncle Garfield the rooins of the watch, so he'd know I done my duty as I seen it.

As we approached the locality where my home cabin stood, who should meet us but Jim Braxton, which tried to conceal his pleasure when I told him in a weak voice that I was a dying man. He was all dressed up in new buckskins and his exuberance was plumb disgustful to a man in my condition.

"Too bad," he said. "Too bad, Breckinridge. I hoped to meet you, but not like this, of course. Yore pap told me to tell you if I seen you about yore Uncle Garfield's watch. He thought I might run into you on my way to Chawed Ear to git a license—"

"Hey?" I said, pricking up my ears.

"Yeah, me and Ellen Reynolds is goin' to git married. Well, as I started to say, seems like one of them bandits which robbed the stage was a fellow whose dad was a friend of yore Uncle Garfield's back in Texas. He reckernized the name in the watch and sent it back, and it got here the day after you left—"

They say it was jealousy which made me rise up on my litter and fracture Jim Braxton's jaw-bone. I denies that. I stoops to no such petty practices. What impelled me was family conventions. I couldn't hit Uncle Garfield—I had to hit somebody—and Jim Braxton just happened to be the nearest one to me.

THE SCALP HUNTER

THE REASON I AM GIVING the full facts of this here affair is to refute a lot of rumors which is circulating about me. I am sick and tired of these lies about me terrorizing the town of Grizzly Claw and ruining their wagon-yard just for spite and trying to murder all their leading citizens. They is more'n one side to anything. These folks which is going around telling about me knocking the mayor of Grizzly Claw down a flight of steps with a kitchen stove ain't yet added that the mayor was trying to blast me with a sawed-off shotgun. As for saying that all I done was with malice afore-thought—if I was a hot-headed man like some I know, I could easy lose my temper over this here slander, but being shy and retiring by nature, I keeps my dignity and merely remarks that these gossipers is blamed liars, and I will kick the ears off of them if I catch them.

I warn't even going to Grizzly Claw in the first place. I'm kind of particular where I go to. I'd been in the settlements along Wild River for several weeks, tending to my own business, and I was headed for Pistol Mountain, when I seen "Tunk" Willoughby setting on a log at the forks where the trail to Grizzly Claw splits off of the Pistol Mountain road. Tunk ain't got no more sense than the law allows anyway, and now he looked plumb discouraged. He had a mangled ear, a couple of black eyes, and a lump on his head so big his hat wouldn't fit. From time to time he spit out a tooth.

I pulled up Cap'n Kidd and said: "What kind of a brawl have you been into?"

"I been to Grizzly Claw," he said, just like that explained it. But I didn't get the drift, because I hadn't never been to Grizzly Claw.

"That's the meanest town in these mountains," he said. "They ain't got no real law there, but they got a feller which claims to be a officer, and if you so much as spit, he says you bust a law and has got to pay a fine. If you puts up a holler, the citizens comes to his assistance. You see what happened to me. I never found out just what law I was supposed to broke," Tunk said, "but it must of been one they was particular fond of. I give 'em a good fight as long as they confined theirselves to rocks and gun butts, but when they interjuiced fence rails and wagon-tongues into the fray, I give up the ghost."

"What you go there for, anyhow?" I demanded.

"Well," he said, mopping off some dried blood, "I was lookin' for you. Three or four days ago I was in the vicinity of Bear Creek, and yore cousin Jack Gordon told me somethin' to tell you."

Him showing no sign of going on, I said: "Well, what was it?"

"I cain't remember," he said. "That lammin' they gimme in Grizzly Claw has plumb addled my brains. Jack told me to tell you to keep a sharp look-out for somebody, but I cain't remember who, or why. But somebody had did somethin' awful to somebody on Bear Creek—seems like it was yore Uncle Jeppard Grimes."

"But why did you go to Grizzly Claw?" I demanded. "I warn't there."

"I dunno," he said. "Seems like the feller which Jack wanted you to get was from Grizzly Claw, or was supposed to go there, or somethin'."

"A great help you be!" I said in disgust. "Here somebody has went and wronged one of my kinfolks, maybe, and you forgets the details. Try to remember the name of the feller, anyway. If I knew who he was, I could lay him out, and then find out what he did later on. Think, can't you?"

"Did you ever have a wagon-tongue busted over yore head?" he said. "I tell you, it's just right recent that I remembered my own name. It was all I could do to rekernize you just now. If you'll come back in a couple of days, maybe by then I'll remember what all Jack told me."

I give a snort of disgust and turned off the road and headed up the trail for Grizzly Claw. I thought maybe I could learn something there. If somebody had done dirt to Uncle Jeppard, I wanted to know it. Us Bear Creek folks may fight amongst ourselves, but we stands for no stranger to impose on any one of us.

Uncle Jeppard was about as old as the Humbolt Mountains, and he'd fit Indians for a living in his younger days. He was still a tough old knot. Anybody that could do him a wrong and get away with it, sure wasn't no ordinary man, so it wasn't no wonder that word had been sent out for me to get on his trail. And now I hadn't no idea who to look for, or why, just because of Tunk Willoughby's weak skull. I despise these here egg-headed weaklings.

WELL, I ARROVE IN GRIZZLY Claw late in the afternoon and went first to the wagon-yard and seen that Cap'n Kidd was put in a good stall and fed proper, and warned the fellow there to keep away from him if he didn't want his brains kicked out. Cap'n Kidd has a disposition like a shark and he don't like strangers. It warn't much of a wagon-yard, and there was only five other horses there, besides me and Cap'n Kidd—a pinto, bay, and piebald, and a couple of pack-horses.

I then went back into the business part of the village, which was one dusty street with stores and saloons on each side, and I didn't pay much attention to the town, because I was trying to figure out how I could go about trying to find out what I wanted to know, and couldn't think of no questions to ask nobody about nothing.

Well, I was approaching a saloon called the Apache Queen, and was looking at the ground in meditation, when I seen a silver dollar laying in the dust close to a hitching rack. I immediately stooped down and picked it up, not noticing how close it was to the hind laigs of a mean-looking mule. When I stooped over he hauled off and kicked me in the head. Then he let out a awful bray and commenced jumping around holding up his hind hoof, and some men come running out of the saloon, and one of 'em hollered: "He's tryin' to kill my mule! Call the law!"

Quite a crowd gathered and the feller which owned the mule hollered like a catamount. He was a mean-looking cuss with mournful whiskers and a cock-eye. He yelled like somebody was stabbing him, and I couldn't get in a word edge-ways. Then a feller with a long skinny neck and two guns come up and said: "I'm the sheriff, what's goin' on here? Who is this big feller? What's he done?"

The whiskered cuss hollered: "He kicked hisself in the head with my mule and crippled the pore critter for life! I demands my rights! He's got to pay me three hundred and fifty dollars for my mule!"

"Aw," I said, "that mule ain't hurt none; his leg's just kinda numbed. Anyway, I ain't got but five bucks, and whoever gets them will take 'em offa my dead body." I then hitched my six-guns forwards, and the crowd kinda fell away.

"I demands that you 'rest him!" howled Drooping-whiskers. "He tried to 'sassinate my mule!"

"You ain't got no star," I told the feller which said he was the law. "You ain't goin' to arrest me."

"Does you dast resist arrest?" he said, fidgeting with his belt.

"Who said anything about resistin' arrest?" I retorted. "All I aim to do is see how far your neck will stretch before it breaks."

"Don't you dast lay hands on a officer of the law!" he squawked, backing away in a hurry.

I was tired of talking and thirsty, so I merely give a snort and turned away through the crowd towards a saloon pushing 'em right and left out of my way. I saw 'em gang up in the street, talking low and mean, but I give no heed.

They wasn't nobody in the saloon except the barman and a gangling cowpuncher which had draped hisself over the bar. I ordered whiskey and when I had drank a few fingers of the rottenest muck I believe I ever tasted, I give it up in disgust and throwed the dollar on the bar which I had found, and was starting out when the barkeeper hollered:

"Hey!"

I turned around and said courteously: "Don't you yell at me like that, you bat-eared buzzard! What you want?"

"This here dollar ain't no good!" he said, banging it on the bar.

"Well, neither is your whiskey," I snarled, because I was getting mad. "So that makes us even!"

I am a long-suffering man but it looked like everybody in Grizzly Claw was out to gyp the stranger in their midst.

"You can't run no blazer over me!" he hollered. "You gimme a real dollar, or else—"

He ducked down behind the bar and come up with a shotgun so I taken it away from him and bent the barrel double across my knee and throwed it after him as he run out the back door hollering help, murder.

The cowpuncher had picked up the dollar and bit on it, and then he looked at me very sharp, and said: "Where did you get this?"

"I found it, if it's any of your dern business," I snapped, because I was mad. Saying no more I strode out the door, and the minute I hit the street somebody let *bam!* at me from behind a rain-barrel across the street and shot my hat off. So I slammed a bullet back through the barrel and the feller hollered and fell out in the open yelling blue murder. It was the feller which called hisself the sheriff and he was drilled through the hind laig. I noticed a lot of heads sticking up over window sills and around doors, so I roared: "Let that be a warnin' to you Grizzly Claw coyotes! I'm Breckinridge Elkins from Bear Creek up in the Humbolts, and I shoot better in my sleep than most men does wide awake!"

I then lent emphasis to my remarks by punctuating a few signboards and knocking out a few winder panes and everybody hollered and ducked. So I shoved my guns back in their scabbards and went into a restaurant. The citizens come out from their hiding-places and carried off my victim, and he made more noise over a broke laig than I thought was possible for a grown man.

There was some folks in the restaurant but they stampeded out the back door as I come in at the front, all except the cook which tried to take refuge somewhere else.

"Come outa there and fry me some bacon!" I commanded, kicking a few slats out of the counter to add point to my request. It disgusts me to see a grown man trying to hide under a stove. I am a very patient and good-natured human, but Grizzly Claw was getting under my hide. So the cook come out and fried me a mess of bacon and ham and aigs and pertaters and sourdough bread and beans and coffee, and I et three cans of cling peaches. Nobody come into the restaurant whilst I was eating but I thought I heard somebody sneaking around outside.

When I got through I asked the feller how much and he told me, and I planked down the cash, and he commenced to bite it. This lack of faith in his feller humans enraged me, so I drawed my bowie knife and said: "They is a limit to any man's patience! I been insulted once tonight and that's enough! You just dast say that coin's phoney and I'll slice off your whiskers plumb at the roots!"

I brandished my bowie under his nose, and he hollered and stampeded back into the stove and upsot it and fell over it, and the coals went down the back of his shirt, so he riz up and run for the creek yelling bloody murder. And that's how the story started that I tried to burn a cook alive, Indian-style, because he fried my bacon too crisp. Matter of fact, I kept his shack from catching fire and burning down, because I stomped out the coals before they did more'n burn a big hole through the floor, and I throwed the stove out the back door.

It ain't my fault if the mayor of Grizzly Claw was sneaking up the back steps with a shotgun just at that moment. Anyway, I hear he was able to walk with a couple of crutches after a few months.

I emerged suddenly from the front door, hearing a suspicious noise, and I seen a feller crouching close to a side window peeking through a hole in the wall. It was the cowboy I seen in the Apache Queen saloon. He whirled when I come out, but I had him covered.

"Are you spyin' on me?" I demanded. "Cause if you are—"

"No, no!" he said in a hurry. "I was just leanin' up against that wall restin'."

"You Grizzly Claw folks is all crazy," I said disgustedly, and looked around to see if anybody else tried to shoot me, but there warn't nobody in sight, which was suspicious, but I give no heed. It was dark by that time so I went to the wagon-yard, and there wasn't nobody there. I guess the man which run it was off somewheres drunk, because that seemed to be the main occupation of most of them Grizzly Claw devils.

THE ONLY PLACE FOR folks to sleep was a kind of double log-cabin. That is, it had two rooms, but there warn't no door between 'em; and in each room there wasn't nothing but a fireplace and a bunk, and just one outer door. I seen Cap'n Kidd was fixed for the night, and then I went into the cabin and brought in my saddle and bridle and saddle blanket because I didn't trust the people thereabouts. I took off my boots and hat and hung 'em on the wall, and hung my guns and bowie on the end of the bunk, and then spread my saddle-blanket on the bunk and laid down glumly.

I dunno why they don't build them dern things for ordinary sized humans. A man six and a half foot tall like me can't never find one comfortable for him. I laid there and was disgusted at the bunk, and at myself too, because I hadn't accomplished nothing. I hadn't learnt who it was done something to Uncle Jeppard, or what he done. It looked like I'd have to go clean to Bear Creek to find out, and that was a good four days ride.

Well, as I contemplated I heard a man come into the wagon-yard, and purty soon I heard him approach the cabin, but I thought nothing of it. Then the door begun to open, and I riz up with a gun in each hand and said: "Who's there? Make yourself knowed before I blasts you down!"

Whoever it was mumbled some excuse about being on the wrong side, and the door closed. But the voice sounded kind of familiar, and the fellow didn't go into the other room. I heard his footsteps sneaking off, and I riz and went to the door, and looked over toward the row of stalls. So purty soon a man led the pinto out of his stall, and swung aboard him and rode off. It was purty dark, but if us folks on Bear Creek didn't have eyes like a hawk, we'd never live to get grown. I seen it was the cowboy I'd seen in the Apache Queen and outside the restaurant. Once he got clear of the wagon-yard, he slapped in the spurs and went racing through the village like they was a red war-party on his trail. I could hear the beat of his horse's hoofs fading south down the rocky trail after he was out of sight.

I knowed he must of follered me to the wagon-yard, but I couldn't make no sense out of it, so I went and laid down on the bunk again. I was just about to go to sleep, when I was woke by the sounds of somebody coming into the other room of the cabin, and I heard somebody strike a match. The bunk was built against the partition wall, so they was only a few feet from me, though with the log wall between us.

They was two of them, from the sounds of their talking.

"I tell you," one of them was saying, "I don't like his looks. I don't believe he's what he pertends to be. We better take no chances, and clear out. After all, we can't stay here forever. These people are beginnin' to git suspicious, and if they find out for shore, they'll be demandin' a cut in the profits, to protect us. The stuff's all packed and ready to jump at a second's notice. Let's run for it tonight. It's a wonder nobody ain't never stumbled on to that hide-out before now."

"Aw," said the other'n, "these Grizzly Claw yaps don't do nothin' but swill licker and gamble and think up swindles to work on such strangers as is unlucky enough to wander in here. They never go into the hills southwest of the village where our cave is. Most of 'em don't even know there's a path past that big rock to the west."

"Well, Bill," said t'other'n, "we've done purty well, countin' that job up in the Bear Creek country."

At that I was wide awake and listening with both ears.

Bill laughed. "That was kind of funny, warn't it, Jim?" he said.

"You ain't never told me the particulars," said Jim. "Did you have any trouble?"

"Well," said Bill. "T'warn't to say easy. That old Jeppard Grimes was a hard old nut. If all Injun fighters was like him, I feel plumb sorry for the Injuns."

"If any of them Bear Creek devils ever catch you—" begun Jim.

Bill laughed again.

"Them hill-billies never strays more'n ten miles from Bear Creek," he said. "I had the sculp and was gone before they knowed what was up. I've collected bounties for wolves and b'ars, but that's the first time I ever got money for a human sculp!"

A icy chill run down my spine. Now I knowed what had happened to poor old Uncle Jeppard! Scalped! After all the Indian scalps he'd lifted! And them cold-blooded murderers could set there and talk about it, like it was the ears of a coyote or a rabbit!

"I told him he'd had the use of that sculp long enough," Bill was saying. "A old cuss like him—"

I waited for no more. Everything was red around me. I didn't stop for my boots, gun nor nothing, I was too crazy mad even to know such things existed. I riz up from that bunk and put my head down and rammed that partition wall like a bull going through a rail fence.

THE DRIED MUD POURED out of the chinks and some of the logs give way, and a howl went up from the other side.

"What's that?" hollered one, and t'other'n yelled: "Look out! It's a b'ar!"

I drawed back and rammed the wall again. It caved inwards and I come head-long through it in a shower of dry mud and splinters, and somebody shot at me and missed. They was a lighted lantern setting on a hand-hewn table, and two men about six feet tall each that hollered and let *bam* at me with their six-shooters. But they was too dumfounded to shoot straight. I gathered 'em to my bosom and we went backwards over the table, taking it and the lantern with us, and you ought to of heard them critters howl when the burning ile splashed down their necks.

It was a dirt floor so nothing caught on fire, and we was fighting in the dark, and they was hollering: "Help! Murder! We are bein' 'sassinated! Release go my ear!" And then one of 'em got his boot heel wedged in my mouth, and whilst I was twisting it out with one hand, the other'n tore out of his shirt which I was gripping with t'other hand, and run out the door. I had hold of the other feller's foot and commenced trying to twist it off, when he wrenched his laig outa the boot, and took it on the run. When I started to foller him I fell over the table in the dark and got all tangled up in it.

I broke off a leg for a club and rushed to the door, and just as I got to it a whole mob of folks come surging into the wagon-yard with torches and guns and dogs and a rope, and they hollered: "There he is, the murderer, the outlaw, the counterfeiter, the house-burner, the mule-killer!"

I seen the man that owned the mule, and the restaurant feller, and the barkeeper and a lot of others. They come roaring and bellering up to the door, hollering, "Hang him! Hang him! String the murderer up!" And they begun shooting at me, so I fell amongst 'em with my table-leg and laid right and left till it busted. They was packed so close together I laid out three and four at a lick and they hollered something awful. The torches was all knocked down and trompled out except them which was held by fellers which danced around on the edge of the mill, hollering: "Lay hold on him! Don't be scared of the big hill-billy! Shoot him! Knock him in the head!" The dogs having more sense than the men, they all run off except one big mongrel that looked like a wolf, and he bit the mob often'er he did me.

They was a lot of wild shooting and men hollering: "Oh, I'm shot! I'm kilt! I'm dyin'!" and some of them bullets burnt my hide they come so close, and the flashes singed my eye-lashes, and somebody broke a knife against my belt buckle. Then I seen the torches was all gone except one, and my club was broke, so I bust right through the mob, swinging right and left with my fists and stomping on them that tried to drag me down. I got clear of everybody except the man with the torch who was so excited he was jumping up and down trying to shoot me without cocking his gun. That blame dog was snapping at my heels, so I swung him by the tail and hit the man over the head with him. They went down in a heap and the torch went out, and the dog clamped on the feller's ear and he let out a squall like a steam-whistle.

They was milling in the dark behind me, and I run straight to Cap'n Kidd's stall and jumped on him bareback with nothing but a hackamore on him. Just as the mob located where I went, we come storming out of the stall like a hurricane and knocked some of 'em galley-west and run over some more, and headed for the gate. Somebody shut the gate but Cap'n Kidd took it in his stride, and we was gone into the darkness before they knowed what hit them.

Cap'n Kidd decided then was a good time to run away, like he usually does, so he took to the hills and run through bushes and clumps of trees trying to scrape me off on the branches. When I finally pulled him up he was maybe a mile south of the village, with Cap'n Kidd no bridle nor saddle nor blanket, and me with no guns, knife, boots nor hat. And what was worse, them devils which scalped Uncle Jeppard had got away from me, and I didn't know where to look for 'em.

I SET MEDITATING WHETHER to go back and fight the whole town of Grizzly Claw for my boots and guns, or what to do, when all at once I remembered what Bill and Jim had said about a cave and a path running to it. I thought: I bet them fellers will go back and get their horses and pull out, just like they was planning, and they had stuff in the cave, so that's the place to look for 'em. I hoped they hadn't already got the stuff, whatever it was, and gone.

I knowed where that rock was, because I'd seen it when I come into town that afternoon—a big rock that jutted up above the trees about a mile to the west of Grizzly Claw. So I started out through the brush, and before long I seen it looming up against the stars, and I made straight for it. Sure enough, there was a narrow trail winding around the base and leading off to the southwest. I follered it, and when I'd went nearly a mile, I come to a steep mountain-side, all clustered with brush.

When I seen that I slipped off and led Cap'n Kidd off the trail and tied him back amongst the trees. Then I crope up to the cave which was purty well masked with bushes. I listened, but everything was dark and still, but all at once, away down the trail, I heard a burst of shots, and what sounded like a lot of horses running. Then everything was still again, and I quick ducked into the cave, and struck a match.

There was a narrer entrance that broadened out after a few feet, and the cave run straight like a tunnel for maybe thirty steps, about fifteen foot wide, and then it made a bend. After that it widened out and got to be purty big—fifty feet wide at least, and I couldn't tell how far back into the mountain it run. To the left the wall was very broken and notched with ledges, might nigh like stair-steps, and when the match went out, away up above me I seen some stars which meant that there was a cleft in the wall or roof away up on the mountain somewheres.

Before the match went out, I seen a lot of junk over in a corner covered up with a tarpaulin, and when I was fixing to strike another match I heard men coming up the trail outside. So I quick clumb up the broken wall and laid on a ledge about ten feet up and listened.

From the sounds as they arriv at the cave mouth, I knowed it was two men on foot, running hard and panting loud. They rushed into the cave and made the turn, and I heard 'em fumbling around. Then a light flared up and I seen a lantern being lit and hung up on a spur of rock.

In the light I seen them two murderers, Bill and Jim, and they looked plumb delapidated. Bill didn't have no shirt on and the other'n was wearing just one boot and limped. Bill didn't have no gun in his belt neither, and both was mauled and bruised, and scratched, too, like they'd been running through briars.

"Look here," said Jim, holding his head which had a welt on it which was likely made by my fist. "I ain't certain in my mind as to just what all *has* happened. Somebody must of hit me with a club some time tonight, and things is happened too fast for my addled wits. Seems like we been fightin' and runnin' all night. Listen, *was* we settin' in the wagon-yard shack talkin' peaceable, and *did* a grizzly b'ar bust through the wall and nigh slaughter us?"

"That's plumb correct," said Bill. "Only it warn't no b'ar. It was some kind of a human critter—maybe a escaped maneyack. We ought to of stopped for our horses—"

"I warn't thinkin' 'bout no horses," broke in Jim. "When I found myself outside that shack my only thought was to cover ground, and I done my best, considerin' that I'd lost a boot and that critter had nigh unhinged my hind laig. I'd lost you in the dark, so I made for the cave, knowin' you would come there eventually, and it seemed like I was forever gettin' through the woods, crippled like I was. I'd no more'n hit the path when you come up it on the run."

"Well," said Bill, "as I went over the wagon-yard wall a lot of people come whoopin' through the gate, and I thought they was after us, but they must of been after the feller we fought, because as I run I seen him layin' into 'em right and left. After I'd got over my panic, I went back after our horses, but I run right into a gang of men on horseback, and one of 'em was that durned feller which passed hisself off as a cowboy. I didn't need no more. I took out through the woods as hard as I could pelt, and they hollered. 'There he goes!' and come hot-foot after me."

"And was them the fellers I shot at back down the trail?" asked Jim.

"Yeah," said Bill. "I thought I'd shooken 'em off, but just as I seen you on the path, I heard horses comin' behind us, so I hollered to let 'em have it, and you did."

"Well, I didn't know who it was," said Jim. "I tell you, my head's buzzin' like a circle-saw."

"Well," said Bill, "we stopped 'em and scattered 'em. I dunno if you hit anybody in the dark, but they'll be mighty cautious about comin' up the trail. Let's clear out."

"On foot?" said Jim. "And me with just one boot?"

"How else?" said Bill. "We'll have to hoof it till we can steal us some broncs. We'll have to leave all this stuff here. We daren't go back to Grizzly Claw after our horses. I *told* you that durned cowboy would do to watch. He ain't no cowpoke at all. He's a blame detective."

"What's that?" broke in Jim.

"Horses' hoofs!" exclaimed Bill, turning pale. "Here, blow out that lantern! We'll climb the ledges and get out of the cleft, and take out over the mountain where they can't foller with horses, and then—"

IT WAS AT THAT INSTANT that I launched myself offa the ledge on top of 'em. I landed with all my two hundred and ninety pounds square on Jim's shoulders and when he hit the ground under me he kind of spread out like a toad when you step on him. Bill give a scream of astonishment and when I riz and come for him, he tore off a hunk of rock about the size of a man's head and lammed me over the ear with it. This irritated me, so I taken him by the neck, and also taken away a knife which he was trying to hamstring me with, and begun sweeping the floor with his carcass.

Presently I paused and kneeling on him, I strangled him till his tongue lolled out, betwixt times hammering his head against the rocky floor.

"You murderin' devil!" I gritted between my teeth. "Before I varnish this here rock with your brains, tell me why you taken my Uncle Jeppard's scalp!"

"Let up!" he gurgled, being purple in the face where he warn't bloody. "They was a dude travelin' through the country and collectin' souvenirs, and he heard about that sculp and wanted it. He hired me to go git it for him."

I was so shocked at that cold-bloodedness that I forgot what I was doing and choked him nigh to death before I remembered to ease up on him.

"Who was he?" I demanded. "Who is the skunk which hires old men murdered so's he can collect their scalps? My God, these Eastern dudes is worse'n Apaches! Hurry up and tell me, so I can finish killin' you."

But he was unconscious; I'd squoze him too hard. I riz up and looked around for some water or whiskey or something to bring him to so he could tell who hired him to scalp Uncle Jeppard, before I twisted his head off, which was my earnest intention of doing, when somebody said: "Han's up!"

I whirled and there at the crook of the cave stood that cowboy which had spied on me in Grizzly Claw, with ten other men. They all had their Winchesters p'inted at me, and the cowboy had a star on his buzum.

"Don't move!" he said. "I'm a Federal detective, and I arrest you for manufactorin' counterfeit money."

"What you mean?" I snarled, backing up to the wall.

"You know," he said, kicking the tarpaulin off the junk in the corner. "Look here, men! All the stamps and dyes he used to make phoney coins and bills! All packed up, ready to light out. I been hangin' around Grizzly Claw for days, knowin' that whoever was passin' this stuff made his, or their, headquarters here somewheres. Today I spotted that dollar you give the barkeep, and I went *pronto* for my men which was camped back in the hills a few miles. I thought you was settled in the wagon-yard for the night, but it seems you give us the slip. Put the cuffs on him, men!"

"No, you don't!" I snarled, bounding back. "Not till I've finished these devils on the floor. I dunno what you're talkin' about, but—"

"Here's a couple of corpses!" hollered one of the men. "He kilt a couple of fellers!"

One of them stooped over Bill, but he had recovered his senses, and now he riz up on his elbows and give a howl. "Save me!" he bellered. "I confesses! I'm a counterfeiter, and so is Jim there on the floor! We surrenders, and you got to pertect us!"

"YOU'RE THE COUNTERFEITERS?" said the detective, took aback as it were. "Why, I was follerin' this giant! I seen him pass fake money myself. We got to the wagon-yard awhile after he'd run off, but we seen him duck in the woods not far from there, and we been chasin' him. He opened fire on us down the trail while ago—"

"That was us," said Bill. "It was me you was chasin'. He musta found that money, if he had fake stuff. I tell you, we're the men you're after, and you got to pertect us! I demands to be put in the strongest jail in this state, which even this here devil can't bust into!"

"And he ain't no counterfeiter?" said the detective.

"He ain't nothin' but a man-eater," said Bill. "Arrest us and take us out of his reach."

"No!" I roared, clean beside myself. "They belongs to me! They scalped my uncle! Give 'em knives or gun or somethin' and let us fight it out."

"Can't do that," said the detective. "They're Federal prisoners. If you got any charge against them, they'll have to be indicted in the proper form."

His men hauled 'em up and handcuffed 'em and started to lead 'em out.

"Blast your souls!" I raved. "Does you mean to pertect a couple of dirty scalpers? I'll—"

I started for 'em and they all p'inted their Winchesters at me.

"Keep back!" said the detective. "I'm grateful for you leadin' us to this den, and layin' out these criminals for us, but I don't hanker after no battle in a cave with a human grizzly like you."

Well, what could a feller do?

If I'd had my guns, or even my knife, I'd of taken a chance with the whole eleven, officers or not, I was that crazy mad. But even I can't fight eleven .45-90's with my bare hands. I stood speechless with rage whilst they filed out, and then I went for Cap'n Kidd in a kind of a daze. I felt wuss'n a horse-thief. Them fellers would be put in the pen safe out of my reach, and Uncle Jeppard's scalp was unavenged! It was awful. I felt like bawling.

Time I got my horse back onto the trail, the posse with their prisoners was out of sight and hearing. I seen the only thing to do was to go back to Grizzly Claw and get my outfit, and then foller the posse and try to take their prisoners away from 'em someway.

Well, the wagon-yard was dark and still. The wounded had been carried away to have their injuries bandaged, and from the groaning that was still coming from the shacks and cabins along the street, the casualties had been plenteous. The citizens of Grizzly Claw must have been shook up something terrible, because they hadn't even stole my guns and saddle and things yet; everything was in the cabin just like I'd left 'em.

I put on my boots, hat and belt, saddled and bridled Cap'n Kidd and sot out on the road I knowed the posse had taken. But they had a long start on me, and when daylight come I hadn't overtook 'em. But I did meet somebody else. It was Tunk Willoughby riding up the trail, and when he seen me he grinned all over his battered features.

"Hey, Breck!" he said. "After you left I sot on that log and thunk, and thunk, and I finally remembered what Jack Gordon told me, and I started out to find you again and tell you. It was this: he said to keep a close lookout for a fellow from Grizzly Claw named Bill Jackson, which had gypped yore Uncle Jeppard in a deal."

"*What?*" I said.

"Yeah," said Tunk. "He bought somethin' from Jeppard and paid him in counterfeit money. Jeppard didn't know it was phoney till after the feller had plumb got away," said Tunk, "and bein' as he was too busy dryin' some b'ar meat to go after him, he sent word for you to git him."

"But the scalp—" I said wildly.

"Oh," said Tunk, "that was what Jeppard sold the feller. It was the scalp Jeppard took offa old Yeller Eagle the Comanche war-chief forty years ago, and been keepin' for a souvenear. Seems like a Eastern dude heard about it and wanted to buy it, but this Jackson must of kept the money he give him to git it with, and give Jeppard phoney cash. So you see everything's all right, even if I did forget a little, and no harm did—"

And that's why Tunk Willoughby is going around saying I am a homicidal maneyack, and run him five miles down a mountain and tried to kill him—which is a exaggeration, of course. I wouldn't of kilt him if I could of caught him. I would merely of raised a few knots on his head and tied his hind laigs in a bow-knot around his fool neck and done a few other little things that might of improved his memory.

A GENT FROM BEAR CREEK

THE FOLKS ON BEAR CREEK ain't what you'd call peaceable by nature, but I was kind of surprised to come onto Erath Elkins and his brother-in-law Joel Gordon locked in mortal combat on the bank of the creek. But there they was, so tangled up they couldn't use their bowies to no advantage, and their cussing was scandalous to hear.

Remonstrances being useless, I kicked their knives out of their hands and threwed 'em bodily into the creek. That broke their holds and they come swarming out with blood-thirsty shrieks and dripping whiskers, and attacked me. Seeing they was too blind mad to have any sense, I bashed their heads together till they was too dizzy to do anything but holler.

"Is this any way for relatives to ack?" I asked disgustedly.

"Lemme at him!" howled Joel, gnashing his teeth whilst blood streamed down his whiskers. "He's broke three of my fangs and I'll have his life!"

"Stand aside, Breckinridge!" raved Erath. "No man can chaw a ear offa me and live to tell the tale!"

"Aw, shut up," I snorted. "One more yap outa either'n of you, and I'll see if yore fool heads are harder'n this." I brandished a fist under their noses and they quieted down. "What's all this about?" I demanded.

"I just discovered my brother-in-law is a thief," said Joel bitterly. At that Erath give a howl and a vi'lent plunge to get at his relative, but I kind of pushed him backwards, and he fell over a willer stump.

"The facts is, Breckinridge," said Joel, "me and this polecat found a buckskin poke full of gold nuggets in a holler oak over on Apache Ridge yesterday. We didn't know whether somebody in these parts had just hid it there for safe-keepin', or whether some old prospector had left it there a long time ago and maybe got sculped by the Injuns and never come back to git it. We agreed to leave it alone for a month, and if it was still there at that time, we'd feel purty shore that the original owner was dead, and we'd split the gold between us. Well, last night I got to worryin' somebody'd find it which wasn't as honest as me, so this mornin' I thought I better go see if it was still there. . . ."

At this point Erath laughed bitterly.

Joel glared at him ominously and continued: "Well, no sooner I hove in sight of the holler tree than this skunk let go at me from the bresh with a rifle-gun—"

"That's a lie!" yelped Erath. "It war jest the other way around!"

"Not bein' armed, Breckinridge," Joel said with dignity, "and realizin' that this coyote was tryin' to murder me so he could claim all the gold, I legged it for home and my weppins. And presently I sighted him sprintin' through the bresh after me."

Erath begun to foam slightly at the mouth. "I warn't chasin' you," he said. "I was goin' home after my rifle-gun."

"What's yore story, Erath?" I inquired.

"Last night I drempt somebody had stole the gold," he answered sullenly. "This mornin' I went to see if it was safe. Just as I got to the tree, this murderer begun shootin' at me with a Winchester. I run for my life, and by some chance I finally run right into him. Likely he thought he'd kilt me and was comin' for the sculp."

"Did either one of you see t'other'n shoot at you?" I asked.

"How could I, with him hid in the bresh?" snapped Joel. "But who else could it been?"

"I didn't have to see him," growled Erath. "I felt the wind of his slug."

"But each one of you says he didn't have no rifle," I said.

"He's a cussed liar," they accused simultaneous, and would have fell on each other tooth and nail if they could have got past my bulk.

"I'm convinced they's been a mistake," I said. "Git home and cool off."

"You're too big for me to lick, Breckinridge," said Erath. "But I warn you, if you cain't prove to me that it wasn't Joel which tried to murder me, I ain't goin' to rest nor sleep nor eat till I've nailed his mangy sculp to the highest pine on Apache Ridge."

"That goes for me, too," said Joel, grinding his teeth. "I'm declarin' truce till tomorrer mornin'. If Breckinridge cain't show me by then that you didn't shoot at me, either my wife or yore'n'll be a widder before midnight."

SO SAYING THEY STALKED off in opposite directions, whilst I stared helplessly after 'em, slightly dazed at the responsibility which had been dumped onto me. That's the drawback of being the biggest man in your settlement. All the relatives pile their troubles onto you. Here it was up to me to stop what looked like the beginnings of a regular family feud which was bound to reduce the population awful.

The more I thought of the gold them idjits had found, the more I felt like I ought to go and take a look to see was it real stuff, so I went back to the corral and saddled Cap'n Kidd and lit out for Apache Ridge, which was about a mile away. From the remarks they'd let fell whilst cussing each other, I had a purty good idea where the holler oak was at, and sure enough I found it without much trouble. I tied Cap'n Kid and clumb up on the trunk till I reached the holler. And then as I was craning my neck to look in, I heard a voice say: "Another dern thief!"

I looked around and seen Uncle Jeppard Grimes p'inting a gun at me.

"Bear Creek is goin' to hell," said Uncle Jeppard. "First it was Erath and Joel, and now it's you. I'm goin' to throw a bullet through yore hind laig just to teach you a little honesty."

With that he started sighting along the barrel of his Winchester, and I said: "You better save yore lead for that Injun over there."

Him being a old Indian fighter he just naturally jerked his head around quick, and I pulled my .45 and shot the rifle out of his hands. I jumped down and, put my foot on it, and he pulled a knife out of his boot, and I taken it away from him and shaken him till he was so addled when I let him go he run in a circle and fell down cussing something terrible.

"Is everybody on Bear Creek gone crazy?" I demanded. "Can't a man look into a holler tree without gettin' assassinated?"

"You was after my gold," swore Uncle Jeppard.

"So it's your gold, hey?" I said. "Well, a holler tree ain't no bank."

"I know it," he growled, combing the pine-needles out of his whiskers. "When I come here early this mornin' to see if it was safe, like I frequent does, I seen right off somebody'd been handlin' it. Whilst I was meditatin' over this, I seen Joel Gordon sneakin' towards the tree. I fired a shot across his bows in warnin' and he run off. But a few minutes later here come Erath Elkins slitherin' through the pines. I was mad by this time, so I combed his whiskers with a chunk of lead and *he* high-tailed it. And now, by golly, here you come—"

"I don't want yore blame gold!" I roared. "I just wanted to see if it was safe, and so did Joel and Erath. If them men was thieves, they'd have took it when they found it yesterday. Where'd you get it, anyway?"

"I panned it, up in the hills," he said sullenly. "I ain't had time to take it to Chawed Ear and git it changed into cash money. I figgered this here tree was as good a place as any. But I done put it elsewhere now."

"Well," I said, "you got to go tell Erath and Joel it was you shot at 'em, so they won't kill each other. They'll be mad at you, but I'll cool 'em off, maybe with a hickory club."

"All right," he said. "I'm sorry I misjedged you, Breckinridge. Just to show you I trusts you, I'll show you whar I hid it."

He led me through the trees till he come to a big rock jutting out from the side of a cliff, and pointed at a smaller stone wedged beneath it.

"I pulled out that rock," he said, "and dug a hole and stuck the poke in. Look!"

He heaved the rock out and bent down. And then he went straight up in the air with a yell that made me jump and pull my gun with cold sweat busting out all over me.

"What's the matter with you?" I demanded. "Are you snake-bit?"

"Yeah, by human snakes!" he hollered. "*It's gone!* I been robbed!"

I looked and seen the impressions the wrinkles in the buckskin poke had made in the soft earth. But there wasn't nothing there now.

UNCLE JEPPARD WAS DOING a scalp dance with a gun in one hand and a bowie knife in the other'n. "I'll fringe my leggins with their mangy sculps!" he raved. "I'll pickle their hearts in a barr'l of brine! I'll feed their livers to my houn' dawgs!"

"Whose livers?" I inquired.

"Whose, you idjit?" he howled. "Joel Gordon and Erath Elkins, dern it! They didn't run off. They snuck back and seen me move the gold! I've kilt better men than them for half as much!"

"Aw," I said, "t'ain't possible they stole yore gold—"

"Then where is it?" he demanded bitterly. "Who else knowed about it?"

"Look here!" I said, pointing to a belt of soft loam near the rocks. "A horse's tracks."

"What of it?" he demanded. "Maybe they had horses tied in the bresh."

"Aw, no," I said. "Look how the Calkins is set. They ain't no horses on Bear Creek shod like that. These is the tracks of a stranger—I bet the feller I seen ride past my cabin just about daybreak. A black-whiskered man with one ear missin'. That hard ground by the big rock don't show where he got off and stomped around, but the man which rode this horse stole yore gold, I'll bet my guns."

"I ain't convinced," said Uncle Jeppard. "I'm goin' home and ile my rifle-gun, and then I'm goin' to go over and kill Joel and Erath."

"Now you lissen," I said forcibly. "I know what a stubborn old jassack you are, Uncle Jeppard, but this time you got to lissen to reason or I'll forget myself and kick the seat outa yore britches. I'm goin' to follow this feller and take yore gold away from him, because I know it was him stole it. And don't you dare to kill nobody till I git back."

"I'll give you till tomorrer mornin'," he compromised. "I won't pull a trigger till then. But," said Uncle Jeppard waxing poetical, "if my gold ain't in my hands by the time the mornin' sun h'ists itself over the shinin' peaks of the Jackass Mountains, the buzzards will rassle their hash on the carcasses of Joel Gordon and Erath Elkins."

I went away from there, mounted Cap'n Kidd and headed west on the trail of the stranger. It was still tolerably early in the morning, and one of them long summer days ahead of me. They wasn't a horse in the Humbolts to equal Cap'n Kidd for endurance. I've rode a hundred miles on him between sun-down and sun-up. But that horse the stranger was riding must have been some chunk of horse-meat hisself. The day wore on, and still I hadn't come up with my man. I was getting into country I wasn't familiar with, but I didn't have much trouble in following the trail, and finally, late in the evening, I come out on a narrow dusty path where the calk-marks of his hoofs was very plain.

The sun sunk lower and my hopes dwindled. Cap'n Kidd was beginning to tire, and even if I got the thief and got the gold, it'd be a awful push to get back to Bear Creek in time to prevent mayhem. But I urged on Cap'n Kidd, and presently we come out onto a road, and the tracks I was following merged with a lot of others. I went on, expecting to come to some settlement, and wondering just where I was. I'd never been that far in that direction before then.

Just at sun-down I rounded a bend in the road and seen something hanging to a tree, and it was a man. There was another man in the act of pinning something to the corpse's shirt, and when he heard me he wheeled and jerked his gun—the man, I mean, not the corpse. He was a mean looking cuss, but he wasn't Black Whiskers. Seeing I made no hostile move, he put up his gun and grinned.

"That feller's still kickin'," I said.

"We just strung him up," said the fellow. "The other boys has rode back to town, but I stayed to put this warnin' on his buzzum. Can you read?"

"No," I said.

"Well," he said, "this here paper says: 'Warnin' to all outlaws and specially them on Grizzly Mountain—Keep away from Wampum.'"

"How far's Wampum from here?" I asked.

"Half a mile down the road," he said. "I'm Al Jackson, one of Bill Ormond's deputies. We aim to clean up Wampum. This is one of them derned outlaws which has denned up on Grizzly Mountain."

BEFORE I COULD SAY anything I heard somebody breathing quick and gaspy, and they was a patter of bare feet in the bresh, and a kid girl about fourteen years old bust into the road.

"You've killed Uncle Joab!" she shrieked. "You murderers! A boy told me they was fixin' to hang him! I run as fast as I could—"

"Git away from that corpse!" roared Jackson, hitting at her with his quirt.

"You stop that!" I ordered. "Don't you hit that young 'un."

"Oh, please, Mister!" she wept, wringing her hands. "You ain't one of Ormond's men. Please help me! He ain't dead—I seen him move!"

Waiting for no more I spurred alongside the body and drawed my knife.

"Don't you cut that rope!" squawk the deputy, jerking his gun. So I hit him under the jaw and knocked him out of his saddle and into the bresh beside the road where he lay groaning. I then cut the rope and eased the hanged man down on my saddle and got the noose offa his neck. He was purple in the face and his eyes was closed and his tongue lolled out, but he still had some life in him. Evidently they didn't drop him, but just hauled him up to strangle to death.

I laid him on the ground and work over him till some of his life begun to come back to him, but I knowed he ought to have medical attention. I said: "Where's the nearest doctor?"

"Doc Richards in Wampum," whimpered the kid. "But if we take him there Ormond will get him again. Won't you please take him home?"

"Where you-all live?" I inquired.

"We been livin' in a cabin on Grizzly Mountain since Ormond run us out of Wampum," she whimpered.

"Well," I said, "I'm goin' to put yore uncle on Cap'n Kidd and you can set behind the saddle and help hold him on, and tell me which way to go."

So I done so and started off on foot leading Cap'n Kidd in the direction the girl showed me, and as we went I seen the deputy Jackson drag hisself out of the bresh and go limping down the road holding his jaw.

I was losing a awful lot of time, but I couldn't leave this feller to die, even if he was a outlaw, because probably the little gal didn't have nobody to take care of her but him. Anyway, I'd never make it back to Bear Creek by daylight on Cap'n Kidd, even if I could have started right then.

It was well after dark when we come up a narrow trail that wound up a thickly timbered mountain side, and purty soon somebody in a thicket ahead of us hollered: "Halt whar you be or I'll shoot!"

"Don't shoot, Jim!" called the girl. "This is Ellen, and we're bringin' Uncle Joab home."

A tall hard-looking young feller stepped out in the open, still p'inting his Winchester at me. He cussed when he seen our load.

"He ain't dead," I said. "But we ought to git him to his cabin."

So Jim led me through the thickets until we come into a clearing where they was a cabin, and a woman come running out and screamed like a catamount when she seen Joab. Me and Jim lifted him off and carried him in and laid him on a bunk, and the women begun to work over him, and I went out to my horse, because I was in a hurry to get gone. Jim follered me.

"This is the kind of stuff we've been havin' ever since Ormond come to Wampum," he said bitterly. "We been livin' up here like rats, afeard to stir in the open. I warned Joab against slippin' down into the village today, but he was sot on it, and wouldn't let any of the boys go with him. Said he'd sneak in, git what he wanted and sneak out again."

"Well," I said, "what's yore business is none of mine. But this here life is hard lines on women and children."

"You must be a friend of Joab's," she said. "He sent a man east some days ago, but we was afraid one of Ormond's men trailed him and killed him. But maybe he got through. Are you the man Joab sent for?"

"Meanin' am I some gunman come in to clean up the town?" I snorted. "Naw, I ain't. I never seen this feller Joab before."

"Well," said Jim, "cuttin' down Joab like you done has already got you in bad with Ormond. Help us run them fellers out of the country! There's still a good many of us in these hills, even if we have been run out of Wampum. This hangin' is the last straw. I'll round up the boys tonight, and we'll have a show-down with Ormond's men. We're outnumbered, and we been licked bad once, but we'll try it again. Won't you throw in with us?"

"Lissen," I said, climbing into the saddle, "just because I cut down a outlaw ain't no sign I'm ready to be one myself. I done it just because I couldn't stand to see the little gal take on so. Anyway, I'm lookin' for a feller with black whiskers and one ear missin' which rides a roan with a big Lazy-A brand."

Jim fell back from me and lifted his rifle. "You better ride on," he said somberly. "I'm obleeged to you for what you've did—but a friend of Wolf Ashley cain't be no friend of our'n."

I give him a snort of defiance and rode off down the mountain and headed for Wampum, because it was reasonable to suppose that maybe I'd find Black Whiskers there.

WAMPUM WASN'T MUCH of a town, but they was one big saloon and gambling hall where sounds of hilarity was coming from, and not many people on the streets and them which was mostly went in a hurry. I stopped one of them and ast him where a doctor lived, and he pointed out a house where he said Doc Richards lived, so I rode up to the door and knocked, and somebody inside said: "What you want? I got you covered."

"Are you Doc Richards?" I said, and he said: "Yes, keep your hands away from your belt or I'll fix you."

"This is a nice, friendly town!" I snorted. "I ain't figgerin' on harmin' you. They's a man up in the hills which needs yore attention."

At that the door opened and a man with red whiskers and a shotgun stuck his head out and said: "Who do you mean?"

"They call him Joab," I said. "He's on Grizzly Mountain."

"Hmmmm!" said Doc Richards, looking at me very sharp where I sot Cap'n Kidd in the starlight. "I set a man's jaw tonight, and he had a lot to say about a certain party who cut down a man that was hanged. If you're that party, my advice to you is to hit the trail before Ormond catches you."

"I'm hungry and thirsty and I'm lookin' for a man," I said. "I aim to leave Wampum when I'm good and ready."

"I never argue with a man as big as you," said Doc Richards. "I'll ride to Grizzly Mountain as quick as I can get my horse saddled. If I never see you alive again, which is very probable, I'll always remember you as the biggest man I ever saw, and the biggest fool. Good night!"

I thought, the folks in Wampum is the queerest acting I ever seen. I took my horse to the barn which served as a livery stable and seen that he was properly fixed. Then I went into the big saloon which was called the Golden Eagle. I was low in my spirits because I seemed to have lost Black Whiskers' trail entirely, and even if I found him in Wampum, which I hoped, I never could make it back to Bear Creek by sun-up. But I hoped to recover that derned gold yet, and get back in time to save a few lives.

They was a lot of tough looking fellers in the Golden Eagle drinking and gambling and talking loud and cussing, and they all stopped their noise as I come in, and looked at me very fishy. But I give 'em no heed and went to the bar, and purty soon they kinda forgot about me and the racket started up again.

Whilst I was drinking me a few fingers of whisky, somebody shouldered up to me and said: "Hey!" I turned around and seen a big, broad-built man with a black beard and blood-shot eyes and a pot-belly with two guns on.

I said: "Well?"

"Who air you?" he demanded.

"Who air you?" I come back at him.

"I'm Bill Ormond, sheriff of Wampum," he said. "That's who!" And he showed me a star on his shirt.

"Oh," I said. "Well, I'm Breckinridge Elkins, from Bear Creek."

I noticed a kind of quiet come over the place, and fellows was laying down their glasses and their billiard sticks, and hitching up their belts and kinda gathering around me. Ormond scowled and combed his beard with his fingers, and rocked on his heels and said: "I got to 'rest you!"

I sot down my glass quick and he jumped back and hollered: "Don't you dast pull no gun on the law!" And they was a kind of movement amongst the men around me.

"What you arrestin' me for?" I demanded. "I ain't busted no law."

"You assaulted one of my deputies," he said, and then I seen that feller Jackson standing behind the sheriff, with his jaw all bandaged up. He couldn't work his chin to talk. All he could do was p'int his finger at me and shake his fists.

"You likewise cut down a outlaw we had just hunged," said Ormond. "Yore under arrest!"

"But I'm lookin' for a man!" I protested. "I ain't got time to be arrested!"

"You should of thunk about that when you busted the law," opined Ormond. "Gimme yore gun and come along peaceable."

A DOZEN MEN HAD THEIR hands on their guns, but it wasn't that which made me give in. Pap had always taught me never to resist no officer of the law, so it was kind of instinctive for me to hand my gun over to Ormond and go along with him without no fight. I was kind of bewildered and my thoughts was addled anyway. I ain't one of these fast thinking sharps.

Ormond escorted me down the street a ways, with a whole bunch of men following us, and stopped at a log building with barred windows which was next to a board shack. A man come out of this shack with a big bunch of keys, and Ormond said he was the jailer. So they put me in the log jail and Ormond went off with everybody but the jailer, who sat down on the step outside the shack and rolled a cigaret.

There wasn't no light in the jail, but I found the bunk and tried to lay down on it, but it wasn't built for a man six and a half foot tall. I sot down on it and at last realized what a infernal mess I was in. Here I ought to be hunting Black Whiskers and getting the gold to take back to Bear Creek and save the lives of a lot of my kin-folks, but instead I was in jail, and no way of getting out without killing a officer of the law. With daybreak Joel and Erath would be at each other's throats, and Uncle Jeppard would be gunning for both of 'em. It was too much to hope that the other relatives would let them three fight it out amongst theirselves. I never seen such a clan for butting into each other's business. The guns would be talking all up and down Bear Creek, and the population would be decreasing with every volley. I thought about it till I got dizzy, and then the jailer stuck his head up to the window and said if I would give him five dollars he'd go get me something to eat.

I give it to him, and he went off and was gone quite a spell, and at last he come back and give me a ham sandwich. I ast him was that all he could get for five dollars, and he said grub was awful high in Wampum. I et the sandwich in one bite, because I hadn't et nothing since morning, and then he said if I'd give him some more money he'd get me another sandwich. But I didn't have no more and told him so.

"What!" he said, breathing licker fumes in my face through the window bars. "No money? And you expect us to feed you for nothin'?" So he cussed me, and went off. Purty soon the sheriff come and looked in at me and said: "What's this I hear about you not havin' no money?"

"I ain't got none left," I said, and he cussed something fierce.

"How you expect to pay yore fine?" he demanded. "You think you can lay up in our jail and eat us out of house and home? What kind of a critter are you, anyway?" Just then the jailer chipped in and said somebody told him I had a horse down at the livery stable.

"Good," said the sheriff. "We'll sell the horse for his fine."

"No, you won't neither," I said, beginning to get mad. "You try to sell Cap'n Kidd, and I'll forgit what pap told me about officers, and take you plumb apart."

I riz up and glared at him through the window, and he fell back and put his hand on his gun. But just about that time I seen a man going into the Golden Eagle which was in easy sight of the jail, and lit up so the light streamed out into the street. I give a yell that made Ormond jump about a foot. It was Black Whiskers!

"Arrest that man, Sheriff!" I hollered. "He's a thief!"

Ormond whirled and looked, and then he said: "Are you plumb crazy? That's Wolf Ashley, my deperty."

"I don't give a dern," I said. "He stole a poke of gold from my Uncle Jeppard up in the Humbolts, and I've trailed him clean from Bear Creek. Do yore duty and arrest him."

"You shut up!" roared Ormond. "You can't tell me my business! I ain't goin' to arrest my best gunman—my star deperty, I mean. What you mean tryin' to start trouble this way? One more yap outa you and I'll throw a chunk of lead through you."

And he turned and stalked off muttering: "Poke of gold, huh? Holdin' out on me is he? I'll see about that!"

I SOT DOWN AND HELD my head in bewilderment. What kind of a sheriff was this which wouldn't arrest a derned thief? My thoughts run in circles till my wits was addled. The jailer had gone off and I wondered if he had went to sell Cap'n Kidd. I wondered what was going on back at Bear Creek, and I shivered to think what would bust loose at daybreak. And here I was in jail, with them fellers fixing to sell my horse whilst that derned thief swaggered around at large. I looked helplessly out the window.

It was getting late, but the Golden Eagle was still going full blast. I could hear the music blaring away, and the fellers yipping and shooting their pistols in the air, and their boot heels stomping on the board walk. I felt like busting down and crying, and then I begun to get mad. I get mad slow, generally, and before I was plumb mad, I heard a noise at the window.

I seen a pale face staring in at me, and a couple of small white hands on the bars.

"Oh, Mister!" a voice whispered. "Mister!"

I stepped over and looked out and it was the kid girl Ellen.

"What you doin' here, gal?" I asked.

"Doc Richards said you was in Wampum," she whispered. "He said he was afraid Ormond and his gang would go for you, because you helped me, so I slipped away on his horse and rode here as hard as I could. Jim was out tryin' to gather up the boys for a last stand, and Aunt Rachel and the other women was busy with Uncle Joab. They wasn't nobody but me to come, but I had to! You saved Uncle Joab, and I don't care if Jim does say you're a outlaw because you're a friend of Wolf Ashley. Oh, I wisht I wasn't just a girl! I wisht I could shoot a gun, so's I could kill Bill Ormond!"

"That ain't no way for a gal to talk," I said. "Leave killin' to the men. But I appreciates you goin' to all this trouble. I got some kid sisters myself—in fact I got seven or eight, as near as I remember. Don't you worry none about me. Lots of men gets throwed in jail."

"But that ain't it!" she wept, wringing her hands. "I listened outside the winder of the back room in the Golden Eagle and heard Ormond and Ashley talkin' about you. I dunno what you wanted with Ashley when you ast Jim about him, but he ain't your friend. Ormond accused him of stealin' a poke of gold and holdin' out on him, and Ashley said it was a lie. Then Ormond said you told him about it, and that he'd give Ashley till midnight to perdooce that gold, and if he didn't Wampum would be too small for both of 'em.

"Then he went out and I heard Ashley talkin' to a pal of his, and Ashley said he'd have to raise some gold somehow, or Ormond would have him killed, but that he was goin' to fix *you,* Mister, for lyin' about him. Mister, Ashley and his bunch are over in the back of the Golden Eagle right now plottin' to bust into the jail before daylight and hang you!"

"Aw," I said, "the sheriff wouldn't let 'em do that."

"You don't understand!" she cried. "Ormond ain't the sheriff! Him and his gunmen come into Wampum and killed all the people that tried to oppose him, or run 'em up into the hills. They got us penned up there like rats, nigh starvin' and afeared to come to town. Uncle Joab come into Wampum this mornin' to git some salt, and you seen what they done to him. *He's* the real sheriff; Ormond is just a bloody outlaw. Him and his gang is usin' Wampum for a hang-out whilst they rob and steal and kill all over the country."

"Then that's what yore friend Jim meant," I said slowly. "And me, like a dumb damn fool, I thought him and Joab and the rest of you-all was just outlaws, like that fake deputy said."

"Ormond took Uncle Joab's badge and called hisself the sheriff to fool strangers," she whimpered. "What honest people is left in Wampum are afeared to oppose him. Him and his gunmen are rulin' this whole part of the country. Uncle Joab sent a man east to git us some help in the settlements on Buffalo River, but none never come, and from what I overheard tonight, I believe Wolf Ashley follered him and killed him over east of the Humbolts somewheres. What are we goin' to do?" she sobbed.

"Ellen," I said, "you git on Doc Richards' horse and ride for Grizzly Mountain. When you git there, tell the Doc to head for Wampum, because there'll be plenty of work for him time he gits there."

"But what about you?" she cried. "I can't go off and leave you to be hanged!"

"Don't worry about me, gal," I said. "I'm Breckinridge Elkins of the Humbolt Mountains, and I'm preparin' for to shake my mane! Hustle!"

SOMETHING ABOUT ME evidently convinced her, because she glided away, whimpering, into the shadows, and presently I heard the clack of horse's hoofs dwindling in the distance. I then riz and I laid hold of the window bars and tore them out by the roots. Then I sunk my fingers into the sill log and tore it out, and three or four more, and the wall give way entirely and the roof fell down on me, but I shook aside the fragments and heaved up out of the wreckage like a bear out of a deadfall.

About this time the jailer come running up, and when he seen what I had did he was so surprised he forgot to shoot me with his pistol. So I taken it away from him and knocked down the door of his shack with him and left him laying in its ruins.

I then strode up the street toward the Golden Eagle and here come a feller galloping down the street. Who should it be but that derned fake deperty, Jackson? He couldn't holler with his bandaged jaw, but when he seen me he jerked loose his lariat and piled it around my neck, and sot spurs to his cayuse aiming for to drag me to death. But I seen he had his rope tied fast to his horn, Texas style, so I laid hold on it with both hands and braced my legs, and when the horse got to the end of the rope, the girths busted and the horse went out from under the saddle, and Jackson come down on his head in the street and laid still.

I threwed the rope off my neck and went on to the Golden Eagle with the jailer's .45 in my scabbard. I looked in and seen the same crowd there, and Ormond r'ared back at the bar with his belly stuck out, roaring and bragging.

I stepped in and hollered: "Look this way, Bill Ormond, and pull iron, you dirty thief!"

He wheeled, paled, and went for his gun, and I slammed six bullets into him before he could hit the floor. I then threwed the empty gun at the dazed crowd and give one deafening roar and tore into 'em like a mountain cyclone. They begun to holler and surge onto me and I threwed 'em and knocked 'em right and left like ten pins. Some was knocked over the bar and some under the tables and some I knocked down stacks of beer kegs with. I ripped the roulette wheel loose and mowed down a whole row of them with it, and I threwed a billiard table through the mirror behind the bar just for good measure. Three or four fellers got pinned under it and yelled bloody murder.

But I didn't have no time to un-pin 'em, for I was busy elsewhere. Four of them hellions come at me in a flyin' wedge and the only thing to do was give them a dose of their own medicine. So I put my head down and butted the first one in the belly. He gave a grunt you could hear across the mountains and I grabbed the other three and squoze them together. I then flung them against the bar and headed into the rest of the mess of them. I felt so good I was yellin' some.

"Come on!" I yelled. "I'm Breckinridge Elkins an' you got my dander roused." And I waded in and poured it to 'em.

Meanwhile they was hacking at me with bowies and hitting me with chairs and brass knuckles and trying to shoot me, but all they done with their guns was shoot each other because they was so many they got in each other's way, and the other things just made me madder. I laid hands on as many as I could hug at once, and the thud of their heads banging together was music to me. I also done good work heaving 'em head-on against the walls, and I further slammed several of 'em heartily against the floor and busted all the tables with their carcasses. In the melee the whole bar collapsed, and the shelves behind the bar fell down when I slang a feller into them, and bottles rained all over the floor. One of the lamps also fell off the ceiling which was beginning to crack and cave in, and everybody begun to yell: "Fire!" and run out through the doors and jump out the windows.

In a second I was alone in the blazing building except for them which was past running. I'd started for a exit myself, when I seen a buckskin pouch on the floor along with a lot of other belongings which had fell out of men's pockets as they will when the men gets swung by the feet and smashed against the wall.

I picked it up and jerked the tie-string, and a trickle of gold dust spilled into my hand. I begun to look on the floor for Ashley, but he wasn't there. But he was watching me from outside, because I looked and seen him just as be let *bam* at me with a .45 from the back room of the place, which wasn't yet on fire much. I plunged after him, ignoring his next slug which took me in the shoulder, and then I grabbed him and taken the gun away from him. He pulled a bowie and tried to stab me in the groin, but only sliced my thigh, so I throwed him the full length of the room and he hit the wall so hard his head went through the boards.

Meantime the main part of the saloon was burning so I couldn't go out that way. I started to go out the back door of the room I was in, but got a glimpse of some fellers which was crouching just outside the door waiting to shoot me as I come out. So I knocked out a section of the wall on another side of the room, and about that time the roof fell in so loud them fellers didn't hear me coming, so I fell on 'em from the rear and beat their heads together till the blood ran out of their ears, and stomped 'em and took their shotguns away from them.

One big fellow with a scarred face tackled me around the knees as I bent over to get the second gun, and a little man hopped on my shoulders from behind at the same time and began clawin' like a catamount. That made me pretty mad again, but I still kept enough presence of mind not to lose my temper. I just grabbed the little man off and hit Scar Face over the head with him, and after that none of the rest bothered me within hand-holt distance.

Then I was aware that people was shooting at me in the light of the burning saloon, and I seen that a bunch was ganged up on the other side of the street, so I begun to loose my shotguns into the thick of them, and they broke and run yelling blue murder.

And as they went out one side of the town, another gang rushed in from the other, yelling and shooting, and I snapped an empty shell at them before one yelled: "Don't shoot, Elkins! We're friends!" And I seen it was Jim and Doc Richards, and a lot of other fellers I hadn't never seen before then.

THEY WENT TEARING around, looking to see if any of Ormond's men was hiding in the village, but none was. They looked like all they wanted to do was get clean out of the country, so most of the Grizzly Mountain men took in after 'em, whoopin' and shoutin'.

Jim looked at the wreckage of the jail, and the remnants of the Golden Eagle, and he shook his head like he couldn't believe it.

"We was on our way to make a last effort to take the town back from that gang," he said. "Ellen met us as we come down and told us you was a friend and a honest man. We hoped to get here in time to save you from gettin' hanged." Again he shook his head with a kind of bewildered look. Then he said: "Oh, say, I'd about forgot. On our way here we run onto a man on the road who said he was lookin' for you. Not knowin' who he was, we roped him and brung him along with us. Bring the prisoner, boys!"

They brung him, tied to his saddle, and it was Jack Gordon, Joel's youngest brother and the fastest gun-slinger on Bear Creek.

"What you doin' here?" I demanded bitterly. "Has the feud begun already and has Joel set you on *my* trail? Well, I got what I started after, and I'm headin' back for Bear Creek. I cain't git there by daylight, but maybe I'll git there in time to keep everybody from killin' everybody else. Here's Uncle Jeppard's cussed gold!" And I waved the pouch in front of him.

"But that cain't be it!" he said. "I been trailin' you all the way from Bear Creek, tryin' to catch you and tell you the gold had been found! Uncle Jeppard and Joel and Erath got together and everything was explained and is all right. Where'd you git that gold?"

"I dunno whether Ashley's pals got it together so he could give it to Ormond and not git killed for holdin' out on his boss, or what," I said. "But I know that the owner ain't got no more use for it now, and probably stole it in the first place. I'm givin' this gold to Ellen," I said. "She shore deserves a reward. And givin' it to her makes me feel like maybe I accomplished *somethin'* on this wild goose chase, after all."

Jim looked around at the ruins of the outlaw hang-out, and murmured something I didn't catch. I said to Jack: "You said Uncle Jeppard's gold was found?

Where was it, anyway?"

"Well," said Jack, "little General William Harrison Grimes, Uncle Jeppard's youngster boy, he seen his pap put the gold under the rock, and he got it out to play with it. He was usin' the nuggets for slugs in his nigger-shooter," Jack said, "and it's plumb cute the way he pops a rattlesnake with 'em. What did you say?"

"Nothin'," I said between my teeth. "Nothin' that'd be fit to repeat, anyway."

THE ROAD TO BEAR CREEK

WHEN PAP GETS RHEUMATISM, he gets remorseful. I remember one time particular. He says to me—him laying on his ba'r-skin with a jug of corn licker at his elbow—he says: "Breckinridge, the sins of my youth is ridin' my conscience heavy. When I was a young man I was free and keerless in my habits, as numerous tombstones on the boundless prairies testifies. I sometimes wonders if I warn't a trifle hasty in shootin' some of the men which disagreed with my principles. Maybe I should of controlled my temper and just chawed their ears off.

"Take Uncle Esau Grimes, for instance." And then pap hove a sigh like a bull, and took a drink, and said: "I ain't seen Uncle Esau for years. Me and him parted with harsh words and gun-smoke. I've often wondered if he still holds a grudge against me for plantin' that charge of buckshot in his hind laig."

"What about Uncle Esau?" I said.

Pap perjuiced a letter and said: "He was brung to my mind by this here letter which Jib Braxton fotched me from War Paint. It's from my sister Elizabeth, back in Devilville, Arizona, whar Uncle Esau lives. She says Uncle Esau is on his way to

Californy, and is due to pass through War Paint about August the tenth—that's tomorrer. She don't know whether he intends turnin' off to see me or not, but suggests that I meet him at War Paint, and make peace with him."

"Well?" I demanded, because from the way pap combed his beard with his fingers and eyed me, I knowed he was aiming to call on me to do something for him.

Which same he was.

"Well," said pap, taking a long swig out of the jug, "I want you to meet the stage tomorrer mornin' at War Paint, and invite Uncle Esau to come up here and visit us. Don't take no for a answer. Uncle Esau is as cranky as hell, and a peculiar old duck, but I think he'll like a fine upstanding young man as big as you be. Specially if you keep yore mouth shet as much as possible, and don't expose yore ignorance."

"But I ain't never seen Uncle Esau," I protested. "How'm I goin' to know him?"

"He ain't a big man," said pap. "Last time I seen him he had a right smart growth of red whiskers. You bring him home, regardless. Don't pay no attention to his belly-achin'. He's a peculiar old cuss, like I said, and awful suspicious, because he's got lots of enemies. He burnt plenty of powder in his younger days, all the way from Texas to Californy. He was mixed up in more feuds and range-wars than any man I ever knowed. He's supposed to have considerable money hid away somewheres, but that ain't got nothin' to do with us. I wouldn't take his blasted money as a gift. All I want is to talk to him, and git his forgiveness for fillin' his hide with buckshot in a moment of youthful passion.

"If he don't forgive me," said pap, taking another pull at the jug, "I'll bend my .45 over his stubborn old skull. Git goin'."

SO I SADDLED CAP'N KIDD and hit out across the mountains, and the next morning found me eating breakfast just outside War Paint. I didn't go right into the town because I was very bashful in them days, being quite young, and scared of sheriffs and things; but I'd stopped with old Bill Polk, an old hunter and trapper which was camped temporary at the edge of the town.

War Paint was a new town which had sprung up out of nothing on account of a small gold rush right recent, and old Bill was very bitter.

"A hell of a come-off this is!" he snorted. "Clutterin' up the scenery and scarin' the animals off with their fool houses and claims. Last year I shot deer right whar their main saloon is now," he said, glaring at me like it was my fault.

I said nothing but chawed my venison which we was cooking over his fire, and he said: "No good'll come of it, you mark my word. These mountains won't be

fit to live in. These camps draws scum like a dead horse draws buzzards. Already
the outlaws is ridin' in from Arizona and Utah, besides the native ones. Grizzly
Hawkins and his thieves is hidin' up in the hills, and no tellin' how many more'll
come in. I'm glad they catched Badger Chisom and his gang after they robbed that
bank at Gunstock. That's one gang which won't bedevil us, becaze they're in jail. If
somebody'd just kill Grizzly Hawkins, now—"

About that time I seen the stagecoach fogging it down the road from the east
in a cloud of dust, so I saddled Cap'n Kidd and left old Bill gorging deer meat and
prophecying disaster and damnation, and I rode into War Paint just as the stage
pulled up at the stand, which was also the post office and a saloon.

They was three passengers, and none of 'em was tenderfeet. Two was big hard-
looking fellows, and t'other'n was a wiry oldish kind of a bird with red whiskers, so
I knowed right off it was Uncle Esau Grimes. They was going into the saloon as I
dismounted, the big men first, and the older fellow follering them. I touched him
on the shoulder and he whirled most amazing quick with a gun in his hand, and
he looked at me very suspicious, and said: "What you want?"

"I'm Breckinridge Elkins," I said. "I want you to come with me. I recognized
you as soon as I seen you—"

I then got a awful surprise, but not as awful as it would have been if pap
hadn't warned me that Uncle Esau was peculiar. He hollered: "Bill! Jim! Help!"
and swung his six-shooter against my head with all his might.

Them two fellows whirled and their hands streaked for their guns, so I
knocked Uncle Esau flat to keep him from getting hit by a stray slug, and shot one
of them through the shoulder before he could unlimber his artillery. The other'n
grazed my neck with a bullet, so I perforated him in the arm and again in the hind
laig and he fell down across the other'n. I was careful not to shoot 'em in no vital
parts, because I seen they was friends of Uncle Esau; but when guns is being drawn
it ain't no time to argue or explain.

Men was hollering and running out of saloons, and I stooped and started to
lift Uncle Esau, who was kind of groggy because he'd hit his head against a
hitching post. He was crawling around on his all-fours cussing something terrible,
and trying to find his gun which he'd dropped. When I laid hold on him he
commenced biting and kicking and hollering, and I said: "Don't ack like that,
Uncle Esau. Here comes a lot of fellers, and the sheriff may be here any minute and
'rest me for shootin' them idjits. We got to get goin'. Pap's waitin' for you, up on
Bear Creek."

But he just fit that much harder and hollered that much louder, so I scooped
him up bodily and jumped onto Cap'n Kidd and throwed Uncle Esau face-down
across the saddle-bow, and headed for the hills. A lot of men yelled at me to stop,

and some of 'em started shooting at me, but I give no heed.

I give Cap'n Kidd the rein and we went tearing down the road and around the first bend, and I didn't even take time to change Uncle Esau's position, because I didn't want to get arrested. I'd heard tell them folks in War Paint would even put a fellow in jail for shooting a man within the city limits.

JUST BEFORE WE REACHED the place where I aimed to turn off up into the hills I seen a man on the road ahead of me, and he must have heard the shooting and Uncle Esau yelling because he whirled his horse and blocked the road. He was a wiry old cuss with gray whiskers.

"Where you goin' with that man?" he yelled as I approached at a thundering gait.

"None of your business," I retorted. "Git outa my way."

"Help! Help!" hollered Uncle Esau. "I'm bein' kidnaped and murdered!"

"Drop that man, you derned outlaw!" roared the stranger, suiting his actions to his words.

Him and me drawed simultaneous, but my shot was a split-second quicker'n his'n. His slug fanned my ear, but his hat flew off and he pitched out of his saddle like he'd been hit with a hammer. I seen a streak of red along his temple as I thundered past him.

"Let that larn you not to interfere in family affairs!" I roared, and turned up the trail that switched off the road and up into the mountains.

"Don't never yell like that," I said irritably to Uncle Esau. "You like to got me shot. That feller thought I was a criminal."

I didn't catch what he said, but I looked back and down over the slopes and shoulders and seen men boiling out of town full tilt, and the sun glinted on six-shooters and rifles, so I urged Cap'n Kidd and we covered the next several miles at a fast clip. They ain't a horse in southern Nevada which can equal Cap'n Kidd for endurance, speed and strength.

Uncle Esau kept trying to talk, but he was bouncing up and down so all I could understand was his cuss words, which was free and fervent. At last he gasped: "For God's sake lemme git off this cussed saddle-horn; it's rubbin' a hole in my belly."

So I pulled up and seen no sign of pursuers, so I said: "All right, you can ride in the saddle and I'll set on behind. I was goin' to hire you a horse at the livery stable, but we had to leave so quick they warn't no time."

"Where you takin' me?" he demanded.

"To Bear Creek," I said. "Where you think?"

"I don't wanta go to Bear Creek," he said fiercely. "I *ain't* goin' to Bear Creek!"

"Yes you are, too," I said. "Pap said not to take 'no' for a answer. I'm goin' to slide over behind the saddle, and you can set in it."

So I pulled my feet outa the stirrups and moved over the cantle, and he slid into the seat—and the first thing I knowed he had a knife out of his boot and was trying to carve my gizzard.

Now I like to humor my relatives, but they is a limit to everything. I taken the knife away from him, but in the struggle, me being handicapped by not wanting to hurt him, I lost hold of the reins and Cap'n Kidd bolted and run for several miles through the pines and brush. What with me trying to grab the reins and keep Uncle Esau from killing me at the same time, and neither one of us in the stirrups, finally we both fell off, and if I hadn't managed to catch hold of the bridle as I went off, we'd had a long walk ahead of us.

I got Cap'n Kidd stopped, after being drug for several yards, and then I went back to where Uncle Esau was laying on the ground trying to get his wind back, because I had kind of fell on him.

"Is that any way to ack, tryin' to stick a knife in a man which is doin' his best to make you comfortable?" I said reproachfully. All he done was gasp, so I said: "Well, pap told me you was a cranky old duck, so I reckon the thing to do is to just not notice your—uh—eccentricities."

I looked around to get my bearings, because Cap'n Kidd had got away off the trail that runs from War Paint to Bear Creek. We was west of the trail, in very wild country, but I seen a cabin off through the trees, and I said: "We'll go over there and see can I hire or buy a horse for you to ride. That'll be more convenient for us both."

I started h'isting him back into the saddle, and he said kind of dizzily: "This here's a free country; I don't have to go to Bear Creek if'n I don't want to."

"Well," I said severely, "you oughtta want to, after all the trouble I've went to, comin' and invitin' you. Set still now; I'm settin' on behind, but I'm holdin' the reins."

"I'll have yore life for this," he promised blood-thirstily, but I ignored it, because pap had said Uncle Esau was peculiar.

PRETTY SOON WE HOVE up to the cabin I'd glimpsed through the trees. Nobody was in sight, but I seen a horse tied to a tree in front of the cabin. I rode up to the door and knocked, but nobody answered. But I seen smoke coming out of the chimney, so I decided I'd go in.

I dismounted and lifted Uncle Esau off, because I seen from the gleam in his eye that he was intending to run off on Cap'n Kidd if I give him half a chance. I got a firm grip on his collar, because I was determined that he was going to visit us up on Bear Creek if I had to tote him on my shoulder all the way, and I went into the cabin with him.

There wasn't nobody in there, though a pot of beans was simmering over some coals in the fireplace, and I seen some rifles in racks on the wall and a belt with two pistols hanging on a nail.

Then I heard somebody walking behind the cabin, and the back door opened and there stood a big black-whiskered man with a bucket of water in his hand and a astonished glare on his face. He didn't have no guns on.

"Who the hell are you?" he demanded, but Uncle Esau give a kind of gurgle, and said: "Grizzly Hawkins!"

The big man jumped and glared at Uncle Esau, and then his black whiskers bristled in a ferocious grin, and he said: "Oh, it's you, is it? Who'd of thunk I'd ever meet you *here!*"

"Grizzly Hawkins, hey?" I said, realizing that I'd stumbled onto the hideout of the worst outlaw in them mountains. "So you all know each other?"

"I'll say we do!" rumbled Hawkins, looking at Uncle Esau like a wolf looks at a fat yearling.

"I'd heard you was from Arizona," I said, being naturally tactful. "Looks to me like they's enough cow-thieves in these hills already without outsiders buttin' in. But your morals ain't none of my business. I want to buy or hire or borrow a horse for this here gent to ride."

"Oh, no, you ain't!" said Grizzly. "You think I'm goin' to let a fortune slip through my fingers like that? Tell you what I'll do, though; I'll split with you. My gang had business over toward Tomahawk this mornin', but they're due back soon. Me and you will work him over before they gits back, and we'll nab all the loot ourselves."

"What you mean?" I asked. "My uncle and me is on our way to Bear Creek—"

"Aw, don't ack innercent with me!" he snorted disgustedly. "Uncle! You think I'm a plumb fool? Cain't I see that he's yore prisoner, the way you got him by the neck? Think I don't know what yo're up to? Be reasonable. Two can work this job better'n one. I know lots of ways to make a man talk. I betcha if we kinda massage his hinder parts with a red-hot brandin' iron he'll tell us quick enough where the money is hid."

Uncle Esau turned pale under his whiskers, and I said indignantly: "Why, you low-lifed polecat! You got the crust to pertend to think I'm kidnapin' my own uncle for his dough? I got a good mind to shoot you!"

"So you're greedy, hey?" he snarled, showing his teeth. "Want all the loot yoreself, hey? I'll show you!" And quick as a cat he swung that water bucket over his head and let it go at me. I ducked and it hit Uncle Esau in the head and stretched him out all drenched with water, and Hawkins give a roar and dived for a .45-90 on the wall. He wheeled with it and I shot it out of his hands. He then come for me wild-eyed with a bowie out of his boot, and my next cartridge snapped, and he was on top of me before I could cock my gun again.

I dropped my gun and grappled with him, and we fit all over the cabin and every now and then we would tromple on Uncle Esau which was trying to crawl toward the door, and the way he would holler was pitiful to hear.

Hawkins lost his knife in the melee, but he was as big as me, and a bear-cat at rough-and-tumble. We would stand up and whale away with both fists, and then clinch and roll around the floor, biting and gouging and slugging, and once we rolled clean over Uncle Esau and kind of flattened him out like a pancake.

Finally Hawkins got hold of the table which he lifted like it was a board and splintered over my head, and this made me mad, so I grabbed the pot off the fire and hit him in the head with it, and about a gallon of red-hot beans went down his back and he fell into a corner so hard he jolted the shelves loose from the logs, and all the guns fell off the walls.

He come up with a gun in his hand, but his eyes was so full of blood and hot beans that he missed me the first shot, and before he could shoot again I hit him on the chin so hard it fractured his jaw bone and sprained both his ankles and stretched him out cold.

THEN I LOOKED AROUND for Uncle Esau, and he was gone, and the front door was open. I rushed out of the cabin and there he was just climbing aboard Cap'n Kidd. I hollered for him to wait, but he kicked Cap'n Kidd in the ribs and went tearing through the trees. Only he didn't head north back toward War Paint. He was p'inted southeast, in the general direction of Hideout Mountain. I jumped on Hawkins' horse, which was tied to a tree nearby, and lit out after him, though I didn't have much hope of catching him. Grizzly's cayuse was a good horse, but he couldn't hold a candle to Cap'n Kidd.

I wouldn't have caught him, neither, if it hadn't been for Cap'n Kidd's distaste of being rode by anybody but me. Uncle Esau was a crack horseman to stay on as long as he did.

But finally Cap'n Kidd got tired of running, and about the time he crossed the trail we'd been follering when he first bolted, he bogged his head and started busting hisself in two, with his snoot rubbing the grass and his heels scraping the clouds offa the sky.

I could see mountain peaks between Uncle Esau and the saddle, and when Cap'n Kidd started sunfishing it looked like the wrath of Judgment Day, but somehow Uncle Esau managed to stay with him till Cap'n Kidd plumb left the earth like he aimed to aviate from then on, and Uncle Esau left the saddle with a shriek of despair and sailed head-on into a blackjack thicket.

Cap'n Kidd give a snort of contempt and trotted off to a patch of grass and started grazing, and I dismounted and went and untangled Uncle Esau from amongst the branches. His clothes was tore and he was scratched so he looked like he'd been fighting with a drove of wildcats, and he left a right smart batch of his whiskers amongst the brush.

But he was full of pizen and hostility.

"I understand this here treatment," he said bitterly, like he blamed me for Cap'n Kidd pitching him into the thicket, "but you'll never git a penny. Nobody but me knows whar the dough is, and you can pull my toe nails out by the roots before I tells you."

"I know you got money hid away," I said, deeply offended, "but I don't want it."

He snorted skeptically and said sarcastic: "Then what're you draggin' me over these cussed hills for?"

"Cause pap wants to see you," I said. "But they ain't no use in askin' me a lot of fool questions. Pap said for me to keep my mouth shet."

I looked around for Grizzly's horse, and seen he had wandered off. He sure hadn't been trained proper.

"Now I got to go look for him," I said disgustedly. "Will you stay here till I git back?"

"Sure," he said. "Sure. Go on and look for the horse. I'll wait here."

But I give him a searching look, and shook my head.

"I don't want to seem like I mistrusts you," I said, "but I see a gleam in your eye which makes me believe that you intends to run off the minute my back's turned. I hate to do this, but I got to bring you safe to Bear Creek; so I'll just kinda hawg-tie you with my lariat till I git back."

Well, he put up a awful holler, but I was firm, and when I rode off on Cap'n Kidd I was satisfied that he couldn't untie them knots by himself. I left him laying in the grass beside the trail, and his language was awful to listen to.

THAT DERNED HORSE had wandered farther'n I thought. He'd moved north along the trail for a short way, and then turned off and headed in a westerly direction, and after a while I heard the sound of horses galloping somewhere behind me, and I got nervous, thinking that if Hawkins' gang had got back to their hang-out and he had told 'em about us, and sent 'em after us, to capture pore Uncle Esau and torture him to make him tell where his savings was hid. I wished I'd had sense enough to shove Uncle Esau back in the thicket so he wouldn't be seen by anybody riding along the trail, and I'd just decided to let the horse go and turn back, when I seen him grazing amongst the trees ahead of me.

I headed back for the trail, leading him, aiming to hit it a short distance north of where I'd left Uncle Esau, and before I got in sight of it, I heard horses and saddles creaking ahead of me.

I pulled up on the crest of a slope, and looked down onto the trail, and there I seen a gang of men riding north, and they had Uncle Esau amongst 'em. Two of the men was ridin' double, and they had him on a horse in the middle of 'em. They'd took the ropes off him, but he didn't look happy. Instantly I realized that my premonishuns was correct. The Hawkins gang had follered us, and now pore Uncle Esau was in their clutches.

I let go of Hawkins' horse and reached for my gun, but I didn't dare fire for fear of hitting Uncle Esau, they was clustered so close about him. I reached up and tore a limb off a oak tree as big as my arm, and I charged down the slope yelling: "I'll save you, Uncle Esau!"

I come so sudden and unexpected them fellows didn't have time to do nothing but holler before I hit 'em. Cap'n Kidd ploughed through their horses like a avalanche through saplings, and he was going so hard I couldn't check him in time to keep him from knocking Uncle Esau's horse sprawling. Uncle Esau hit the turf with a shriek.

All around me men was yelling and surging and pulling guns and I riz in my stirrups and laid about me right and left, and pieces of bark and oak leaves and blood flew in showers and in a second the ground was littered with writhing figures, and the groaning and cussing was awful to hear. Knives was flashing and pistols was banging, but them outlaws' eyes was too full of bark and stars and blood for them to aim, and right in the middle of the brawl, when the guns was roaring and men was yelling and horses neighing and my oak-limb going *crack! crack!* on human skulls, down from the north swooped *another* gang, howling like hyeners!

"There he is!" one of 'em yelled. "I see him crawlin' around under them horses! After him, boys! We got as much right to his dough as anybody!"

The next minute they'd dashed in amongst us and embraced the members of the other gang and started hammering 'em over the heads with their pistols, and in a second was the damndest three-cornered war you ever seen, men fighting on the ground and on the horses, all mixed and tangled up, two gangs trying to extermi-nate each other, and me whaling hell out of both of 'em.

Now I have been mixed up in ruckuses like this before, despite of the fact that I am a peaceful and easy-goin' feller which never done harm to man or beast unless provoked beyond reason. I always figger the best thing to do in a brawl is to hold your temper, and I done just that. When this one feller fired a pistol plumb in my face and singed my eyebrows I didn't get mad. When this other 'un come from somewhere to start biting my leg I only picked him up by the scruff of the neck and knocked a horse over with him. But I must of lost control a little, I guess, when two fellers at once started bashing at my head with rifle-butts. I swung at them so hard I turned Cap'n Kidd plumb around, and my club broke and I had to grab a bigger and tougher one.

Then I really laid into 'em.

Meanwhile Uncle Esau was on the ground under us, yelling bloody murder and being stepped on by the horses, but finally I cleared a space with a devastating sweep of my club, and leaned down and scooped him up with one hand and hung him over my saddle horn and started battering my way clear.

But a big feller which was one of the second gang come charging through the melee yelling like a Injun, with blood running down his face from a cut in his scalp. He snapped a empty cartridge at me, and then leaned out from his saddle and grabbed Uncle Esau by the foot.

"Leggo!" he howled. "He's my meat!"

"Release Uncle Esau before I does you a injury!" I roared, trying to jerk Uncle Esau loose, but the outlaw hung on, and Uncle Esau squalled like a catamount in a wolf-trap. So I lifted what was left of my club and splintered it over the outlaw's head, and he gave up the ghost with a gurgle. I then wheeled Cap'n Kidd and rode off like the wind. Them fellows was too busy fighting each other to notice my flight. Somebody did let *bam* at me with a Winchester, but all it done was to nick Uncle Esau's ear.

THE SOUNDS OF CARNAGE faded out behind us as I headed south along the trail. Uncle Esau was belly-aching about something. I never seen such a cuss for finding fault, but I felt they was no time to be lost, so I didn't slow up for some miles. Then I pulled Cap'n Kidd down and said: "What did you say, Uncle Esau?"

"I'm a broken man!" he gasped. "Take my secret, and lemme go back to the posse. All I want now is a good, safe prison term."

"What posse?" I asked, thinking he must be drunk, though I couldn't figure where he'd got any booze.

"The posse you took me away from," he said. "Anything's better'n bein' dragged through these hellish mountains by a homicidal maneyack."

"Posse?" I gasped wildly. "But who was the second gang?"

"Grizzly Hawkins' outlaws," he said, and added bitterly: "Even they would be preferable to what I been goin' through. I give up. I know when I'm licked. The dough's hid in a holler oak three miles south of Gunstock."

I didn't pay no attention to his remarks, because my head was in a whirl. A

posse! Of course; the sheriff and his men had follered us from War Paint, along the
Bear Creek trail, and finding Uncle Esau tied up, had thought he'd been kidnaped
by a outlaw instead of merely being invited to visit his relatives. Probably he was
too cussed ornery to tell 'em any different. I hadn't rescued him from no bandits;
I'd took him away from a posse which thought *they* was rescuing him.

Meanwhile Uncle Esau was clamoring: "Well, why'n't you lemme go? I've
told you whar the dough is; what else you want?"

"You got to go on to Bear Creek with me—" I begun; and Uncle Esau give a
shriek and went into a kind of convulsion, and the first thing I knowed he'd
twisted around and jerked my gun out of its scabbard and let *bam!* right in my face
so close it singed my hair. I grabbed his wrist and Cap'n Kidd bolted like he always
does when he gets the chance.

"They's a limit to everything!" I roared. "A hell of a relative you be, you old
maneyack!"

We was tearing over slopes and ridges at breakneck speed and fighting all
over Cap'n Kidd's back—me to get the gun away from him, and him to commit
murder. "If you warn't kin to me, Uncle Esau, I'd plumb lose my temper!"

"What you keep callin' me that fool name for?" he yelled, frothing at the
mouth. "What you want to add insult to injury—" Cap'n Kidd swerved sudden and
Uncle Esau tumbled over his neck. I had him by the shirt and tried to hold him
on, but the shirt tore. He hit the ground on his head and Cap'n Kidd run right
over him. I pulled up as quick as I could and hove a sigh of relief to see how close
to home I was.

"We're nearly there, Uncle Esau," I said, but he made no comment. He was
out cold.

A short time later I rode up to the cabin with my eccentric relative slung over
my saddle-bow, and took him and stalked into where pap was laying on his b'ar-
skin, and slung my burden down on the floor in disgust. "Well, here he is," I said.

Pap stared and said: "Who's this?"

"When you wipe the blood off," I said, "you'll find it's your Uncle Esau
Grimes. And," I added bitterly, "the next time you want to invite him to visit us,
you can do it yourself. A more ungrateful cuss I never seen. Peculiar ain't no name
for him; he's as crazy as a locoed jackass."

"But *that* ain't Uncle Esau!" said pap.

"What you mean?" I said irritably. "I know most of his clothes is tore off, and
his face is kinda scratched and skinned and stomped outa shape, but you can see
his whiskers is red, in spite of the blood."

"Red whiskers turn gray, in time," said a voice, and I wheeled and pulled my
gun as a man loomed in the door.

It was the gray-whiskered old fellow I'd traded shots with on the edge of War Paint. He didn't go for his gun, but stood twisting his mustache and glaring at me like I was a curiosity or something.

"Uncle Esau!" said pap.

"What?" I hollered. "Air *you* Uncle Esau?"

"Certainly I am!" he snapped.

"But you warn't on the stagecoach—" I begun.

"Stagecoach!" he snorted, taking pap's jug and beginning to pour licker down the man on the floor. "Them things is for wimmen and childern. I travel horse-back. I spent last night in War Paint, and aimed to ride on up to Bear Creek this mornin'. In fact, Bill," he addressed pap, "I was on the way here when this young maneyack creased me." He indicated a bandage on his head.

"You mean Breckinridge shot you?" ejaculated pap.

"It seems to run in the family," grunted Uncle Esau.

"But who's this?" I hollered wildly, pointing at the man I'd thought was Uncle Esau, and who was just coming to.

"I'm Badger Chisom," he said, grabbing the jug with both hands. "I demands to be pertected from this lunatick and turned over to the sheriff."

"HIM AND BILL REYNOLDS and Jim Hopkins robbed a bank over at Gunstock three weeks ago," said Uncle Esau; the real one, I mean. "A posse captured 'em, but they'd hid the loot somewhere and wouldn't say where. They escaped several days ago, and not only the sheriffs was lookin' for 'em, but all the outlaw gangs too, to find out where they'd hid their plunder. It was a awful big haul. They must of figgered that escapin' out of the country by stage coach would be the last thing folks would expect 'em to do, and they warn't known in this part of the country.

"But I recognized Bill Reynolds when I went back to War Paint to have my head dressed, after you shot me, Breckinridge. The doctor was patchin' him and Hopkins up, too. The sheriff and a posse lit out after you, and I follered 'em when I'd got my head fixed. Course, I didn't know who you was. I come up while the posse was fightin' with Hawkins' gang, and with my help we corralled the whole bunch. Then I took up yore trail again. Purty good day's work, wipin' out two of the worst gangs in the West. One of Hawkins' men said Grizzly was laid up in his cabin, and the posse was goin' to drop by for him."

"What you goin' to do about me?" clamored Chisom.

"Well," said pap, "we'll bandage yore wounds, and then I'll let Breckinridge here take you back to War Paint—hey, what's the matter with him?"

Badger Chisom had fainted.

THE HAUNTED MOUNTAIN

THE REASON I DESPISES tarantulas, stinging lizards, and hydrophobia skunks is because they reminds me so much of Aunt Lavaca, which my Uncle Jacob Grimes married in a absent-minded moment, when he was old enough to know better.

That-there woman's voice plumb puts my teeth on aidge, and it has the same effect on my horse, Cap'n Kidd, which don't generally shy at nothing less'n a rattlesnake. So when she stuck her head out of her cabin as I was riding by and yelled "Breck*in*ri-i-idge," Cap'n Kidd jumped straight up in the air, and then tried to buck me off.

"Stop tormentin' that pore animal and come here," Aunt Lavaca commanded, whilst I was fighting for my life against Cap'n Kidd's spine-twisting sunfishing. "I never see such a cruel, worthless, no-good—"

She kept right on yapping away until I finally wore him down and reined up alongside the cabin stoop and said: "What you want, Aunt Lavaca?"

She give me a scornful snort, and put her hands onto her hips and glared at

TH E HAUNTED MOUNTAIN ⟶ 153

me like I was something she didn't like the smell of.

"I want you should go git yore Uncle Jacob and bring him home," she said at last. "He's off on one of his idiotic prospectin' sprees again. He snuck out before daylight with the bay mare and a pack mule—I wisht I'd woke up and caught him. I'd of fixed him! If you hustle you can catch him this side of Haunted Mountain Gap. You bring him back if you have to lasso him and tie him to his saddle. Old fool! Off huntin' gold when they's work to be did in the alfalfa fields. Says he ain't no farmer. Huh! I 'low I'll make a farmer outa him yet. You git goin'.'"

"But I ain't got time to go chasin' Uncle Jacob all over Haunted Mountain," I protested. "I'm headin' for the rodeo over to Chawed Ear. I'm goin' to win me a prize bull-doggin' some steers—"

"Bull-doggin'!" she snapped. "A fine ockerpashun! Gwan, you worthless loafer! I ain't goin' to stand here all day argyin' with a big ninny like you be. Of all the good-for-nothin', triflin', lunkheaded—"

When Aunt Lavaca starts in like that you might as well travel. She can talk steady for three days and nights without repeating herself, her voice getting louder and shriller all the time till it nigh splits a body's eardrums. She was still yelling at me as I rode up the trail toward Haunted Mountain Gap, and I could hear her long after I couldn't see her no more.

Pore Uncle Jacob! He never had much luck prospecting, but trailing around through the mountains with a jackass is a lot better'n listening to Aunt Lavaca. A jackass's voice is mild and soothing alongside of hers.

Some hours later I was climbing the long rise that led up to the Gap, and I realized I had overtook the old coot when something went *ping!* up on the slope, and my hat flew off. I quick reined Cap'n Kidd behind a clump of bresh, and looked up toward the Gap, and seen a packmule's rear-end sticking out of a cluster of boulders.

"You quit that shootin' at me, Uncle Jacob!" I roared.

"You stay whar you be," his voice come back, sharp as a razor. "I know Lavacky sent you after me, but I ain't goin' home. I'm onto somethin' big at last, and I don't aim to be interfered with."

"What you mean?" I demanded.

"Keep back or I'll ventilate you," he promised. "I'm goin' for the Lost Haunted Mine."

"You been huntin' that thing for thirty years," I snorted.

"This time I finds it," he says. "I bought a map off'n a drunk Mex down to Perdition. One of his ancestors was a Injun which helped pile up the rocks to hide the mouth of the cave where it is."

"Why didn't he go find it and git the gold?" I asked.

"He's skeered of ghosts," said Uncle Jacob. "All Mexes is awful superstitious. This-un 'ud ruther set and drink, nohow. They's millions in gold in that-there mine. I'll shoot you before I'll go home. Now will you go on back peaceable, or will you throw-in with me? I might need you, in case the pack mule plays out."

"I'll come with you," I said, impressed. "Maybe you have got somethin', at that. Put up yore Winchester. I'm comin'."

He emerged from his rocks, a skinny leathery old cuss, and he said: "What about Lavacky? If you don't come back with me, she'll foller us herself. She's that strong-minded."

"I'll leave a note for her," I said. "Joe Hopkins always comes down through the Gap onct a week on his way to Chawed Ear. He's due through here today. I'll stick the note on a tree, where he'll see it and take it to her."

I had a pencil-stub in my saddle-bag, and I tore a piece of wrapping paper off'n a can of tomaters Uncle Jacob had in his pack, and I writ:

> Dere Ant Lavaca:
> I am takin uncle Jacob way up in the mountins dont try to foler us it wont do no good gold is what Im after. Breckinridge.

I folded it and writ on the outside:

> Dere Joe: pleeze take this here note to Miz Lavaca Grimes on the Chawed Ear rode.

THEN ME AND UNCLE JACOB sot out for the higher ranges, and he started telling me all about the Lost Haunted Mine again, like he'd already did about forty times before. Seems like they was onct a old prospector which stumbled onto a cave about fifty years before then, which the walls was solid gold and nuggets all over the floor till a body couldn't walk, as big as mushmelons. But the Indians jumped him and run him out and he got lost and nearly starved in the desert, and went crazy. When he come to a settlement and finally regained his mind, he tried to lead a party back to it, but never could find it. Uncle Jacob said the Indians had took rocks and bresh and hid the mouth of the cave so nobody could tell it was there. I asked him how he knowed the Indians done that, and he said it was common knowledge. Any fool oughta know that's just what they done.

"This-here mine," says Uncle Jacob, "is located in a hidden valley which lies away up amongst the high ranges. I ain't never seen it, and I thought I'd explored these mountains plenty. Ain't nobody more familiar with 'em than me except old Joshua Braxton. But it stands to reason that the cave is awful hard to find, or somebody'd already found it. Accordin' to this-here map, that lost valley must lie just beyond Apache Canyon. Ain't many white men knows whar that is, even. We're headin' there."

We had left the Gap far behind us, and was moving along the slanting side of a sharp-angled crag whilst he was talking. As we passed it, we seen two figgers with horses emerge from the other side, heading in the same direction we was, so our trails converged. Uncle Jacob glared and reached for his Winchester.

"Who's that?" he snarled.

"The big un's Bill Glanton," I said. "I never seen t'other'n."

"And nobody else, outside of a freak museum," growled Uncle Jacob.

This other feller was a funny-looking little maverick, with laced boots and a cork sun-helmet and big spectacles. He sot his horse like he thought it was a rocking chair, and held his reins like he was trying to fish with 'em. Glanton hailed us. He was from Texas, original, and was rough in his speech and free with his weapons, but me and him had always got along very well.

"Where you-all goin'?" demanded Uncle Jacob.

"I am Professor Van Brock, of New York," said the tenderfoot, whilst Bill was getting rid of his tobaccer wad. "I have employed Mr. Glanton, here, to guide me up into the mountains. I am on the track of a tribe of aborigines, which, according to fairly well substantiated rumor, have inhabited the Haunted Mountains since time immemorial."

"Lissen here, you four-eyed runt," said Uncle Jacob in wrath, "are you givin' me the horse-laugh?"

"I assure you that equine levity is the furthest thing from my thoughts," says Van Brock. "Whilst touring the country in the interests of science, I heard the rumors to which I have referred. In a village possessing the singular appellation of Chawed Ear, I met an aged prospector who told me that he had seen one of the aborigines, clad in the skin of a wild animal and armed with a bludgeon. The wildman, he said, emitted a most peculiar and piercing cry when sighted, and fled into the recesses of the hills. I am confident that it is some survivor of a pre-Indian race, and I am determined to investigate."

"They ain't no such critter in these hills," snorted Uncle Jacob. "I've roamed all over 'em for thirty year, and I ain't seen no wildman."

"Well," says Glanton, "they's *somethin'* onnatural up there, because I been hearin' some funny yarns myself. I never thought I'd be huntin' wildmen," he says, "but since that hash-slinger in Perdition turned me down to elope with a travelin' salesman, I welcomes the chance to lose myself in the mountains and forget the perfidy of women-kind. What you-all doin' up here? Prospectin'?" he said, glancing at the tools on the mule.

"Not in earnest," said Uncle Jacob hurriedly. "We're just kinda whilin' away our time. They ain't no gold in these mountains."

"Folks says that Lost Haunted Mine is up here somewhere," said Glanton.

"A pack of lies," snorted Uncle Jacob, busting into a sweat. "Ain't no such mine. Well, Breckinridge, let's be shovin'. Got to make Antelope Peak before sundown."

"I thought we was goin' to Apache Canyon," I says, and he give me a awful glare, and said: "Yes, Breckinridge, that's right, Antelope Peak, just like you said. So long, gents."

"So long," said Glanton.

So we turned off the trail almost at right-angles to our course, me follering Uncle Jacob bewilderedly. When we was out of sight of the others, he reined around again.

"When Nature give you the body of a giant, Breckinridge," he said, "she plumb forgot to give you any brains to go along with yore muscles. You want everybody to know what we're lookin' for?"

"Aw," I said, "them fellers is just lookin' for wildmen."

"Wildmen!" he snorted. "They don't have to go no further'n Chawed Ear on payday night to find more wildmen than they could handle. I ain't swallerin' no such stuff. Gold is what they're after, I tell you. I seen Glanton talkin' to that Mex in Perdition the day I bought that map from him. I believe they either got wind of that mine, or know I got that map, or both."

"What you goin' to do?" I asked him.

"Head for Apache Canyon by another trail," he said.

SO WE DONE SO AND ARRIV there after night, him not willing to stop till we got there. It was deep, with big high cliffs cut with ravines and gulches here and there, and very wild in appearance. We didn't descend into the canyon that night, but camped on a plateau above it. Uncle Jacob 'lowed we'd begin exploring next morning. He said they was lots of caves in the canyon, and he'd been in all of 'em. He said he hadn't never found nothing except b'ars and painters and rattlesnakes; but he believed one of them caves went on through into another, hidden canyon, and there was where the gold was at.

Next morning I was awoke by Uncle Jacob shaking me, and his whiskers was curling with rage.

"What's the matter?" I demanded, setting up and pulling my guns.

"They're here!" he squalled. "Daw-gone it, I suspected 'em all the time! Git up, you big lunk. Don't set there gawpin' with a gun in each hand like a idjit! They're here, I tell you!"

"Who's here?" I asked.

"That dern tenderfoot and his cussed Texas gunfighter," snarled Uncle Jacob. "I was up just at daylight, and purty soon I seen a wisp of smoke curlin' up from behind a big rock t'other side of the flat. I snuck over there, and there was Glanton fryin' bacon, and Van Brock was pertendin' to be lookin' at some flowers with a magnifyin' glass—the blame fake. He ain't no perfessor. I bet he's a derned crook. They're follerin' us. They aim to murder us and rob us of my map."

"Aw, Glanton wouldn't do that," I said. And Uncle Jacob said: "You shet up! A man will do anything whar gold is consarned. Dang it all, git up and do somethin'! Air you goin' to set there, you big lummox, and let us git murdered in our sleep?"

That's the trouble of being the biggest man in yore clan; the rest of the family always dumps all the onpleasant jobs onto yore shoulders. I pulled on my boots and headed across the flat, with Uncle Jacob's war-songs ringing in my ears, and I didn't notice whether he was bringing up the rear with his Winchester or not.

They was a scattering of trees on the flat, and about halfway across a figger emerged from amongst them, headed my direction with fire in his eye. It was Glanton.

"So, you big mountain grizzly," he greeted me rambunctiously, "you was goin' to Antelope Peak, hey? Kinda got off the road, didn't you? Oh, we're on to you, we are!"

"What you mean?" I demanded. He was acting like he was the one which oughta feel righteously indignant, instead of me.

"You know what I mean!" he says, frothing slightly at the mouth. "I didn't believe it when Van Brock first said he suspicioned you, even though you hombres did act funny yesterday when we met you on the trail. But this mornin' when I glimpsed yore fool Uncle Jacob spyin' on our camp, and then seen him sneakin' off through the bresh, I knowed Van Brock was right. Yo're after what we're after, and you-all resorts to dirty onderhanded tactics. Does you deny yo're after the same thing we are?"

"Naw, I don't," I said. "Uncle Jacob's got more right to it than you-all. And when you says we uses underhanded tricks, yo're a liar."

"That settles it!" gnashed he. "Go for yore gun!"

"I don't want to perforate you," I growled.

"I ain't hankerin' to conclude yore mortal career," he admitted. "But Haunted Mountain ain't big enough for both of us. Take off yore guns and I'll maul the livin' daylights outa you, big as you be."

I unbuckled my gun-belt and hung it on a limb, and he laid off his'n, and hit me in the stummick and on the ear and in the nose, and then he socked me in the jaw and knocked out a tooth. This made me mad, so I taken him by the neck and throwed him against the ground so hard it jolted all the wind outa him. I then sot on him and started banging his head against a convenient boulder, and his cussing was terrible to hear.

"If you all had acted like white men," I gritted, "we'd of *give* you a share in that there mine."

"What you talkin' about?" he gurgled, trying to haul his bowie out of his boot which I had my knee on.

"The Lost Haunted Mine, of course," I snarled, getting a fresh grip on his ears.

"Hold on," he protested. "You mean you-all are just lookin' for gold? On the level?"

I was so astonished I quit hammering his skull against the rock.

"Why, what else?" I demanded. "Ain't you-all follerin' us to steal Uncle Jacob's map which shows where at the mine is hid?"

"Git offa me," he snorted disgustfully, taking advantage of my surprize to push me off. "Hell!" he said, starting to knock the dust offa his britches. "I might of knowed that tenderfoot was wool-gatherin'. After we seen you-all yesterday, and he heard you mention 'Apache Canyon' he told me he believed you was follerin' us. He said that yarn about prospectin' was just a blind. He said he believed you was workin' for a rival scientific society to git ahead of us and capture that-there wildman yoreselves."

"What?" I said. "You mean that wildman yarn is straight?"

"So far as we're consarned," said Bill. "Prospectors is been tellin' some onusual stories about Apache Canyon. Well, I laughed at him at first, but he kept on usin' so many .45-caliber words that he got me to believin' it might be so. 'Cause, after all, here was me guidin' a tenderfoot on the trail of a wildman, and they wasn't no reason to think you and Jacob Grimes was any more sensible than me.

"Then, this mornin' when I seen Joab peekin' at me from the bresh, I decided Van Brock must be right. You-all hadn't never went to Antelope Peak. The more I thought it over, the more sartain I was that you was follerin' us to steal our wildman, so I started over to have a showdown."

"Well," I said, "we've reached a understandin' at last. You don't want our mine, and we shore don't want yore wildman. They's plenty of them amongst my relatives on Bear Creek. Le's git Van Brock and lug him over to our camp and explain things to him and my weak-minded uncle."

"All right," said Glanton, buckling on his guns. "Hey, what's that?"

From down in the canyon come a yell: "Help! Aid! Assistance!"

"It's Van Brock!" yelped Glanton. "He's wandered down into the canyon by hisself! Come on!"

*   *   *

RIGHT NEAR THEIR CAMP they was a ravine leading down to the floor of the canyon. We pelted down that at full speed, and emerged near the wall of the cliffs. They was the black mouth of a cave showing nearby, in a kind of cleft, and just outside this cleft Van Brock was staggering around, yowling like a hound dawg with his tail caught in the door.

His cork helmet was laying on the ground all bashed outa shape, and his specs was lying near it. He had a knob on his head as big as a turnip and he was doing a kind of ghost-dance or something all over the place.

He couldn't see very good without his specs, 'cause when he sighted us he give a shriek and starting legging it for the other end of the canyon, seeming to think we was more enemies. Not wanting to indulge in no sprint in that heat, Bill shot a heel offa his boot, and that brung him down squalling blue murder.

"Help!" he shrieked. "Mr. Glanton! Help! I am being attacked! Help!"

"Aw, shet up," snorted Bill. "I'm Glanton. Yo're all right. Give him his specs, Breck. Now what's the matter?"

He put 'em on, gasping for breath, and staggered up, wild-eyed, and p'inted at the cave and hollered: "The wildman! I saw him, as I descended into the canyon on a private exploring expedition! A giant with a panther-skin about his waist, and a club in his hand. He dealt me a murderous blow with the bludgeon when I sought to apprehend him, and fled into that cavern. He should be arrested!"

I looked into the cave. It was too dark to see anything except for a hoot-owl.

"He must of saw *somethin'*, Breck," said Glanton, hitching his gun-harness. "Somethin' shore cracked him on the conk. I've been hearin' some queer tales about this canyon, myself. Maybe I better sling some lead in there—"

"No, no, no!" broke in Van Brock. "We must capture him alive!"

"What's goin' on here?" said a voice, and we turned to see Uncle Jacob approaching with his Winchester in his hands.

"Everything's all right, Uncle Jacob," I said. "They don't want yore mine. They're after the wildman, like they said, and we got him cornered in that there cave."

"All right, huh?" he snorted. "I reckon you thinks it's all right for you to waste yore time with such dern foolishness when you oughta be helpin' me look for my mine. A big help you be!"

"Where was you whilst I was arguin' with Bill here?" I demanded.

"I knowed you could handle the sityation, so I started explorin' the canyon," he said. "Come on, we got work to do."

"But the wildman!" cried Van Brock. "Your nephew would be invaluable in securing the specimen. Think of science! Think of progress! Think of—"

"Think of a striped skunk!" snorted Uncle Jacob. "Breckinridge, air you comin'?"

"Aw, shet up," I said disgustedly. "You both make me tired. I'm goin' in there and run that wildman out, and Bill, you shoot him in the hind-laig as he comes out, so's we can catch him and tie him up."

"But you left yore guns hangin' onto that limb up on the plateau," objected Glanton.

"I don't need 'em," I said. "Didn't you hear Van Brock say we was to catch him alive? If I started shootin' in the dark I might rooin him."

"All right," says Bill, cocking his six-shooters. "Go ahead. I figger yo're a match for any wildman that ever come down the pike."

So I went into the cleft and entered the cave, and it was dark as all get-out. I groped my way along and discovered the main tunnel split into two, so I taken the biggest one. It seemed to get darker the further I went, and purty soon I bumped into something big and hairy and it went "Wump!" and grabbed me.

Thinks I, it's the wildman, and he's on the war-path. We waded into each other and tumbled around on the rocky floor in the dark, biting and mauling and tearing. I'm the biggest and the fightingest man on Bear Creek, which is famed far and wide for its ring-tailed scrappers, but this wildman shore give me my hands full. He was the biggest hairiest critter I ever laid hands on, and he had more teeth and talons than I thought a human could possibly have. He chawed me with vigor and enthusiasm, and he waltzed up and down my frame free and hearty, and swept the floor with me till I was groggy.

For a while I thought I was going to give up the ghost, and I thought with despair of how humiliated my relatives on Bear Creek would be to hear their champion battler had been clawed to death by a wildman in a cave.

That made me plumb ashamed for weakening, and the socks I give him ought to of laid out any man, wild or tame, to say nothing of the pile-driver kicks in his belly, and butting him with my head so he gasped. I got what felt like a ear in my mouth and commenced chawing on it, and presently, what with this and other mayhem I committed on him, he give a most inhuman squall and bust away and went lickety-split for the outside world.

I riz up and staggered after him, hearing a wild chorus of yells break forth outside, but no shots. I bust out into the open, bloody all over, and my clothes hanging in tatters.

"Where is he?" I hollered. "Did you let him git away?"

"Who?" said Glanton, coming out from behind a boulder, whilst Van Brock and Uncle Jacob dropped down out of a tree nearby.

"The wildman, damn it!" I roared.

"We ain't seen no wildman," said Glanton.

"Well, what was that thing I just run outa the cave?" I hollered.

"That was a grizzly b'ar," said Glanton. "Yeah," sneered Uncle Jacob, "and that was Van Brock's 'wildman'! And now, Breckinridge, if yo're through playin', we'll—"

"No, no!" hollered Van Brock, jumping up and down. "It was a human being which smote me and fled into the cavern. Not a bear! It is still in there somewhere, unless there is another exit to the cavern."

"Well, he ain't in there now," said Uncle Jacob, peering into the mouth of the cave. "Not even a wildman would run into a grizzly's cave, or if he did, he wouldn't stay long—ooomp!"

A rock come whizzing out of the cave and hit Uncle Jacob in the belly, and he doubled up on the ground.

"Aha!" I roared, knocking up Glanton's ready six-shooter. "I know! They's two tunnels in here. He's in that smaller cave. I went into the wrong one! Stay here, you-all, and gimme room! This time I gets him!"

WITH THAT I RUSHED INTO the cave mouth again, disregarding some more rocks which emerged, and plunged into the smaller opening. It was dark as pitch, but I seemed to be running along a narrer tunnel, and ahead of me I heered bare feet pattering on the rock. I follered 'em at full lope, and presently seen a faint hint of light. The next minute I rounded a turn and come out into a wide place, which was lit by a shaft of light coming in through a cleft in the wall, some yards up. In the light I seen a fantastic figger climbing up on a ledge, trying to reach that cleft.

"Come down offa that!" I thundered, and give a leap and grabbed the ledge by one hand and hung on, and reached for his legs with t'other hand. He give a squall as I grabbed his ankle and splintered his club over my head. The force of the lick broke off the lip of the rock ledge I was holding to, and we crashed to the floor together, because I didn't let loose of him. Fortunately, I hit the rock floor headfirst which broke my fall and kept me from fracturing any of my important limbs, and his head hit my jaw, which rendered him unconscious.

I riz up and picked up my limp captive and carried him out into the daylight where the others was waiting. I dumped him on the ground and they stared at him like they couldn't believe it. He was a ga'nt old cuss with whiskers about a foot long and matted hair, and he had a mountain lion's hide tied around his waist.

"A white man!" enthused Van Brock, dancing up and down. "An unmistakable Caucasian! This is stupendous! A prehistoric survivor of a pre-Indian epoch! What an aid to anthropology! A wildman! A veritable wildman!"

"Wildman, hell!" snorted Uncle Jacob. "That-there's old Joshua Braxton, which was tryin' to marry that old maid schoolteacher down at Chawed Ear all last winter."

"*I* was tryin' to marry her!" said Joshua bitterly, setting up suddenly and glaring at all of us. "That-there is good, that-there is! And me all the time fightin' for my life against it. Her and all her relations was tryin' to marry *her* to me. They made my life a curse. They was finally all set to kidnap me and marry me by force. That's why I come away off up here, and put on this rig to scare folks away. All I craves is peace and quiet and no dern women."

Van Brock begun to cry because they wasn't no wildman, and Uncle Jacob said: "Well, now that this dern foolishness is settled, maybe I can git to somethin' important. Joshua, you know these mountains even better'n I do. I want you to help me find the Lost Haunted Mine."

"There ain't no such mine," said Joshua. "That old prospector imagined all that stuff whilst he was wanderin' around over the desert crazy."

"But I got a map I bought from a Mexican in Perdition," hollered Uncle Jacob.

"Lemme see that map," said Glanton. "Why, hell," he said, "that-there is a fake. I seen that Mexican drawin' it, and he said he was goin' to try to sell it to some old jassack for the price of a drunk."

Uncle Jacob sot down on a rock and pulled his whiskers. "My dreams is bust," he said weakly. "I'm goin' home to my wife."

"You must be desperate if it's come to that," said old Joshua acidly. "You better stay up here. If they ain't no gold, they ain't no women to torment a body, either."

"Women is a snare and a delusion," agreed Glanton. "Van Brock can go back with these fellers. I'm stayin' with Joshua."

"You-all oughta be ashamed talkin' about women that way," I reproached 'em. "What, in this here lousy and troubled world can compare to women's gentle sweetness—"

"There the scoundred is!" screeched a familiar voice. "Don't let him git away! Shoot him if he tries to run!"

WE TURNED SUDDEN. We'd been argyin' so loud amongst ourselves we hadn't noticed a gang of folks coming down the ravine. There was Aunt Lavaca and the sheriff of Chawed Ear with ten men, and they all p'inted sawed-off shotguns at me.

"Don't get rough, Elkins," warned the sheriff nervously. "They're all loaded with buckshot and ten-penny nails. I knows yore repertation and I takes no chances. I arrests you for the kidnapin' of Jacob Grimes."

"Are you plumb crazy?" I demanded.

"Kidnapin'!" hollered Aunt Lavaca, waving a piece of paper. "Abductin' yore pore old uncle! Aimin' to hold him for ransom! It's all writ down in yore own handwritin' right here on this-here paper! Sayin' yo're takin' Jacob away off into the mountains—warnin' me not to try to foller! Same as threatenin' me! I never heered of such doin's! Soon as that good-for-nothin' Joe Hopkins brung me that there insolent letter, I went right after the sheriff. . . . Joshua Braxton, what *air* you doin' in them ondecent togs? My land, I dunno what we're comin' to! Well, sheriff, what you standin' there for like a ninny? Why'n't you put some handcuffs and chains and shackles on him? Air you skeered of the big lunkhead?"

"Aw, heck," I said. "This is all a mistake. I warn't threatenin' nobody in that there letter—"

"Then where's Jacob?" she demanded. "Prejuice him imejitately, or—"

"He ducked into that cave," said Glanton.

I stuck my head in and roared: "Uncle Jacob! You come outa there and explain before I come in after you!"

He snuck out looking meek and down-trodden, and I says: "You tell these idjits that I ain't no kidnaper."

"That's right," he said. "I brung him along with me."

"Hell!" said the sheriff, disgustedly. "Have we come all this way on a wild goose chase? I should of knew better'n to listen to a woman—"

"You shet yore fool mouth!" squalled Aunt Lavaca. "A fine sheriff you be. Anyway—what was Breckinridge doin' up here with you, Jacob?"

"He was helpin' me look for a mine, Lavacky," he said.

"*Helpin'* you?" she screeched. "Why, I sent him to fetch you back! Breckin-ridge Elkins, I'll tell yore pap about this, you big, lazy, good-for-nothin', low-down, ornery—"

"Aw, *shet up!*" I roared, exasperated beyond endurance. I seldom lets my voice go its full blast. Echoes rolled through the canyon like thunder, the trees shook and the pine cones fell like hail, and rocks tumbled down the mountainsides. Aunt Lavaca staggered backwards with a outraged squall.

"Jacob!" she hollered. "Air you goin' to 'low that ruffian to use that-there tone of voice to me? I demands that you flail the livin' daylights outa the scoun-drel right now!"

Uncle Jacob winked at me.

"Now, now, Lavacky," he started soothing her, and she give him a clip under the ear that changed ends with him. The sheriff and his posse and Van Brock took out up the ravine like the devil was after 'em, and Glanton bit off a chaw of tobaccer and says to me, he says: "Well, what was you fixin' to say about women's gentle sweetness?"

"Nothin'," I snarled. "Come on, let's git goin'. I yearns to find a more quiet and secluded spot than this-here'n. I'm stayin' with Joshua and you and the grizzly."

WAR ON BEAR CREEK

PAP DUG THE NINETEENTH buckshot out of my shoulder and said, "Pigs is more disturbin' to the peace of a community than scandal, divorce, and corn licker put together. And," says pap, pausing to strop his bowie on my scalp where the hair was all burnt off, "when the pig is a razorback hawg, and is mixed up with a lady schoolteacher, a English tenderfoot, and a passle of bloodthirsty relatives, the result is appallin' for a peaceable man to behold. Hold still till John gits yore ear sewed back on."

Pap was right. I warn't to blame for what happened. Breaking Joel Gordon's laig was a mistake, and Erath Elkins is a liar when he says I caved in them five ribs of his'n plumb on purpose. If Uncle Jeppard Grimes had been tending to his own business he wouldn't have got the seat of his britches filled with bird-shot, and I don't figger it was my fault that cousin Bill Kirby's cabin got burned down. And I don't take no blame for Jim Gordon's ear which Jack Grimes shot off, neither. I figger everybody was more to blame than I was, and I stand ready to wipe up the earth with anybody which disagrees with me.

But it was that derned razorback hawg of Uncle Jeppard Grimes' which started the whole mess.

It begun when that there tenderfoot come riding up the trail with Tunk Willoughby, from War Paint. Tunk ain't got no more sense than the law allows, but he shore showed good jedgement that time, because having delivered his charge to his destination, he didn't tarry. He merely handed me a note, and p'inted dumbly at the tenderfoot, whilst holding his hat reverently in his hand meanwhile.

"What you mean by that there gesture?" I ast him rather irritably, and he said: "I doffs my sombrero in respect to the departed. Bringin' a specimen like that onto Bear Creek is just like heavin' a jackrabbit to a pack of starvin' loboes."

He hove a sigh and shook his head, and put his hat back on. "Rassle a cat in pieces," he says, gathering up the reins.

"What the hell are you talkin' about?" I demanded.

"That's Latin," he said. "It means rest in peace."

And with that he dusted it down the trail and left me alone with the tenderfoot which all the time was setting his cayuse and looking at me like I was a curiosity or something.

I called my sister Ouachita to come read that there note for me, which she did and it run as follows:

Dere Breckinridge:
This will interjuice Mr. J. Pembroke Pemberton a English sportsman which I met in Frisco recent. He was disapinted because he hadn't found no adventures in America and was fixin to go to Aferker to shoot liuns and elerfants but I perswaded him to come with me because I knowed he would find more hell on Bear Creek in a week than he would find in a yere in Aferker or any other place. But the very day we hit War Paint I run into a old ackwaintance from Texas I will not speak no harm of the ded but I wish the son of a buzzard had shot me somewheres besides in my left laig which already had three slugs in it which I never could get cut out. Anyway I am lade up and not able to come on to Bear Creek with J. Pembroke Pemberton. I am dependin on you to show him some good bear huntin and other excitement and pertect him from yore relatives I know what a awful responsibility I am puttin on you but I am askin' this as yore frend,
William Harrison Glanton. Esqy.

I looked J. Pembroke over. He was a medium sized young feller and looked kinda soft in spots. He had yaller hair and very pink cheeks like a gal; and he had on whip-cord britches and tan riding boots which was the first I ever seen. And he had on a funny kinda coat with pockets and a belt which he called a shooting jacket, and a big hat like a mushroom made outa cork with a red ribbon around it. And he had a pack-horse loaded with all kinds of plunder, and four or five different kinds of shotguns and rifles.

"So yo're J. Pembroke," I says, and he says, "Oh, rahther! And you, no doubt, are the person Mr. Glanton described to me, Breckinridge Elkins?"

"Yeah," I said. "Light and come in. We got b'ar meat and honey for supper."

"I say," he said, climbing down. "Pardon me for being a bit personal, old chap, but may I ask if your—ah—magnitude of bodily stature is not a bit unique?"

"I dunno," I says, not having the slightest idee what he was talking about. "I always votes a straight Democratic ticket, myself."

He started to say something else, but just then pap and my brothers John and Bill and Jim and Buckner and Garfield come to the door to see what the noise was about, and he turned pale and said faintly: "I beg your pardon; giants seem to be the rule in these parts."

"Pap says men ain't what they was when he was in his prime," I said, "but we manage to git by."

Well, J. Pembroke laid into them b'ar steaks with a hearty will, and when I told him we'd go after b'ar next day, he ast me how many days travel it'd take till we got to the b'ar country.

"Heck!" I said. "You don't have to travel to git b'ar in these parts. If you forgit to bolt yore door at night yo're liable to find a grizzly sharin' yore bunk before mornin'. This here'n we're eatin' was ketched by my sister Ellen there whilst tryin' to rob the pig-pen out behind the cabin last night."

"My word!" he says, looking at her peculiarly. "And may I ask, Miss Elkins, what caliber of firearm you used?"

"I knocked him in the head with a wagon tongue," she said, and he shook his head to hisself and muttered: "Extraordinary!"

J. PEMBROKE SLEPT IN my bunk and I took the floor that night; and we was up at daylight and ready to start after the b'ar. Whilst J. Pembroke was fussing over his guns, pap come out and pulled his whiskers and shook his head and said: "That there is a perlite young man, but I'm afeared he ain't as hale as he oughta be. I just give him a pull at my jug, and he didn't gulp but one good snort and like to choked to death."

"Well," I said, buckling the cinches on Cap'n Kidd, "I've done learnt not to jedge outsiders by the way they takes their licker on Bear Creek. It takes a Bear Creek man to swig Bear Creek corn juice."

"I hopes for the best," sighed pap. "But it's a dismal sight to see a young man which cain't stand up to his licker. Whar you takin' him?"

"Over toward Apache Mountain," I said. "Erath seen a exter big grizzly over there day before yesterday."

"Hmmmm!" says pap. "By pecooliar coincidence the schoolhouse is over on the side of Apache Mountain, ain't it, Breckinridge?"

"Maybe it is and maybe it ain't," I replied with dignerty, and rode off with J. Pembroke ignoring pap's sourcastic comment which he hollered after me: "Maybe they is a connection between book-larnin' and b'ar-huntin', but who am I to say?"

J. Pembroke was a purty good rider, but he used a funny looking saddle without no horn nor cantle, and he had the derndest gun I ever seen. It was a double-barrel rifle, and he said it was a elerfant-gun. It was big enough to knock a hill down. He was surprised I didn't tote no rifle and ast me what would I do if we met a b'ar. I told him I was depending on him to shoot it, but I said if it was necessary for me to go into action, my six-shooter was plenty.

"My word!" says he. "You mean to say you can bring down a grizzly with a shot from a pistol?"

"Not always," I said. "Sometimes I have to bust him over the head with the butt to finish him."

He didn't say nothing for a long time after that.

Well, we rode over on the lower slopes of Apache Mountain, and tied the horses in a holler and went through the bresh on foot. That was a good place for b'ars, because they come there very frequently looking for Uncle Jeppard Grimes' pigs which runs loose all over the lower slopes of the mountain.

But just like it always is when yo're looking for something, we didn't see a cussed b'ar.

The middle of the evening found us around on the south side of the mountain where they is a settlement of Kirbys and Grimeses and Gordons. Half a dozen families has their cabins within a mile of each other, and I dunno what in hell they want to crowd up together that way for, it would plumb smother me, but pap says they was always peculiar that way.

We warn't in sight of the settlement, but the schoolhouse warn't far off, and I said to J. Pembroke: "You wait here a while and maybe a b'ar will come by. Miss Margaret Ashley is teachin' me how to read and write, and it's time for my lesson."

I left J. Pembroke setting on a log hugging his elerfant-gun, and I strode through the bresh and come out at the upper end of the run which the settlement was at the other'n, and school had just turned out and the chillern was going home, and Miss Ashley was waiting for me in the log schoolhouse.

That was the first school that was ever taught on Bear Creek, and she was the first teacher. Some of the folks was awful sot agen it at first, and said no good would come of book larning, but after I licked six or seven of them they allowed it might be a good thing after all, and agreed to let her take a whack at it.

Miss Margaret was a awful purty gal and come from somewhere away back East. She was setting at her hand-made desk as I come in, ducking my head so as not to bump it agen the top of the door and perlitely taking off my coonskin cap. She looked kinda tired and discouraged, and I said: "Has the young'uns been raisin' any hell today, Miss Margaret?"

"Oh, no," she said. "They're very polite—in fact I've noticed that Bear Creek people are always polite except when they're killing each other. I've finally gotten used to the boys wearing their bowie knives and pistols to school. But somehow it seems so futile. This is all so terribly different from everything to which I've always been accustomed. I get discouraged and feel like giving up."

"You'll git used to it," I consoled her. "It'll be a lot different once yo're married to some honest reliable young man."

She give me a startled look and said: "Married to someone here on Bear Creek?"

"Shore," I said, involuntarily expanding my chest under my buckskin shirt. "Everybody is just wonderin' when you'll set the date. But le's git at the lesson. I done learnt the words you writ out for me yesterday."

But she warn't listening, and she said: "Do you have any idea of why Mr. Joel Grimes and Mr. Esau Gordon quit calling on me? Until a few days ago one or the other was at Mr. Kirby's cabin where I board almost every night."

"Now don't you worry none about them," I soothed her. "Joel'll be about on crutches before the week's out, and Esau can already walk without bein' helped. I always handles my relatives as easy as possible."

"You fought with them?" she exclaimed.

"I just convinced 'em you didn't want to be bothered with 'em," I reassured her. "I'm easy-goin', but I don't like competition."

"Competition!" Her eyes flared wide open and she looked at me like she never seen me before. "Do you mean, that you —that I—that—"

"Well," I said modestly, "everybody on Bear Creek is just wonderin' when you're goin' to set the day for us to git hitched. You see gals don't stay single very long in these parts, and—hey, what's the matter?"

Because she was getting paler and paler like she'd et something which didn't agree with her.

"Nothing," she said faintly. "You—you mean people are expecting me to marry you?"

"Shore," I said.

She muttered something that sounded like "My God!" and licked her lips with her tongue and looked at me like she was about ready to faint. Well, it ain't every gal which has a chance to get hitched to Breckinridge Elkins, so I didn't blame her for being excited.

"You've been very kind to me, Breckinridge," she said feebly. "But I—this is so sudden—so unexpected—I never thought—I never *dreamed—*"

"I don't want to rush you," I said. "Take yore time. Next week will be soon enough. Anyway, I got to build us a cabin, and—"

Bang! went a gun, too loud for a Winchester.

"Elkins!" It was J. Pembroke yelling for me up the slope. "Elkins! Hurry!"

"Who's that?" she exclaimed, jumping to her feet like she was working on a spring.

"Aw," I said in disgust, "it's a fool tenderfoot Bill Glanton wished on me. I reckon a b'ar is got him by the neck. I'll go see."

"I'll go with you!" she said, but from the way Pembroke was yelling I figgered I better not waste no time getting to him, so I couldn't wait for her, and she was some piece behind me when I mounted the lap of the slope and met him running out from amongst the trees. He was gibbering with excitement.

"I winged it!" he squawked. "I'm sure I winged the blighter! But it ran in among the underbrush and I dared not follow it, for the beast is most vicious when wounded. A friend of mine once wounded one in South Africa, and—"

"A b'ar?" I ast.

"No, no!" he said. "A wild boar! The most vicious brute I have ever seen! It ran into that brush there!"

"Aw, they ain't no wild boars in the Humbolts," I snorted. "You wait here. I'll go see just what you did shoot."

I seen some splashes of blood on the grass, so I knowed he'd shot *something*. Well, I hadn't gone more'n a few hunderd feet and was just out of sight of J. Pembroke when I run into Uncle Jeppard Grimes.

Uncle Jeppard was one of the first white men to come into the Humbolts. He's as lean and hard as a pine-knot, and wears fringed buckskins and moccasins just like he done fifty years ago. He had a bowie knife in one hand and he waved something in the other'n like a flag of revolt, and he was frothing at the mouth.

"The derned murderer!" he howled. "You see this? That's the tail of Daniel Webster, the finest derned razorback boar which ever trod the Humbolts! That danged tenderfoot of your'n tried to kill him! Shot his tail off, right spang up to the hilt! He cain't muterlate my animals like this! I'll have his heart's blood!"

And he done a war-dance waving that pig-tail and his bowie and cussing in English and Spanish and Apache Injun an at once.

"You ca'm down, Uncle Jeppard," I said sternly. "He ain't got no sense, and he thought Daniel Webster was a wild boar like they have in Aferker and England

and them foreign places. He didn't mean no harm."

"No harm!" said Uncle Jeppard fiercely. "And Daniel Webster with no more tail onto him than a jackrabbit!"

"Well," I said, "here's a five dollar gold piece to pay for the dern hawg's tail, and you let J. Pembroke alone."

"Gold cain't satisfy honor," he said bitterly, but nevertheless grabbing the coin like a starving man grabbing a beefsteak. "I'll let this outrage pass for the time. But I'll be watchin' that maneyack to see that he don't muterlate no more of my prize razorbacks."

And so saying he went off muttering in his beard.

I WENT BACK TO WHERE I left J. Pembroke, and there he was talking to Miss Margaret which had just come up. She had more color in her face than I'd saw recent.

"Fancy meeting a girl like you here!" J. Pembroke was saying.

"No more surprizing than meeting a man like you!" says she with a kind of fluttery laugh.

"Oh, a sportsman wanders into all sorts of out-of-the-way places," says he, and seeing they hadn't noticed me coming up, I says: "Well, J. Pembroke, I didn't find yore wild boar, but I met the owner."

He looked at me kinda blank, and said vaguely: "Wild boar? *What* wild boar?"

"That-un you shot the tail off of with that there fool elerfant gun," I said. "Listen: next time you see a hawg-critter you remember there ain't no wild boars in the Humbolts. They is critters called haverleeners in South Texas, but they ain't even none of them in Nevada. So next time you see a hawg, just reflect that it's merely one of Uncle Jeppard Grimes' razorbacks and refrain from shootin' at it."

"Oh, quite!" he agreed absently, and started talking to Miss Margaret again.

So I picked up the elerfant gun which he'd absent-mindedly laid down, and said: "Well, it's gittin' late. Let's go. We won't go back to pap's cabin tonight, J. Pembroke. We'll stay at Uncle Saul Garfield's cabin on t'other side of the Apache Mountain settlement."

As I said, them cabins was awful close together. Uncle Saul's cabin was below the settlement, but it warn't much over three hundred yards from cousin Bill Kirby's cabin where Miss Margaret boarded. The other cabins was on t'other side of Bill's, mostly, strung out up the run, and up and down the slopes.

I told J. Pembroke and Miss Margaret to walk on down to the settlement whilst I went back and got the horses.

They'd got to the settlement time I catched up with 'em, and Miss Margaret had gone into the Kirby cabin, and I seen a light spring up in her room. She had one of them new-fangled ile lamps she brung with her, the only one on Bear Creek. Candles and pine chunks was good enough for us folks. And she'd hanged rag things over the winders which she called curtains. You never seen nothing like it, I tell you she was that elegant you wouldn't believe it.

We walked on toward Uncle Saul's, me leading the horses, and after a while J. Pembroke says: "A wonderful creature!"

"You mean Daniel Webster?" I ast.

"No!" he said. "No, no, I mean Miss Ashley."

"She shore is," I said. "She'll make me a fine wife."

He whirled like I'd stabbed him and his face looked pale in the dusk.

"You?" he said, *"You* a wife?"

"Well," I said bashfully, "she ain't sot the day yet, but I've shore sot my heart on that gal."

"Oh!" he says, *"Oh!"* says he, like he had the toothache. Then he said kinda hesitatingly: "Suppose—er, just suppose, you know! Suppose a rival for her affections should appear? What would you do?"

"You mean if some dirty, low-down son of a mangy skunk was to try to steal my gal?" I said, whirling so sudden he staggered backwards.

"Steal my gal?" I roared, seeing red at the mere thought. "Why, I'd—I'd—"

Words failing me I wheeled and grabbed a good-sized sapling and tore it up by the roots and broke it acrost my knee and throwed the pieces clean through a rail fence on the other side of the road.

"That there is a faint idee!" I said, panting with passion.

"That gives me a very good conception," he said faintly, and he said nothing more till we reached the cabin and seen Uncle Saul Garfield standing in the light of the door combing his black beard with his fingers.

NEXT MORNING J. PEMBROKE seemed like he'd kinda lost interest in b'ars. He said all that walking he done over the slopes of Apache Mountain had made his laig muscles sore. I never heard of such a thing, but nothing that gets the matter with these tenderfeet surprizes me much, they is such a effemernate race, so I ast him would he like to go fishing down the run and he said all right.

But we hadn't been fishing more'n a hour when he said he believed he'd go back to Uncle Saul's cabin and take him a nap, and he insisted on going alone, so I stayed where I was and ketched me a nice string of trout.

I went back to the cabin about noon, and ast Uncle Saul if J. Pembroke had got his nap out.

"Why, heck," said Uncle Saul. "I ain't seen him since you and him started down the run this mornin'. Wait a minute—yonder he comes from the other direction."

Well, J. Pembroke didn't say where he'd been all morning, and I didn't ast him, because a tenderfoot don't generally have no reason for anything he does.

We et the trout I ketched, and after dinner he perked up a right smart and got his shotgun and said he'd like to hunt some wild turkeys. I never heard of anybody hunting anything as big as a turkey with a shotgun, but I didn't say nothing, because tenderfeet is like that.

So we headed up the slopes of Apache Mountain, and I stopped by the schoolhouse to tell Miss Margaret I probably wouldn't get back in time to take my reading and writing lesson, and she said: "You know, until I met your friend, Mr. Pembroke, I didn't realize what a difference there was between men like him, and— well, like the men on Bear Creek."

"I know," I said. "But don't hold it agen him. He means well. He just ain't got no sense. Everybody cain't be smart like me. As a special favor to me, Miss Margaret, I'd like for you to be exter nice to the poor sap, because he's a friend of my friend Bill Glanton down to War Paint."

"I will, Breckinridge," she replied heartily, and I thanked her and went away with my big manly heart pounding in my gigantic bosom.

Me and J. Pembroke headed into the heavy timber, and we hadn't went far till I was convinced that somebody was follering us. I kept hearing twigs snapping, and oncet I thought I seen a shadowy figger duck behind a bush. But when I run back there, it was gone, and no track to show in the pine needles. That sort of thing would of made me nervous, anywhere else, because they is a awful lot of people which would like to get a clean shot at my back from the bresh, but I knowed none of them dast come after me in my own territory. If anybody was trailing us it was bound to be one of my relatives and to save my neck I couldn't think of no reason why anyone of 'em would be gunning for me.

But I got tired of it, and left J. Pembroke in a small glade while I snuck back to do some shaddering of my own. I aimed to cast a big circle around the opening and see could I find out who it was, but I'd hardly got out of sight of J. Pembroke when I heard a gun bang.

I turned to run back and here come J. Pembroke yelling: "I got him! I got him! I winged the bally aborigine!"

He had his head down as he busted through the bresh and he run into me in his excitement and hit me in the belly with his head so hard he bounced back like a rubber ball and landed in a bush with his riding boots brandishing wildly in the air.

"Assist me, Breckinridge!" he shrieked. "Extricate me! They will be hot on our trail!"

"Who?" I demanded, hauling him out by the hind laig and setting him on his feet.

"The Indians!" he hollered, jumping up and down and waving his smoking shotgun frantically. "The bally redskins! I shot one of them! I saw him sneaking through the bushes! I saw his legs! I know it was an Indian because he had on moccasins instead of boots! Listen! That's him now!"

"A Injun couldn't cuss like that," I said. "You've shot Uncle Jeppard Grimes!"

TELLING HIM TO STAY there, I run through the bresh, guided by the maddened howls which riz horribly on the air, and busting through some bushes I seen Uncle Jeppard rolling on the ground with both hands clasped to the rear bosom of his buckskin britches which was smoking freely. His langwidge was awful to hear.

"Air you in misery, Uncle Jeppard?" I inquired solicitously. This evoked another ear-splitting squall.

"I'm writhin' in my death-throes," he says in horrible accents, "and you stands there and mocks my mortal agony! My own blood-kin!" he says. "ae&ae&ae&ae&!" says Uncle Jeppard with passion.

"Aw," I says, "that there bird-shot wouldn't hurt a flea. It cain't be very deep under yore thick old hide. Lie on yore belly, Uncle Jeppard," I said, stropping my bowie on my boot, "and I'll dig out them shot for you."

"Don't tech me!" he said fiercely, painfully climbing onto his feet. "Where's my rifle-gun? Gimme it! Now then, I demands that you bring that English murderer here where I can git a clean lam at him! The Grimes honor is besmirched and my new britches is rooint. Nothin' but blood can wipe out the stain on the family honor!"

"Well," I said, "you hadn't no business sneakin' around after us thataway—"

Here Uncle Jeppard give tongue to loud and painful shrieks.

"Why shouldn't I?" he howled. "Ain't a man got no right to pertect his own property? I was follerin' him to see that he didn't shoot no more tails offa my hawgs. And now he shoots me in the same place! He's a fiend in human form—a monster which stalks ravelin' through these hills bustin' for the blood of the innercent!"

"Aw, J. Pembroke thought you was a Injun," I said.

"He thought Daniel Webster was a wild wart-hawg," gibbered Uncle Jeppard. "He thought I was Geronimo. I reckon he'll massacre the entire population of Bear Creek under a misapprehension, and you'll uphold and defend him! When the cabins of yore kinfolks is smolderin' ashes, smothered in the blood of yore own relatives, I hope you'll be satisfied—bringin' a foreign assassin into a peaceful community!"

Here Uncle Jeppard's emotions choked him, and he chawed his whiskers and then yanked out the five-dollar gold piece I give him for Daniel Webster's tail, and throwed it at me.

"Take back yore filthy lucre," he said bitterly. "The day of retribution is close onto hand, Breckinridge Elkins, and the Lord of battles shall jedge between them which turns agen their kinfolks in their extremerties!"

"In their which?" I says, but he merely snarled and went limping off through the trees, calling back over his shoulder: "They is still men on Bear Creek which will see justice did for the aged and helpless. I'll git that English murderer if it's the last thing I do, and you'll be sorry you stood up for him, you big lunkhead!"

I went back to where J. Pembroke was waiting bewilderedly, and evidently still expecting a tribe of Injuns to bust out of the bresh and sculp him, and I said in disgust: "Let's go home. Tomorrer I'll take you so far away from Bear Creek you can shoot in any direction without hittin' a prize razorback or a antiquated gunman with a ingrown disposition. When Uncle Jeppard Grimes gits mad enough to throw away money, it's time to ile the Winchesters and strap your scabbard-ends to yore laigs."

"Legs?" he said mistily, "But what about the Indian?"

"There warn't no Injun, gol-dern it!" I howled. "They ain't been any on Bear Creek for four or five year. They—aw, hell! What's the use? Come on. It's gittin' late. Next time you see somethin' you don't understand, ast me before you shoot it. And remember, the more ferocious and woolly it looks, the more likely it is to be a leadin' citizen of Bear Creek."

It was dark when we approached Uncle Saul's cabin, and J. Pembroke glanced back up the road, toward the settlement, and said: "My word, is it a political rally? Look! A torchlight parade!"

I looked, and I said: "Quick! Git into the cabin and stay there."

He turned pale, and said: "If there is danger, I insist on—"

"Insist all you dern please," I said. "But git in that house and stay there. I'll handle this. Uncle Saul, see he gits in there."

Uncle Saul is a man of few words. He taken a firm grip on his pipe stem and grabbed J. Pembroke by the neck and seat of the britches and throwed him bodily into the cabin, and shet the door, and sot down on the stoop.

"They ain't no use in you gittin' mixed up in this, Uncle Saul," I said.

"You got yore faults, Breckinridge," he grunted. "You ain't got much sense, but yo're my favorite sister's son—and I ain't forgot that lame mule Jeppard traded me for a sound animal back in '69. Let 'em come!"

*   *   *

THEY COME ALL RIGHT, and surged up in front of the cabin—Jeppard's boys Jack and Buck and Esau and Joash and Polk County. And Erath Elkins, and a mob of Gordons and Buckners and Polks, all more or less kin to me, except Joe Braxton who wasn't kin to any of us, but didn't like me because he was sweet on Miss Margaret. But Uncle Jeppard warn't with 'em. Some had torches and Polk County Grimes had a rope with a noose in it.

"Where-at air you all goin' with that there lariat?" I ast them sternly, planting my enormous bulk in their path.

"Perjuice the scoundrel!" said Polk County, waving his rope around his head. "Bring out the foreign invader which shoots hawgs and defenseless old men from the bresh!"

"What you aim to do?" I inquired.

"We aim to hang him!" they replied with hearty enthusiasm.

Uncle Saul knocked the ashes out of his pipe and stood up and stretched his arms which looked like knotted oak limbs, and he grinned in his black beard like a old timber wolf, and he says: "Whar is dear cousin Jeppard to speak for hisself?"

"Uncle Jeppard was havin' the shot picked outa his hide when we left," says Joel Gordon. "He'll be along directly. Breckinridge, we don't want no trouble with you, but we aims to have that Englishman."

"Well," I snorted, "you all cain't. Bill Glanton is trustin' me to return him whole of body and limb, and—"

"What you want to waste time in argyment for, Breckinridge?" Uncle Saul reproved mildly. "Don't you know it's a plumb waste of time to try to reason with the off-spring of a lame-mule trader?"

"What would you suggest, old man?" sneeringly remarked Polk County.

Uncle Saul beamed on him benevolently, and said gently: "I'd try moral suasion—like this!" And he hit Polk County under the jaw and knocked him clean acrost the yard into a rain barrel amongst the ruins of which he reposed until he was rescued and revived some hours later.

But they was no stopping Uncle Saul oncet he took the war-path. No sooner had he disposed of Polk County than he jumped seven foot into the air, cracked his heels together three times, give the rebel yell and come down with his arms around the necks of Esau Grimes and Joe Braxton, which he went to the earth with and starting mopping up the cabin yard with 'em.

That started the fight, and they is no scrap in the world where mayhem is committed as free and fervent as in one of these here family rukuses.

Polk County had hardly crashed into the rain barrel when Jack Grimes stuck a pistol in my face. I slapped it aside just as he fired and the bullet missed me and taken a ear offa Jim Gordon. I was scared Jack would hurt somebody if he kept on shooting reckless that way, so I kinda rapped him with my left fist and how was I to know it would dislocate his jaw. But Jim Gordon seemed to think I was to blame about his ear because he give a maddened howl and jerked up his shotgun and let *bam* with both barrels. I ducked just in time to keep from getting my head blowed off, and catched most of the double-charge in my shoulder, whilst the rest hived in the seat of Steve Kirby's britches. Being shot that way by a relative was irritating, but I controlled my temper and merely taken the gun away from Jim and splintered the stock over his head.

In the meantime Joel Gordon and Buck Grimes had grabbed one of my laigs apiece and was trying to rassle me to the earth, and Joash Grimes was trying to hold down my right arm, and cousin Pecos Buckner was beating me over the head from behind with a ax-handle, and Erath Elkins was coming at me from the front with a bowie knife. I reached down and got Buck Grimes by the neck with my left hand, and I swung my right and hit Erath with it, but I had to lift Joash clean off his feet and swing him around with the lick, because he wouldn't let go, so I only knocked Erath through the rail fence which was around Uncle Saul's garden.

About this time I found my left laig was free and discovered that Buck Grimes was unconscious, so I let go of his neck and begun to kick around with my left laig and it ain't my fault if the spur got tangled up in Uncle Jonathan Polk's whiskers and jerked most of 'em out by the roots. I shaken Joash off and taken the ax-handle away from Pecos because I seen he was going to hurt somebody if he kept on swinging it around so reckless, and I dunno why he blames me because his skull got fractured when he hit that tree. He oughta look where he falls when he gets throwed across a cabin yard. And if Joel Gordon hadn't been so stubborn trying to gouge me he wouldn't of got his laig broke neither.

I was handicapped by not wanting to kill any of my kinfolks, but they was so mad they all wanted to kill me, so in spite of my carefulness the casualties was increasing at a rate which would of discouraged anybody but Bear Creek folks. But they are the stubbornnest people in the world. Three or four had got me around the laigs again, refusing to be convinced that I couldn't be throwed that way, and Erath Elkins, having pulled hisself out of the ruins of the fence, come charging back with his bowie.

By this time I seen I'd have to use violence in spite of myself, so I grabbed Erath and squoze him with a grizzly-hug and that was when he got them five ribs caved in, and he ain't spoke to me since. I never seen such a cuss for taking offense over trifles.

For a matter of fact, if he hadn't been so bodaciously riled up—if he had of kept his head like I did—he would have seen how kindly I felt toward him even in the fever of that there battle. If I had dropped him underfoot he might have been tromped on fatally for I was kicking folks right and left without caring where they fell. So I carefully flung Erath out of the range of that ruckus—and if he thinks I aimed him at Ozark Grimes and his pitchfork—well, I just never done it. It was Ozark's fault more than mine for toting that pitchfork, and it ought to be Ozark that Erath cusses when he starts to sit down these days.

It was at this moment that somebody swung at me with a ax and ripped my ear nigh offa my head, and I begun to lose my temper. Four or five other relatives was kicking and hitting and biting at me all at oncet, and they is a limit even to my timid manners and mild nature. I voiced my displeasure with a beller of wrath, and lashed out with both fists, and my misguided relatives fell all over the yard like persimmons after a frost. I grabbed Joash Grimes by the ankles and begun to knock them ill-advised idjits in the head with him, and the way he hollered you'd of thought somebody was manhandling him. The yard was beginning to look like a battle-field when the cabin door opened and a deluge of b'iling water descended on us.

I got about a gallon down my neck, but paid very little attention to it, however the others ceased hostilities and started rolling on the ground and hollering and cussing, and Uncle Saul riz up from amongst the ruins of Esau Grimes and Joe Braxton, and bellered: "Woman! What air you at?"

Aunt Zavalla Garfield was standing in the doorway with a kettle in her hand, and she said: "Will you idjits stop fightin'? The Englishman's gone. He run out the back door when the fightin' started, saddled his nag and pulled out. Now will you born fools stop, or will I give you another deluge? Land save us! What's that light?"

Somebody was yelling toward the settlement, and I was aware of a peculiar glow which didn't come from such torches as was still burning. And here come Medina Kirby, one of Bill's gals, yelping like a Comanche.

"Our cabin's burnin'!" she squalled. "A stray bullet went through the winder and busted Miss Margaret's ile lamp!"

WITH A YELL OF DISMAY I abandoned the fray and headed for Bill's cabin, follered by everybody which was able to foller me. They had been several wild shots fired during the melee and one of 'em must have hived in Miss Margaret's winder. The Kirbys had dragged most of their belongings into the yard and some was bringing water from the creek, but the whole cabin was in a blaze by now.

"Whar's Miss Margaret?" I roared.

"She must be still in there!" shrilled Miss Kirby. "A beam fell and wedged her door so we couldn't open it, and—"

I grabbed a blanket one of the gals had rescued and plunged it into the rain barrel and run for Miss Margaret's room. They wasn't but one door in it, which led into the main part of the cabin, and was jammed like they said, and I knowed I couldn't never get my shoulders through either winder, so I just put down my head and rammed the wall full force and knocked four or five logs outa place and made a hole big enough to go through.

The room was so full of smoke I was nigh blinded but I made out a figger fumbling at the winder on the other side. A flaming beam fell outa the roof and broke acrost my head with a loud report and about a bucketful of coals rolled down the back of my neck, but I paid no heed.

I charged through the smoke, nearly fracturing my shin on a bedstead or something, and enveloped the figger in the wet blanket and swept it up in my arms. It kicked wildly and fought and though its voice was muffled in the blanket I ketched some words I never would of thought Miss Margaret would use, but I figgered she was hysterical. She seemed to be wearing spurs, too, because I felt 'em every time she kicked.

By this time the room was a perfect blaze and the roof was falling in and we'd both been roasted if I'd tried to get back to the hole I knocked in the oppersite wall. So I lowered my head and butted my way through the near wall, getting all my eyebrows and hair burnt off in the process, and come staggering through the ruins with my precious burden and fell into the arms of my relatives which was thronged outside.

"I've saved her!" I panted. "Pull off the blanket! Yo're safe, Miss Margaret!"

"$ae&ae&ae&ae$ae!" said Miss Margaret, and Uncle Saul groped under the blanket and said: "By golly, if this is the schoolteacher she's growed a remarkable set of whiskers since I seen her last!"

He yanked off the blanket—to reveal the bewhiskered countenance of Uncle Jeppard Grimes!

"Hell's fire!" I bellered. "What *you* doin' here?"

"I was comin' to jine the lynchin', you blame fool!" he snarled. "I seen Bill's cabin was afire so I clumb in through the back winder to save Miss Margaret. She was gone, but they was a note she'd left. I was fixin' to climb out the winder when this maneyack grabbed me."

"Gimme that note!" I bellered, grabbing it. "Medina! Come here and read it for me."

That note run:

> Dear Breckinridge:
> I am sorry, but I can't stay on Bear Creek any longer. It was tough enough anyway, but being expected to marry you was the last straw.

You've been very kind to me, but it would be too much like marrying a grizzly bear. Please forgive me. I am eloping with J. Pembroke Pemberton. We're going out the back window to avoid any trouble, and ride away on his horse. Give my love to the children. We are going to Europe on our honeymoon.

   With love,

      Margaret Ashley.

"Now what you got to say?" sneered Uncle Jeppard.

"I'm a victim of foreign entanglements," I said dazedly. "I'm goin' to chaw Bill Glanton's ears off for saddlin' that critter on me. And then I'm goin' to lick me a Englishman if I have to go all the way to Californy to find one."

Which same is now my aim, object and ambition. This Englishman took my girl and ruined my education, and filled my neck and spine with burns and bruises. A Elkins never forgets?and the next one that pokes his nose into the Bear Creek country had better be a fighting fool or a powerful fast runner.

THE FEUD BUSTER

THESE HERE DERNED LIES which is being circulated around is making me sick and tired. If this slander don't stop I'm liable to lose my temper, and anybody in the Humbolts can tell you when I loses my temper the effect on the population is wuss'n fire, earthquake, and cyclone.

First-off, it's a lie that I rode a hundred miles to mix into a feud which wasn't none of my business. I never heard of the Hopkins-Barlow war before I come in the Mezquital country. I hear tell the Barlows is talking about suing me for destroying their property. Well, they ought to build their cabins solider if they don't want 'em tore down. And they're all liars when they says the Hopkinses hired me to exterminate 'em at five dollars a sculp. I don't believe even a Hopkins would pay five dollars for one of their mangy sculps. Anyway, I don't fight for hire for nobody. And the Hopkinses needn't bellyache about me turning on 'em and trying to massacre the entire clan. All I wanted to do was kind of disable 'em so they couldn't interfere with my business. And my business, from first to last, was defending the family honor. If I had to wipe up the earth with a couple of feuding clans whilst so doing, I can't help it. Folks which is particular of their hides ought to stay out of the way of torna-does, wild bulls, devastating torrents, and a insulted Elkins.

But it was Uncle Jeppard Grimes' fault to begin with, like it generally is. Dern near all the calamities which takes places in southern Nevada can be traced back to that old lobo. He's got a ingrown disposition and a natural talent for pestering his feller man. Specially his relatives.

I was setting in a saloon in War Paint, enjoying a friendly game of kyards with a horse-thief and three train-robbers, when Uncle Jeppard come in and spied me, and he come over and scowled down on me like I was the missing lynx or something. Purty soon he says, just as I was all sot to make a killing, he says: "How can you set there so free and keerless, with four ace-kyards into yore hand, when yore family name is bein' besmirched?"

I flang down my hand in annoyance, and said: "Now look what you done! What you mean blattin' out information of sech a private nature? What you talkin' about, anyhow?"

"Well," he says, "durin' the three months you been away from home roisterin' and wastin' yore substance in riotous livin'—"

"I been down on Wild River punchin' cows at thirty a month!" I said fiercely. "I ain't squandered nothin' nowheres. Shut up and tell me whatever yo're a-talkin' about."

"Well," says he, "whilst you been gone young Dick Jackson of Chawed Ear has been courtin' yore sister Ellen, and the family's been expectin' 'em to set the day, any time. But now I hear he's been braggin' all over Chawed Ear about how he done jilted her. Air you goin' to set there and let yore sister become the laughin' stock of the country? When I was a young man—"

"When you was a young man Dan'l Boone warn't whelped yet!" I bellered, so mad I included him and everybody else in my irritation. They ain't nothing upsets me like injustice done to some of my close kin. "Git out of my way! I'm headin' for Chawed Ear—what *you* grinnin' at, you spotted hyener?" This last was addressed to the horse-thief in which I seemed to detect signs of amusement.

"I warn't grinnin'," he said.

"So I'm a liar, I reckon!" I said. I felt a impulse to shatter a demi-john over his head, which I done, and he fell under a table hollering bloody murder, and all the fellers drinking at the bar abandoned their licker and stampeded for the street hollering: "Take cover, boys! Breckinridge Elkins is on the rampage!"

So I kicked all the slats out of the bar to relieve my feelings, and stormed out of the saloon and forked Cap'n Kidd. Even he seen it was no time to take liberties with me—he didn't pitch but seven jumps—then he settled down to a dead run, and we headed for Chawed Ear.

* * *

EVERYTHING KIND OF floated in a red haze all the way, but them folks which claims I tried to murder 'em in cold blood on the road between War Paint and Chawed Ear is just narrer-minded and super-sensitive. The reason I shot every- body's hats off that I met was just to kind of ca'm my nerves, because I was afraid if I didn't cool off some by the time I hit Chawed Ear I might hurt somebody. I am that mild-mannered and retiring by nature that I wouldn't willing hurt man, beast, nor Injun unless maddened beyond endurance.

That's why I acted with so much self-possession and dignity when I got to Chawed Ear and entered the saloon where Dick Jackson generally hung out.

"Where's Dick Jackson?" I said, and everybody must of been nervous, because when I boomed out they all jumped and looked around, and the bartender dropped a glass and turned pale.

"Well," I hollered, beginning to lose patience. "Where is the coyote?"

"G—gimme time, will ya?" stuttered the bar-keep. "I—uh—he—uh—"

"So you evades the question, hey?" I said, kicking the foot-rail loose. "Friend of his'n, hey? Tryin' to pertect him, hey?" I was so overcome by this perfidy that I lunged for him and he ducked down behind the bar and I crashed into it bodily with all my lunge and weight, and it collapsed on top of him, and all the customers run out of the saloon hollering, "Help, murder, Elkins is killin' the bartender!"

This feller stuck his head up from amongst the ruins of the bar and begged: "For God's sake, lemme alone! Jackson headed south for the Mezquital Mountains yesterday."

I throwed down the chair I was fixing to bust all the ceiling lamps with, and run out and jumped on Cap'n Kidd and headed south, whilst behind me folks emerged from their cyclone cellars and sent a rider up in the hills to tell the sheriff and his deputies they could come on back now.

I knowed where the Mezquitals was, though I hadn't never been there. I crossed the Californy line about sundown, and shortly after dark I seen Mezquital Peak looming ahead of me. Having ca'med down somewhat, I decided to stop and rest Cap'n Kidd. He warn't tired, because that horse has got alligator blood in his veins, but I knowed I might have to trail Jackson clean to The Angels, and they warn't no use in running Cap'n Kidd's laigs off on the first lap of the chase.

It warn't a very thickly settled country I'd come into, very mountainous and thick timbered, but purty soon I come to a cabin beside the trail and I pulled up and hollered, "Hello!"

The candle inside was instantly blowed out, and somebody pushed a rifle barrel through the winder and bawled: "Who be you?"

"I'm Breckinridge Elkins from Bear Creek, Nevada," I said. "I'd like to stay all night, and git some feed for my horse."

"Stand still," warned the voice. "We can see you agin the stars, and they's four rifle-guns a-kiverin' you."

"Well, make up yore minds," I said, because I could hear 'em discussing me. I reckon they thought they was whispering. One of 'em said: "Aw, he can't be a Barlow. Ain't none of 'em that big." T'other'n said: "Well, maybe he's a derned gun-fighter they've sent for to help 'em out. Old Jake's nephew's been up in Nevady."

"Le's let him in," said a third. "We can mighty quick tell what he is."

So one of 'em come out and 'lowed it would be all right for me to stay the night, and he showed me a corral to put Cap'n Kidd in, and hauled out some hay for him.

"We got to be keerful," he said. "We got lots of enemies in these hills."

We went into the cabin, and they lit the candle again, and sot some corn pone and sow-belly and beans on the table and a jug of corn licker. They was four men, and they said their names was Hopkins—Jim, Bill, Joe, and Joshua, and they was brothers. I'd always heard tell the Mezquital country was famed for big men, but these fellers wasn't so big—not much over six foot high apiece. On Bear Creek they'd been considered kind of puny and undersized.

They warn't very talkative. Mostly they sot with their rifles across their knees and looked at me without no expression onto their faces, but that didn't stop me from eating a hearty supper, and would of et a lot more only the grub give out; and I hoped they had more licker somewheres else because I was purty dry. When I turned up the jug to take a snort of it was brim-full, but before I'd more'n dampened my gullet the dern thing was plumb empty.

When I got through I went over and sot down on a raw-hide bottomed chair in front of the fire-place where they was a small fire going, though they warn't really no need for it, and they said: "What's yore business, stranger?"

"Well," I said, not knowing I was going to get the surprize of my life, "I'm lookin' for a feller named Dick Jackson—"

By golly, the words wasn't clean out of my mouth when they was four men onto my neck like catamounts!

"He's a spy!" they hollered. "He's a cussed Barlow! Shoot him! Stab him! Hit him in the head!"

All of which they was endeavoring to do with such passion they was getting in each other's way, and it was only his over-eagerness which caused Jim to miss me with his bowie and sink it into the table instead, but Joshua busted a chair over my head and Bill would of shot me if I hadn't jerked back my head so he just singed my eyebrows. This lack of hospitality so irritated me that I riz up amongst 'em like a b'ar with a pack of wolves hanging onto him, and commenced committing mayhem on my hosts, because I seen right off they was critters which couldn't be persuaded to respect a guest no other way.

WELL, THE DUST OF BATTLE hadn't settled, the casualities was groaning all over the place, and I was just re-lighting the candle when I heard a horse galloping down the trail from the south. I wheeled and drawed my guns as it stopped before the cabin. But I didn't shoot, because the next instant they was a bare-footed gal standing in the door. When she seen the rooins she let out a screech like a catamount.

"You've kilt 'em!" she screamed. "You murderer!"

"Aw, I ain't neither," I said. "They ain't hurt much—just a few cracked ribs, and dislocated shoulders and busted laigs and sech-like trifles. Joshua's ear'll grow back on all right, if you take a few stitches into it."

"You cussed Barlow!" she squalled, jumping up and down with the hystericals. "I'll kill you! You damned Barlow!"

"I ain't no Barlow," I said. "I'm Breckinridge Elkins, of Bear Creek. I ain't never even heard of no Barlows."

At that Jim stopped his groaning long enough to snarl: "If you ain't a friend of the Barlows, how come you askin' for Dick Jackson? He's one of 'em."

"He jilted my sister!" I roared. "I aim to drag him back and make him marry her!"

"Well, it was all a mistake," groaned Jim. "But the damage is done now."

"It's wuss'n you think," said the gal fiercely. "The Hopkinses has all forted theirselves over at pap's cabin, and they sent me to git you all. We got to make a stand. The Barlows is gatherin' over to Jake Barlow's cabin, and they aims to make a foray onto us tonight. We was outnumbered to begin with, and now here's our best fightin' men laid out! Our goose is cooked plumb to hell!"

"Lift me on my horse," moaned Jim. "I can't walk, but I can still shoot." He tried to rise up, and fell back cussing and groaning.

"You got to help us!" said the gal desperately, turning to me. "You done laid out our four best fightin' men, and you owes it to us. It's yore duty! Anyway, you says Dick Jackson's yore enemy—well, he's Jake Barlow's nephew, and he come back here to help 'em clean out us Hopkinses. He's over to Jake's cabin right now. My brother Bill snuck over and spied on 'em, and he says every fightin' man of the clan is gatherin' there. All we can do is hold the fort, and you got to come help us hold it! Yo're nigh as big as all four of these boys put together."

Well, I figgered I owed the Hopkinses something, so, after setting some bones and bandaging some wounds and abrasions of which they was a goodly lot, I saddled Cap'n Kidd and we sot out.

As we rode along she said: "That there is the biggest, wildest, meanest-lookin' critter I ever seen. Where'd you git him?"

"He was a wild horse," I said. "I catched him up in the Humbolts. Nobody ever rode him but me. He's the only horse west of the Pecos big enough to carry my weight, and he's got painter's blood and a shark's disposition. What's this here feud about?"

"I dunno," she said. "It's been goin' on so long everybody's done forgot what started it. Somebody accused somebody else of stealin' a cow, I think. What's the difference?"

"They ain't none," I assured her. "If folks wants to have feuds its their own business."

We was following a winding path, and purty soon we heard dogs barking and about that time the gal turned aside and got off her horse, and showed me a pen hid in the brush. It was full of horses.

"We keep our mounts here so's the Barlows ain't so likely to find 'em and run 'em off," she said, and she turned her horse into the pen, and I put Cap'n Kidd in, but tied him over in one corner by hisself—otherwise he would of started fighting all the other horses and kicked the fence down.

Then we went on along the path and the dogs barked louder and purty soon we come to a big two-story cabin which had heavy board-shutters over the winders. They was just a dim streak of candle light come through the cracks. It was dark, because the moon hadn't come up. We stopped in the shadder of the trees, and the gal whistled like a whippoorwill three times, and somebody answered from up on the roof. A door opened a crack in the room which didn't have no light at all, and somebody said: "That you, Elizerbeth? Air the boys with you?"

"It's me," says she, starting toward the door. "But the boys ain't with me."

Then all to once he throwed open the door and hollered: "Run, gal! They's a grizzly b'ar standin' up on his hind laigs right behind you!"

"Aw, that ain't no b'ar," says she. "That there's Breckinridge Elkins, from up in Nevady. He's goin' to help us fight the Barlows."

WE WENT ON INTO A ROOM where they was a candle on the table, and they was nine or ten men there and thirty-odd women and chillern. They all looked kinda pale and scairt, and the men was loaded down with pistols and Winchesters.

They all looked at me kind of dumb-like, and the old man kept staring like he warn't any too sure he hadn't let a grizzly in the house, after all. He mumbled something about making a natural mistake, in the dark, and turned to the gal.

"Whar's the boys I sent you after?" he demanded, and she says: "This gent mussed 'em up so's they ain't fitten for to fight. Now, don't git rambunctious, pap. It war just a honest mistake all around. He's our friend, and he's gunnin' for Dick Jackson."

"Ha! Dick Jackson!" snarled one of the men, lifting his Winchester. "Just lemme line my sights on him! I'll cook his goose!"

"You won't, neither," I said. "He's got to go back to Bear Creek and marry my sister Ellen. . . . Well," I says, "what's the campaign?"

"I don't figger they'll git here till well after midnight," said Old Man Hopkins. "All we can do is wait for 'em."

"You means you all sets here and waits till they comes and lays siege?" I says.

"What else?" says he. "Lissen here, young man, don't start tellin' me how to conduck a feud. I growed up in this here'n. It war in full swing when I was born, and I done spent my whole life carryin' it on."

"That's just it," I snorted. "You lets these dern wars drag on for generations. Up in the Humbolts we brings such things to a quick conclusion. Mighty near everybody up there come from Texas, original, and we fights our feuds Texas style, which is short and sweet—a feud which lasts ten years in Texas is a humdinger. We winds 'em up quick and in style. Where-at is this here cabin where the Barlow's is gatherin'?"

"'Bout three mile over the ridge," says a young feller they called Bill.

"How many is they?" I ast.

"I counted seventeen," says he.

"Just a fair-sized mouthful for a Elkins," I said. "Bill, you guide me to that there cabin. The rest of you can come or stay, it don't make no difference to me."

Well, they started jawing with each other then. Some was for going and some for staying. Some wanted to go with me and try to take the Barlows by surprize, but the others said it couldn't be done—they'd git ambushed theirselves, and the only sensible thing to be did was to stay forted and wait for the Barlows to come. They given me no more heed—just sot there and augered.

But that was all right with me. Right in the middle of the dispute, when it looked like maybe the Hopkinses' would get to fighting amongst theirselves and finish each other before the Barlows could git there, I lit out with the boy Bill, which seemed to have considerable sense for a Hopkins.

He got him a horse out of the hidden corral, and I got Cap'n Kidd, which was a good thing. He'd somehow got a mule by the neck, and the critter was almost at its last gasp when I rescued it. Then me and Bill lit out.

We follered winding paths over thick-timbered mountainsides till at last we come to a clearing and they was a cabin there, with light and profanity pouring out of the winders. We'd been hearing the last mentioned for half a mile before we sighted the cabin.

We left our horses back in the woods a ways, and snuck up on foot and stopped amongst the trees back of the cabin.

"They're in there tankin' up on corn licker to whet their appetites for Hopkins blood!" whispered Bill, all in a shiver. "Lissen to 'em! Them fellers ain't hardly human! What you goin' to do? They got a man standin' guard out in front of the door at the other end of the cabin. You see they ain't no doors nor winders at the back. They's winders on each side, but if we try to rush it from the front or either side, they'll see us and fill us full of lead before we could git in a shot. Look! The moon's comin' up. They'll be startin' on their raid before long."

I'll admit that cabin looked like it was going to be harder to storm than I'd figgered. I hadn't had no idee in mind when I sot out for the place. All I wanted was to get in amongst them Barlows—I does my best fighting at close quarters. But at the moment I couldn't think of no way that wouldn't get me shot up. Of course I could just rush the cabin, but the thought of seventeen Winchesters blazing away at me from close range was a little stiff even for me, though I was game to try it, if they warn't no other way.

Whilst I was studying over the matter, all to once the horses tied out in front of the cabin snorted, and back up the hills something went *Oooaaaw-w-w!* And a idee hit me.

"Git back in the woods and wait for me," I told Bill, as I headed for the thicket where we'd left the horses.

I MOUNTED AND RODE up in the hills toward where the howl had come from. Purty soon I lit and throwed Cap'n Kidd's reins over his head, and walked on into the deep bresh, from time to time giving a long squall like a cougar. They ain't a catamount in the world can tell the difference when a Bear Creek man imitates one. After a while one answered, from a ledge just a few hundred feet away.

I went to the ledge and clumb up on it, and there was a small cave behind it, and a big mountain lion in there. He give a grunt of surprise when he seen I was a human, and made a swipe at me, but I give him a bat on the head with my fist, and whilst he was still dizzy I grabbed him by the scruff of the neck and hauled him out of the cave and lugged him down to where I left my horse.

Cap'n Kidd snorted at the sight of the cougar and wanted to kick his brains out, but I give him a good kick in the stummick hisself, which is the only kind of reasoning Cap'n Kidd understands, and got on him and headed for the Barlow hangout.

I can think of a lot more pleasant jobs than toting a full-growed mountain lion down a thick-timbered mountain side on the back of a iron jaw outlaw at midnight. I had the cat by the back of the neck with one hand, so hard he couldn't squall, and I held him out at arm's length as far from the horse as I could, but every now and then he'd twist around so he could claw Cap'n Kidd with his hind laigs, and when this would happen Cap'n Kidd would squall with rage and start bucking all over the place. Sometimes he would buck the derned cougar onto me, and pulling him loose from my hide was wuss'n pulling cockle-burrs out of a cow's tail.

But presently I arriv close behind the cabin. I whistled like a whippoorwill for Bill, but he didn't answer and warn't nowheres to be seen, so I decided he'd got scairt and pulled out for home. But that was all right with me. I'd come to fight the Barlows, and I aimed to fight 'em, with or without assistance. Bill would just of been in the way.

I got off in the trees back of the cabin and throwed the reins over Cap'n Kidd's head, and went up to the back of the cabin on foot, walking soft and easy. The moon was well up, by now, and what wind they was, was blowing toward me, which pleased me, because I didn't want the horses tied out in front to scent the cat and start cutting up before I was ready.

The fellers inside was still cussing and talking loud as I approached one of the winders on the side, and one hollered out: "Come on! Let's git started! I craves Hopkins gore!" And about that time I give the cougar a heave and throwed him through the winder.

He let out a awful squall as he hit, and the fellers in the cabin hollered louder'n he did. Instantly a most awful bustle broke loose in there and of all the whooping and bellering and shooting I ever heard, and the lion squalling amongst it all, and clothes and hides tearing so you could hear it all over the clearing, and the horses busting loose and tearing out through the bresh.

As soon as I hove the cat I run around to the door and a man was standing there with his mouth open, too surprized at the racket to do anything. So I takes his rifle away from him and broke the stock off on his head, and stood there at the door with the barrel intending to brain them Barlows as they run out. I was plumb certain they *would* run out, because I have noticed that the average man is funny that way, and hates to be shut up in a cabin with a mad cougar as bad as the cougar would hate to be shut up in a cabin with a infuriated settler of Bear Creek.

But them scoundrels fooled me. 'Pears like they had a secret door in the back wall, and whilst I was waiting for them to storm out through the front door and get their skulls cracked, they knocked the secret door open and went piling out that way.

BY THE TIME I REALIZED what was happening and run around to the other end of the cabin, they was all out and streaking for the trees, yelling blue murder, with their clothes all tore to shreds and them bleeding like stuck hawgs.

That there catamount sure improved the shining hours whilst he was corralled with them Barlows. He come out after 'em with his mouth full of the seats of men's britches, and when he seen me he give a kind of despairing yelp and taken out up the mountain with his tail betwixt his laigs like the devil was after him with a red-hot branding iron.

I taken after the Barlows, sot on scuttling at least a few of 'em, and I was on the p'int of letting *bam* at 'em with my six-shooters as they run, when, just as they reached the trees, all the Hopkins men riz out of the bresh and fell on 'em with piercing howls.

That fray was kind of peculiar. I don't remember a single shot being fired. The Barlows had dropped their guns in their flight, and the Hopkinses seemed bent on whipping out their wrongs with their bare hands and gun butts. For a few seconds they was a hell of a scramble—men cussing and howling and bellering, and rifle-stocks cracking over heads, and the bresh crashing underfoot, and then before I could get into it, the Barlows broke every which-way and took out through the woods like jack-rabbits squalling Jedgment Day.

Old Man Hopkins come prancing out of the bresh waving his Winchester and his beard flying in the moonlight and he hollered: "The sins of the wicked shall return onto 'em! Elkins, we have hit a powerful lick for righteousness this here night!"

"Where'd you all come from?" I ast. "I thought you was still back in yore cabin chawin' the rag."

"Well," he says, "after you pulled out we decided to trail along and see how you come out with whatever you planned. As we come through the woods expectin' to git ambushed every second, we met Bill here who told us he believed you had a idee of circumventin' them devils, though he didn't know what it was. So we come on and hid ourselves at the aidge of the trees to see what'd happen. I see we been too timid in our dealin's with these heathens. We been lettin' them force the fightin' too long. You was right. A good offense is the best defense.

"We didn't kill any of the varmints, wuss luck," he said, "but we give 'em a prime lickin'. Hey, look there! The boys has caught one of the critters! Take him into that cabin, boys!"

They lugged him into the cabin, and by the time me and the old man got there, they had the candles lit, and a rope around the Barlow's neck and one end throwed over a rafter.

That cabin was a sight, all littered with broke guns and splintered chairs and tables, pieces of clothes and strips of hide. It looked just about like a cabin ought to look where they has just been a fight between seventeen polecats and a mountain lion. It was a dirt floor, and some of the poles which helped hold up the roof was splintered, so most of the weight was resting on a big post in the center of the hut.

All the Hopkinses was crowding around their prisoner, and when I looked over their shoulders and seen the feller's pale face in the light of the candle I give a yell: "Dick Jackson!"

"So it is!" said Old Man Hopkins, rubbing his hands with glee. "So it is! Well, young feller, you got any last words to orate?"

"Naw," said Jackson sullenly. "But if it hadn't been for that derned lion spilin' our plans we'd of had you danged Hopkinses like so much pork. I never heard of a cougar jumpin' through a winder before."

"That there cougar didn't jump," I said, shouldering through the mob. "He was hev. I done the heavin'."

His mouth fell open and he looked at me like he'd saw the ghost of Sitting Bull. "Breckinridge Elkins!" says he. "I'm cooked now, for sure!"

"I'll say you air!" gritted the feller who'd spoke of shooting Jackson earlier in the night. "What we waitin' for? Le's string him up."

The rest started howlin'.

"Hold on," I said. "You all can't hang him. I'm goin' to take him back to Bear Creek."

"You ain't neither," said Old Man Hopkins. "We're much obleeged to you for the help you've give us tonight, but this here is the first chance we've had to hang a Barlow in fifteen year, and we aim to make the most of it. String him, boys!"

"Stop!" I roared, stepping for'ard.

IN A SECOND I WAS COVERED by seven rifles, whilst three men laid hold of the rope and started to heave Jackson's feet off the floor. Them seven Winchesters didn't stop me. But for one thing I'd of taken them guns away and wiped up the floor with them ungrateful mavericks. But I was afeared Jackson would get hit in the wild shooting that was certain to foller such a plan of action.

What I wanted to do was something which would put 'em all horse-de-combat as the French say, without killing Jackson. So I laid hold on the center-post and before they knowed what I was doing, I tore it loose and broke it off, and the roof caved in and the walls fell inwards on the roof.

In a second they wasn't no cabin at all—just a pile of lumber with the Hopkinses all underneath and screaming blue murder. Of course I just braced my laigs and when the roof fell my head busted a hole through it, and the logs of the falling walls hit my shoulders and glanced off, so when the dust settled I was standing waist-deep amongst the ruins and nothing but a few scratches to show for it.

The howls that riz from beneath the ruins was blood-curdling, but I knowed nobody was hurt permanent because if they was they wouldn't be able to howl like that. But I expect some of 'em would of been hurt if my head and shoulders hadn't kind of broke the fall of the roof and wall-logs.

I located Jackson by his voice, and pulled pieces of roof board and logs off until I come onto his laig, and I pulled him out by it and laid him on the ground to get his wind back, because a beam had fell acrost his stummick and when he tried to holler he made the funniest noise I ever heard.

I then kind of rooted around amongst the debris and hauled Old Man Hopkins out, and he seemed kind of dazed and kept talking about earthquakes.

"You better git to work extricatin' yore misguided kin from under them logs, you hoary-haired old sarpent," I told him sternly. "After that there display of ingratitude I got no sympathy for you. In fact, if I was a short-tempered man I'd feel inclined to violence. But bein' the soul of kindness and generosity, I controls my emotions and merely remarks that if I *wasn't* mild-mannered as a lamb, I'd hand you a boot in the pants—like this!"

I kicked him gentle.

"Owww!" says he, sailing through the air and sticking his nose to the hilt in the dirt. "I'll have the law on you, you derned murderer!" He wept, shaking his fists at me, and as I departed with my captive I could hear him chanting a hymn of hate as he pulled chunks of logs off of his bellering relatives.

Jackson was trying to say something, but I told him I warn't in no mood for perlite conversation and the less he said the less likely I was to lose my temper and tie his neck into a knot around a black jack.

CAP'N KIDD MADE THE hundred miles from the Mezquital Mountains to Bear Creek by noon the next day, carrying double, and never stopping to eat, sleep, nor drink. Them that don't believe that kindly keep their mouths shet. I have already licked nineteen men for acting like they didn't believe it.

I stalked into the cabin and throwed Dick Jackson down on the floor before Ellen which looked at him and me like she thought I was crazy.

"What you finds attractive about this coyote," I said bitterly, "is beyond the grasp of my dust-coated brain. But here he is, and you can marry him right away."

She said: "Air you drunk or sun-struck? Marry that good-for-nothin', whiskey-swiggin', card-shootin' loafer? Why, ain't been a week since I run him out of the house with a buggy whip."

"Then he didn't jilt you?" I gasped.

"Him jilt me?" she said. "I jilted him!"

I turned to Dick Jackson more in sorrer than in anger.

"Why," said I, "did you boast all over Chawed Ear about jiltin' Ellen Elkins?"

"I didn't want folks to know she turned me down," he said sulkily. "Us Jacksons is proud. The only reason I ever thought about marryin' her was I was ready to settle down, on the farm pap gave me, and I wanted to marry me a Elkins gal so I wouldn't have to go to the expense of hirin' a couple of hands and buyin' a span of mules and—"

They ain't no use in Dick Jackson threatening to have the law on me. He got off light to what's he'd have got if pap and my brothers hadn't all been off hunting. They've got terrible tempers. But I was always too soft-hearted for my own good. In spite of Dick Jackson's insults I held my temper. I didn't do nothing to him at all, except escort him in sorrow for five or six miles down the Chawed Ear trail, kicking the seat of his britches.

CUPID FROM BEAR CREEK

SOME DAY, MAYBE, WHEN I'm a old man, I'll have sense enough to stay away from these new mining camps which springs up overnight like mushroomers. There was that time in Teton Gulch, for instance. It was a ill-advised moment when I stopped there on my way back to the Humbolts from the Yavapai country. I was a sheep for the shearing and I was shore plenty. And if some of the shearers got fatally hurt in the process, they needn't to blame me. I was acting in self-defense all the way through.

At first I aimed to pass right through Teton Gulch without stopping. I was in a hurry to git back to my home-country and find out was any misguided idjits trying to court Dolly Rixby, the belle of War Paint, in my absence. I hadn't heard from her since I left Bear Creek, five weeks before, which warn't surprizing, seeing as how she couldn't write, nor none of her family, and I couldn't of read it if they had. But they was a lot of young bucks around War Paint which could be counted on to start shining around her the minute my back was turnt.

But my thirst got the best of me, and I stopped in the camp. I was drinking me a dram at the bar of the Yaller Dawg Saloon and Hotel, when the bar-keep says, after studying me a spell, he says: "You must be Breckinridge Elkins, of Bear Creek."

I give the matter due consideration, and 'lowed as how I was.

"How come you knowed me?" I inquired suspiciously, because I hadn't never been in Teton Gulch before, and he says: "Well, I've heard tell of Breckinridge Elkins, and when I seen you, I figgered you must be him, because I don't see how they can be two men in the world that big. By the way, there's a friend of yore'n upstairs—Blink Wiltshaw, from War Paint. I've heered him brag about knowin' you personal. He's upstairs now, fourth door from the stair-head, on the left."

Now that there news interested me, because Blink was the most persistent of all them young mavericks which was trying to spark Dolly Rixby. Just the night before I left for Yavapai, I catched him coming out of her house, and was fixing to sweep the street with him when Dolly come out and stopped me and made us shake hands.

It suited me fine for him to be in Teton Gulch, or anywheres just so he warn't no-wheres nigh Dolly Rixby, so I thought I'd pass the time of day with him.

I went upstairs and knocked on the door, and *bam!* went a gun inside and a .45 slug ripped through the door and taken a nick out of my off-ear. Getting shot in the ear always did irritate me, so without waiting for no more exhibitions of hospitality, I give voice to my displeasure in a deafening beller and knocked the door off its hinges and busted into the room over its ruins.

For a second I didn't see nobody, but then I heard a kind of gurgle going on, and happened to remember that the door seemed kind of squishy underfoot when I tromped over it, so I knowed that whoever was in the room had got pinned under the door when I knocked it down.

So I reached under it and got him by the collar and hauled him out, and shore enough it was Blink Wiltshaw. He was limp as a lariat, and glassy-eyed and pale, and was still kind of trying to shoot me with his six-shooter when I taken it away from him.

"What the hell's the matter with you?" I demanded sternly, dangling him by the collar with one hand, whilst shaking him till his teeth rattled. "Didn't Dolly make us shake hands? What you mean by tryin' to 'sasserinate me through a hotel door?"

"Lemme down, Breck," he gasped. "I didn't know it was you. I thought it was Rattlesnake Harrison comin' after my gold."

SO I SOT HIM DOWN. HE grabbed a jug of licker and taken a swig, and his hand shook so he spilled half of it down his neck.

"Well?" I demanded. "Ain't you goin' to offer me a snort, dern it?"

"Excuse me, Breckinridge," he apolergized. "I'm so derned jumpy I dunno what I'm doin'. You see them buckskin pokes?" says he, p'inting at some bags on the bed. "Them is plumb full of nuggets. I been minin' up the Gulch, and I hit a regular bonanza the first week. But it ain't doin' me no good."

"What you mean?" I demanded.

"These mountains is full of outlaws," says he. "They robs, and murders every man which makes a strike. The stagecoach has been stuck up so often nobody sends their dust out on it no more. When a man makes a pile he sneaks out through the mountains at night, with his gold on pack-mules. I aimed to do that last night. But them outlaws has got spies all over the camp, and I know they got me spotted. Rattlesnake Harrison's their chief, and he's a ring-tailed he-devil. I been squattin' over this here gold with my pistol in fear and tremblin', expectin' 'em to come right into camp after me. I'm dern nigh loco!"

And he shivered and cussed kind of whimpery, and taken another dram, and cocked his pistol and sot there shaking like he'd saw a ghost or two.

"You got to help me, Breckinridge," he said desperately. "*You* take this here gold out for me, willya? The outlaws don't know you. You could hit the old Injun path south of the camp and foller it to Hell-Wind Pass. The Chawed-Ear–Wahpeton stage goes through there about sun-down. You could put the gold on the stage there, and they'd take it on to Wahpeton. Harrison wouldn't never think of holdin' it up *after* it left Hell-Wind. They always holds it up this side of the Pass."

"What I want to risk my neck for you for?" I demanded bitterly, memories of Dolly Rixby rising up before me. "If you ain't got the guts to tote out yore own gold—"

"T'ain't altogether the gold, Breck," says he. "I'm tryin' to git married, and—"

"*Married?*" says I. "Here? In Teton Gulch? To a gal in Teton Gulch?"

"Married to a gal in Teton Gulch," he avowed. "I was aimin' to git hitched tomorrer, but they ain't a preacher or justice of the peace in camp to tie the knot. But her uncle the Reverant Rembrandt Brockton is a circuit rider, and he's due to pass through Hell-Wind on his way to Wahpeton today. I was aimin' to sneak out last night, hide in the hills till the stage come through, then put the gold on the stage and bring Brother Rembrandt back with me. But yesterday I learnt Harrison's spies was watchin' me, and I'm scairt to go. Now Brother Rembrandt will go on to Wahpeton, not knowin' he's needed here, and no tellin' when I'll be able to git married—"

"Hold on," I said hurried, doing some quick thinking. I didn't want this here wedding to fall through. The more Blink was married to some gal in Teton, the less he could marry Dolly Rixby.

"Blink," I said, grasping his hand warmly, "let it never be said that a Elkins ever turned down a friend in distress. I'll take yore gold to Hell-Wind Pass and bring back Brother Rembrandt."

Blink fell onto my neck and wept with joy. "I'll never forget this, Breckinridge," says he, "and I bet you won't neither! My hoss and pack-mule are in the stables behind the saloon."

"I don't need no pack-mule," I says. "Cap'n Kidd can pack the dust easy."

CAP'N KIDD WAS GETTING fed out in the corral next to the hotel. I went out there and got my saddle-bags, which is a lot bigger'n most saddle-bags, because all my plunder has to be made to fit my size. They're made outa three-ply elkskin, stitched with rawhide thongs, and a wildcat couldn't claw his way out of 'em.

I noticed quite a bunch of men standing around the corral looking at Cap'n Kidd, but thought nothing of it, because he is a hoss which naturally attracts attention. But whilst I was getting my saddle-bags, a long lanky cuss with long yaller whiskers come up and said, says he: "Is that yore hoss in the corral?"

If he ain't he ain't nobody's," I says.

"Well, he looks a whole lot like a hoss that was stole off my ranch six months ago," he said, and I seen ten or fifteen hard-looking hombres gathering around me. I laid down my saddle-bags sudden-like and reached for my guns, when it occurred to me that if I had a fight there I might git arrested and it would interfere with me bringing Brother Rembrandt in for the wedding.

"If that there is yore hoss," I said, "you ought to be able to lead him out of that there corral."

"Shore I can," he says with a oath. "And what's more, I aim'ta."

He looked at me suspiciously, but he taken up a rope and clumb the fence and started toward Cap'n Kidd which was chawing on a block of hay in the middle of the corral. Cap'n Kidd threwed up his head and laid back his ears and showed his teeth, and Jake stopped sudden and turned pale.

"I—I don't believe that there is my hoss, after all!" says he.

"Put that lasso on him!" I roared, pulling my right-hand gun. "You say he's yore'n; I say he's mine. One of us is a liar and a hoss-thief, and I aim to prove which. Gwan, before I festoons yore system with lead polka-dots!"

He looked at me and he looked at Cap'n Kidd, and he turned bright green all over. He looked agen at my .45 which I now had cocked and p'inted at his long neck, which his adam's apple was going up and down like a monkey on a pole, and he begun to aidge toward Cap'n Kidd again, holding the rope behind him and sticking out one hand.

"Whoa, boy," he says kind of shudderingly. "Whoa—good old feller—nice hossie—whoa, boy—*ow!*"

He let out a awful howl as Cap'n Kidd made a snap and bit a chunk out of his hide. He turned to run but Cap'n Kidd wheeled and let fly both heels which caught Jake in the seat of the britches, and his shriek of despair was horrible to hear as he went head-first through the corral fence into a hoss-trough on the other side. From this he ariz dripping water, blood and profanity, and he shook a quivering fist at me and croaked: "You derned murderer! I'll have yore life for this!"

"I don't hold no conversation with hoss-thieves," I snorted, and picked up my saddle-bags and stalked through the crowd which give back in a hurry.

I TAKEN THE SADDLE-BAGS up to Blink's room, and told him about Jake, thinking he'd be amoosed, but got a case of aggers again, and said: "That was one of Harrison's men! He meant to take yore hoss. It's a old trick, and honest folks don't dare interfere. Now they got you spotted! What'll you do?"

"Time, tide and a Elkins waits for no man!" I snorted, dumping the gold into the saddle-bags. "If that yaller-whiskered coyote wants any trouble, he can git a bellyfull. Don't worry, yore gold will be safe in my saddle-bags. It's as good as in the Wahpeton stage right now. And by midnight I'll be back with Brother Rembrandt Brockton to hitch you up with his niece."

"Don't yell so loud," begged Blink. "The cussed camp's full of spies. Some of 'em may be downstairs now, listenin'."

"I warn't speakin' above a whisper," I said indignantly.

"That bull's beller may pass for a whisper on Bear Creek," says he, wiping off the sweat, "but I bet they can hear it from one end of the Gulch to the other, at least."

It's a pitable sight to see a man with a case of the scairts; I shook hands with him and left him pouring red licker down his gullet like it was water, and I swung the saddle-bags over my shoulder and went downstairs, and the bar-keep leaned over the bar and whispered to me: "Look out for Jake Roman! He was in here a minute ago, lookin' for trouble. He pulled out just before you come down, but he won't be forgittin' what yore hoss done to him!"

"Not when he tries to set down, he won't," I agreed, and went on out to the corral, and they was a crowd of men watching Cap'n Kidd eat his hay, and one of 'em seen me and hollered: "Hey, boys, here comes the giant! He's goin' to saddle that man-eatin' monster! Hey, Bill! Tell the boys at the bar!"

And here come a whole passel of fellers running out of all the saloons, and they lined the corral fence solid, and started laying bets whether I'd git the saddle on Cap'n Kidd or git my brains kicked out. I thought miners must all be crazy. They ought've knowed I was able to saddle my own hoss.

Well, I saddled him and throwed on the saddle-bags and clumb aboard, and he pitched about ten jumps like he always does when I first fork him—t'warn't nothing, but them miners hollered like wild Injuns. And when he accidentally bucked hisself and me through the fence and knocked down a section of it along with fifteen men which was setting on the top-rail, the way they howled you'd of thought something terrible had happened. Me and Cap'n Kidd don't generally bother about gates. We usually makes our own through whatever happens to be in front of us. But them miners is a weakly breed, because as I rode out of town I seen the crowd dipping four or five of 'em into a hoss-trough to bring 'em to, on account of Cap'n Kidd having accidentally tromped on 'em.

WELL, I RODE OUT OF THE Gulch and up the ravine to the south, and come out into the high timbered country, and hit the old Injun trail Blink had told me about. It warn't traveled much. I didn't meet nobody after I left the Gulch. I figgered to hit Hell-Wind Pass at least a hour before sun-down which would give me plenty of time. Blink said the stage passed through there about sun-down. I'd have to bring back Brother Rembrandt on Cap'n Kidd, I reckoned, but that there hoss can carry double and still out-run and out-last any other hoss in the State of Nevada. I figgered on getting back to Teton about midnight or maybe a little later.

After I'd went several miles I come to Apache Canyon, which was a deep, narrer gorge, with a river at the bottom which went roaring and foaming along betwixt rock walls a hundred and fifty feet high. The old trail hit the rim at a place where the canyon warn't only about seventy foot wide, and somebody had felled a whopping big pine tree on one side so it fell acrost and made a foot-bridge, where a man could walk acrost. They'd once been a gold strike in Apache Canyon, and a big camp there, but now it was plumb abandoned and nobody lived anywheres near it.

I turned east and follered the rim for about half a mile. Here I come into a old wagon road which was just about growed up with saplings now, but it run down into a ravine into the bed of the canyon, and they was a bridge acrost the river which had been built during the days of the gold rush. Most of it had done been washed away by head-rises, but a man could still ride a horse across what was left. So I done so and rode up a ravine on the other side, and come out on high ground again.

I'd rode a few hundred yards past the ravine when somebody said: "Hey!" and I wheeled with both guns in my hands. Out of the bresh s'antered a tall gent in a long frock tail coat and broad-brimmed hat.

"Who air you and what the hell you mean by hollerin' 'Hey!' at me?" I demanded courteously, p'inting my guns at him. A Elkins is always perlite.

"I am the Reverant Rembrandt Brockton, my good man," says he. "I am on my way to Teton Gulch to unite my niece and a young man of that camp in the bonds of holy matrimony."

"The he—you don't say!" I says. "Afoot?"

"I alit from the stage-coach at—ah—Hades-Wind Pass," says he. "Some very agreeable cowboys happened to be awaiting the stage there, and they offered to escort me to Teton."

"How come you knowed yore niece was wantin' to be united in acrimony?" I ast.

"The cowboys informed me that such was the case," says he.

"Where-at are they now?" I next inquore.

"The mount with which they supplied me went lame a little while ago," says he. "They left me here while they went to procure another from a near-by ranch-house."

"I dunno who'd have a ranch anywheres near here," I muttered. "They ain't got much sense leavin' you here by yore high lonesome."

"You mean to imply there is danger?" says he, blinking mildly at me.

"These here mountains is lousy with outlaws which would as soon kyarve a preacher's gullet as anybody's," I said, and then I thought of something else. "Hey!" I says. "I thought the stage didn't come through the Pass till sun-down?"

"Such was the case," says he. "But the schedule has been altered."

"Heck!" I says. "I was aimin' to put this here gold on it which my saddle-bags is full of. Now I'll have to take it back to Teton with me. Well, I'll bring it out tomorrer and catch the stage then. Brother Rembrandt, I'm Breckinridge Elkins, of Bear Creek, and I come out here to meet you and escort you back to the Gulch, so's you could unite yore niece and Blink Wiltshaw in the holy bounds of alimony. Come on. We'll ride double."

"But I must await my cowboy friends!" he said. "Ah, here they come now!"

I looked over to the east and seen about fifteen men ride into sight out of the bresh and move toward us. One was leading a hoss without no saddle onto it.

"Ah, my good friends!" beamed Brother Rembrandt. "They have procured a mount for me, even as they promised."

He hauled a saddle out of the bresh, and says: "Would you please saddle my horse for me when they get here? I should be delighted to hold your rifle while you did so."

I started to hand him my Winchester, when the snap of a twig under a hoss's hoof made me whirl quick. A feller had just rode out of a thicket about a hundred yards south of me, and he was raising a Winchester to his shoulder. I recognized him instantly. If us Bear Creek folks didn't have eyes like a hawk, we'd never live to git growed. It was Jake Roman!

Our Winchesters banged together. His lead fanned my ear and mine knocked him end-ways out of his saddle.

"Cowboys, hell!" I roared. "Them's Harrison's outlaws! I'll save you, Brother Rembrandt!"

I SWOOPED HIM UP WITH one arm and gouged Cap'n Kidd with the spurs and he went from there like a thunderbolt with its tail on fire. Them outlaws come on with wild yells. I ain't in the habit of running from people, but I was afeared they might do the Reverant harm if it come to a close fight, and if he stopped a hunk of lead, Blink might not git to marry his niece, and might git disgusted and go back to War Paint and start sparking Dolly Rixby again.

I was heading back for the canyon, aiming to make a stand in the ravine if I had to, and them outlaws was killing their hosses trying to git to the bend of the trail ahead of me, and cut me off. Cap'n Kidd was running with his belly to the ground, but I'll admit Brother Rembrandt warn't helping me much. He was laying acrost my saddle with his arms and laigs waving wildly because I hadn't had time to set him comfortable, and when the horn jobbed him in the belly he uttered some words I wouldn't of expected to hear spoke by a minister of the gospel.

Guns begun to crack and lead hummed past us, and Brother Rembrandt twisted his head around and screamed: "Stop that shootin', you — sons of —! You'll hit me!"

I thought it was kind of selfish of Brother Rembrandt not to mention me, too, but I said: "T'ain't no use to remonstrate with them skunks, Reverant. They ain't got no respeck for a preacher even."

But to my amazement the shooting stopped, though them bandits yelled louder'n ever and flogged their cayuses. But about that time I seen they had me cut off from the lower canyon crossing, so I wrenched Cap'n Kidd into the old Injun trace and headed straight for the canyon rim as hard as he could hammer, with the bresh lashing and snapping around us and slapping Brother Rembrandt in the face when it whipped back. The outlaws yelled and wheeled in behind us, but Cap'n Kidd drawed away from them with every stride, and the canyon rim loomed just ahead of us.

"Pull up, you jack-eared son of Baliol!" howled Brother Rembrandt. "You'll go over the edge!"

"Be at ease, Reverant," I reassured him. "We're goin' over the log."

"Lord have mercy on my soul!" he squalled, and shet his eyes and grabbed a stirrup leather with both hands, and then Cap'n Kidd went over that log like thunder rolling on Jedgment Day.

I doubt if they is another hoss west of the Pecos which would bolt out onto a log foot-bridge acrost a canyon a hundred fifty foot deep like that, but they ain't nothing in this world Cap'n Kidd's scairt of except maybe me. He didn't slacken his speed none. He streaked acrost that log like it was a quarter-track, with the bark and splinters flying from under his hoofs, and if one foot had slipped a inch, it would of been Sally bar the door. But he didn't slip, and we was over and on the other side almost before you could catch yore breath.

"You can open yore eyes now, Brother Rembrandt," I said kindly, but he didn't say nothing. He'd fainted. I shook him to wake him up, and in a flash he come to and give a shriek and grabbed my laig like a b'ar trap. I reckon he thought we was still on the log. I was trying to pry him loose when Cap'n Kidd chose that moment to run under a low-hanging oak tree limb. That's his idee of a joke. That there hoss has got a great sense of humor.

I looked up just in time to see the limb coming, but not in time to dodge it. It was as big around as my thigh, and it took me smack acrost the wish-bone. We was going full speed, and something had to give way. It was the girths—both of 'em. Cap'n Kidd went out from under me, and me and Brother Rembrandt and the saddle hit the ground together.

I JUMPED UP BUT BROTHER Rembrandt laid there going: "Wug wug wug!" like water running out of a busted jug. And then I seen them outlaws had dismounted off of their hosses and was corning acrost the bridge single file, with their Winchesters in their hands.

I didn't waste no time shooting them misguided idjits. I run to the end of the foot-bridge, ignoring the slugs they slung at me. It was purty pore shooting, because they warn't shore of their footing, and didn't aim good. So I only got one bullet in the hind laig and was creased three or four other unimportant places—not enough to bother about.

I bent my knees and got hold of the end of the tree and heaved up with it, and them outlaws hollered and fell along it like ten pins, and dropped their Winchesters and grabbed holt of the log. I given it a shake and shook some of 'em off like persimmons off a limb after a frost, and then I swung the butt around clear of the rim and let go, and it went down end over end into the river a hundred and fifty feet below, with a dozen men still hanging onto it and yelling blue murder.

A regular geyser of water splashed up when they hit, and the last I seen of 'em they was all swirling down the river together in a thrashing tangle of arms and laigs and heads.

I remember Brother Rembrandt and run back to where he'd fell, but was already onto his feet. He was kind of pale and wild-eyed and his laigs kept bending under him, but he had hold of the saddle-bags and was trying to drag 'em into a thicket, mumbling kind of dizzily to hisself.

"It's all right now, Brother Rembrandt," I said kindly. "Them outlaws is plumb horse-de-combat now, as the French say. Blink's gold is safe."

"—!" says Brother Rembrandt, pulling two guns from under his coat tails, and if I hadn't grabbed him, he would of undoubtedly shot me. We rassled around and I protested: "Hold on, Brother Rembrandt! I ain't no outlaw. I'm yore friend, Breckinridge Elkins. Don't you remember?"

His only reply was a promise to eat my heart without no seasoning, and he then sunk his teeth into my ear and started to chaw it off, whilst gouging for my eyes with both thumbs and spurring me severely in the hind laigs. I seen he was out of his head from fright and the fall he got, so I said sorrerfully: "Brother Rembrandt, I hate to do this. It hurts me more'n it does you, but we cain't waste time like this. Blink is waitin' to git married." And with a sigh I busted him over the head with the butt of my six-shooter, and he fell over and twitched a few times and then lay limp.

"Pore Brother Rembrandt," I sighed sadly. "All I hope is I ain't addled yore brains so you've forgot the weddin' ceremony."

So as not to have no more trouble with him when, and if, he come to, I tied his arms and laigs with pieces of my lariat, and taken his weppins which was most surprizing arms for a circuit rider. His pistols had the triggers out of 'em, and they was three notches on the butt of one, and four on the other'n. Moreover he had a bowie knife in his boot, and a deck of marked kyards and a pair of loaded dice in his hip-pocket. But that warn't none of my business.

About the time I finished tying him up, Cap'n Kidd come back to see if he'd killed me or just crippled me for life. To show him I can take a joke too, I give him a kick in the belly, and when he could git his breath again, and undouble hisself, I throwed the saddle on him. I spliced the girths with the rest of my lariat, and put Brother Rembrandt in the saddle and clumb on behind and we headed for Teton Gulch.

After a hour or so Brother Rembrandt come to and says kind of dizzily: "Was anybody saved from the typhoon?"

"Yo're all right, Brother Rembrandt," I assured him. "I'm takin' you to Teton Gulch."

"I remember," he muttered. "It all comes back to me. Damn Jake Roman! I thought it was a good idea, but it seems I was mistaken. I thought we had an ordinary human being to deal with. I know when I'm licked. I'll give you a thousand dollars to let me go."

"Take it easy, Brother Rembrandt," I soothed, seeing he was still delirious.

"We'll be to Teton in no time."

"I don't want to go to Teton!" he hollered.

"You got to," I said. "You got to unite yore niece and Blink Wiltshaw in the holy bums of parsimony."

"To hell with Blink Wiltshaw and my — niece!" he yelled.

"You ought to be ashamed usin' sech langwidge, and you a minister of the gospel," I reproved him sternly. His reply would of curled a Piute's hair.

I was so scandalized I made no reply. I was just fixing to untie him, so's he could ride more comfortable, but I thought if he was that crazy, I better not. So I give no heed to his ravings which growed more and more unbearable. In all my born days I never seen such a preacher.

IT WAS SHORE A RELIEF to me to sight Teton at last. It was night when we rode down the ravine into the Gulch, and the dance halls and saloons was going full blast. I rode up behind the Yaller Dawg Saloon and hauled Brother Rembrandt off with me and sot him on his feet, and he said, kind of despairingly: "For the last time, listen to reason. I got fifty thousand dollars cached up in the hills. I'll give you every cent if you'll untie me."

"I don't want no money," I said. "All I want is for you to marry yore niece and Blink Wiltshaw. I'll untie you then."

"All right," he said. "All right! But untie me now!"

I was just fixing to do it, when the bar-keep come out with a lantern and he shone it on our faces and said in a startled tone: "Who the hell is that with you, Elkins?"

"You wouldn't never suspect it from his langwidge," I says, "but it's the Reverant Rembrandt Brockton."

"Are you crazy?" says the bar-keep. "That's Rattlesnake Harrison!"

"I give up," said my prisoner. "I'm Harrison. I'm licked. Lock me up somewhere away from this lunatic."

I was standing in a kind of daze, with my mouth open, but now I woke up and bellered: "*What?* Yo're Harrison? I see it all now! Jake Roman overheard me talkin' to Blink Wiltshaw, and rode off and fixed it with you to fool me like you done, so's to git Blink's gold! That's why you wanted to hold my Winchester whilst I saddled yore cayuse."

"How'd you ever guess it?" he sneered. "We ought to have shot you from ambush like I wanted to, but Jake wanted to catch you alive and torture you to death account of your horse bitin' him. The fool must have lost his head at the last minute and decided to shoot you after all. If you hadn't recognized him we'd had you surrounded and stuck up before you knew what was happening."

"But now the real preacher's gone on to Wahpeton!" I hollered. "I got to foller him and bring him back—"

"Why, he's here," said one of the men which was gathering around us. "He come in with his niece a hour ago on the stage from War Paint."

"War Paint?" I howled, hit in the belly by a premonition. I run into the saloon, where they was a lot of people, and there was Blink and a gal holding hands in front of a old man with a long white beard, and he had a book in his hand, and t'other'in lifted in the air. He was saying: "—And I now pronounces you-all man and wife. Them which God had j'ined together let no snake-hunter put asunder."

"Dolly!" I yelled. Both of 'em jumped about four foot and whirled, and Dolly Rixby jumped in front of Blink and spread her arms like she was shooing chickens.

"Don't you tech him, Breckinridge Elkins!" she hollered. "I just married him and I don't aim for no Humbolt grizzly to spile him!"

"But I don't *sabe* all this—" I said dizzily, nervously fumbling with my guns which is a habit of mine when upsot.

Everybody in the wedding party started ducking out of line, and Blink said hurriedly: "It's this way, Breck. When I made my pile so onexpectedly quick, I sent for Dolly to come and marry me like she'd promised the day after you left for the Yavapai. I *was* aimin' to take my gold out today, like I told you, so me and Dolly could go to San Francisco on our honeymoon, but I learnt Harrison's gang was watchin' me, just like I told you. I wanted to git my gold out, and I wanted to git you out of the way before Dolly and her uncle got here on the War Paint stage, so I told you that lie about Brother Rembrandt bein' on the Wahpeton stage. It was the only lie."

"You said you was marryin' a gal in Teton," I accused fiercely.

"Well," says he, "I did marry her in Teton. You know, Breck, all's fair in love and war."

"Now, now, boys," said Brother Rembrandt—the real one, I mean. "The gal's married, yore rivalry is over, and they's no use holdin' grudges. Shake hands and be friends."

"All right," I said heavily. No man cain't say I ain't a good loser. I was cut deep but I concealed my busted heart.

Leastways I concealed it all I was able to. Them folks which says I crippled Blink Wiltshaw with malice aforethought is liars which I'll sweep the road with when I catches 'em. When my emotions is wrought up I unconsciously uses more of my strength than I realizes. I didn't aim to break Blink's arm when I shook hands with him; it was just the stress of my emotions. Likewise it was Dolly's fault that her Uncle Rembrandt got throwed out a winder and some others got their heads banged. When she busted me with that cuspidor I knew that our love was dead forever. Tears come into my eyes as I waded through the crowd, and I had to move fast to keep from making a fool of myself. Them that was flang out of my way ought to have knowed it was done more in sorrer than in anger.

THE RIOT AT COUGAR PAW

I WAS OUT IN THE BLACKSMITH shop by the corral beating out some shoes for Cap'n Kidd, when my brother John come sa'ntering in. He'd been away for a few weeks up in the Cougar Paw country, and he'd evidently done well, whatever he'd been doing, because he was in a first class humor with hisself, and plumb spilling over with high spirits and conceit. When he feels prime like that he wants to rawhide everybody he meets, especially me. John thinks he's a wit, but I figger he's just half right.

"Air you slavin' over a hot forge for that mangy, flea-bit hunk of buzzard-meat again?" he greeted me. "That broom-tail ain't wuth the iron you wastes on his splayed-out hooves!"

He knows the easiest way to git under my hide is to poke fun at Cap'n Kidd. But I reflected it was just envy on his part, and resisted my natural impulse to bend the tongs over his head. I taken the white-hot iron out of the forge and put it on the anvil and started beating it into shape with the sixteen-pound sledge I always uses. I got no use for the toys which most blacksmiths uses for hammers.

"If you ain't got nothin' better to do than criticize a animal which is a damn sight better hoss than you'll ever be a man," I said with dignerty, between licks, "I calls yore attention to a door right behind you which nobody ain't usin' at the moment."

He bust into loud rude laughter and said: "You call that thing a hossshoe? It's big enough for a snow plow! Here, long as yo're in the business, see can you fit a shoe for that!"

He sot his foot up on the anvil and I give it a good slam with the hammer. John let out a awful holler and begun hopping around over the shop and cussing fit to curl yore hair. I kept on hammering my iron.

Just then pap stuck his head in the door and beamed on us, and said: "You boys won't never grow up! Always playin' yore childish games, and sportin' in yore innercent frolics!"

"He's busted my toe," said John blood-thirstily, "and I'll have his heart's blood if it's the last thing I do."

"Chips off the old block," beamed pap. "It takes me back to the time when, in the days of my happy childhood, I emptied a sawed-off shotgun into the seat of brother Joel's britches for tellin' our old man it was me which put that b'ar-trap in his bunk."

"He'll rue the day," promised John, and hobbled off to the cabin with moans and profanity. A little later, from his yells, I gathered that he had persuaded maw or one of the gals to rub his toe with hoss-liniment. He could make more racket about nothing then any Elkins I ever knowed.

I went on and made the shoes and put 'em on Cap'n Kidd, which is a job about like roping and hawg-tying a mountain cyclone, and by the time I got through and went up to the cabin to eat, John seemed to have got over his mad spell. He was laying on his bunk with his foot up on it all bandaged up, and he says: "Breckinridge, they ain't no use in grown men holdin' a grudge. Let's fergit about it."

"Who's holdin' any grudge?" I ast, making sure he didn't have a bowie knife in his left hand. "I dunno why they should be so much racket over a trifle that didn't amount to nothin', nohow."

"Well," he said, "this here busted foot discommodes me a heap. I won't be able to ride for a day or so, and they is business up to Cougar Paw I ought to 'tend to."

"I thought you just come from there," I says.

"I did," he said, "but they is a man up there which has promised me somethin' which is due me, and now I ain't able to go collect. Whyn't you go collect for me, Breckinridge? You ought to, dern it, because its yore fault I cain't ride. The man's name is Bill Santry, and he lives up in the mountains a few miles from Cougar Paw. You'll likely find him in Cougar Paw any day, though."

"What's this he promised you?" I ast.

"Just ask for Bill Santry," he said. "When you find him say to him: 'I'm John Elkins' brother, and you can give me what you promised him.'"

My family always imposes onto my good nature; generally I'd rather go do what they want me to do than to go to the trouble with arguing with 'em.

"Oh, all right," I said. "I ain't got nothin' to do right now."

"Thanks, Breckinridge," he said. "I knowed I could count on you."

SO A COUPLE OF DAYS later I was riding through the Cougar Range, which is very thick-timbered mountains, and rapidly approaching Cougar Paw. I hadn't never been there before, but I was follering a winding wagon-road which I knowed would eventually fetch me there.

The road wound around the shoulder of a mountain, and ahead of me I seen a narrer path opened into it, and just before I got there I heard a bull beller, and a gal screamed: "Help! Help! Old Man Kirby's bull's loose!"

They came a patter of feet, and behind 'em a smashing and crashing in the underbrush, and a gal run out of the path into the road, and a rampaging bull was right behind her with his head lowered to toss her. I reined Cap'n Kidd between her and him, and knowed Cap'n Kidd would do the rest without no advice from me. He done so by wheeling and lamming his heels into that bull's ribs so hard he kicked the critter clean through a rail fence on the other side of the road. Cap'n Kidd hates bulls, and he's too big and strong for any of 'em. He would of then jumped on the critter and stomped him, but I restrained him, which made him mad, and whilst he was trying to buck me off, the bull ontangled hisself and high-tailed it down the mountain, bawling like a scairt yearling.

When I had got Cap'n Kidd in hand, I looked around and seen the gal looking at me very admiringly. I swept off my Stetson and bowed from my saddle and says: "Can I assist you any father, m'am?"

She blushed purty as a pitcher and said: "I'm much obliged, stranger. That there critter nigh had his hooks into my hide. Whar you headin'? If you ain't in no hurry I'd admire to have you drop by the cabin and have a snack of b'ar meat and honey. We live up the path about a mile."

They ain't nothin' I'd ruther do," I assured her. "But just at the present I got business in Cougar Paw. How far is it from here?"

"'Bout five mile down the road," says she. "My name's Joan; what's yore'n?"

"Breckinridge Elkins, of Bear Creek," I said. "Say, I got to push on to Cougar Paw, but I'll be ridin' back this way tomorrer mornin' about sun-up. If you could–"

"I'll be waitin' right here for you," she said so promptly it made my head swim. No doubt about it; it was love at first sight. "I—I got store-bought shoes," she added shyly. "I'll be a-wearin' 'em when you come along."

"I'll be here if I have to wade through fire, flood and hostile Injuns," I assured her, and rode on down the wagon-trace with my manly heart swelling with pride in my bosom. They ain't many mountain men which can awake the fire of love in a gal's heart at first sight—a gal, likewise, which was as beautiful as that there gal, and rich enough to own store-bought shoes. As I told Cap'n Kidd, they was just something *about* a Elkins.

It was about noon when I rode into Cougar Paw which was a tolerably small village sot up amongst the mountains, with a few cabins where folks lived, and a few more which was a grocery store and a jail and a saloon. Right behind the saloon was a good-sized cabin with a big sign onto it which said: *Jonathan Middleton, Mayor of Cougar Paw.*

They didn't seem to be nobody in sight, not even on the saloon porch, so I rode on to the corrals which served for a livery stable and wagon yard, and a man come out of the cabin nigh it, and took charge of Cap'n Kidd. He wanted to turn him in with a couple of mules which hadn't never been broke, but I knowed what Cap'n Kidd would do to them mules, so the feller give him a corral to hisself, and belly-ached just because Cap'n Kidd playfully bit the seat out of his britches.

He ca'med down when I paid for the britches. I ast him where I could find Bill Santry, and he said likely he was up to the store.

SO I WENT UP TO THE store, and it was about like all them stores you see in them kind of towns—groceries, and dry-goods, and grindstones, and harness and such-like stuff, and a wagon-tongue somebody had mended recent. They warn't but the one store in the town and it handled a little of everything. They was a sign onto it which said: *General Store; Jonathan Middleton, Prop.*

They was a bunch of fellers setting around on goods boxes and benches eating sody crackers and pickles out of a barrel, and they was a tolerable hard-looking gang. I said: "I'm lookin' for Bill Santry."

The biggest man in the store, which was setting on a bench, says: "You don't have to look no farther. I'm Bill Santry."

"Well," I says, "I'm Breckinridge Elkins, John Elkins' brother. You can give me what you promised him."

"Ha!" he says with a snort like a hungry catamount rising sudden. "They is nothin' which could give me more pleasure! Take it with my blessin'!" And so saying he picked up the wagon tongue and splintered it over my head.

It was so onexpected that I lost my footing and fell on my back, and Santry give a wolfish yell and jumped into my stummick with both feet, and the next thing I knowed nine or ten more fellers was jumping up and down on me with their boots.

Now I can take a joke as well as the next man, but it always did make me mad for a feller to twist a spur into my hair and try to tear the sculp off. Santry having did this, I throwed off them lunatics which was trying to tromp out my innards, and riz up amongst them with a outraged beller. I swept four or five of 'em into my arms and give 'em a grizzly-hug, and when I let go all they was able to do was fall on the floor and squawk about their busted ribs.

I then turned onto the others which was assaulting me with pistols and bowie knives and the butt ends of quirts and other villainous weppins, and when I laid into 'em you should of heard 'em howl. Santry was trying to dismember my ribs with a butcher knife he'd got out of the pork barrel, so I picked up the pickle barrel and busted it over his head. He went to the floor under a avalanche of splintered staves and pickles and brine, and then I got hold of a grindstone and really started getting destructive. A grindstone is a good comforting implement to have hold of in a melee, but kind of clumsy. For instance when I hove it at a feller which was trying to cock a sawed-off shotgun, it missed him entirely and knocked all the slats out of the counter and nigh squashed four or five men which was trying to shoot me from behind it. I settled the shotgun-feller's hash with a box of canned beef, and then I got hold of a double-bitted axe, and the embattled citizens of Cougar Paw quit the field with blood-curdling howls of fear—them which was able to quit and howl.

I stumbled over the thickly-strewn casualties to the door, taking a few casual swipes at the shelves as I went past, and knocking all the cans off of them. Just as I emerged into the street, with my axe lifted to chop down anybody which opposed me, a skinny looking human bobbed up in front of me and hollered: "Halt, in the name of the law!"

Paying no attention to the double-barreled shotgun he shoved in my face, I swung back my axe for a swipe, and accidentally hit the sign over the door and knocked it down on top of him. He let out a squall as he went down and let *bam!* with the shotgun right in my face so close it singed my eyebrows. I pulled the sign-board off of him so I could git a good belt at him with my axe, but he hollered: "I'm the sheriff! I demands that you surrenders to properly constupated authority!"

I then noticed that he had a star pinned onto one gallus, so I put down my axe and let him take my guns. I never resists a officer of the law—well, seldom ever, that is.

He p'inted his shotgun at me and says: "I fines you ten dollars for disturbin' the peace!"

About this time a lanky maverick with side-whiskers come prancing around the corner of the building, and he started throwing fits like a locoed steer.

"The scoundrel's rooint my store!" he howled. "He's got to pay me for the counters and winders he busted, and the shelves he knocked down, and the sign he rooint, and the pork-keg he busted over my clerk's head!"

"What you think he ought to pay, Mr. Middleton?" ast the sheriff.

"Five hundred dollars," said the mayor bloodthirstily.

"Five hundred hell!" I roared, stung to wrath. "This here whole dern town ain't wuth five hundred dollars. Anyway, I ain't got no money but fifty cents I owe to the feller that runs the wagon yard."

"Gimme the fifty cents," ordered the mayor. "I'll credit that onto yore bill."

"I'll credit my fist onto yore skull," I snarled, beginning to lose my temper, because the butcher knife Bill Santry had carved my ribs with had salt on the blade, and the salt got into the cuts and smarted. "I owes this fifty cents and I gives it to the man I owes it to."

"Throw him in jail!" raved Middleton. "We'll keep him there till we figures out a job of work for him to do to pay out his fine."

So the sheriff marched me down the street to the log cabin which they used for a jail, whilst Middleton went moaning around the rooins of his grocery store, paying no heed to the fellers which lay groaning on the floor. But I seen the rest of the citizens packing them out on stretchers to take 'em into the saloon to bring 'em to. The saloon had a sign; *Square Deal Saloon; Jonathan Middleton, Prop.* And I heard fellers cussing Middleton because he made 'em pay for the licker they poured on the victims' cut and bruises. But they cussed under their breath. Middleton seemed to pack a lot of power in that there town.

Well, I laid down on the jail-house bunk as well as I could, because they always build them bunks for ordinary-sized men about six foot tall, and I wondered what in hell Bill Santry had hit me with that wagon tongue for. It didn't seem to make no sense.

I laid there and waited for the sheriff to bring me my supper, but he didn't bring none, and purty soon I went to sleep and dreamed about Joan, with her store-bought shoes.

What woke me up was a awful racket in the direction of the saloon. I got up and looked out of the barred winder. Night had fell, but the cabins and the saloon was well lit up, but too far away for me to tell what was going on. But the noise was so familiar I thought for a minute I must be back on Bear Creek again, because men was yelling and cussing, and guns was banging, and a big voice roaring over the din. Once it sounded like somebody had got knocked through a door, and it made me right home-sick, it was so much like a dance on Bear Creek.

I pulled the bars out of the winder trying to see what was going on, but all I could see was what looked like men flying headfirst out of the saloon, and when they hit the ground and stopped rolling, they jumped up and run off in all directions, hollering like the Apaches was on their heels.

Purty soon I seen somebody running toward the jail as hard as he could leg it, and it was the sheriff. Most of his clothes was tore off, and he had blood on his face, and he was gasping and panting.

"We got a job for you, Elkins!" he panted. "A wild man from Texas just hit town, and is terrorizin' the citizens! If you'll pertect us, and layout this fiend from the prairies, we'll remit yore fine! Listen at that!"

From the noise I jedged the aforesaid wild man had splintered the panels out of the bar.

"What started him on his rampage?" I ast.

"Aw, somebody said they made better chili con carne in Santa Fe than they did in El Paso," says the sheriff. "So this maneyack starts cleanin' up the town—"

"Well, I don't blame him," I said. "That was a dirty lie and a low-down slander. My folks all come from Texas, and if you Cougar Paw coyotes thinks you can slander the State and git away with it—"

"We don't think nothin'!" wailed the sheriff, wringing his hands and jumping like a startled deer every time a crash resounded up the street. "We admits the Lone Star State is the cream of the West in all ways! Lissen, will you lick this homicidal lunatic for us? You got to, dern it. You got to work out yore fine, and—"

"Aw, all right," I said, kicking the door down before he could unlock it. "I'll do it. I cain't waste much time in this town. I got a engagement down the road tomorrer at sun-up."

The street was deserted, but heads was sticking out of every door and winder. The sheriff stayed on my heels till I was a few feet from the saloon, and then he whispered: "Go to it, and make it a good job! If anybody can lick that grizzly in there, it's you!" He then ducked out of sight behind the nearest cabin after handing me my gun-belt.

I stalked into the saloon and seen a gigantic figger standing at the bar and just fixing to pour hisself a dram out of a demijohn. He had the place to hisself, but it warn't near as much of a wreck as I'd expected.

As I come in he wheeled with a snarl, as quick as a cat, and flashing out a gun. I drawed one of mine just as quick, and for a second we stood there, glaring at each other over the barrels.

"Breckinridge Elkins!" says he. "My own flesh and blood kin!"

"Cousin Bearfield Buckner!" I says, shoving my gun back in its scabbard. "I didn't even know you was in Nevada."

"I GOT A RAMBLIN' FOOT," says he, holstering his shooting iron. "Put 'er there, Cousin Breckinridge!"

"By golly, I'm glad to see you!" I said, shaking with him. Then I recollected. "Hey!" I says. "I got to lick you."

"What you mean?" he demanded.

"Aw," I says, "I got arrested, and ain't got no money to pay my fine, and I got to work it out. And lickin' you was the job they gimme."

"I ain't got no use for law," he said grumpily. "Still and all, if I had any dough, I'd pay yore fine for you."

"A Elkins don't accept no charity," I said slightly nettled. "We works for what we gits. I pays my fine by lickin' the hell out of you, Cousin Bearfield."

At this he lost his temper; he was always hot-headed that way. His black brows come down and his lips curled up away from his teeth and he clenched his fists which was about the size of mallets.

"What kind of kinfolks air you?" he scowled. "I don't mind a friendly fight between relatives, but yore intentions is mercenary and unworthy of a true Elkins. You put me in mind of the fact that yore old man had to leave Texas account of a hoss gittin' its head tangled in a lariat he was totin' in his absent-minded way."

"That there is a cussed lie," I said with heat. "Pap left Texas because he wouldn't take the Yankee oath after the Civil War, and you know it. Anyway," I added bitingly, "nobody can ever say a Elkins ever stole a chicken and roasted it in a chaparral thicket."

He started violently and turned pale.

"What you hintin' at, you son of Baliol?" he hollered.

"Yore iniquities ain't no family secret," I assured him bitterly. "Aunt Atascosa writ Uncle Jeppard Grimes about you stealin' that there Wyandotte hen off of Old Man Westfall's roost."

"Shet up!" he bellered, jumping up and down in his wrath, and clutching his six-shooters convulsively. "I war just a yearlin' when I lifted that there fowl and et it, and I war plumb famished, because a posse had been chasin' me six days. They was after me account of Joe Richardson happenin' to be in my way when I was emptyin' my buffalo rifle. Blast yore soul, I have shot better men than you for talkin' about chickens around me."

"Nevertheless," I said, "the fact remains that yo're the only one of the clan which ever swiped a chicken. No Elkins never stole no hen."

"No," he sneered, "they prefers hosses."

Just then I noticed that a crowd had gathered timidly outside the doors and winders and was listening eagerly to this exchange of family scandals, so I said: "We've talked enough. The time for action has arriv. When I first seen you, Cousin Bearfield, the thought of committin' mayhem onto you was very distasteful. But after our recent conversation, I feels I can scramble yore homely features with a free and joyful spirit. Le's have a snort and then git down to business."

"Suits me," he agreed, hanging his gun belt on the bar. "Here's a jug with about a gallon of red licker into it."

So we each taken a medium-sized snort, which of course emptied the jug, and then I hitched my belt and says: "Which does you desire first, Cousin Bearfield—a busted laig or a fractured skull?"

"Wait a minute," he requested as I approached him. "What's, that on yore boot?"

I stooped over to see what it was, and he swung his laig and kicked me in the mouth as hard as he could, and imejitately busted into a guffaw of brutal mirth. Whilst he was thus employed I spit his boot out and butted him in the belly with a vi'lence which changed his haw-haw to a agonized grunt, and then we laid hands on each other and rolled back and forth acrost the floor, biting and gouging, and that was how the tables and chairs got busted. Mayor Middleton must of been watching through a winder because I heard him squall: "My Gawd, they're wreckin' my saloon! Sheriff, arrest 'em both."

And the sheriff hollered back: "I've took yore orders all I aim to, Jonathan Middleton! If you want to stop that double-cyclone git in there and do it yoreself!"

Presently we got tired scrambling around on the floor amongst the cuspidors, so we riz simultaneous and I splintered the roulette wheel with his carcass, and he hit me on the jaw so hard he knocked me clean through the bar and all the bottles fell off the shelves and showered around me, and the ceiling lamp come loose and spilled about a gallon of red hot ile down his neck.

Whilst he was employed with the ile I clumb up from among the debris of the bar and started my right fist in a swing from the floor, and after it traveled maybe nine feet it took Cousin Bearfield under the jaw, and he hit the oppersite wall so hard he knocked out a section and went clean through it, and that was when the roof fell in.

I started kicking and throwing the rooins off me, and then I was aware of Cousin Bearfield lifting logs and beams off of me, and in a minute I crawled out from under 'em.

"I could of got out all right," I said. "But just the same I'm much obleeged to you."

"Blood's thicker'n water," he grunted, and hit me under the jaw and knocked me about seventeen feet backwards toward the mayor's cabin. He then rushed forward and started kicking me in the head, but I riz up in spite of his efforts.

"Git away from that cabin!" screamed the mayor, but it was too late. I hit Cousin Bearfield between the eyes and he crashed into the mayor's rock chimney and knocked the whole base loose with his head, and the chimney collapsed and the rocks come tumbling down on him.

BUT BEING A TEXAS BUCKNER, Bearfield riz out of the rooins. He not only riz, but he had a rock in his hand about the size of a watermelon and he busted it over my head. This infuriated me, because I seen he had no intention of fighting fair, so I tore a log out of the wall of the mayor's cabin and belted him over the ear with it, and Cousin Bearfield bit the dust. He didn't git up that time.

Whilst I was trying to git my breath back and shaking the sweat out of my eyes, all the citizens of Cougar Paw come out of their hiding places and the sheriff yelled: "You done a good job, Elkins! Yo're a free man!"

"He is like hell!" screamed Mayor Middleton, doing a kind of war-dance, whilst weeping and cussing together. "Look at my cabin! I'm a rooint man! Sheriff, arrest that man!"

"Which 'un?" inquired the sheriff.

"The feller from Texas," said Middleton bitterly. "He's unconscious, and it won't be no trouble to drag him to jail. Run the other'n out of town. I don't never want to see him no more."

"Hey!" I said indignantly. "You cain't arrest Cousin Bearfield. I ain't goin' to stand for it."

"Will you resist a officer of the law?" ast the sheriff, sticking his gallus out on his thumb.

"You represents the law whilst you wear yore badge?" I inquired.

"As long as I got that badge on," boasts he, "I am the law!"

"Well," I said, spitting on my hands, "you ain't got it on now. You done lost it somewhere in the shuffle tonight, and you ain't nothin' but a common citizen like me! Git ready, for I'm comin' head-on and wide-open!"

I whooped me a whoop.

He glanced down in a stunned sort of way at his empty gallus, and then he give a scream and took out up the street with most of the crowd streaming out behind him.

"Stop, you cowards!" screamed Mayor Middleton. "Come back here and arrest these scoundrels—"

"Aw, shet up," I said disgustedly, and give him a kind of push and how was I to know it would dislocate his shoulder blade. It was just beginning to git light by now, but Cousin Bearfield wasn't showing no signs of consciousness, and I heard them Cougar Paw skunks yelling to each other back and forth from the cabins where they'd forted themselves, and from what they said I knowed they figgered on opening up on us with their Winchesters as soon as it got light enough to shoot good.

Just then I noticed a wagon standing down by the wagon-yard, so I picked up Cousin Bearfield and lugged him down there and threw him into the wagon. Far be it from a Elkins to leave a senseless relative to the mercy of a Cougar Paw mob. I went into the corral where them two wild mules was and started putting harness onto 'em, and it warn't no child's play. They hadn't never been worked before, and they fell onto me with a free and hearty enthusiasm. Onst they had me down stomping on me, and the citizens of Cougar Paw made a kind of half-hearted sally. But I unlimbered my .45s and threw a few slugs in their direction and they all hollered and run back into their cabins.

I finally had to stun them fool mules with a bat over the ear with my fist, and before they got their senses back, I had 'em harnessed to the wagon, and Cap'n Kidd and Cousin Bearfield's hoss tied to the rear end.

"He's stealin' our mules!" howled somebody, and taken a wild shot at me, as I headed down the street, standing up in the wagon and keeping them crazy critters straight by sheer strength on the lines.

"I ain't stealin' nothin'!" I roared as we thundered past the cabins where spurts of flame was already streaking out of the winders. "I'll send this here wagon and these mules back tomorrer!"

The citizens answered with blood-thirsty yells and a volley of lead, and with their benediction singing past my ears, I left Cougar Paw in a cloud of dust and profanity.

THEM MULES, AFTER A vain effort to stop and kick loose from the harness, laid their bellies to the ground and went stampeding down that crooking mountain road like scairt jackrabbits. We went around each curve on one wheel, and sometimes we'd hit a stump that would throw the whole wagon several foot into the air, and that must of been what brung Cousin Bearfield to hisself. He was laying sprawled in the bed, and finally we taken a bump that throwed him in a somersault clean to the other end of the wagon. He hit on his neck and riz up on his hands and knees and looked around dazedly at the trees and stumps which was flashing past, and bellered: "What the hell's happenin'? Where-at am I, anyway?"

"Yo're on yore way to Bear Creek, Cousin Bearfield!" I yelled, cracking my whip over them fool mules' backs. "Yippee ki-yi! This here is fun, ain't it, Cousin Bearfield?"

I was thinking of Joan waiting with her store-bought shoes for me down the road, and in spite of my cuts and bruises, I was rolling high and handsome.

"Slow up!" roared Cousin Bearfield, trying to stand up. But just then we went crashing down a steep bank, and the wagon tilted, throwing Cousin Bearfield to the other end of the wagon where he rammed his head with great force against the front-gate. "#$%&*?@¢!" says Cousin Bearfield. "Glug!" Because we had hit the creek bed going full speed and knocked all the water out of the channel, and about a hundred gallons splashed over into the wagon and nearly washed Cousin Bearfield out.

"If I ever git out of this alive," promised Cousin Bearfield, "I'll kill you if it's the last thing I do—"

But at that moment the mules stampeded up the bank on the other side and Cousin Bearfield was catapulted to the rear end of the wagon so hard he knocked out the end-gate with his head and nearly went out after it, only he just managed to grab hisself.

We went plunging along the road and the wagon hopped from stump to stump and sometimes it crashed through a thicket of bresh. Cap'n Kidd and the other hoss was thundering after us, and the mules was braying and I was whooping and Cousin Bearfield was cussing, and purty soon I looked back at him and hollered: "Hold on, Cousin Bearfield! I'm goin' to stop these critters. We're close to the place where my gal will be waitin' for me—"

"Look out, you blame fool!" screamed Cousin Bearfield, and then the mules left the road and went one on each side of a white oak tree, and the tongue splintered, and they run right out of the harness and kept high-tailing it, but the wagon piled up on that tree with a jolt that throwed me and Cousin Bearfield headfirst into a blackjack thicket.

Cousin Bearfield vowed and swore, when he got back home, that I picked this thicket special on account of the hornets' nest that was there, and drove into it plumb deliberate. Which same is a lie which I'll stuff down his gizzard next time I cut his sign. He claimed they was trained hornets which I educated not to sting me, but the fact was I had sense enough to lay there plumb quiet. Cousin Bearfield was fool enough to run.

Well, he knows by this time, I reckon, that the fastest man afoot can't noways match speed with a hornet. He taken out through the bresh and thickets, yelpin' and hollerin' and hoppin' most bodacious. He run in a circle, too, for in three minutes he come bellerin' back, gave one last hop and dove back into the thicket. By this time I figgered he'd wore the hornets out, so I came alive again.

I extricated myself first and locating Cousin Bearfield by his profanity, I laid hold onto his hind laig and pulled him out. He lost most of his clothes in the process, and his temper wasn't no better. He seemed to blame me for his misfortunes.

"Don't tech me," he said fiercely. "Leave me be. I'm as close to Bear Creek right now as I want to be. Whar's my hoss?"

The hosses had broke loose when the wagon piled up, but they hadn't gone far, because they was fighting with each other in the middle of the road. Bearfield's hoss was about as big and mean as Cap'n Kidd. We separated 'em and Bearfield clumb aboard without a word.

"Where you goin', Cousin Bearfield?" I ast.

"As far away from you as I can," he said bitterly. "I've saw all the Elkinses I can stand for awhile. Doubtless yore intentions is good, but a man better git chawed by lions than rescued by a Elkins!"

And with a few more observations which highly shocked me, and which I won't repeat, he rode off at full speed, looking very pecooliar, because his pants was about all that hadn't been tore off of him, and he had scratches and bruises all over him.

I WAS SORRY COUSIN Bearfield was so sensitive, but I didn't waste no time brooding over his ingratitude. The sun was up and I knowed Joan would be waiting for me where the path come down into the road from the mountain.

Sure enough, when I come to the mouth of the trail, there she was, but she didn't have on her store-bought shoes, and she looked flustered and scairt.

"Breckinridge!" she hollered, running up to me before I could say a word. "Somethin' terrible's happened! My brother was in Cougar Paw last night, and a big bully beat him up somethin' awful! Some men are bringin' him home on a stretcher! One of 'em rode ahead to tell me!"

"How come I didn't pass 'em on the road?" I said, and she said: "They walked and taken a short cut through the hills. There they come now."

I seen some men come into the road a few hundred yards away and come toward us, lugging somebody on a stretcher like she said.

"Come on!" she says, tugging at my sleeve. "Git down off yore hoss and come with me. I want him to tell you who done it, so you can whup the scoundrel!"

"I got a idee, I know who done it," I said, climbing down. "But I'll make sure." I figgered it was one of Cousin Bearfield's victims.

"Why, look!" said Joan. "How funny the men are actin' since you started toward 'em! They've sot down the litter and they're runnin' off into the woods! Bill!" she shrilled as we drawed nigh. "Bill, air you hurt bad?"

"A busted laig and some broke ribs," moaned the victim on the litter, which also had his head so bandaged I didn't recognize him. Then he sot up with a howl.

"What's that ruffian doin' with you?" he roared, and to my amazement I recognized Bill Santry.

"Why, he's a friend of our'n, Bill—" Joan begun, but he interrupted her loudly and profanely: "Friend, hell! He's John Elkins' brother, and furthermore he's the one which is responsible for the crippled and mutilated condition in which you now sees me!"

Joan said nothing. She turned and looked at me in a very pecooliar manner, and then dropped her eyes shyly to the ground.

"Now, Joan," I begun, when all at once I saw what she was looking for. One of the men had dropped a Winchester before he run off. Her first bullet knocked off my hat as I forked Cap'n Kidd, and her second, third and fourth missed me so close I felt their hot wind. Then Cap'n Kidd rounded a curve with his belly to the ground, and my busted romance was left far behind me. . . .

A couple of days later a mass of heartaches and bruises which might of been recognized as Breckinridge Elkins, the pride of Bear Creek, rode slowly down the trail that led to the settlements on the afore-said creek. And as I rode, it was my fortune to meet my brother John coming up the trail on foot.

"Where you been?" he greeted me hypocritically. "You look like you been rasslin' a pack of mountain lions."

I eased myself down from the saddle and said without heat: "John, just what was it that Bill Santry promised you?"

"Oh," says John with a laugh, "I skinned him in a hoss-trade before I left Cougar Paw, and he promised if he ever met me, he'd give me the lickin' of my life. I'm glad you don't hold no hard feelin's, Breck. It war just a joke, me sendin' you up there. You can take a joke, cain't you?"

"Sure," I said. "By the way, John, how's yore toe?"

"It's all right," says he.

"Lemme see," I insisted. "Set yore foot on that stump."

He done so and I give it a awful belt with the butt of my Winchester.

"That there is a receipt for yore joke," I grunted, as he danced around on one foot and wept and swore. And so saying, I mounted and rode on in gloomy grandeur. A Elkins always pays his debts.

THE APACHE MOUNTAIN WAR

SOME DAY, MAYBE, when I'm old and gray in the whiskers, I'll have sense
enough not to stop when I'm riding by Uncle Shadrach Polk's cabin, and Aunt
Tascosa Polk hollers at me. Take the last time, for instance. I ought to of spurred
Cap'n Kidd into a high run when she stuck her head out'n the winder and yelled:
"Breck*in*ridge! Oh, *Breck*inri*ddd*gggge!"

But I reckon pap's right when he says Nater gimme so much muscle she
didn't have no room left for brains. Anyway, I reined Cap'n Kidd around,
ignoring his playful efforts to bite the muscle out of my left thigh, and I rode up to
the stoop and taken off my coonskin-cap. I said: "Well, Aunt Tascosa, how air you
all?"

"You may well ast how air we," she said bitterly. "How should a pore weak
woman be farin' with a critter like Shadrach for a husband? It's a wonder I got a
roof over my head, or so much as a barr'l of b'ar meat put up for the winter. The
place is goin' to rack and rooin. Look at that there busted axe-handle, for a
instance. Is a pore weak female like me got to endure sech abuse?"

"You don't mean to tell me Uncle Shadrach's been beatin' you with that axe-handle?" I says, scandalized.

"No," says this pore weak female. "I busted it over his head a week ago, and he's refused to mend it. It's licker is been Shadrach's rooin. When he's sober he's a passable figger of a man, as men go. But swiggin' blue rooin is brung him to shame an' degradation."

"He looks fat and sassy," I says.

"Beauty ain't only skin-deep," she scowls. "Shadrach's like Dead Sea fruit—fair and fat-bellied to look on, but ready to dissolve in dust and whiskey fumes when prodded. Do you know whar he is right now?" And she glared at me so accusingly that Cap'n Kidd recoiled and turned pale.

"Naw," says I. "Whar?"

"He's over to the Apache Mountain settlement a-lappin' up licker," she snarled. "Just a-rootin' and a-wallerin' in sin and corn juice, riskin' his immortal soul and blowin' in the money he got off'n his coon hides. I had him locked in the corn crib, aimin' to plead with him and appeal to his better nater, but whilst I was out behind the corral cuttin' me a hickory club to do the appealin' with, he kicked the door loose and skun out. I know whar he's headin'—to Joel Garfield's stillhouse, which is a abomination in the sight of the Lord and oughta be burnt to the ground and the ashes skwenched with the blood of the wicked. But I cain't stand here listenin' to yore gab. I got hominy to make. What you mean wastin' my time like this for? I got a good mind to tell yore pap on you. You light a shuck for Apache Mountain and bring Shadrach home."

"But—" I said.

"Don't you give me no argyments, you imperdent scoundrel!" she hollered. "I should think you'd be glad to help a pore, weak female critter 'stead of wastin' yore time gamblin' and fightin', in such dens of iniquity as War Paint. I want you to fix some way so's to disgust Shadrach with drink for the rest of his nateral life, and if you don't you'll hear from me, you good-for-nothin'—"

"All right!" I yelled. "*All right!* Anything for a little peace! I'll git him and bring him home, and make a teetotaler outa him if I have to strangle the old son of a—"

"How dast you use sech langwidge in front of me?" she hollered. "Ain't you got no respect for a lady? I'll be #4%*¢@?-!'d if I know what the &%$@*¢ world's comin' to! Git outa here and don't show yore homely mug around here again onless you git Shadrach off of rum for good!"

WELL, IF UNCLE SHADRACH ever took a swig of rum in his life it was because they warn't no good red corn whiskey within reach, but I didn't try to argy with

Aunt Tascosa. I lit out down the trail feeling like I'd been tied up to a Apache stake with the whole tribe sticking red-hot Spanish daggers into my hide. Aunt Tascosa affects a man that way. I heard Cap'n Kidd heave a sigh of relief plumb up from his belly, too, as we crossed a ridge and her distant voice was drowned out by the soothing noises of a couple of bobcats fighting with a timber wolf. I thought what ca'm and happy lives them simple critters lived, without no Aunt Tascosa.

I rode on, forgetting my own troubles in feeling sorry for pore Uncle Shadrach. They warn't a mean bone in his carcass. He was just as good-natered and hearty a critter as you'd ever meet even in the Humbolts. But his main object in life seemed to be to stow away all the corn juice they is in the world.

As I rode along I racked my brain for a plan to break Uncle Shadrach of this here habit. I like a dram myself, but in moderation, never more'n a gallon or so at a time, unless it's a special occasion. I don't believe in a man making a hawg out of hisself, and anyway I was sick and tired running Uncle Shadrach down and fetching him home from his sprees.

I thought so much about it on my way to Apache Mountain that I got so sleepy I seen I was gitting into no state to ride Cap'n Kidd. He got to looking back at me now and then, and I knowed if he seen me dozing in the saddle he'd try his derndest to break my neck. I was passing Cousin Bill Gordon's barn about that time, so I thought I'd go in and take me a nap up in the hayloft, and maybe I'd dream about a way to make a water-drinker out of Uncle Shadrach or something.

I tied Cap'n Kidd and started into the barn, and what should I see but Bill's three youngest boys engaged in daubing paint on Uncle Jeppard Grimes' favorite jackass, Joshua.

"What air you all a-doin' to Joshua?" I demanded, and they jumped back and looked guilty. Joshua was a critter which Uncle Jeppard used for a pack-mule when he went prospecting. He got the urge maybe every three or four year, and between times Joshua just et and slept. He was the sleepin'est jackass I ever seen. He was snoozing now, whilst them young idjits was working on him.

I seen what they was at. Bill had loaned a feller some money which had a store down to War Paint, and the feller went broke, and give Bill a lot of stuff outa the store for pay. They was a lot of paint amongst it. Bill packed it home, though I dunno what he aimed to do with it, because all the houses in the Humbolts was log cabins which nobody ever painted, or if they did, they just white-washed 'em. But anyway, he had it all stored in his barn, and his boys was smearing it on Joshua.

He was the derndest sight you ever seen. They'd painted a big stripe down his spine, like a Spanish mustang, only this stripe was green instead of black, and more stripes curving over his ribs and down under his belly, red, white and blue, and they'd painted his ears green.

"What you all mean by sech doin's?" I ast. "Uncle Jeppard'll plumb skin you all alive. He sets a lot of store by that there jack."

"Aw, it's just funnin'," they said. "He won't know who done it."

"You go scrub that paint off," I ordered 'em. "Joshua'll lick it off and git pizened."

"It won't hurt him," they assured me. "He got in here yesterday and et three cans of paint and a bucket of whitewash. That's what give us the idee. He kin eat anything. Eatin'est jack you ever seen."

"Heh, heh, heh!" snickered one of 'em. "He looks like a drunkard's dream!"

Instantly a idee hit me.

"Gimme that jackass!" I exclaimed. "He's just what I need to kyore Uncle Shadrach Polk of drinkin' licker. One glimpse of that there jack in his present state and Uncle Shadrach'll think he's got the delerious trimmin's and git so scairt he'll swear off whiskey for life."

"If you aims to lead Joshua to Joel's stillhouse," they said, "you'll be all day gittin' there. You cain't hustle Joshua."

"I ain't goin to lead him," I said. "You all hitch a couple of mules to yore pa's spring wagon. I'll leave Cap'n Kidd here till I git back."

"We'll put him in the corral behind the barn," they says. "Them posts are set four foot deep in concrete and the fence is braced with railroad iron, so maybe it'll hold him till you git back, if you ain't gone too long."

WHEN THEY GOT THE mules hitched, I tied Joshua's laigs and laid him in the wagon bed, where he went to sleep, and I climbed onto the seat and lit out for Apache Mountain. I hadn't went far when I run over a rock and woke Joshua up and he started braying and kept it up till I stopped and give him a ear of corn to chew on. As I started off again I seen Dick Grimes' youngest gal peeping at me from the bresh, and when I called to her she run off. I hoped she hadn't heard Joshua braying. I knowed she couldn't see him, laying down in the wagon bed, but he had a very pecooliar bray and anybody in the Humbolts could recognize him by it. I hoped she didn't know I had Joshua, because she was the derndest tattletale in the Bear Creek country, and Uncle Jeppard is such a cross-grained old cuss you can't explain nothing to him. He was born with the notion that the whole world was plotting agen him.

It hadn't been much more'n good daylight when I rode past Uncle Shadrach's house, and I'd pushed Cap'n Kidd purty brisk from there; the mules made good time, so it warn't noon yet when I come to Apache Mountain. As I approached the settlement, which was a number of cabins strung up and down a breshy run, I swung wide of the wagon-road and took to the trails, because I didn't want nobody to see me with Joshua. It was kind of tough going, because the trails was mostly footpaths and not wide enough for the wagon, and I had to stop and pull up saplings every few yards. I was scairt the noise would wake up Joshua and he'd start braying again, but that jackass could sleep through a bombardment, long as he warn't being jolted personal.

I was purty close to the settlement when I had to git out of the wagon and go ahead and break down some bresh so the wheels wouldn't foul, and when I laid hold of it, a couple of figgers jumped up on the other side. One was Cousin Buckner Kirby's gal Kit, and t'other'n was young Harry Braxton from the other side of the mountain, and no kin to none of us.

"Oh!" says Kit, kind of breathless.

"What you all doin' out here?" I scowled, fixing Harry with a eye which made him shiver and fuss with his gun-belt. "Air yore intentions honorable, Braxton?"

"I dunno what business it is of yore'n," said Kit bitterly.

"I makes it mine," I assured her. "If this young buck cain't come sparkin' you at a respectable place and hour, why, I figgers—"

"Yore remarks is ignorant and insultin'," says Harry, sweating profusely, but game. "I aims to make this here young lady my wife, if it warn't for the toughest prospective father-in-law ever blighted young love's sweet dream with a number twelve boot in the seat of the pants."

"To put it in words of one syllable so's even you can understand, Breckin-ridge," says Kit, "Harry wants to marry me, but pap is too derned mean and stub-born to let us. He don't like the Braxtons account of one of 'em skun him in a hoss-swap thirty years ago."

"I don't love 'em myself," I grunted. "But go on."

"Well," she says, "after pap had kicked Harry out of the house five or six times, and dusted his britches with birdshot on another occasion, we kind of got the idee that he was prejudiced agen Harry. So we has to take this here method of seein' each other."

"Whyn't you all run off and git married anyway?" I ast.

Kit shivered. "We wouldn't dare try it. Pap might wake up and catch us, and he'd shoot Harry. I taken a big chance sneakin' out here today. Ma and the kids are all over visitin' a few days with Aunt Ouachita, but pap wouldn't let me go for fear I'd meet Harry over there. I snuck out here for a few minutes—pap thinks I'm gatherin' greens for dinner—but if I don't hustle back he'll come lookin' for me with a hickory gad."

"Aw, shucks," I said. "You all got to use yore brains like I do. You leave it to me. I'll git yore old man out of the way for the night, and give you a chance to skip."

"How'll you do that?" Kit ast skeptically.

"Never mind," I told her, not having the slightest idee how I was going to do it. "I'll 'tend to that. You git yore things ready, and you, Harry, you come along the road in a buckboard just about moonrise, and Kit'll be waitin' for you. You all can git hitched over to War Paint. Buckner won't do nothin' after yo're hitched."

"Will you, shore enough?" says Harry, brightening up.

"Shore I will," I assured him. "Vamoose now, and git that buckboard."

HE HUSTLED OFF, AND I said to Kit: "Git in the wagon and ride to the settlement with me. This time tomorrer you'll be a happy married woman shore enough."

"I hope so," she said sad-like. "But I'm bettin' somethin' will go wrong and pap'll catch us, and I'll eat my meals off the mantel-board for the next week."

"Trust me," I assured her, as I helped her in the wagon.

She didn't seem much surprised when she looked down in the bed and seen Joshua all tied up and painted and snoring his head off. Humbolt folks expects me to do onusual things.

"You needn't look like you thought I was crazy," I says irritably. "That critter is for Uncle Shadrach Polk."

"If Uncle Shadrach sees that thing," says she, "he'll think he's seein' worse'n snakes."

"That's what I aim for him to think," I says. "Who's he stayin' with?"

"Us," says she.

"Hum!" I says. "That there complicates things a little. Whar-at does he sleep?"

"Upstairs," she says.

"Well," I says, "he won't interfere with our elopement none. You git outa here and go on home, and don't let yore pap suspect nothin'."

"I'd be likely to, wouldn't I?" says she, and clumb down and pulled out.

I'd stopped in a thicket at the aidge of the settlement, and I could see the roof of Cousin Buckner's house from where I was. I could also hear Cousin Buckner bellering: "Kit! Kit! Whar air you? I know you ain't in the garden. If I have to come huntin' you, I 'low I'll—"

"Aw, keep yore britches on," I heard Kit call. "I'm a-comin'!"

I heard Cousin Buckner subside into grumblings and rumblings like a grizzly talking to hisself. I figgered he was out on the road which run past his house, but I couldn't see him and neither he couldn't see me, nor nobody could which might happen to be passing along the road. I onhitched the mules and tied 'em where they could graze and git water, and I h'isted Joshua outa the wagon, and taken the ropes offa his laigs and tied him to a tree, and fed him and the mules with some corn I'd brung from Cousin Bill Gordon's. Then I went through the bresh till I come to Joel Garfield's stillhouse, which was maybe half a mile from there, up the run. I didn't meet nobody.

Joel was by hisself in the stillhouse, for a wonder, but he was making up for lack of trade by his own personal attention to his stock.

"Ain't Uncle Shadrach Polk nowhere around?" I ast, and Joel lowered a jug of white corn long enough to answer me.

"Naw," he says, "he ain't right now. He's likely still sleepin' off the souse he was on last night. He didn't leave here till after midnight," says Joel, with another pull at the jug, "and he was takin' all sides of the road to onst. He'll pull in about the middle of the afternoon and start in to fillin' his hide so full he can just barely stagger back to Buckner Kirby's house by midnight or past. I bet he has a fine old time navigatin' them stairs Buckner's got into his house. I'd be afeared to tackle 'em myself, even when I was sober. A pole ladder is all I want to git into a loft with, but Buckner always did have high-falutin' idees. Lately he's been argyin' with Uncle Shadrach to cut down on his drinkin'—specially when he's full hisself."

Speakin' of Cousin Buckner," I says, "has he been around for his regular dram yet?"

"Not yet," says Joel. "He'll be in right after dinner, as usual."

"He wouldn't if he knowed what I knowed," I opined, because I'd thought up a way to git Cousin Buckner out of the way that night. "He'd be headin' for Wolf Canyon fast as he could spraddle. I just met Harry Braxton with a pack-mule headin' for there."

"You don't mean somebody's made a strike in Wolf Canyon?" says Joel, pricking up his ears.

"You never heard nothin' like it," I assured him. "Alder Gulch warn't nothin' to this."

"Hum!" says Joel, absent-mindedly pouring hisself a quart-size tin cup full of corn juice.

"I'm a Injun if it ain't!" I says, and dranken me a dram and went back to lay in the bresh and watch the Kirby house. I was well pleased with myself, because I knowed what a wolf Cousin Buckner was after gold. If anything could draw him away from home and his daughter, it would be news of a big strike. I was willing to bet my six-shooters against a prickly pear that as soon as Joel told him the news, he'd light out for Wolf Canyon. More especially as he'd think Harry Braxton was going there, too, and no chance of him sneaking off with Kit whilst the old man was gone.

*　　　*　　　*

AFTER A WHILE I SEEN Cousin Buckner leave the house and go down the road towards the stillhouse, and purty soon Uncle Shadrach emerged and headed the same way. Purty well satisfied with myself, I went back to where I left Cousin Bill's wagon, and fried me five or six pounds of venison I'd brung along for provisions and et it, and drunk at the creek, and then laid down and slept for a few hours.

It was right at sundown when I woke up. I went on foot through the bresh till I come out behind Buckner's cow-pen and seen Kit milking. I ast her if anybody was in the house.

"Nobody but me," she said. "And I'm out here. I ain't seen neither pap nor Uncle Shadrach since they left right after dinner. Can it be yore scheme is actually workin' out?"

"Certainly," I says. "Uncle Shadrach'll be swillin' at Joel's stillhouse till past midnight, and yore pap is ondoubtedly on his way towards Wolf Canyon. You git through with yore chores, and git ready to skip. Don't have no light in yore room, though. It's just likely yore pap told off one of his relatives to lay in the bresh and watch the house—him bein' of a suspicious nater. We don't want to have no bloodshed. When I hear Harry's buckboard I'll come for you. And if you hear any pecooliar noises before he gits here, don't think nothin' of it. It'll just be me luggin' Joshua upstairs."

"That critter'll bray fit to wake the dead," says she.

"He won't, neither," I said. "He'll go to sleep and keep his mouth shet. Uncle Shadrach won't suspect nothin' till he lights him a candle to go to bed by. Or if he's too drunk to light a candle, and just falls down on the bed in the dark, he'll wake up durin' the night some time to git him a drink of water. He's bound to see Joshua some time between midnight and mornin'. All I hope is the shock won't prove fatal. You go git ready to skip now."

I went back to the wagon and cooked me some more venison, also about a dozen aigs Kit had give me along with some corn pone and a gallon of buttermilk. I managed to make a light snack out of them morsels, and then, as soon as it was good and dark, I hitched up the mules and loaded Joshua into the wagon and went slow and easy down the road. I stopped behind the corral and tied the mules.

The house was dark and still. I toted Joshua into the house and carried him upstairs. I heard Kit moving around in her room, but they warn't nobody else in the house.

COUSIN BUCKNER HAD regular stairs in his house like what they have in big towns like War Paint and the like. Most folks in the Bear Creek country just has a ladder going up through a trap-door, and some said they would be a jedgment onto Buckner account of him indulging in such vain and sinful luxury, but I got to admit that packing a jackass up a flight of stairs was a lot easier than what it would have been to lug him up a ladder.

Joshua didn't bray nor kick none. He didn't care what was happening to him so long as he didn't have to do no work personal. I onfastened his laigs and tied a rope around his neck and t'other end to the foot of Uncle Shadrach's bunk, and give him a hat I found on a pag to chaw on till he went to sleep, which I knowed he'd do pronto.

I then went downstairs and heard Kit fussing around in her room, but it warn't time for Harry, so I went back out behind the corral and sot down and leaned my back agen the fence, and I reckon I must of gone to sleep. Just associating with Joshua give a man the habit. First thing I knowed I heard a buckboard rumbling over a bridge up the draw, and knowed it was Harry coming in fear and trembling to claim his bride. The moon warn't up yet but they was a glow above the trees on the eastern ridges.

I jumped up and ran quick and easy to Kit's winder—I can move light as a cougar in spite of my size—and I said: "Kit, air you ready?"

"I'm ready!" she whispered, all of a tremble. "Don't talk so loud!"

"They ain't nothin' to be scairt of," I soothed her, but lowered my voice just to humor her. "Yore pap is in Wolf Canyon by this time. Ain't nobody in the house but us. I been watchin' out by the corral."

Kit sniffed.

"Warn't that you I heard come into the house while ago?" she ast.

"You been dreamin'," I said. "Come on! That's Harry's buckboard comin' up the road."

"Lemme get just a few more things together!" she whispered, fumbling around in the dark. That's just like a woman. No matter how much time they has aforehand, they always has something to do at the last minute.

I waited by the winder and Harry druv on past the house a few rods and tied the hoss and come back, walking light and soft, and plenty pale in the starlight.

"Go on out the front door and meet him," I told her. "No, wait!"

Because all to onst Harry had ducked back out of the road, and he jumped over the fence and come to the winder where I was. He was shaking like a leaf.

"Somebody comin' up the road afoot!" he says.

"It's pap!" gasped Kit. Her and Harry was shore scairt of the old man. They hadn't said a word above a whisper you could never of heard three yards away, and I was kinda suiting my voice to their'n.

"Aw, it cain't be!" I said. "He's in Wolf Canyon. That's Uncle Shadrach comin' home to sleep off his drunk, but he's back a lot earlier'n what I figgered he would be. He ain't important, but we don't want no delay. Here, Kit, gimme that bag. Now lemme lift you outa the winder. So! Now you all skin out. I'm goin' to climb this here tree whar I can see the fun. Git!"

They crope out the side-gate of the yard just as Uncle Shadrach come in at the front gate, and he never seen 'em because the house was between 'em. They went so soft and easy I thought if Cousin Buckner had been in the house he wouldn't of woke up. They was hustling down the road towards the buckboard as Uncle Shadrach was coming up on the porch and going into the hall. I could hear him climbing the stair. I could of seen him if they'd been a light in the house, because I could look into a winder in his room and one in the downstairs hall, too, from the tree where I was setting.

He got into his room about the time the young folks reached their buck-board, and I seen a light flare up as he struck a match. They warn't no hall upstairs. The stairs run right up to the door of his room. He stood in the doorway and lit a candle on a shelf by the door. I could see Joshua standing by the bunk with his head down, asleep, and I reckon the light must of woke him up, because he throwed up his head and give a loud and ringing bray. Uncle Shadrach turned and seen Joshua and he let out a shriek and fell backwards downstairs.

THE CANDLE LIGHT STREAMED down into the hall, and I got the shock of my life. Because as Uncle Shadrach went pitching down them steps, yelling bloody murder, they sounded a bull's roar below, and out of the room at the foot of the stair come prancing a huge figger waving a shotgun in one hand and pulling on his britches with the other'n. It was Cousin Buckner which I thought was safe in Wolf Canyon! That'd been him which Kit heard come in and go to bed awhile before!

"What's goin' on here?" he roared. "What you doin', Shadrach?"

"Git outa my way!" screamed Uncle Shadrach. "I just seen the devil in the form of a zebray jackass! Lemme outa here!"

He busted out of the house, and jumped the fence and went up the road like a quarter-hoss, and Cousin Buckner run out behind him. The moon was just comin' up, and Kit and Harry was just starting down the road. When she seen her old man irrupt from the house, Kit screeched like a scairt catamount, and Buckner heard her. He whirled and seen the buckboard rattling down the road and he knowed what was happening. He give a beller and let *bam* at 'em with his shotgun, but it was too long a range.

"Whar's my hoss?" he roared, and started for the corral. I knowed if he got astraddle of that derned long-laigged bay gelding of his'n, he'd ride them pore infants down before they'd went ten miles. I jumped down out of the tree and yelled: "Hey, there, Cousin Buckner! Hey, Buck—"

He whirled and shot the tail offa my coonskin cap before he seen who it was.

"What you mean jumpin' down on me like that?" he roared. "What you doin' up that tree? Whar you come from?"

"Never-mind that," I said. "You want to catch Harry Braxton before he gits away with yore gal, don't you? Don't stop to saddle a hoss. I got a light wagon hitched up behind the corral. We can run 'em down easy in that."

"Let's go!" he roared, and in no time at all we was off, him standing up in the bed and cussing and waving his shotgun.

"I'll have his sculp!" he roared. "I'll pickle his heart and feed it to my houn' dawgs! Cain't you go no faster?"

Them dern mules was a lot faster than I'd thought. I didn't dare hold 'em back for fear Buckner would git suspicious, and the first thing I knowed we was overhauling the buckboard foot by foot. Harry's critters warn't much account, and Cousin Bill Gordon's mules was laying their bellies to the ground.

I dunno what Kit thought when she looked back and seen us tearing after 'em, but Harry must of thought I was betraying 'em, otherwise he wouldn't of opened up on me with his six-shooter. But all he done was to knock some splinters out of the wagon and nick my shoulder. The old man would of returned the fire with his shotgun but he was scairt he might hit Kit, and both vehicles was bounding and bouncing along too fast and furious for careful aiming.

All to onst we come to a place where the road forked, and Kit and Harry taken the right-hand turn. I taken the left.

"Are you crazy, you blame fool?" roared Cousin Buckner. "Turn back and take the other road!"

"I cain't!" I responded. "These mules is runnin' away!"

"Yo're a liar!" howled Cousin Buckner. "Quit pourin' leather into them mules, you blasted #$%&@¢*, and turn back! Turn back, cuss you!" With that he started hammering me in the head with the stock of his shotgun.

WE WAS THUNDERING along a road which run along the rim of a sloping bluff, and when Buckner's shotgun went off accidentally the mules really did git scairt and started running away, just about the time I reached back to take the shotgun away from Cousin Buckner. Being beat in the head with the butt was getting awful monotonous, because he'd been doing nothing else for the past half mile.

I yanked the gun out of his hand and just then the left hind wheel hit a stump and the hind end of the wagon went straight up in the air and the pole splintered. The mules run right out of the harness and me and the wagon and Cousin Buckner went over the bluff and down the slope in a whirling tangle of wheels and laigs and heads and profanity.

We brung up against a tree at the bottom, and I throwed the rooins off of me and riz, swearing fervently when I seen how much money I'd have to pay Cousin Bill Gordon for his wagon. But Cousin Buckner give me no time for meditation. He'd ontangled hisself from a hind wheel and was doing a war-dance in the moonlight and frothing at the mouth.

"You done that on purpose!" he raged. "You never aimed to ketch them wretches! You taken the wrong road on purpose! You turned us over on purpose! Now I'll never ketch the scoundrel which run away with my datter—the pore, dumb, trustin' #$%&f!@* innercent!"

"Be ca'm, Cousin Buckner," I advised. "He'll make her a good husband. They're well onto their way to War Paint and a happy married life. Best thing you can do is forgive 'em and give 'em yore blessin'."

"Well," he snarled, "you ain't neither my datter nor my son-in-law. Here's my blessin' to you!"

It was a pore return for all the trouble I'd taken for him to push me into a cactus bed and hit me with a rock the size of a watermelon. However, I taken into consideration that he was overwrought and not hisself, so I ignored his incivility and made no retort whatever, outside of splintering a wagon spoke over his head.

I then clumb the bluff, making no reply to his impassioned and profane comments, and looked around for the mules. They hadn't run far. I seen 'em grazing down the road, and I started after 'em, when I heard horses galloping back up the road toward the settlement, and around a turn in the road come Uncle Jeppard Grimes with his whiskers streaming in the moonlight, and nine or ten of his boys riding hard behind him.

"Thar he is!" he howled, impulsively discharging his six-shooter at me. "Thar's the fiend in human form! Thar's the kidnaper of helpless jassacks! Boys, do yore duty!"

They pulled up around me and started piling off their horses with blood in their eyes and weppins in their hands.

"Hold on!" I says. "If it's Joshua you fools are after—"

"He admits the crime!" howled Uncle Jeppard. "Is it Joshua, says you! You know dern well it is! We been combin' the hills for you, ever since my gran'datter brought me the news! What you done with him, you scoundrel?"

"Aw," I said, "he's all right. I was just goin' to—"

"He evades the question!" screamed Uncle Jeppard. "Git him, boys!"

"I TELL YOU HE'S ALL right!" I roared, but they give me no chance to explain. Them Grimeses is all alike; you cain't tell 'em nothing. You got to knock it into their fool heads. They descended on me with fence rails and rocks and wagon spokes and loaded quirts and gun stocks in a way which would of tried the patience of a saint. I always try to be as patient with my erring relatives as I can be. I merely taken their weppins away from 'em and kind of pushed 'em back away from me, and if they'd looked where they fell Jim and Joe and Erath wouldn't of fell down that bluff and broke their arms and laigs and Bill wouldn't of fractured his skull agen that tree.

I handled 'em easy as babies, and kept my temper in spite of Uncle Jeppard dancing around on his hoss and yelling: "Lay into him, boys! Don't be scairt of the big grizzly! He cain't hurt us!" and shooting at me every time he thought he could shoot without hitting one of his own offspring. He did puncture two or three of 'em, and then blamed me for it, the old jackass.

Nobody could of acted with more restraint than I did when Dick Grimes broke the blade of his bowie knife off on my hip bone, and the seven fractured ribs I give his brother Jacob was a mild retaliation for chawing my ear like he done. But it was a ill-advised impulse which prompted Esau Grimes to stab me in the seat of the britches with a pitchfork. There ain't nothing which sours the milk of human kindness in a man's veins any more'n getting pitchforked by a raging relative behind his back.

I give a beller which shook the acorns out of the oaks all up and down the run, and whirled on Esau so quick it jerked the pitchfork out of his hands and left it sticking in my hide. I retched back and pulled it out and wrapped the handle around Esau's neck, and then I taken him by the ankles and started remodeling the landscape with him. I mowed down a sapling thicket with him, and leveled a cactus bed with him, and swept the road with him, and when his brothers tried to rescue him, I beat 'em over the head with him till they was too groggy to do anything but run in circles.

Uncle Jeppard come spurring at me, trying to knock me down with his hoss and trample me, and Esau was so limp by this time he warn't much good for a club no more, so I whirled him around my head a few times and throwed him at Uncle Jeppard. Him and Uncle Jeppard and the hoss all went down in a heap together, and from the way Uncle Jeppard hollered you'd of thought somebody was trying to injure him. It was plumb disgusting.

Five or six of his boys recovered enough to surge onto me then, and I knocked 'em all down on top of him and Esau and the hoss, and the hoss was trying to git up, and kicking around right and left, and his hoofs was going *bam, bam, bam* on human heads, and Uncle Jeppard was hollering so loud I got to thinking maybe he was hurt or something. So I retched down in the heap and got him by the whiskers and pulled him out from under the hoss and four or five of his fool boys.

"Air you hurt, Uncle Jeppard?" I inquired.

"#$%&¢@*!" responded Uncle Jeppard, rewarding my solicitude by trying to stab me with his bowie knife. This ingratitude irritated me, and I tossed him from me fretfully, and as he was pulling hisself outa the prickley pear bed where he landed, he suddenly give a louder scream than ever. Something come ambling up the road and I seen it was that fool jackass Joshua, which had evidently et his rope and left the house looking for more grub. He looked like a four-laigged nightmare in the moonlight, but all Uncle Jeppard noticed was the red paint on him.

"Halp! Murder!" howled Uncle Jeppard. "They've wounded him mortally! He's bleedin' to death! Git a tourniquet, quick!"

With that they all deserted the fray, them which was able to hobble, and run to grab Joshua and stanch his bleeding. But when he seen all them Grimeses coming for him, Joshua got scairt and took out through the bresh. They all pelted after him, and the last thing I heard as they passed out of hearing was Uncle Jeppard wailing: "Joshua! Stop, dern it! This here's yore friends! Pull up, dang you! We wants to help you, you cussed fool!"

I turned to see what I could do for the casualties which lay groaning in the road and at the foot of the bluff, but they said unanamous they didn't want no help from a enemy—which they meant me. They one and all promised to pickle my heart and eat it as soon as they was able to git about on crutches, so I abandoned my efforts and headed for the settlement.

THE FIGHTING HAD SCAIRT the mules up the road a ways, but I catched 'em and made a hackamore outa one of my galluses, and rode one and led t'other'n, and lit out straight through the bresh for Bear Creek. I'd had a belly-full of Apache Mountain. But I swung past Joel's stillhouse to find out how come Cousin Buckner didn't go to Wolf Canyon. When I got there the stillhouse was dark and the door was shet, and they was a note on the door. I could read a little by then, and I spelt it out. It said:

> Gone to Wolf Canyon.
> Joel Garfield.

That selfish polecat hadn't told Cousin Buckner nor nobody about the strike. He'd got hisself a pack-mule and lit out for Wolf Canyon hisself. A hell of a relative he was, maybe doing pore Cousin Buckner outa a fortune, for all he knowed.

A mile from the settlement I met Jack Gordon coming from a dance on t'other side of the mountain, and he said he seen Uncle Shadrach Polk fogging down the trail on a mule he was riding bare-back without no bridle, so I thought well, anyway my scheme for scairing him out of a taste for licker worked. Jack said Uncle Shadrach looked like he'd saw a herd of ha'nts.

It was about daylight when I stopped at Bill Gordon's ranch to leave him his mules. I paid him for his wagon and also for the damage Cap'n Kidd had did to his corral. Bill had to build a new one, and Cap'n Kidd had also run his prize stallion offa the ranch, an chawed the ears off of a longhorn bull, and busted into the barn and gobbled up about ten dollars worth of oats. When I lit out for Bear Creek again I warn't feeling in no benevolent mood, but, thinks I, it's worth it if it's made a water-swigger outa Uncle Shadrach.

It was well along toward noon when I pulled up at the door and called for Aunt Tascosa. Jedge my scandalized amazement when I was greeted by a deluge of b'iling water from the winder and Aunt Tascosa stuck her head out and says: "You buzzard in the form of a human bein'! How you got the brass to come bulgin' around here? If I warn't a lady I'd tell you just what I thought of you, you $#*&¢?@! Git, before I opens up on you with this here shotgun!"

"Why, Aunt Tascosa, what you talkin' about?" I ast, combing the hot water outa my hair with my fingers.

"You got the nerve to ast!" she sneered. "Didn't you promise me you'd kyore Shadrach of drinkin' rum? Didn't you, hey? Well, come in here and look at him! He arriv home about daylight on one of Buckner Kirby's mules and it about ready to drop, and he's been rasslin' every since with a jug he had hid. I cain't git no sense out'n him."

I went in and Uncle Shadrach was setting by the back door and he had hold of that there jug like a drownding man clutching a straw-stack.

"I'm surprised at you, Uncle Shadrach," I said. "What in the—"

"Shet the door, Breckinridge," he says. "They is more devils onto the earth than is dreamed of in our philosophy. I've had a narrer escape, Breckinridge! I let myself be beguiled by the argyments of Buckner Kirby, a son of Baliol which is without understandin'. He's been rasslin' with me to give up licker. Well, yesterday I got so tired of his argyments I said I'd try it a while, just to have some peace. I never taken a drink all day yesterday, and Breckinridge, I give you my word when I started to go to bed last night I seen a red, white and blue jackass with green ears standin' at the foot of my bunk, just as plain as I sees you now! It war the water that done it, Breckinridge," he says, curling his fist lovingly around the handle of the jug. "Water's a snare and a delusion. I drunk water all day yesterday, and look what it done to me! I don't never want to see no water no more, again."

"Well," I says, losing all patience, "you're a-goin' to, by golly, if I can heave you from here to that hoss-trough in the backyard."

I done it, and that's how come the rumor got started that I tried to drown Uncle Shadrach Polk in a hoss-trough because he refused to swear off licker. Aunt Tascosa was responsible for that there slander, which was a pore way to repay me for all I'd did for her. But people ain't got no gratitude.

PILGRIMS TO THE PECOS

THAT THERE WAGON rolled up the trail and stopped in front of our cabin one morning jest after sun-up. We all come out to see who it was, because strangers ain't common on Bear Creek—and not very often welcome, neither. They was a long, hungry-looking old coot driving, and four or five growed boys sticking their heads out.

"Good mornin', folks," said the old coot, taking off his hat. "My name is Joshua Richardson. I'm headin' a wagon-train of immigrants which is lookin' for a place to settle. The rest of 'em's camped three miles back down the trail. Everybody we met in these here Humbolt Mountings told us we'd hev to see Mister Roaring Bill Elkins about settlin' here-abouts. Be you him?"

"I'm Bill Elkins," says pap suspiciously.

"Well, Mister Elkins," says Old Man Richardson, wagging his chin-whiskers, "we'd admire it powerful if you folks would let us people settle somewheres about."

"Hmmmm!" says pap, pulling his beard. "Whar you all from?"

"Kansas," says Old Man Richardson.

"Ouachita," says pap, "git my shotgun."

"Don't you do no sech thing, Ouachie," says maw. "Don't be stubborn, Willyum. The war's been over for years."

"That's what I say," hastily spoke up Old Man Richardson. "Let bygones be bygones, I says!"

"What," says pap ominously, "is yore honest opinion of General Sterlin' Price?"

"One of nature's noblemen!" declares Old Man Richardson earnestly.

"Hmmmmm!" says pap. "You seem to have considerable tact and hoss-sense for a Red-laig. But they hain't no more room on Bear Creek fer no more settlers, even if they was Democrats. They's nine er ten families now within a rech of a hunnert square miles, and I don't believe in over-crowdin' a country."

"But we're plumb tuckered out!" wailed Old Man Richardson. "And nowheres to go! We hev been driv from pillar to post, by settlers which got here ahead of us and grabbed all the best land. They claims it whether they got any legal rights or not."

"Legal rights be damned," snorted pap. "Shotgun rights is what goes in this country. But I know jest the place fer you. It's ten er fifteen days' travel from here, in Arizony. It's called Bowie Knife Canyon, and hit's jest right fer farmin' people, which I jedge you all be."

"We be," says Old Man Richardson. "But how we goin' to git there?"

"My son Breckinridge will be plumb delighted to guide you there," says pap. "Won't you, Breckinridge?"

"No, I won't," I said. "Why the tarnation have *I* got to be picked on to ride herd on a passle of tenderfooted mavericks—"

"He'll git you there safe," says pap, ignoring my remarks. "He dotes on lendin' folks a helpin' hand, don't you, Breckinridge?"

Seeing the futility of argyment, I merely snarled and went to saddle Cap'n Kidd. I noticed Old Man Richardson and his boys looking at me in a very pecooliar manner all the time, and when I come out on Cap'n Kidd, him snorting and bucking and kicking the rails out of the corral like he always does, they turnt kind of pale and Old Man Richardson said: "I wouldn't want to impose on yore son, Mister Elkins. After all, we wasn't intendin' to go to that there canyon, in the first place—"

"I'm guidin' you to Bowie Knife Canyon!" I roared. "Maybe you warn't goin' there before I saddled my hoss, but you air now! C'm'on."

I then cut loose under the mules' feet with my .45s to kind of put some ginger in the critters, and they brayed and sot off down the trail jest hitting the high places with Old Man Richardson hanging onto the lines and bouncing all over the seat and his sons rolling in the wagon-bed.

WE COME INTO CAMP full tilt, and some of the men grabbed their guns and the women hollered and jerked up their kids, and one feller was so excited he fell into a big pot of beans which was simmering over a fire and squalled out that the Injuns was trying to burn him alive.

Old Man Richardson had his feet braced again the front-gate, pulling back on the lines as hard as he could and yelling bloody murder, but the mules had the bits betwixt their teeth. So I rode to their heads and grabbed 'em by the bridles and throwed 'em back onto their haunches, and Old Man Richardson ought to of knew the stop would be sudden. T'warn't my fault he done a dive off of the seat and hit on the wagon-tongue on his head. And it warn't my fault neither that one of the mules kicked him and t'other'n bit him before I could ontangle him from amongst them. Mules is mean critters howsoever you take 'em.

Everybody hollered amazing, and he riz up and mopped the blood offa his face and waved his arms and hollered: "Ca'm down, everybody! This hain't nawthin' to git excited about. This gent is Mister Breckinridge Elkins, which has kindly agreed to guide us to a land of milk and honey down in Arizony."

They received the news without enthusiasm. They was about fifty of 'em, mostly women, chillern, and half-grown young 'uns. They warn't more'n a dozen fit fighting men in the train. They all looked like they'd been on the trail a long time. And they was all some kin to Old Man Richardson—sons and daughters, and grandchillern, and nieces and nephews, and their husbands and wives, and sech like. They was one real purty gal, the old man's youngest daughter Betty, who warn't yet married.

They'd jest et breakfast and was hitched up when we arrove, so we pulled out without no more delay. I rode along of Old Man Richardson's wagon, which went ahead with the others strung out behind, and he says to me: "If this here Bowie Knife Canyon is sech a remarkable place, why ain't it already been settled?"

"Aw, they was a settlement there," I said, "but the Apaches kilt some, and Mexicans bandits kilt some, and about three years ago the survivors got to fightin' amongst theirselves and jest kind of kilt each other off."

He yanked his beard nervously and said: "I dunno! I dunno! Maybe we had ought to hunt a more peaceful spot than that there sounds like."

"You won't find no peaceful spots west of the Pecos," I assured him. "Say no more about it. I've made up our minds that Bowie Knife Canyon is the place for you all, and we're goin' there!"

"I wouldn't think of argyin' the p'int," he assured me hastily. "What towns does we pass on our way."

"Jest one," I said. "War Smoke, right on the Arizona line. Tell yore folks to keep out of it. It's a hangout for every kind of a outlaw. I jedge yore boys ain't handy enough with weppins to mix in sech company."

"We don't want no trouble," says he. "I'll tell 'em."

SO WE ROLLED ALONG, and the journey was purty uneventful except for the usual mishaps which generally happens to tenderfeet. But we progressed, until we was within striking distance of the Arizona border. And there we hit a snag. The rear wagon bogged in a creek we had to cross a few miles north of the line. They'd been a head rise, and the wagons churned the mud so the last one stuck fast. It was getting on toward sun-down, and I told the others to go on and make camp a mile west of War Smoke, and me and the folks in the wagon would foller when we got it out.

But that warn't easy. It was mired clean to the hubs, and the mules was up to their bellies. We pried and heaved and hauled, and night was coming on, and finally I said: "If I could git them cussed mules out of my way, I might accomplish somethin'."

So we unhitched 'em from the wagon, but they was stuck too, and I had to wade out beside 'em and lift 'em out of the mud one by one and tote 'em to the bank. A mule is a helpless critter. But then, with them out of the way, I laid hold of the tongue and hauled the wagon out of the creek in short order. Them Kansas people sure did look surprized, I dunno why.

Time we'd scraped the mud offa the wagon and us, and hitched up the mules again, it was night, and so it was long after dark when we come up to the camp the rest of the train had made in the place I told 'em. Old Man Richardson come up to me looking worried, and he says: "Mister Elkins, some of the boys went into that there town in spite of what I told 'em."

"Don't worry," I says. "I'll go git 'em."

I clumb on Cap'n Kidd without stopping to eat supper, and rode over to War Smoke, and tied my hoss outside the only saloon they was there. It was a small town, and awful hard looking. As I went into the saloon I seen the four Richardson boys, and they was surrounded by a gang of cut-throats and outlaws. They was a Mexican there, too, a tall, slim cuss, with a thin black mustash, and gilt braid onto his jacket.

"So you theenk you settle in Bowie Knife Canyon, eh?" he says, and one of the boys said: "Well, that's what we was aimin' to do."

"I theenk not," he said, grinning like a cougar, and I seen his hands steal to the ivory-handled guns at his hips. "You never heard of Se?or Gonzales Zamora? No? Well, he is a beeg *hombre* in thees country, and he has use for thees canyon in hees business."

"Start the fireworks whenever yo're ready, Gomez," muttered a white desperado. "We're backin' yore play."

The Richardson boys didn't know what the deal was about, but they seen they was up agen real trouble, and they turnt pale and looked around like trapped critters, seeing nothing but hostile faces and hands gripping guns.

"Who tell you you could settle thees canyon?" ast Gomez. "Who breeng you here? Somebody from Kansas? Yes? No?"

"No," I said, shouldering my way through the crowd. "My folks come from Texas. My granddaddy was at San Jacinto. You remember that?"

His hands fell away from his guns and his brown hide turnt ashy. The rest of them renegades give back, muttering: "Look out, boys! It's Breckinridge Elkins!"

They all suddenly found they had business at the bar, or playing cards, or something, and Gomez found hisself standing alone. He licked his lips and looked sick, but he tried to keep up his bluff.

"You maybe no like what I say about Se?or Zamora?" says he. "But ees truth. If I tell him gringoes come to Bowie Knife Canyon, he get very mad!"

"Well, suppose you go tell him now," I said, and so as to give him a good start, I picked him up and throwed him through the nearest winder.

He picked hisself up and staggered away, streaming blood and Mex profanity, and them in the saloon maintained a kind of pallid silence. I hitched my guns forard, and said to the escaped convict which was tending bar, I says: "You don't want me to pay for that winder, do you?"

"Oh, no!" says he, polishing away with his rag at a spittoon he must of thought was a beer mug. "Oh, no, no, no, no! We needed that winder busted fer the ventilation!"

"Then everybody's satisfied," I suggested, and all the hoss-thieves and stage-coach bandits in the saloon give me a hearty agreement.

"That's fine," I says. "Peace is what I aim to have, if I have to lick every — in the joint to git it. You boys git back to the camp."

They was glad to do so, but I lingered at the bar, and bought a drink for a train-robber I'd knowed at Chawed Ear onst, and I said: "Jest who is this cussed Zamora that Mex was spielin' about?"

"I dunno," says he. "I never heard of him before."

"I wouldn't say you was lyin'," I said tolerantly. "Yo're jest sufferin' from loss of memory. Frequently cases like that is cured and their memory restored by a severe shock or jolt like a lick onto the head. Now then, if I was to take my six-shooter butt and drive yore head through that whiskey barrel with it, I bet it'd restore yore memory right sudden."

"Hold on!" says he in a hurry. "I jest remembered that Zamora is the boss of a gang of Mexicans which claims Bowie Knife Canyon. He deals in hosses."

"You mean he steals hosses," I says, and he says: "I ain't argyin'. Anyway, the canyon is very convenient for his business, and if you dump them immigrants in his front yard, he'll be very much put out."

"He sure will," I agreed. "As quick as I can git my hands onto him."

I finished my drink and strode to the door and turnt suddenly with a gun in each hand. The nine or ten fellers which had drawed their guns aiming to shoot me in the back as I went through the door, they dropped their weppins and throwed up their hands and yelled: "Don't shoot!" So I jest shot the lights out, and then went out and got onto Cap'n Kidd whilst them idjits was hollering and falling over each other in the dark, and rode out of War Smoke, casually shattering a few winder lights along the street as I went.

When I got back to camp the boys had already got there, and the whole wagon train was holding their weppins and scairt most to death.

"I'm mighty relieved to see you back safe, Mister Elkins," says Old Man Richardson. "We heard the shootin' and was afeared them bullies had kilt you. Le's hitch up and pull out right now!"

Them tenderfoots is beyond my comprehension. They'd of all pulled out in the dark if I'd let 'em, and I believe most of 'em stayed awake all night, expecting to be butchered in their sleep. I didn't say nothing to them about Zamora. The boys hadn't understood what Gomez was talking about, and they warn't no use getting 'em worse scairt than what they generally was.

WELL, WE PULLED OUT before daylight, because I aimed to rech the canyon without another stop. We kept rolling and got there purty late that night. It warn't really no canyon at all, but a whopping big valley, well timbered, and mighty good water and grass. It was a perfect place for a settlement, as I p'inted out, but tenderfoots is powerful pecooliar. I happened to pick our camp site that night on the spot where the Apaches wiped out a mule-train of Mexicans six years before, and it was too dark to see the bones scattered around till next morning. Old Man Richardson was using what he thought was a round rock for a piller, and when he woke up the next morning and found he'd been sleeping with his head onto a human skull he like to throwed a fit.

And when I wanted to stop for the noonday meal in that there grove where the settlers hanged them seven cattle-rustlers three years before, them folks got the willies when they seen some of the ropes still sticking onto the limbs, and wouldn't on no account eat their dinner there. You got no idee what pecooliar folks them immigrants is till you've saw some.

Well, we stopped a few miles further on, in another grove in the midst of a wide rolling country with plenty of trees and tall grass, and I didn't tell 'em that was where them outlaws murdered the three Grissom boys in their sleep. Old Man Richardson said it looked like as good a place as any to locate the settlement. But I told him we was going to look over the whole derned valley before we chosed a spot. He kind of wilted and said at least for God's sake let 'em rest a few days.

I never seen folks which tired out so easy, but I said all right, and we camped there that night. I hadn't saw no signs of Zamora's gang since we come into the valley, and thought likely they was all off stealing hosses somewhere. Not that it made any difference.

Early next morning Ned and Joe, the old man's boys, they wanted to look for deer, and I told 'em not to go more'n a mile from camp, and be keerful, and they said they would, and sot out to the south.

I went back of the camp a mile or so to the creek where Jim Dornley ambushed Tom Harrigan four years before, and taken me a swim. I stayed longer'n I intended to, it was sech a relief to get away from them helpless tenderfoots for a while, and when I rode back into camp, I seen Ned approaching with a stranger—a young white man, which carried hisself with a air of great importance.

"Hey, pap!" hollered young Ned as they dismounted. "Where's Mister Elkins? This feller says we can't stay in Bowie Knife Canyon!"

"Who're you?" I demanded, emerging from behind a wagon, and the stranger's eyes bugged out as he seen me.

"My name's George Warren," says he. "A wagon train of us just came into the valley from the east yesterday. We're from Illinois."

"And by what right does you order people outa this canyon?" I ast.

"We got the fightin'est man in the world guidin' us," says he. "I thought he was the biggest man in the world till I seen you. But he ain't to be fooled with. When he heard they was another train in the valley, he sent me to tell you to git. You better, too, if you got any sense!"

"We don't want no trouble!" quavered Old Man Richardson.

"You got a nerve!" I snorted, and I pulled George Warren's hat down so the brim come off and hung around his neck like a collar, and turnt him around and lifted him off the ground with a boot in the pants, and then throwed him bodily onto his hoss. "Go back and tell yore champeen that Bowie Knife Canyon belongs to us!" I roared, slinging a few bullets around his hoss' feet. "And we gives him one hour to hitch up and clear out!"

"I'll git even for this!" wept George Warren, as he streaked it for his home range. "You'll be sorry, you big polecat! Jest wait'll I tell Mister—" I couldn't catch what else he said.

"Now I bet he's mad," says Old Man Richardson. "We better go. After all—"

"Shet up!" I roared. "This here valley's our'n, and I intends to defend our rights to the last drop of yore blood! Hitch them mules and swing the wagons in a circle! Pile yore saddles and plunder betwixt the wheels. I got a idee you all fights better behind breastworks. Did you see their camp, Ned?"

"Naw," says he, "but George Warren said it lies about three miles east of our'n. Me and Joe got separated and I was swingin' east around the south end of that ridge over there, when I met this George Warren. He said he was out lookin' for a hoss before sun-up and seen our camp and went back and told their guide, and he sent him over to tell us to git out."

"I'm worried about Joe," said Old Man Richardson. "He ain't come back."

"I'll go look for him," I said. "I'll also scout their camp, and if the odds ain't more'n ten to one, we don't wait for 'em to attack. We goes over and wipes 'em out *pronto*. Then we hangs their fool sculps to our wagon bows as a warnin' to other sech scoundrels."

Old Man Richardson turnt pale and his knees knocked together, but I told him sternly to get to work swinging them wagons, and clumb onto Cap'n Kidd and lit out.

REASON I HADN'T SAW the smoke of the Illinois camp was on account of a thick-timbered ridge which lay east of our camp. I swung around the south end of that ridge and headed east, and I'd gone maybe a mile and a half when I seen a man riding toward me.

When he seen me he come lickety-split, and I could see the sun shining on his Winchester barrel. I cocked my .45-90 and rode toward him and we met in the middle of a open flat. And suddenly we both lowered our weppins and pulled up, breast to breast, glaring at each other.

"Breckinridge Elkins!" says he.

"Cousin Bearfield Buckner!" says I. "Air you the man which sent that unlicked cub of a George Warren to bring *me* a defiance?"

"Who else?" he snarled. He always had a awful temper.

"Well," I says, "this here is our valley. You all got to move on."

"What you mean, move on?" he yelled. "I brung them pore critters all the way from Dodge City, Kansas, where I encountered 'em bein' tormented by some wuthless buffalo hunters which is no longer in the land of the livin'. I've led 'em through fire, flood, hostile Injuns and white renegades. I promised to lead 'em into a land of milk and honey, and I been firm with 'em, even when they weakened theirselves. Even when they begged on bended knees to be allowed to go back to Illinois, I wouldn't hear of it, because, as I told 'em, I knowed what was best for 'em. I had this canyon in mind all the time. And now you tells me to move on!"

Cousin Bearfield rolled an eye and spit on his hand. I jest waited.

"What sort of a reply does you make to my request to go on and leave us in peace?" he goes on. "George Warren come back to camp wearin' his hat brim around his neck and standin' up in the stirrups because he was too sore to set in the saddle. So I set 'em fortifyin' the camp whilst I went forth to reconnoiter. That word I sent you, I now repeats in person. Yo're my blood-kin, but principles comes first!"

"Me, too," I said. "A Nevada Elkins' principles is as loftey as a Texas Buckner's any day. I whupped you a year ago in Cougar Paw—"

"That's a cussed lie!" gnashed he. "You taken a base advantage and lammed me with a oak log when I warn't expectin' it!"

"Be that as it may," says I, "—ignorin' the fack that you had jest beaned me with a rock the size of a water-bucket—the only way to settle this dispute is to fight it out like gents. But we got to determine what weppins to use. The matter's too deep for fists."

"I'd prefer butcher knives in a dark room," says he, "only they ain't no room. If we jest had a couple of sawed-off shotguns, or good double-bitted axes—I tell you, Breck, le's tie our left hands together and work on each other with our bowies."

"Naw," I says, "I got a better idee. We'll back our hosses together, and then ride for the oppersite sides of the flat. When we git there we'll wheel and charge back, shootin' at each other with our Winchesters. Time they're empty we'll be clost enough to use our pistols, and when we've emptied them we'll be clost enough to finish the fight with our bowies."

"Good idee!" agreed Bearfield. "You always was a brainy, cultured sort of a lobo, if you wasn't so damn stubborn. Now, me, I'm reasonable. When I'm wrong, I admit it."

"You ain't never admitted it so far," says I.

"I ain't never been wrong yet!" he roared. "And I'll kyarve the gizzard of the buzzard which says I am! Come on! Le's git goin'."

So we started to gallop to the oppersite sides of the flat when I heard a voice hollering: "Mister Elkins! Mister Elkins!"

"Hold on!" I says. "That's Joe Richardson."

NEXT MINUTE JOE COME tearing out of the bresh from the south on a mustang I hadn't never seen before, with a Mexican saddle and bridle on. He didn't have no hat nor shirt, and his back was criss-crossed with bloody streaks. He likewise had a cut in his sculp which dribbled blood down his face.

"Mexicans!" he panted. "I got separated from Ned and rode further'n I should ought to had. About five miles down the canyon I run into a big gang of Mexicans—about thirty of 'em. One was that feller Gomez. Their leader was a big feller they called Zamora.

"They grabbed me and taken my hoss, and whupped me with their quirts. Zamora said they was goin' to wipe out every white man in the canyon. He said his scouts had brung him news of our camp, and another'n east of our'n, and he aimed to destroy both of 'em at one sweep. Then they all got onto their hosses and headed north, except one man which I believe they left there to kill me before he follered 'em. He hit me with his six-shooter and knocked me down, and then put up his gun and started to cut my throat with his knife. But I wasn't unconscious like he thought, and I grabbed his gun and knocked *him* down with it, and jumped on his hoss and lit out. As I made for camp I heard you and this gent talkin' loud to each other, and headed this way."

"Which camp was they goin' for first?" I demanded.

"I dunno," he said. "They talked mostly in Spanish I can't understand."

"The duel'll have to wait," I says. "I'm headin' for our camp."

"And me for mine," says Bearfield. "Lissen: le's decide it this way: one that scuppers the most Greasers wins and t'other'n takes his crowd and pulls out!"

"*Bueno!*" I says, and headed for camp.

The trees was dense. Them bandits could of passed either to the west or the east of us without us seeing 'em. I quickly left Joe, and about a quarter of a mile further on I heard a sudden burst of firing and screaming, and then silence. A little bit later I bust out of the trees into sight of the camp, and I cussed earnestly. Instead of being drawed up in a circle, with the men shooting from between the wheels and holding them bandits off like I expected, them derned wagons was strung out like they was heading back north. The hosses was cut loose from some of 'em, and mules was laying acrost the poles of the others, shot full of lead. Women was screaming and kids was squalling, and I seen young Jack Richardson laying face down in the ashes of the campfire with his head in a puddle of blood.

Old Man Richardson come limping toward me with tears running down his face. "Mexicans!" he blubbered. "They hit us like a harrycane jest a little while ago! They shot Jack down like he was a dog! Three or four of the other boys is got knife slashes or bullet marks or bruises from loaded quirt-ends! As they rode off they yelled they'd come back and kill us all!"

"Why'n't you throw them wagons round like I told you?" I roared.

"We didn't want no fightin'!" he bawled. "We decided to pull out of the valley and find some more peaceful place—"

"And now Jack's dead and yore stock's scattered!" I raged. "Jest because you didn't want to fight! What the hell you ever cross the Pecos for if you didn't aim to fight nobody? Set the boys to gatherin' sech stock as you got left—"

"But them Mexicans taken Betty!" he shrieked, tearing his scanty locks. "Most of 'em headed east, but six or seven grabbed Betty right out of the wagon and rode off south with her, drivin' the hosses they stole from us!"

"Well, git yore weppins and foller me!" I roared. "For Lord's sake forgit they is places where sheriffs and policemen pertecks you, and make up yore minds to *fight!* I'm goin' after Betty."

I HEADED SOUTH AS HARD as Cap'n Kidd could run. The reason I hadn't met them Mexicans as I rode back from the flat where I met Cousin Bearfield was because they swung around the north end of the ridge when they headed east. I hadn't gone far when I heard a sudden burst of firing, off to the east, and figgered they'd hit the Illinois camp. But I reckoned Bearfield had got there ahead of 'em. Still, it didn't seem like the shooting was far enough off to be at the other camp. But I didn't have no time to study it.

Them gal-thieves had a big start, but it didn't do no good. I hadn't rode over three miles till I heard the stolen hosses running ahead of me, and in a minute I bust out into a open flat and seen six Mexicans driving them critters at full speed, and one of 'em was holding Betty on the saddle in front of him. It was that blasted Gomez.

I come swooping down onto 'em, with a six-shooter in my right hand and a bowie knife in my left. Cap'n Kidd needed no guiding. He'd smelt blood and fire and he come like a hurricane on Jedgment Day, with his mane flying and his hoofs burning the grass.

The Mexicans seen I'd ride 'em down before they could get acrost the flat and they turnt to meet me, shooting as they come. But Mexicans always was rotten shots. As we come together I let *bam* three times with my .45, and: "Three!" says I.

One of 'em rode at me from the side and clubbed his rifle and hit at my head, but I ducked and made one swipe with my bowie. "Four!" says I. Then the others turnt and high-tailed it, letting the stolen hosses run where they wanted to. One of 'em headed south, but I was crowding Gomez so clost he whirled around and lit a shuck west.

"Keep back or I keel the girl!" he howled, lifting a knife, but I shot it out of his hand, and he give a yowl and let go of her and she fell off into the high grass. He kept fogging it.

I pulled up to see if Betty was hurt, but she warn't—jest scairt. The grass cushioned her fall. I seen her pap and sech of the boys as was able to ride was all coming at a high run, so I left her to 'em and taken in after Gomez again. Purty soon he looked back and seen me overhauling him, so he reched for his Winchester which he'd evidently jest thought of using, when about that time his hoss stepped into a prairie dog hole and throwed him over his head. Gomez never twitched after he hit the ground. I turnt around and rode back, cussing disgustedly, because a Elkins is ever truthful, and I couldn't honestly count Gomez in my record.

But I thought I'd scuttle that coyote that run south, so I headed in that direction. I hadn't gone far when I heard a lot of hosses running somewhere ahead of me and to the east, and then presently I bust out of the trees and come onto a flat which run to the mouth of a narrer gorge opening into the main canyon.

On the left wall of this gorge-mouth they was a ledge about fifty foot up, and they was a log cabin on that ledge with loop-holes in the walls. The only way up onto the ledge was a log ladder, and about twenty Mexicans was running their hosses toward it, acrost the flat. Jest as I reched the aidge of the bushes, they got to the foot of the wall and jumped off their hosses and run up that ladder like monkeys, letting their hosses run any ways. I seen a big feller with gold ornaments on his sombrero which I figgered was Zamora, but before I could unlimber my Winchester they was all in the cabin and slammed the door.

THE NEXT MINUTE COUSIN Bearfield busted out of the trees a few hundred yards east of where I was and started recklessly acrost the flat. Imejitely all them Mexicans started shooting at him, and he grudgingly retired into the bresh again, with terrible language. I yelled, and rode toward him, keeping to the trees.

"How many you got?" he bellered as soon as he seen me.

"Four," I says, and he grinned like a timber wolf and says: "I got five! I was ridin' for my camp when I heard the shootin' behind me, and so I knowed it was yore camp they hit first. I turnt around to go back and help you out—"

"When did I ever ast you for any help?" I bristled, but he said: "But purty soon I seen a gang of Mexicans comin' around the north end of the ridge, so I taken cover and shot five of 'em out of their saddles. They must of knowed it was me, because they high-tailed it."

"How could they know that, you conceited jackass?" I snorted. "They run off because they probably thought a whole gang had ambushed 'em."

Old Man Richardson and his boys had rode up whilst we was talking, and now he broke in with some heat, and said: "That hain't the question! The p'int is we got 'em hemmed up on that ledge for the time bein', and can git away before they come down and massacre us."

"What you talkin' about?" I roared. *"They're* the ones which is in need of gittin' away. If any massacrein' is did around here, we does it!"

"It's flyin' in the face of Providence!" he bleated, but I told him sternly to shet up, and Bearfield says: "Send somebody over to my camp to bring my warriors," so I told Ned to go and he pulled out.

Then me and Bearfield studied the situation, setting our hosses in the open whilst bullets from the cabin whistled all around us, and the Richardsons hid in the bresh and begged us to be keerful.

"That ledge is sheer on all sides," says Bearfield. "Nobody couldn't climb down onto it from the cliff. And anybody tryin' to climb that ladder in the teeth of twenty Winchesters would be plum crazy."

But I says, "Look, Bearfield, how the ledge overhangs about ten foot to the left of that ladder. A man could stand at the foot of the bluff there and them coyotes couldn't see to shoot him."

"And," says Bearfield, "he could sling his rope up over that spur of rock at the rim, and they couldn't shoot it off. Only way to git to it would be to come out of the cabin and rech down and cut it with a knife. Door opens toward the ladder, and they ain't no door in the wall on that side. A man could climb right up onto the ledge before they knowed it—if they didn't shoot him through the loop-holes as he come over the rim."

"You stay here and shoot 'em when they tries to cut the rope," I says.

"You go to hell!" he roared. "I see through yore hellish plot. You aims to git up there and kill all them Mexes before I has a chance at 'em. You thinks you'll outwit me! By golly, I got my rights, and—"

"Aw, shet up," I says disgustedly. "We'll both go." I hollered to Old Man Richardson: "You all lay low in the bresh and shoot at every Mex which comes outa the cabin."

"What you goin' to do now?" he hollered. "Don't be rash—"

But me and Bearfield was already headed for the ledge at a dead run.

THIS MOVE SURPRIZED the Mexicans, because they knowed we couldn't figger to ride our hosses up that ladder. Being surprized they shot wild and all they done was graze my sculp and nick Bearfield's ear. Then, jest as they begun to get their range and started trimming us clost, we swerved aside and thundered in under the overhanging rock.

We clumb off and tied our hosses well apart, otherwise they'd of started fighting each other. The Mexicans above us was yelling most amazing but they couldn't even see us, much less shoot us. I whirled my lariat, which is plenty longer and stronger than the average lasso, and roped the spur of rock which jutted up jest below the rim.

"I'll go up first," says I, and Bearfield showed his teeth and drawed his bowie knife.

"You won't neither!" says he. "We'll cut kyards! High man wins!"

So we squatted, and Old Man Richardson yelled from the trees: "For God's sake, what are you doin' now? They're fixin' to roll rocks down onto you!"

"You tend to yore own business," I advised him, and shuffled the cards which Bearfield hauled out of his britches. As it turnt out, the Mexes had a supply of boulders in the cabin. They jest opened the door and rolled 'em toward the rim. But they shot off the ledge and hit beyond us.

Bearfield cut, and yelped: "A ace! You cain't beat that!"

"I can equal it," I says, and drawed a ace of diamonds.

"I wins!" he clamored. "Hearts beats diamonds!"

"That rule don't apply here," I says. "It war a draw, and—"

"Why, you ——!" says Bearfield, leaning for'ard to grab the deck, and jest then a rock about the size of a bushel basket come bounding over the ledge and hit a projection which turnt its course, so instead of shooting over us, it fell straight down and hit Bearfield smack between the ears.

It stunned him for a instant, and I jumped up and started climbing the rope, ignoring more rocks which come thundering down. I was about half-way up when Bearfield come to, and he riz with a beller of rage. "Why, you dirty, double-crossin' so-and-so!" says he, and started throwing rocks at me.

They was a awful racket, the Mexicans howling, and guns banging, and Bearfield cussing, and Old Man Richardson wailing: "They're crazy, I tell you! They're both crazy as mudhens! I think everybody west of the Pecos must be maneyacks!"

Bearfield grabbed the rope and started climbing up behind me, and about that time one of the Mexicans run to cut the rope. But for onst my idiotic follerers was on the job. He run into about seven bullets that hit him all to onst, and fell down jest above the spur where the loop was caught onto.

So when I reched my arm over the rim to pull myself up they couldn't see me on account of the body. But jest as I was pulling myself up, they let go a boulder at random and it bounded along and bounced over the dead Mexican and hit me right smack in the face. It was about as big as a pumpkin.

I give a infuriated beller and swarmed up onto the ledge and it surprised 'em so that most of them missed me clean. I only got one slug through the arm. Before they had time to shoot again I made a jump to the wall and flattened myself between the loop-holes, and grabbed the rifle barrels they poked through the loop-holes and bent 'em and rooint 'em. Bearfield was coming up the rope right behind me, so I grabbed hold of the logs and tore that whole side of the wall out, and the roof fell in and the other walls come apart.

*   *   *

IN A INSTANT ALL YOU could see was logs falling and rolling and Mexicans busting out into the open. Some got pinned by the falling logs and some was shot by my embattled Kansans and Bearfield's Illinois warriors which had jest come up, and some fell offa the ledge and broke their fool necks.

One of 'em run agen me and tried to stab me so I throwed him after them which had already fell off the ledge, and hollered: "Five for me, Bearfield!"

"——!" says Bearfield, arriving onto the scene with blood in his eye and his bowie in his hand. Seeing which a big Mexican made for him with a butcher knife, which was pore jedgment on his part, and in about the flick of a mustang's tail Bearfield had a sixth man to his credit.

This made me mad. I seen some of the Mexicans was climbing down the ladder, so I run after 'em, and one turnt around and missed me so close with a shotgun he burnt my eyebrows. I taken it away from him and hit him over the head with it, and yelled: "Six for me, too, Cousin Bearfield!"

"Lookout!" he yelled. "Zamora's gittin' away!"

I seen Zamora had tied a rope to the back side of the ledge and was sliding down it. He dropped the last ten feet and run for a corral which was full of hosses back up the gorge, behind the ledge.

We seen the other Mexicans was all laid out or running off up the valley, persued by our immigrants, so I went down the ladder and Bearfield slid down my rope. Zamora's rope wouldn't of held our weight. We grabbed our hosses and lit out up the gorge, around a bend of which Zamora was jest disappearing.

He had a fast hoss and a long start, but I'd of overtook him within the first mile, only Cap'n Kidd kept trying to stop and fight Bearfield's hoss, which was about as big and mean as he was. After we'd run about five miles, and come out of the gorge onto a high plateau, I got far enough ahead of Bearfield so Cap'n Kidd forgot about his hoss, and then he settled down to business and run Zamora's hoss right off his laigs.

They was a steep slope on one side of us, and a five hundred foot drop on the other, and Zamora seen his hoss was winded, so he jumped off and started up the slope on foot. Me and Bearfield jumped off, too, and run after him. Each one of us got him by a laig as he was climbing up a ledge.

"Leggo my prisoner!" roared Bearfield.

"He's my meat," I snarled. "This makes me seven! I wins!"

"You lie!" bellered Bearfield, jerking Zamora away from me and hitting me over the head with him. This made me mad so I grabbed Zamora and throwed him in Bearfield's face. His spurs jabbed Bearfield in the belly, and my cousin give a maddened beller and fell on me fist and tush, and in the battle which follered we forgot all about Zamora till we heard a man scream. He'd snuck away and tried to mount Cap'n Kidd. We stopped fighting and looked around jest in time to see Cap'n Kidd kick him in the belly and knock him clean over the aidge of the cliff.

"Well," says Bearfield disgustedly, "that decides nothin', and our score is a draw."

"It was my hoss which done it," I said. "It ought a count for me."

"Over my corpse it will!" roared Bearfield. "But look here, it's nearly night. Le's git back to the camps before my follerers start cuttin' yore Kansans' throats. Whatever fight is to be fought to decide who owns the canyon, it's betwixt you and me, not them."

"All right," I said. "If my Kansas boys ain't already kilt all yore idjits, we'll fight this out somewhere where we got better light and more room. But I jest expect to find yore Illinoisans writhin' in their gore."

"Don't worry about them," he snarled. "They're wild as painters when they smells gore. I only hope they ain't kilt *all* yore Kansas mavericks."

SO WE PULLED FOR THE valley. When we got there it was dark, and as we rode outa the gorge, we seen fires going on the flat, and folks dancing around 'em, and fiddles was going at a great rate.

"What the hell is this?" bellered Bearfield, and then Old Man Richardson come up to us, overflowing with good spirits. "Glad to see you gents!" he says. "This is a great night! Jack warn't kilt, after all. Jest creased. We come out of that great fight whole and sound—"

"But what you doin'?" roared Bearfield. "What's my people doin' here?"

"Oh," says Old Man Richardson, "we got together after you gents left and agreed that the valley was big enough for both parties, so we decided to jine together into one settlement, and we're celebratin'. Them Illinois people is fine folks. They're as peace-lovin' as we are."

"Blood-thirsty painters!" I sneers to Cousin Bearfield.

"I ain't no bigger liar'n you air," he says, more in sorrer than in anger. "Come on. They ain't nothin' more we can do. We air swamped in a mess of pacifism. The race is degeneratin'. Le's head for Bear Creek. This atmosphere of brotherly love is more'n I can stand."

We set our hosses there a minnit and watched them pilgrims dance and listened to 'em singing. I squints across at Cousin Bearfield's face and doggoned if it don't look almost human in the firelight. He hauls out his plug of tobacco and offers me first chaw. Then we headed yonderly, riding stirrup to stirrup.

Must of been ten miles before Cap'n Kidd retches over and bites Cousin Bearfield's hoss on the neck. Bearfield's hoss bites back, and by accident Cap'n Kidd kicks Cousin Bearfield on the ankle. He lets out a howl and thumps me over the head, and I hit him, and then we gits our arms around each other and roll in the bresh in a tangle.

We fit fer two hours, I reckon, and we'd been fighting yet if we hadn't scrambled under Cap'n Kidd's hoofs where he was feeding. He kicked Cousin Bearfield one way and me the other.

I got up after a while and went hunting my hat. The bresh crackled, and in the moonlight I could see Cousin Bearfield on his hands and knees. "Whar air ye, Cousin Breckinridge?" says he. "Air you all right?"

Well, mebbe my clothes was tore more'n his was and a lip split and a rib or two busted, but I could still see, which was more'n he could say with both his eyes swole that way. "Shore I'm all right," I says. "How air *you*, Cousin Bearfield?"

He let out a groan and tried to git up. He made 'er on the second heave and stood there swaying. "Why, I'm fine," he says. "Plumb fine. I feel a whole lot better, Breck. I was afraid fer a minnit back there, whilst we was ridin' along, that that daggone brotherly love would turn out to be catchin'."

PISTOL POLITICS

POLITICS AND BOOK-LEARNING is bad enough took separate; together they're a blight and a curse. Take Yeller Dog for a instance, a mining camp over in the Apache River country, where I was rash enough to take up my abode in onst.

Yeller Dog was a decent camp till politics reared its head in our midst and education come slithering after. The whiskey was good and middling cheap. The poker and faro games was honest if you watched the dealers clost. Three or four piddlin' fights a night was the usual run, and a man hadn't been shot dead in more than a week by my reckoning. Then, like my Aunt Tascosa Polk would say, come the deluge.

It all begun when Forty-Rod Harrigan moved his gambling outfit over to Alderville and left our one frame building vacant, and Gooseneck Wilkerson got the idee of turning it into a city hall. Then he said we ought to have a mayor to go with it, and announced hisself as candidate. Naturally Bull Hawkins, our other leading citizen, come out agen him. The election was sot for April 11. Gooseneck established his campaign headquarters in the Silver Saddle saloon, and Bull taken up his'n in the Red Tomahawk on t'other side of the street. First thing we knowed, Yeller Dog was in the grip of politics.

The campaign got under way, and the casualties was mounting daily as public interest become more and more fatally aroused, and on the afternoon of the 9th Gooseneck come into his headquarters. and says: "We got to make a sweepin' offensive, boys. Bull Hawkins is outgeneralin' us. That shootin' match he put on for a prime beef steer yesterday made a big hit with the common herd. He's tryin' to convince Yeller Dog that if elected he'd pervide the camp with more high-class amusement than I could. Breck Elkins, will you pause in yore guzzlin' and lissen here a minute? As chief of this here political organization I demand yore attention!"

"I hear you," I says. "I was to the match, and they barred me on a tecknicality, otherwise I would of won the whole steer. It warn't so excitin', far as I could see. Only one man got shot."

"And he was one of my voters," scowled Gooseneck. "But we got to outshine Bull's efforts to seduce the mob. He's resortin' to low, onder-handed tactics by buyin' votes outright. I scorns sech measures—anyway, I've bought all I'm able to pay for. We got to put on a show which out-dazzles his dern' shootin' match."

"A rodeo, maybe," suggested Mule McGrath. "Or a good dog-fight."

"Naw, naw," says Gooseneck. "My show will be a symbol of progress and culture. We stages a spellin' match tomorrow night in the city hall. Next mornin' when the polls opens the voters'll still be so dazzled by the grandeur of our entertainment they'll eleck me by a vast majority."

"How many men in this here camp can spell good enough to git into a spellin' bee?" says I.

"I'm confident they's at least thirty-five men in this camp which can read and write," says Gooseneck. "That's plenty. But we got to find somebody to give out the words. It wouldn't look right for me—it'd be beneath my offishul dignity. Who's educated enough for the job?"

"I am!" says Jerry Brennon and Bill Garrison simultaneous. They then showed their teeth at each other. They warn't friends nohow.

"Cain't but one git the job," asserted Gooseneck. "I tests yore ability. Can either one of you spell Constantinople?"

"K-o-n-" begun Garrison, and Brennon burst into a loud and mocking guffaw, and said something pointed about ignoramuses.

"You $%#&*!" says Garrison blood-thirstily.

"Gentlemen!" squawked Gooseneck—and then ducked as they both went for their guns.

✳   ✳   ✳

THEY CLEARED LEATHER about the same time. When the smoke oozed away Gooseneck crawled out from under the roulette table and cussed fervently.

"Two more reliable voters gone to glory!" he raged. "Breckinridge, whyn't you stop 'em?"

"'T'warn't none of my business," says I, reaching for another drink, because a stray bullet had knocked my glass out a my hand. "Hey!" I addressed the barkeep sternly. "I see you fixin' to chalk up that there spilt drink agen me. Charge it to Jerry Brennon. He spilt it."

"Dead men pays no bills," complained the bartender.

"Cease them petty squabbles!" snarled Gooseneck. "You argys over a glass of licker when I've jest lost two good votes! Drag 'em out, boys," he ordered the other members of the organization which was emerging from behind the bar and the whiskey barrels where they'd took refuge when the shooting started. "Damn!" says Gooseneck with bitterness. "This here is a deadly lick to my campaign! I not only loses two more votes, but them was the best educated men in camp, outside of me. Now who we goin' to git to conduck the spellin' match?"

"Anybody which can read can do it," says Lobo Harrison a hoss-thief with a mean face and a ingrown disposition. He'd go a mile out of his way jest to kick a dog. "Even Elkins there could do it."

"Yeah, if they was anything to read from," snorted Gooseneck. "But they ain't a line of writin' in camp except on whiskey bottles. We got to have a man with a lot of long words in his head. Breckinridge, dammit, jest because I told the barkeep to charge yore drinks onto campaign expenses ain't no reason for you to freeze onto that bar permanent. Ride over to Alderville and git us a educated man."

"How'll he know whether he's educated or not?" sneered Lobo, which seemed to dislike me passionately for some reason or another.

"Make him spell Constantinople," says Gooseneck.

"He cain't go over there," says Soapy Jackson. "The folks has threatened to lynch him for cripplin' their sheriff."

"I didn't cripple their fool sheriff," I says indignantly. "He crippled hisself fallin' through a wagon wheel when I give him a kind of a push with a rock. How you spell that there Constance Hopple word?"

Well, he spelt it thirty or forty times till I had it memorized, so I rode over to Alderville. When I rode into town the folks looked at me coldly and bunched up and whispered amongst theirselves, but I paid no attention to 'em. I never seen the deputy sheriff, unless that was him I seen climbing a white oak tree as I hove in sight. I went into the White Eagle saloon and drunk me a dram, and says to the barkeep: "Who's the best educated man in Alderville?"

Says he: "Snake River Murgatroyd, which deals monte over to the Elite

Amusement Palace." So I went over there and jest as I went through the door I happened to remember that Snake River had swore he was going to shoot me on sight next time he seen me, account of some trouble we'd had over a card game. But sech things is too trivial to bother about. I went up to where he was setting dealing monte, and I says: "Hey!"

"Place your bet," says he. Then he looked up and said: "You! $#/0&*@!" and reched for his gun, but I got mine out first and shoved the muzzle under his nose.

"Spell Constantinople!" I tells him.

He turnt pale and said: "Are you crazy?"

"Spell it!" I roared, and he says: "C-o-n-s-t-a-n-t-i-n-o-p-l-e! What the hell?"

"Good," I said, throwing his gun over in the corner out of temptation's way. "We wants you to come over to Yeller Dog and give out words at a spellin' match."

EVERYBODY IN THE PLACE was holding their breath. Snake River moved his hands nervous-like and knocked a jack of diamonds off onto the floor. He stooped like he was going to pick it up, but instead he jerked a bowie out of his boot and tried to stab me in the belly. Well, much as I would of enjoyed shooting him, I knowed it would spile the spelling match, so merely taken the knife away from him, and held him upside down to shake out whatever other weppins he might have hid, and he begun to holler: "Help! Murder! Elkins is killin' me!"

"It's a Yeller Dog plot!" somebody howled, and the next instant the air was full of beer mugs and cuspidors. Some of them spittoons was quite heavy, and when one missed me and went bong on Snake River's head, he curled up like a angleworm which has been tromped on.

"Lookit there!" they hollered, like it was my fault. "He's tryin' to kill Snake River! Git him, boys!"

They then fell on me with billiard sticks and chair laigs in a way which has made me suspicious of Alderville's hospitality ever since.

Argyment being useless, I tucked Snake River under my left arm and started knocking them fool critters right and left with my right fist, and I reckon that was how the bar got wrecked. I never seen a bar a man's head would go through easier'n that'n. So purty soon the survivors abandoned the fray and run out of the door hollering: "Help! Murder! Rise up, citizens! Yeller Dog is at our throats! Rise and defend yore homes and loved ones!"

You would of thought the Apaches was burning the town, the way folks was hollering and running for their guns and shooting at me, as I clumb aboard Cap'n Kidd and headed for Yeller Dog. I left the main road and headed through the bresh for a old trail I knowed about, because I seen a whole army of men getting on their hosses to lick out after me, and while I knowed they couldn't catch Cap'n Kidd, I was a feared they might hit Snake River with a stray bullet if they got within range. The bresh was purty thick and I reckon it was the branches slapping him in the face which brung him to, because all to onst he begun hollering blue murder.

"You ain't takin' me to Yeller Dog!" he yelled. "You're takin' me out in the hills to murder me! Help! Help!"

"Aw, shet up," I snorted. "This here's a short cut."

"You can't get across Apache River unless you follow the road to the bridge," says he.

"I can, too," I says. "We'll go acrost on the foot-bridge."

With that he give a scream of horror and a convulsive wrench which tore hisself clean out of his shirt which I was holding onto. The next thing I knowed all I had in my hand was a empty shirt and he was on the ground and scuttling through the bushes. I taken in after him, but he was purty tricky dodging around stumps and trees, and I begun to believe I was going to have to shoot him in the hind laig to catch him, when he made the mistake to trying to climb a tree. I rode up onto him before he could get out of rech, and reched up and got him by the laig and pulled him down, and his langwidge was painful to hear.

It was his own fault he slipped outa my hand, he kicked so vi'lent. I didn't go to drop him on his head.

But jest as I was reching down for him, I heard hosses running, and looked up and here come that derned Alderville posse busting through the bresh right on me. I'd lost so much time chasing Snake River they'd catched up with me. So I scooped him up and hung him over my saddle horn, because he was out cold, and headed for Apache River. Cap'n Kidd drawed away from them hosses like they was hobbled, so they warn't scarcely in pistol-range of us when we busted out on the east bank. The river was up, jest a-foaming and a-b'ling, and the footbridge warn't nothing only jest a log.

But Cap'n Kidd's sure-footed as a billy goat. We started acrost it, and everything went all right till we got about the middle of it, and then Snake River come to and seen the water booming along under us. He lost his head and begun to struggle and kick and holler, and his spurs scratched Cap'n Kidd's hide. That made Cap'n Kidd mad, and he turnt his head and tried to bite my laig, because he always blames me for everything that happens, and lost his balance and fell off.

That would of been all right, too, because as we hit the water I got hold of Cap'n Kidd's tail with one hand, and Snake River's undershirt with the other'n, and Cap'n Kidd hit out for the west bank. They is very few streams he cain't swim, flood or not. But jest as we was nearly acrost the posse appeared on the hind bank and started shooting at me, and they was apparently in some doubt as to which head in the water was me, because some of 'em shot at Snake River, too, jest to make sure. He opened his mouth to holler at 'em, and got it full of water and dern near strangled.

Then all to onst somebody in the bresh on the west shore opened up with a Winchester, and one of the posse hollered: "Look out, boys! It's a trap! Elkins has led us into a ambush!"

They turnt around and high-tailed it for Alderville.

WELL, WHAT WITH THE shooting and a gullet full of water, Snake River was having a regular fit and he kicked and thrashed so he kicked hisself clean out of his undershirt, and jest as my feet hit bottom, he slipped out of my grip and went whirling off downstream.

I jumped out on land, ignoring the hearty kick Cap'n Kidd planted in my midriff, and grabbed my lariat off my saddle. Gooseneck Wilkerson come prancing outa the bresh, waving a Winchester and yelling: "Don't let him drownd, dang you! My whole campaign depends on that spellin' bee! Do somethin'!"

I run along the bank and made a throw and looped Snake River around the ears. It warn't a very good catch, but the best I could do under the circumstances, and skin will always grow back onto a man's ears.

I hauled him out of the river, and it was plumb ungrateful for him to accuse me later of dragging him over them sharp rocks on purpose. I like to know how he figgered I could rope him outa Apache River without skinning him up a little. He'd swallered so much water he was nigh at his last gasp. Gooseneck rolled him onto his belly and jumped up and down on his back with both feet to git the water out; Gooseneck said that was artifishul respiration, but from the way Snake River hollered I don't believe it done him much good.

Anyway, he choked up several gallons of water. When he was able to threaten our lives betwixt cuss-words, Gooseneck says: "Git him on yore hoss and le's git started. Mine run off when the shootin' started. I jest suspected you'd be pursued by them dumb-wits and would take the short-cut. That's why I come to meet you. Come on. We got to git Snake River some medical attention. In his present state he ain't in no shape to conduck no spellin' match."

Snake River was too groggy to set in the saddle, so we hung him acrost it like a cow-hide over a fence, and started out, me leading Cap'n Kidd. It makes Cap'n Kidd very mad to have anybody but me on his back, so we hadn't went more'n a mile when he reched around and sot his teeth in the seat of Snake River's pants. Snake River had been groaning very weak and dismal and commanding us to stop and let him down so's he could utter his last words, but when Cap'n Kidd bit him he let out a remarkable strong yell and bust into langwidge unfit for a dying man.

"$%/#&¢!" quoth he passionately. "Why have *I* got to be butchered for a

Yeller Dog holiday?"

We was reasoning with him, when Old Man Jake Hanson hove out of the bushes. Old Jake had a cabin a hundred yards back from the trail. He was about the width of a barn door, and his whiskers was marvelous to behold. "What's this ungodly noise about?" he demanded. "Who's gittin' murdered?"

"I am!" says Snake River fiercely. "I'm bein' sacrificed to the passions of the brutal mob!"

"You shet up," said Gooseneck severely. "Jake, this is the gent we've consented to let conduck the spellin' match."

"Well, well!" says Jake, interested. "A educated man, hey? Why, he don't look no different from us folks, if the blood war wiped offa him. Say, lissen, boys, bring him over to my cabin! I'll dress his wounds and feed him and take keer of him and git him to the city hall tomorrer night in time for the spellin' match. In the meantime he can teach my datter Salomey her letters."

"I refuse to tutor a dirty-faced cub—" began Snake River w hen he seen a face peeking eagerly at us from the trees. "Who's that?" he demanded.

"My datter Salomey," says Old Jake. "Nineteen her last birthday and cain't neither read nor write. None of my folks ever could, far back as family history goes, but I wants her to git some education."

"It's a human obligation," says Snake River. "I'll do it!"

So we left him at Jake's cabin, propped up on a bunk, with Salomey feeding him spoon-vittles and whiskey, and me and Gooseneck headed for Yeller Dog, which warn't hardly a mile from there.

Gooseneck says to me: "We won't say nothin' about Snake River bein' at Jake's shack. Bull Hawkins is sweet on Salomey and he's so dern jealous-minded it makes him mad for another man to even stop there to say hello to the folks. We don't want nothin' to interfere with our show."

"You ack like you got a lot of confidence in it," I says.

"I banks on it heavy," says he. "It's a symbol of civilization."

WELL, JEST AS WE COME into town we met Mule McGrath with fire in his eye and corn-juice on his breath. "Gooseneck, lissen!" says he. "I jest got wind of a plot of Hawkins and Jack Clanton to git a lot of our voters so drunk election day that they won't be able to git to the polls. Le's call off the spellin' match and go over to the Red Tomahawk and clean out that rat-nest!"

"Naw," says Gooseneck, "we promised the mob a show, and we keeps our word. Don't worry; I'll think of a way to circumvent the heathen."

Mule headed back for the Silver Saddle, shaking his head, and Gooseneck sot down on the aidge of a hoss-trough and thunk deeply. I'd begun to think he'd drapped off to sleep, when he riz up and said: "Breck, git hold of Soapy Jackson and tell him to sneak out of camp and stay hid till the mornin' of the eleventh. Then he's to ride in jest before the polls open and spread the news that they has been a big gold strike over in Wild Ross Gulch. A lot of fellers will stampede for there without waitin' to vote. Meanwhile you will have circulated amongst the men you know air goin' to vote for me, and let 'em know we air goin' to work this campaign strategy. With all my men in camp, and most of Bull's headin' for Wild Ross Gulch, right and justice triumphs and I wins."

So I went and found Soapy and told him what Gooseneck said, and on the strength of it he imejitly headed for the Silver Saddle, and begun guzzling on campaign credit. I felt it was my duty to go along with him and see that he didn't get so full he forgot what he was supposed to do, and we was putting down the sixth dram apiece when in come Jack McDonald, Jim Leary, and Tarantula Allison, all Hawkins men. Soapy focused his wandering eyes on 'em, and says: "W-who's this here clutterin' up the scenery? Whyn't you mavericks stay over to the Red Tomahawk whar you belong?"

"It's a free country," asserted Jack McDonald. "What about this here derned spellin' match Gooseneck's braggin' about all over town?"

"Well, what about it?" I demanded, hitching my harness for'ard. The political foe don't live which can beard a Elkins in his lair.

"We demands to know who conducks it," stated Leary. "At least half the men in camp eligible to compete is in our crowd. We demands fair play!"

"We're bringin' in a cultured gent from another town," I says coldly.

"Who?" demanded Allison.

"None of yore dang business!" trumpeted Soapy, which gets delusions of valor when he's full of licker. "As a champion of progress and civic pride I challenges the skunk-odored forces of corrupt politics, and—"

Bam! McDonald swung with a billiard ball and Soapy kissed the sawdust.

"Now look what you done," I says peevishly. "If you coyotes cain't ack like gents, you'll oblige me by gittin' to hell outa here."

"If you don't like our company suppose you tries to put us out!" they challenged.

So when I'd finished my drink I taken their weppins away from 'em and throwed 'em headfirst out the side door. How was I to know somebody had jest put up a new cast-iron hitching-rack out there? Their friends carried 'em over to the Red Tomahawk to sew up their sculps, and I went back into the Silver Saddle to see if Soapy had come to yet. Jest as I reched the door he come weaving out, muttering in his whiskers and waving his six-shooter.

"Do you remember what all I told you?" I demanded.

"S-some of it!" he goggled, with his glassy eyes wobbling in all directions.

"Well, git goin' then," I urged, and helped him up onto his hoss. He left town at full speed, with both feet outa the stirrups and both arms around the hoss' neck.

"Drink is a curse and a delusion," I told the barkeep in disgust. "Look at that sickenin' example and take warnin'! Gimme me a bottle of rye."

WELL, GOOSENECK DONE a good job of advertising the show. By the middle of the next afternoon men was pouring into town from claims all up and down the creek. Half an hour before the match was sot to begin the hall was full. The benches was moved back from the front part, leaving a space clear all the way acrost the hall. They had been a lot of argyment about who was to compete, and who was to choose sides, but when it was finally settled, as satisfactory as anything ever was settled in Yeller Dog, they was twenty men to compete, and Lobo Harrison and Jack Clanton was to choose up.

By a peculiar coincidence, half of that twenty men was Gooseneck's, and half was Bull's. So naturally Lobo choosed his pals, and Clanton choosed his'n.

"I don't like this," Gooseneck whispered to me. "I'd ruther they'd been mixed up. This is beginnin' to look like a contest between my gang and Bull's. If they win, it'll make me look cheap. Where the hell is Snake River?"

"I ain't seen him," I said, "You ought to of made 'em take off their guns."

"Shucks," says he. "What could possibly stir up trouble at sech a lady-like affair as a spellin' bee. Dang it, where is Snake River? Old Jake said he'd git him here on time."

"Hey, Gooseneck!" yelled Bull Hawkins from where he sot amongst his coharts. "Why'n't you start the show?"

Bull was a big broad-shouldered hombre with black mustashes like a walrus. The crowd begun to holler and cuss and stomp their feet and this pleased Bull very much.

"Keep 'em amused," hissed Gooseneck. "I'll go look for Snake River."

He snuck out a side door and I riz up and addressed the throng. "Gents," I said, "be patient! They is a slight delay, but it won't be long. Meantime I'll be glad to entertain you all to the best of my ability. Would you like to hear me sing *Barbary Allen?*"

"No, by grab!" they answered in one beller.

"Well, yo're a-goin' to!" I roared, infuriated by this callous lack of the finer feelings. "I will now sing," I says, drawing my .45s "and I blows the brains out of the first coyote which tries to interrupt me."

I then sung my song without interference, and when I was through I bowed and waited for the applause, but all I heard was Lobo Harrison saying: "Imagine what the pore wolves on Bear Creek has to put up with!"

This cut me to the quick, but before I could make a suitable reply, Gooseneck slid in, breathing heavy. "I can't find Snake River," he hissed. "But the bar-keep gimme a book he found somewheres. Most of the leaves is tore out, but there's plenty left. I've marked some of the longest words, Breck. You can read good enough to give 'em out. You got to! If we don't start the show right away, this mob'll wreck the place. Yo're the only man not in the match which can even read a little, outside of me and Bull. It wouldn't look right for me to do it, and I shore ain't goin' to let Bull run my show."

I knew I was licked.

"Aw, well, all right," I said. "I might of knew I'd be the goat. Gimme the book."

"Here it is," he said. "'The Adventures of a French Countess.' Be dern shore you don't give out no words except them I marked."

"Hey!" bawled Jack Clanton. "We're gittin' tired standin' up here. Open the ball."

"All right," I says. "We commences."

"Hey!" said Bull. "Nobody told us Elkins was goin' to conduck the ceremony. We was told a cultured gent from outa town was to do it."

"Well," I says irritably, "Bear Creek is my home range, and I reckon I'm as cultured as any snake-hunter here. If anybody thinks he's better qualified than me, step up whilst I stomp his ears off."

Nobody volunteered, so I says "All right. I tosses a dollar to see who gits the first word." It fell for Harrison's gang, so I looked in the book at the first word marked, and it was a gal's name.

"Catharine," I says.

Nobody said nothing.

"Catharine!" I roared, glaring at Lobo Harrison,

"What you lookin' at me for?" he demanded. "I don't know no gal by that name."

"%$&*@!" I says with passion. "That's the word I give out. Spell it, dammit!"

"Oh," says he. "All right. K-a-t-h-a-r-i-n-n."

"That's wrong," I says.

"What you mean wrong?" he roared. "That's right!"

"'Tain't accordin' to the book," I said.

"Dang the book," says he. "I knows my rights and I ain't to be euchered by no ignorant grizzly from Bear Creek!"

"Who you callin' ignorant?" I demanded, stung, "Set down! You spelt it wrong."

"You lie!" he howled, and went for his gun. But I fired first.

⁕   ⁕   ⁕

WHEN THE SMOKE CLEARED away I seen everybody was on their feet preparing for to stampede, sech as warn't trying to crawl under the benches, so I said: "Set
down, everybody. They ain't nothin' to git excited about. The spellin' match con-
tinues—and I'll shoot the first scoundrel which tries to leave the hall before the entertainment's over."

Gooseneck hissed fiercely at me: "Dammit, be careful who you shoot,
cain't'cha? That was another one of my voters!"

"Drag him out!" I commanded, wiping off some blood where a slug had
notched my ear. "The spellin' match is ready to commence again."

They was a kind of tension in the air, men shuffling their feet and twisting
their mustashes and hitching their gun-belts, but I give no heed. I now approached
the other side, with my hand on my pistol, and says to Clanton: "Can you spell
Catharine?"

"C-a-t-h-a-r-i-n-e!" says he.

"Right, by golly!" I says, consulting *The French Countess*, and the audience
cheered wildly and shot off their pistols into the roof.

"Hey!" says Bill Stark, on the other side. "That's wrong. Make him set down!
It spells with a 'K'!"

"He spelt it jest like it is in the book," I says. "Look for yoreself."

"I don't give a damn!" he yelled, rudely knocking The French Countess outa
my hand. "It's a misprint! It spells with a 'K' or they'll be more blood on the floor!
He spelt it wrong and if he don't set down I shoots him down!"

"I'm runnin' this show!" I bellered, beginning to get mad. "You got to shoot
me before you shoots anybody else!"

"With pleasure!" snarled he, and went for his gun. . . . Well, I hit him on the
jaw with my fist and he went to sleep amongst a wreckage of busted benches.
Gooseneck jumped up with a maddened shriek.

"Dang yore soul, Breckinridge!" he squalled. "Quit cancelin' my votes! Who
air you workin' for—me or Hawkins?"

"Haw! haw! haw!" bellered Hawkins. "Go on with the show! This is the
funniest thing I ever seen!"

Wham! The door crashed open and in pranced Old Jake Hanson, waving a
shotgun.

"Welcome to the festivities, Jake," I greeted him, "Where's—"

"You son of a skunk!" quoth he, and let go at me with both barrels. The shot
scattered remarkable. I didn't get more'n five or six of 'em and the rest distributed
freely amongst the crowd. You ought to of heard 'em holler—the folks, I mean, not
the buckshot.

"What in tarnation air you doin'?" shrieked Gooseneck. "Where's Snake River?"

"Gone!" howled Old Jake. "Run off! Eloped with my datter!"

Bull Hawkins riz with a howl of anguish, convulsively clutching his whiskers.

"Salomey?" he bellered. "Eloped?"

"With a cussed gambolier they brung over from Alderville!" bleated Old Jake, doing a war-dance in his passion. "Elkins and Wilkerson persuaded me to take that snake into my boozum! In spite of my pleas and protests they forced him into my peaceful $# %*¢ household, and he stole the pore, mutton-headed innercent's blasted heart with his cultured airs and his slick talk! They've run off to git married!"

"It's a political plot!" shrieked Hawkins, going for his gun, "Wilkerson done it a-purpose!"

I shot the gun out of his hand, but Jack Clanton crashed a bench down on Gooseneck's head and Gooseneck kissed the floor. Clanton come down on top of him, out cold, as Mule McGrath swung with a pistol butt, and the next instant somebody lammed Mule with a brick bat and he flopped down acrost Clanton. And then the fight was on. Them rival political factions jest kind of riz up and rolled together in a wave of profanity, gun-smoke and splintering benches.

I HAVE ALWAYS NOTICED that the best thing to do in sech cases is to keep yore temper, and that's what I did for some time, in spite of the efforts of nine or ten wild-eyed Hawkinites. I didn't even shoot one of 'em; I kept my head and battered their skulls with a joist I tore outa the floor, and when I knocked 'em down I didn't stomp 'em hardly any. But they kept coming, and Jack McDonald was obsessed with the notion that he could ride me to the floor by jumping up astraddle of my neck. So he done it, and having discovered his idee was a hallucination, he got a fistful of my hair with his left, and started beating me in the head with his pistol-barrel.

It was very annoying. Simultaneous, several other misfits got hold of my laigs, trying to rassle me down, and some son of Baliol stomped severely on my toe. I had bore my afflictions as patient as Job up to that time, but this perfidy maddened me.

I give a roar which loosened the shingles on the roof, and kicked the toe-stomper in the belly with sech fury that he curled up on the floor with a holler groan and taken no more interest in the proceedings. I likewise busted my timber on somebody's skull, and reched up and pulled Jack McDonald off my neck like pulling a tick off a bull's hide, and hev him through a convenient winder. He's a liar when he says I aimed him deliberate at that rain barrel. I didn't even know they was a rain barrel till I heard his head crash through the staves. I then shaken nine or ten idjits loose from my shoulders and shook the blood outa my eyes and preceived that Gooseneck's men was getting the worst of it, particularly including Gooseneck hisself. So I give another roar and prepared to wade through them fool Hawkinites like a b'ar through a pack of hound-dogs, when I discovered that some perfidious side-winder had got my spur tangled in his whiskers.

I stooped to ontangle myself, jest as a charge of buckshot ripped through the air where my head had been a instant before. Three or four critters was rushing me with bowie knives, so I give a wrench and tore loose by main force. How could I help it if most of the whiskers come loose too? I grabbed me a bench to use for a club, and I mowed the whole first rank down with one swipe, and then as I drawed back for another lick, I heard somebody yelling above the melee.

"*Gold!*" he shrieked.

Everybody stopped like they was froze in their tracks. Even Bull Hawkins shook the blood outa his eyes and glared up from where he was kneeling on Gooseneck's wishbone with one hand in Gooseneck's hair and a bowie in the other'n. Everybody quit fighting everybody else, and looked at the door—and there was Soapy Jackson, a-reeling and a-weaving with a empty bottle in one hand, and hollering.

"Big gold strike in Wild Hoss Gulch," he blats. "Biggest the West ever seen! Nuggets the size of osteridge aigs—*gulp!*"

He disappeared in a wave of frenzied humanity as Yeller Dog's population abandoned the fray and headed for the wide open spaces. Even Hawkins ceased his efforts to sculp Gooseneck alive and j'ined the stampede. They tore the whole front out of the city hall in their flight, and even them which had been knocked stiff come to at the howl of "Gold!" and staggered wildly after the mob, shrieking pitifully for their picks, shovels and jackasses. When the dust had settled and the thunder of boot-heels had faded in the distance, the only human left in the city hall was me and Gooseneck, and Soapy Jackson, which riz unsteadily with the prints of hob-nails all over his homely face. They shore trompled him free and generous in their rush.

Gooseneck staggered up, glared wildly about him, and went into convulsions. At first he couldn't talk at all; he jest frothed at the mouth. When he found speech his langwidge was shocking.

"What you spring it this time of night for?" he howled. "Breckinridge, I said tell him to bring the news in the mornin', not tonight!"

"I did tell him that," I says.

"Oh, so that was what I couldn't remember!" says Soapy. "That lick

McDonald gimme so plumb addled my brains I knowed they was somethin' I forgot, but couldn't remember what it was."

"Oh sole mio!" gibbered Gooseneck, or words to that effeck.

"Well, what you kickin' about?" I demanded peevishly, having jest discovered that somebody had stabbed me in the hind laig during the melee. My boot was full of blood, and they was brand-new boots. "It worked, didn't it?" I says. "They're all headin' for Wild Hoss Gulch, includin' Hawkins hisself, and they cain't possibly git back afore day after tomorrer."

"Yeah!" raved Gooseneck. "They're all gone, includin' my gang! The damn camp's empty! How can I git elected with nobody here to hold the election, and nobody to vote?"

"Oh," I says. "That's right. I hadn't thunk of that."

He fixed me with a awful eye.

"Did you," says he in a blood-curdling voice, "did you tell my voters Soapy was goin' to enact a political strategy?"

"By golly!" I said. "You know it plumb slipped my mind! Ain't that a joke on me?"

"Git out of my life!" says Gooseneck, drawing his gun.

That was a genteel way for him to ack, trying to shoot me after all I'd did for him! I taken his gun away from him as gentle as I knowed how and it was his own fault he got his arm broke. But to hear him rave you would of thought he considered I was to blame for his misfortunes or something. I was so derned disgusted I clumb onto Cap'n Kidd and shaken the dust of that there camp offa my boots, because I seen they was no gratitude in Yeller Dog.

I likewise seen I wasn't cut out for the skullduggery of politics. I had me a notion one time that I'd make a hiyu sheriff but I learnt my lesson. It's like my pap says, I reckon.

"All the law a man needs," says he, "is a gun tucked into his pants. And the main l'arnin' he needs is to know which end of that gun the bullet comes out of."

What's good enough for pap, gents, is good enough for me.

EVIL DEEDS AT RED COUGAR

I BEEN ACCUSED OF prejudice agen the town of Red Cougar, on account of my habit of avoiding it if I have to ride fifty miles outen my way to keep from going through there. I denies the slander. It ain't no more prejudiced for me to ride around Red Cougar than it is for a lobo to keep his paw out of a jump-trap. My experiences in that there lair of iniquity is painful to recall. I was a stranger and took in. I was a sheep for the fleecing, and if some of the fleecers got their fingers catched in the shears, it was their own fault. If I shuns Red Cougar like a plague, that makes it mutual, because the inhabitants of Red Cougar shuns me with equal enthusiasm, even to the p'int of deserting their wagons and taking to the bresh if they happen to meet me on the road.

I warn't intending to go there in the first place. I been punching cows over in Utah and was heading for Bear Creek, with the fifty bucks a draw poker game had left me outa my wages. When I seen a trail branching offa the main road I knowed it turnt off to Red Cougar, but it didn't make no impression on me.

But I hadn't gone far past it when I heard a hoss running, and the next thing it busted around a bend in the road with foam flying from the bit rings. They was a gal on it, looking back over her shoulder down the road. Jest as she rounded the turn her hoss stumbled and went to its knees, throwing her over its head.

I was offa Cap'n Kidd in a instant and catched her hoss before it could run off. I helped her up, and she grabbed holt of me and hollered: "Don't let 'em get me!"

"Who?" I said, taking off my hat with one hand and drawing a .45 with the other'n.

"A gang of desperadoes!" she panted. "They've chased me for five miles! Oh, please don't let 'em get me!"

"They'll tech you only over my dead carcass," I assured her.

She gimme a look which made my heart turn somersets. She had black curly hair and big innercent gray eyes, and she was the purtiest gal I'd saw in a coon's age.

"Oh, thank you!" she panted. "I knowed you was a gent the minute I seen you. Will you help me up onto my hoss?"

"You shore you ain't hurt none?" I ast, and she said she warn't, so I helped her up, and she gathered up her reins and looked back down the road very nervous. "Don't let 'em foller me!" she begged. "I'm goin' on."

"You don't need to do that," I says. "Wait till I exterminate them scoundrels, and I'll escort you home."

But she started convulsively as the distant pound of hoofs reched us, and said: "Oh, I dast not! They mustn't even see me again!"

"But *I* want to," I said. "Where you live?"

"Red Cougar," says she. "My name's Sue Pritchard. If you happen up that way, drop in."

"I'll be there!" I promised, and she flashed me a dazzling smile and loped on down the road and outa sight up the Red Cougar trail.

SO I SET TO WORK. I USES a rope wove outa buffalo hide, a right smart longer and thicker and stronger'n the average riata because a man my size has got to have a rope to match. I tied said lariat acrost the road about three foot off the ground.

Then I backed Cap'n Kidd into the bushes, and purty soon six men swept around the bend. The first hoss fell over my rope and the others fell over him, and the way they piled up in the road was beautiful to behold. Before you could bat yore eye they was a most amazing tangle of kicking hosses and cussing men. I chose that instant to ride out of the bresh and throw my pistols down on 'em.

"Cease that scandalous langwidge and rise with yore hands up!" I requested, and they done so, but not cheerfully. Some had been kicked right severe by the hosses, and one had pitched over his cayuse's neck and lit on his head, and his conversation warn't noways sensible.

"What's the meanin' of this here hold-up?" demanded a tall maverick with long yaller whiskers.

"Shet up!" I told him sternly. "Men which chases a he'pless gal like a pack of Injuns ain't fittin' for to talk to a white man."

"Oh, so that's it!" says he. "Well, lemme tell yuh—"

"I said shet up!" I roared, emphasizing my request by shooting the left tip offa his mustash. "I don't aim to powwow with no dern women-chasin' coyotes! In my country we'd decorate a live oak with yore carcasses!"

"But you don't—" began one of the others, but Yaller Whiskers profanely told him to shet up.

"Don't yuh see he's one of Ridgeway's men?" snarled he. "He's got the drop on us, but our turn'll come. Till it does, save yore breath!"

"That's good advice," I says. "Onbuckle yore gun-belts and hang 'em on yore saddle-horns, and keep yore hands away from them guns whilst you does it. I'd plumb welcome a excuse to salivate the whole mob of you."

So they done it, and then I fired a few shots under the hosses' feet and stampeded 'em, and they run off down the road the direction they'd come from. Yaller Whiskers and his pals cussed something terrible.

"Better save yore wind," I advised 'em. "You likely got a good long walk ahead of you, before you catches yore cayuses."

"I'll have yore heart's blood for this," raved Yaller Whiskers. "I'll have yore sculp if I have to trail yuh from here to Jedgment Day! Yuh don't know who yo're monkeyin' with."

"And I don't care!" I snorted. "Vamoose!"

They taken out down the road after their hosses, and I shot around their feet a few times to kinda speed 'em on their way. They disappeared down the road in a faint blue haze of profanity, and I turnt around and headed for Red Cougar.

I hoped to catch up with Miss Pritchard before she got to Red Cougar, but she had too good a start and was going at too fast a gait. My heart pounded at the thought of her and my corns begun to ache. It shore was love at first sight.

Well, I'd follered the trail for maybe three miles when I heard guns banging ahead of me. A little bit later I came to where the trail forked and I didn't know which'n led to Red Cougar. Whilst I was setting there wondering which branch to take, I heard hosses running again, and purty soon a couple of men hove in sight, spurring hard and bending low like they was expecting to be shot from behind. When they approached me I seen they had badges onto their vests, and bullet holes in their hats.

"Which is the road to Red Cougar?" I ast perlitely.

"That'n," says the older feller, p'inting back the way they'd come. "But if yo're aimin' to go there I advises yuh to reflect deeply on the matter. Ponder, young man, ponder and meditate! Life is sweet, after all!"

"What you mean?" I ast. "Who're you all chasin'?"

"Chasin' hell!" says he, polishing his sheriff's badge with his sleeve. "We're bein' chased! Buck Ridgeway's in town!"

"Never heard of him," I says.

"Well," says the sheriff, "Buck don't like strangers no more'n he does law-officers. And yuh see how well he likes *them!*"

"This here's a free country!" I snorted. "When I stays outa town on account of this here Ridgeway or anybody else they'll be ice in hell thick enough for the devil to skate on. I'm goin' to visit a young lady—Miss Sue Pritchard. Can you tell me where she lives?"

They looked at me very pecooliar, and the sheriff says: "Oh, in that case—well, she lives in the last cabin north of the general store, on the left-hand side of the street."

"Le's git goin'," urged his deputy nervously. "They may foller us!"

They started spurring again, and as they rode off, I heard the deputy say: "Reckon he's one of 'em?" And the sheriff said: "If he ain't he's the biggest damn fool that ever lived, to come sparkin' Sue Pritchard—" Then they rode outa hearing. I wondered who they was talking about, but soon forgot it as I rode on into Red Cougar.

I COME IN ON the south end of the town, and it was about like all them little mountain villages. One straggling street, hound dogs sleeping in the dust of the wagon ruts, and a general store and a couple of saloons.

I seen some hosses tied at the hitching rack outside the biggest saloon which said "Mac's Bar" on it, but I didn't see nobody on the streets, although noises of hilarity was coming outa the saloon. I was thirsty and dusty, and I decided I better have me a drink and spruce up some before I called on Miss Pritchard. So I watered Cap'n Kidd at the trough, and tied him to a tree (if I'd tied him to the hitch rack he'd of kicked the tar outa the other hosses) and went into the saloon. They warn't nobody in there but a old coot with gray whiskers tending bar, and the noise was all coming from another room. From the racket I jedged they was a bowling alley in there and the gents was bowling.

I beat the dust outa my pants with my hat and called for whiskey. Whilst I was drinking it the feller said: "Stranger in town, hey?"

I said I was and he said: "Friend of Buck Ridgeway's?"

"Never seen him in my life," says I, and he says: "Then you better git outa town fast as you can dust it. Him and his bunch ain't here—he pulled out jest a little while ago—but Jeff Middleton's in there, and Jeff's plenty bad."

I started to tell him I warn't studying Jeff Middleton, but jest then a lot of whooping bust out in the bowling alley like somebody had made a ten-strike or something, and here come six men busting into the bar whooping and yelling and slapping one of 'em on the back.

"Decorate the mahogany, McVey!" they whooped. "Jeff's buyin'! He jest beat Tom Grissom here six straight games!"

They surged up to the bar and one of 'em tried to jostle me aside, but as nobody ain't been able to do that successful since I got my full growth, all he done was sprain his elbow. This seemed to irritate him, because he turnt around and said heatedly: "What the hell you think yo're doin'?"

"I'm drinkin' me a glass of corn squeezin's," I replied coldly, and they all turnt around and looked at me, and they moved back from the bar and hitched at their pistol-belts. They was a hard looking gang, and the feller they called Middleton was the hardest looking one of 'em.

"Who're you and where'd you come from?" he demanded.

"None of yore damn business," I replied with a touch of old Southern curtesy.

He showed his teeth at this and fumbled at his gun-belt.

"Air you tryin' to start somethin'?" he demanded, and I seen McVey hide behind a stack of beer kaigs.

"I ain't in the habit of startin' trouble," I told him. "All I does is end it. I'm in here drinkin' me a quiet dram when you coyotes come surgin' in hollerin' like you was the first critter which ever hit a pin."

"So you depreciates my talents, hey?" he squalled like he was stung to the quick. "Maybe you think you could beat me, hey?"

"I ain't yet seen the man which could hold a candle to my game," I replied with my usual modesty.

"All right!" he yelled, grinding his teeth. "Come into the alley, and I'll show you some action, you big mountain grizzly!"

"Hold on!" says McVey, sticking his head up from behind the kaigs. "Be keerful, Jeff! I believe that's—"

"I don't keer who he is!" raved Middleton. "He has give me a mortal insult! Come on, you, if you got the nerve!"

"You be careful with them insults!" I roared menacingly, striding into the alley. "I ain't the man to be bulldozed." I was looking back over my shoulder when

I shoved the door open with my palm and I probably pushed harder'n I intended to, and that's why I tore the door offa the hinges. They all looked kinda startled, and McVey give a despairing squeak, but I went on into the alley and picked up a bowl ball which I brandished in defiance.

"Here's fifty bucks!" I says, waving the greenbacks. "We puts up fifty each and rolls for five dollars a game. That suit you?"

I couldn't understand what he said, because he jest made a noise like a wolf grabbing a beefsteak, but he snatched up a bulldog, and perjuiced ten five-dollar bills, so I jedged it was agreeable with him.

But he had a awful temper, and the longer we played, the madder he got, and when I had beat him five straight games and taken twenty-five outa his fifty, the veins stood out purple onto his temples.

"It's yore roll," I says, and he throwed his bowl ball down and yelled: "Blast yore soul, I don't like yore style! I'm through and I'm takin' down my stake! You gits no more of my money, damn you!"

"Why, you cheap-heeled piker!" I roared. "I thought you was a sport, even if you was a hoss-thief, but—"

"Don't you call me a hoss-thief!" he screamed.

"Well, cow-thief then," I says. "If yo're so dern particular—"

IT WAS AT THIS INSTANT that he lost his head to the p'int of pulling a pistol and firing at me p'int-blank. He would of ondoubtedly shot me, too, if I hadn't hit him in the head with my bowl ball jest as he fired. His bullet went into the ceiling and his friends begun to display their disapproval by throwing pins and bulldogs at me. This irritated me almost beyond control, but I kept my temper and taken a couple of 'em by the neck and beat their heads together till they was limp. The matter would of ended there, without any vi'lence, but the other three insisted on taking the thing serious, and I defy any man to remain tranquil when three hoss-thieves are kyarving at him with bowies and beating him over the head with ten-pins.

But I didn't intend to bust the big ceiling lamp; I jest hit it by accident with the chair which I knocked one of my enermies stiff with. And it warn't my fault if one of 'em got blood all over the alley. All I done was break his nose and knock out seven teeth with my fist. How'd I know he was going to fall in the alley and bleed on it. As for that section of wall which got knocked out, all I can say is it's a derned flimsy wall which can be wrecked by throwing a man through it. I thought I'd throwed him through a winder until I looked closer and seen it was a hole he busted through the wall. And can I help it if them scalawags blowed holes in the roof till it looked like a sieve trying to shoot me?

It wasn't my fault, nohow.

But when the dust settled and I looked around to see if I'd made a clean sweep, I was jest in time to grab the shotgun which old man McVey was trying to shoot me through the barroom door with.

"You oughta be ashamed," I reproved. "A man of yore age and venerable whiskers, tryin' to shoot a defenseless stranger in the back."

"But my bowlin' alley's wrecked!" he wept, tearing the aforesaid whiskers. "I'm a rooint man! I sunk my wad in it—and now look at it!"

"Aw, well," I says, "it warn't my fault, but I cain't see a honest man suffer. Here's seventy-five dollars, all I got."

"'Tain't enough," says he, nevertheless making a grab for the dough like a kingfisher diving after a pollywog. "'Tain't near enough."

"I'll collect the rest from them coyotes," I says.

"Don't do it!" he shuddered. "They'd kill me after you left!"

"I wanta do the right thing," I says. "I'll work out the rest of it."

He looked at me right sharp then, and says: "Come into the bar."

But I seen three of 'em was coming to, so I hauled 'em up and told 'em sternly to tote their friends out to the hoss trough and bring 'em to. They done so, kinda wabbling on their feet. They acted like they was still addled in the brains, and McVey said it looked to him like Middleton was out for the day, but I told him it was quite common for a man to be like that which has jest had a fifteen-pound bowling ball split in two over his head.

Then I went into the bar with McVey and he poured out the drinks.

"Air you in earnest about workin' out that debt?" says he.

"Sure," I said. "I always pays my debts, by fair means or foul."

"Ain't you Breckinridge Elkins?" says he, and when I says I was, he says: "I thought I rekernized you when them fools was badgerin' you. Look out for 'em. That ain't all of 'em. The whole gang rode into town a hour or so ago and run the sheriff and his deperty out, but Buck didn't stay long. He seen his gal, and then he pulled out for the hills again with four men. They's a couple more besides them you fit hangin' around somewheres. I dunno where."

"Outlaws?" I said, and he said: "Shore. But the local law-force ain't strong enough to deal with 'em, and anyway, most of the folks in town is in cahoots with 'em, and warns 'em if officers from outside come after 'em. They hang out in the hills ordinary, but they come into Red Cougar regular. But never mind them. I was jest puttin' you on yore guard.

"This is what I want you to do. A month ago I was comin' back to Red Cougar with a tidy fortune in gold dust I'd panned back up in the hills, when I was held up and robbed. It warn't one of Ridgeway's men; it was Three-Fingers

Clements, a old lone wolf and the wust killer in these parts. He lives by hisself up in the hills and nobody knows where.

"But I jest recent learnt by accident. He sent a message by a sheepherder and the sheepherder got drunk in my saloon and talked. I learnt he's still got my gold, and aims to sneak out with it as soon as he's j'ined by a gang of desperadoes from Tomahawk. It was them the sheepherder was takin' the message to. I cain't git no help from the sheriff; these outlaws has got him plumb buffaloed. I want you to ride up in the hills and git my gold. Of course, if yo're scairt of him—"

"Who said I was scairt of him or anybody else?" I demanded irritably. "Tell me how to git to his hide-out and I'm on my way."

McVey's eyes kinda gleamed, and he says: "Good boy! Foller the trail that leads outa town to the northwest till you come to Diablo Canyon. Foller it till you come to the fifth branch gulch openin' into it on the right. Turn off the trail then and foller the gulch till you come to a big white oak nigh the left-hand wall. Climb up outa the gulch there and head due west up the slope. Purty soon you'll see a crag like a chimney stickin' out above a clump of spruces. At the foot of that crag they's a cave, and Clements is livin' there. And he's a tough old—"

"It's as good as did," I assured him, and had another drink, and went out and clumb aboard Cap'n Kidd and headed out of town.

BUT AS I RODE PAST THE last cabin on the left, I suddenly remembered about Sue Pritchard, and I 'lowed Three Fingers could wait long enough for me to pay my respecks on her. Likely she was expecting me and getting nervous and impatient because I was so long coming. So I reined up to the stoop and hailed, and somebody looked at me through a winder. They also appeared to be a rifle muzzle trained on me, too, but who could blame folks for being cautious with them Ridgeway coyotes in town.

"Oh, it's you!" said a female voice, and then the door opened and Sue Pritchard said: "Light and come in! Did you kill any of them rascals?"

"I'm too soft-hearted for my own good," I says apologetically. "I jest merely only sent 'em down the road on foot. But I ain't got time to come in now. I'm on my way up in the mountains to see Three Fingers Clements. I aimed to stop on my way back, if it's agreeable with you."

"Three Fingers Clements?" says she in a pecooliar voice. "Do you know where he is?"

"McVey told me," I said. "He's got a poke of dust he stole from McVey. I'm goin' after it."

She said something under her breath which I must have misunderstood because I was sure Miss Pritchard wouldn't use the word it sounded like.

"Come in jest a minute," she begged. "You got plenty of time. Come in and have a snort of corn juice. My folks is all visitin' and it gets mighty lonesome to a gal. Please come in!"

Well, I never could resist a purty gal, so I tied Cap'n Kidd to a stump that looked solid, and went in, and she brung out her old man's jug. It was tolerable licker. She said she never drunk none, personal.

We set and talked, and there wasn't a doubt we cottoned to each other right spang off. There is some that says that Breckinridge Elkins hain't got a lick of sense when it comes to wimmin-folks—among these bein' my cousin, Bearfield Buckner—but I vow and declare that same is my only weakness, if any, and that likewise it is manly weakness.

This Sue Pritchard was plumb sensible I seen. She wasn't one of these flighty kind that a feller would have to court with a banjo or geetar. We talked around about bear-traps and what was the best length barrel on shotguns and similar subjects of like nature. I likewise told her one or two of my mild experiences and her eyes boogered big as saucers. We finally got around to my latest encounter.

"Tell me some more about Three Fingers," she coaxed. "I didn't know anybody knowed his hide-out." So I told her what all McVey said, and she was a heap interested, and had me repeat the instructions how to get there two or three times. Then she ast me if I'd met any badmen in town, and I told her I'd met six and they was now recovering on pallets in the back of the general store. She looked startled at this, and purty soon she ast me to excuse her because she heard one of the neighbor women calling her. I didn't hear nobody, but I said all right, and she went out of the back door, and I heard her whistle three times. I sot there and had another snort or so and reflected that the gal was ondoubtedly taken with me.

She was gone quite a spell, and finally I got up and looked out the back winder and seen her standing down by the corral talking to a couple of fellers. As I looked one of 'em got on a bobtailed roan and headed north at a high run, and t'other'n come on back to the cabin with Sue.

"This here's my cousin Jack Montgomery," says she. "He wants to go with you. He's jest a boy, and likes excitement."

He was about the hardest-looking boy I ever seen, and he seemed remarkable mature for his years, but I said: "All right. But we got to git goin'."

"Be careful, Breckinridge," she advised. "You, too, Jack."

"I won't hurt Three Fingers no more'n I got to," I promised her, and we went on our way yonderly, headed for the hideout.

WE GOT TO DIABLO CANYON in about a hour, and went up it about three miles till we come to the gulch mouth McVey had described. All to onst Jack

Montgomery pulled up and p'inted down at a pool we was passing in a holler of the rock, and hollered: "Look there! Gold dust scattered at the aidge of the water!"

"I don't see none," I says.

"Light," he urged, getting off his cayuse. "I see it! It's thick as butter along the aidge!"

Well, I got down and bent over the pool but I couldn't see nothing and all to onst something hit me in the back of the head and knocked my hat off. I turnt around and seen Jack Montgomery holding the bent barrel of a Winchester carbine in his hands. The stock was busted off and pieces was laying on the ground. He looked awful surprized about something; his eyes was wild and his hair stood up.

"Air you sick?" I ast. "What you want to hit me for?"

"You ain't human!" he gasped, dropping the bent barrel and jerking out his pistol. I grabbed him and taken it away from him.

"What's the matter with you?" I demanded. "Air you locoed?"

For answer he run off down the canyon shrieking like a lost soul. I decided he must have went crazy like sheepherders does sometimes, so I pursued him and catched him. He fit and hollered like a painter.

"Stop that!" I told him sternly. "I'm yore friend. It's my duty to yore cousin to see that you don't come to no harm."

"Cousin, hell!" says he with frightful profanity. "She ain't no more my cousin than you be."

"Pore feller," I sighed, throwing him on his belly and reaching for his lariat. "Yo're outa yore head and sufferin' from hallucernations. I knowed a sheepherder jest like you onst, only he thought he was Sittin' Bull."

"What you doin'?" he hollered, as I started tying him with his rope.

"Don't you worry," I soothed him. "I cain't let you go tearin' around over these mountains in yore condition. I'll fix you so's you'll be safe and comfortable till I git back from Three Fingers' cave. Then I'll take you to Red Cougar and we'll send you to some nice, quiet insane asylum."

"Blast yore soul!" he shrieked. "I'm sane as you be! A damn sight saner, because no man with a normal brain could ignore gittin' a rifle stock broke off over his skull like you done!"

Whereupon he tries to kick me between the eyes and otherwise give evidence of what I oncet heard a doctor call his derangement. It was a pitiful sight to see, especially since he was a cousin to Miss Sue Pritchard and would ondoubtedly be my cousin-in-law one of these days. He jerked and rassled and some of his words was downright shocking.

But I didn't pay no attention to his ravings. I always heard the way to get along with crazy people was to humor 'em. I was afeared if I left him laying on the ground the wolves might chaw him, so I tied him up in the crotch of a big tree where they couldn't rech him. I likewise tied his hoss by the pool where it could drink and graze.

"Lissen!" Jack begged as I clumb onto Cap'n Kidd. "I give up! Ontie me and I'll spill the beans! I'll tell you everything!"

"You jest take it easy," I soothed. "I'll be back soon."

"$#%&*@!" says he, frothing slightly at the mouth.

With a sigh of pity I turnt up the gulch, and his langwidge till I was clean outa sight ain't to be repeated. A mile or so on I come to the white oak tree, and clumb outa the gulch and went up a long slope till I seen a jut of rock like a chimney rising above the trees. I slid offa Cap'n Kidd and drawed my pistols and snuck for'ard through the thick bresh till I seen the mouth of a cave ahead of me. And I also seen something else, too.

A man was laying in front of it with his head in a pool of blood.

I rolled him over and he was still alive. His sculp was cut open, but the bone didn't seem to be caved in. He was a lanky old coot, with reddish gray whiskers, and he didn't have but three fingers onto his left hand. They was a pack tore up and scattered on the ground nigh him, but I reckon the pack mule had run off. They was also hoss-tracks leading west.

They was a spring nearby and I brung my hat full of water and sloshed it into his face, and tried to pour some into his mouth, but it warn't no go. When I throwed the water over him he kinda twitched and groaned, but when I tried to pour the water down his gullet he kinda instinctively clamped his jaws together like a bulldog.

Then I seen a jug setting in the cave, so I brung it out and pulled out the cork. When it popped he opened his mouth convulsively and reched out his hand.

So I poured a pint or so down his gullet, and he opened his eyes and glared wildly around till he seen his busted pack, and then he clutched his whiskers and shrieked: "They got it! My poke of dust! I been hidin' up here for weeks, and jest when I was goin' to make a jump for it, they finds me!"

"Who?" I ast.

"Buck Ridgeway and his gang!" he squalled. "I was keerless. When I heard hosses I thought it was the men which was comin' to help me take my gold out. Next thing I knowed Ridgeway's bunch had run outa the bresh and was beatin' me over the head with their Colts. I'm a rooint man!"

"Hell's fire!" quoth I with passion. Them Ridgeways was beginning to get on my nerves. I left old man Clements howling his woes to the skies like a timber wolf with the bellyache, and I forked Cap'n Kidd and headed west. They'd left a trail the youngest kid on Bear Creek could foller.

IT LED FOR FIVE MILES through as wild a country as I ever seen outside the Humbolts, and then I seen a cabin ahead, on a wide benchland and that backed agen a steep mountain slope. I could jest see the chimney through the tops of a dense thicket. It warn't long till sun-down and smoke was coming outa the chimney.

I knowed it must be the Ridgeway hideout, so I went busting through the thicket in sech a hurry that I forgot they might have a man on the look-out. I'm powerful absent minded thataway. They was one all right, but I was coming so fast he missed me with his buffalo gun, and he didn't stop to reload but run into the cabin yelling: "Bar the door quick! Here comes the biggest man in the world on the biggest hoss in creation!"

They done so. When I emerged from amongst the trees they opened up on me through the loop-holes with sawed-off shotguns. If it'd been Winchesters I'd of ignored 'em, but even I'm a little bashful about buckshot at close range, when six men is shooting at me all to onst. So I retired behind a big tree and begun to shoot back with my pistols, and the howls of them worthless critters when my bullets knocked splinters in their faces was music to my ears.

They was a corral some distance behind the cabin with six hosses in it. To my surprise I seen one of 'em was a bob-tailed roan the feller was riding which I seen talking with Sue Pritchard and Jack Montgomery, and I wondered if them blame outlaws had captured him.

But I warn't accomplishing much, shooting at them loop-holes, and the sun dipped lower and I began to get mad. I decided to rush the cabin anyway and to hell with their derned buckshot, and I dismounted and stumped my toe right severe on a rock. It always did madden me to stump my toe, and I uttered some loud and profane remarks, and I reckon them scoundrels must of thunk I'd stopped some lead, the way they whooped. But jest then I had a inspiration. A big thick smoke was pouring outa the rock chimney so I knowed they was a big fire on the fireplace where they was cooking supper, and I was sure they warn't but one door in the cabin. So I taken up the rock which was about the size of a ordinary pig and throwed it at the chimney.

Boys on Bear Creek is ashamed if they have to use more'n one rock on a squirrel in a hundred-foot tree acrost the creek, and I didn't miss. I hit her center and she buckled and come crashing down in a regular shower of rocks, and most of 'em fell down into the fireplace as I knowed by the way the sparks flew. I jedged that the coals was scattered all over the floor, and the chimney hole was blocked so the smoke couldn't get out that way. Anyway, the smoke begun to pour outa the winders and the Ridgewayers stopped shooting and started hollering.

Somebody yelled: "The floor's on fire! Throw that bucket of water on it!" And somebody else shrieked: "Wait, you damn fool! That ain't water, it's whiskey!"

But he was too late; I heard the splash and then a most amazing flame sprung up and licked outa the winders and the fellers hollered louder'n ever and yelled: "Lemme out! I got smoke in my eyes! I'm chokin' to death!"

I left the thicket and run to the door just as a man throwed it open and staggered out blind as a bat and cussing and shooting wild. I was afeared he'd hurt hisself if he kept tearing around like that, so I taken his shotgun away from him and bent the barrel over his head to kinda keep him quiet, and then I seen to my surprize that he was the feller which rode the bob-tailed roan. I thunk how surprized Sue'd be to know a friend of her'n was a cussed outlaw.

I then went into the cabin which was so full of smoke and gun-powder fumes a man couldn't hardly see nothing. The walls and roof was on fire by now, and them idjits was tearing around with their eyes full of smoke trying to find the door, and one of 'em run head-on into the wall and knocked hisself stiff. I throwed him outside, and got hold of another'n to lead him out, and he cut me acrost the boozum with his bowie. I was so stung by this ingratitude that when I tossed him out to safety I maybe throwed him further'n I aimed to, and it appears they was a stump which he hit his head on. But I couldn't help it being there.

I THEN TURNT AROUND and located the remaining three, which was fighting with each other evidently thinking they was fighting me. Jest as I started for 'em a big log fell outa the roof and knocked two of 'em groggy and sot their clothes on fire, and a regular sheet of flame sprung up and burnt off most of my hair, and whilst I was dazzled by it the surviving outlaw run past me out the door, leaving his smoking shirt in my hand.

Well, I dragged the other two out and stomped on 'em to put out the fire, and the way they hollered you'd of thought I was injuring 'em instead of saving their fool lives.

"Shet up and tell me where the gold is," I ordered, and one of 'em gurgled: "Ridgeway's got it!"

I ast which'n of 'em was him and they all swore they wasn't, and I remembered the feller which run outa the cabin. So I looked around and seen him jest leading a hoss outa the corral to ride off bareback.

"You stop!" I roared, letting my voice out full, which I seldom does. The acorns rattled down outa the trees, and the tall grass bent flat, and the hoss Ridgeway was fixing to mount got scairt and jerked away from him and bolted, and the other hosses knocked the corral gate down and stampeded. Three or four of 'em run over Ridgeway before he could git outa the way.

He jumped up and headed out acrost the flat on foot, wabbling some but going strong. I could of shot him easy but I was afeared he'd hid the gold somewheres, and if I kilt him he couldn't tell me where. So I run and got my lariat and taken out after him on foot, because I figgered he'd duck into the thick bresh to get away. But when he seen I was overhauling him he made for the mountain side and began to climb a steep slope.

I follered him, but before he was much more'n half way up he taken refuge on a ledge behind a dead tree and started shooting at me. I got behind a boulder about seventy-five foot below him, and ast him to surrender, like a gent, but his only reply was a direct slur on my ancestry and more bullets, one of which knocked off a sliver of rock which gouged my neck.

This annoyed me so much that I pulled my pistols and started shooting back at him. But all I could hit was the tree, and the sun was going down and I was afeared if I didn't get him before dark he'd manage to sneak off. So I stood up, paying no attention to the slug he put in my shoulder, and swang my lariat. I always uses a ninety-foot rope; I got no use for them little bitsy pieces of string most punchers uses.

I threw my noose and looped that tree, and sot my feet solid and heaved, and tore the dern tree up by the roots. But them roots went so deep most of the ledge come along with 'em, and that started a landslide. The first thing I knowed here come the tree and Ridgeway and several tons of loose rock and shale, gathering weight and speed as they come. It sounded like thunder rolling down the mountain, and Ridgeway's screams was frightful to hear. I jumped out from behind the boulder intending to let the landslide split on me and grab him out as it went past me, but I stumbled and fell and that dern tree hit me behind the ear and the next thing I knowed I was traveling down the mountain with Ridgeway and the rest of the avalanche. It was very humiliating.

I was right glad at the time, I recollect, that Miss Sue Pritchard wasn't nowheres near to witness this catastrophe. It's hard for a man to keep his dignity, I found, when he's scootin' in a hell-slue of trees and bresh and rocks and dirt, and I become aware, too, that a snag had tore the seat outa my pants, which made me some despondent. This, I figgered, is what a man gets for losing his self-control. I recollected another time or two when I'd exposed myself to the consequences by exertin' my full strength, and I made me a couple of promises then and there.

It's all right for a single young feller to go hellin' around and let the chips fall where they may, but it's different with a man like me who was almost just the same as practically married. You got to look before you leap, was the way I reckoned it. A man's got to think of his wife and children.

We brung up at the foot of the slope in a heap of boulders and shale, and I throwed a few hundred pounds of busted rocks offa me and riz up and shaken the blood outa my eyes and looked around for Ridgeway.

I presently located a boot sticking outa the heap, and I laid hold onto it and hauled him out and he looked remarkable like a skint rabbit. About all the clothes he had left onto him beside his boots was his belt, and I seen a fat buckskin poke stuck under it. So I dragged it out, and about that time he sot up groggy and looked around dizzy and moaned feeble: "Who the hell are you?"

"Breckinridge Elkins, of Bear Creek," I said.

"And with all the men they is in the State of Nevada," he says weakly, "I *had* to tangle with you. What you goin' to do?"

"I think I'll turn you and yore gang over to the sheriff," I says. "I don't hold much with law—we ain't never had none on Bear Creek—but sech coyotes as you all don't deserve no better."

"A hell of a right you got to talk about law!" he said fiercely. "After plottin' with Badger McVey to rob old man Clements! That's all I done!"

"What you mean?" I demanded. "Clements robbed McVey of this here dust—"

"Robbed hell!" says Ridgeway. "McVey is the crookedest cuss that ever lived, only he ain't got the guts to commit robbery hisself. Why, Clements is a honest miner, the old jackass, and he panned that there dust up in the hills. He's been hidin' for weeks, scairt to try to git outa the country, we was huntin' him too industrious."

"McVey put me up to committin' robbery?" I ejaculated, aghast.

"That's jest what he did!" declared Ridgeway, and I was so overcome by this perfidy that I was plumb paralyzed. Before I could recover Ridgeway give a convulsive flop and rolled over into the bushes and was gone in a instant.

THE NEXT THING I KNOWED I heard hosses running and I turnt in time to see a bunch of men riding up on me. Old man Clements was with 'em, and I rekernized the others as the fellers I stopped from chasing Sue Pritchard on the road below Red Cougar.

I reched for a pistol, but Clements yelled: "Hold on! They're friends!" He then jumped off and grabbed the poke outa my limp hand and waved it at them triumphantly. "See that?" he hollered. "Didn't I tell you he was a friend? Didn't I tell you he come up here to bust up that gang? He got my gold back for me, jest like I said he would!" He then grabbed my hand and shaked it energetic, and says: "These is the men I sent to Tomahawk for, to help me git my gold out. They got to my cave jest a while after you left. They're prejudiced agen you, but—"

"No, we ain't!" denied Yaller Whiskers, which I now seen was wearing a deputy's badge. And *he* got off and shaken my hand heartily. "You didn't know we was special law-officers, and I reckon it did look bad, six men chasin' a woman. We thought *you* was a outlaw! We was purty mad at you when we finally caught our hosses and headed back. But I begun to wonder about you when we found them six disabled outlaws in the store at Red Cougar. Then when we got to Clements' cave, and found you'd befriended him, and had lit out on Ridgeway's trail, it looked still better for you, but I still thought maybe you was after that gold on yo're own account. But, of course, I see now I was all wrong, and I apolergizes. Where's Ridgeway?"

"He got away," I said.

"Never mind!" says Clements, pumping my hand again. "Kirby here and his men has got Jeff Middleton and five more men in the jail at Red Cougar. McVey, the old hypocrite, taken to the hills when Kirby rode into town. And we got six more of Ridgeway's gang tied up over at Ridgeway's cabin—or where it was till you burnt it down. They're shore a battered mob! It musta been a awful fight! You look like you been through a tornado yoreself. Come on with us and our prisoners to Tomahawk. I buys you a new suit of clothes, and we celebrates!"

"I got to git a feller I left tied up in a tree down the gulch," I said. "Jack Montgomery. He's et loco weed or somethin'. He's crazy."

They laughed hearty, and Kirby says: "You got a great sense of humor, Elkins. We found him when we come up the gulch, and brung him on with us. He's tied up with the rest of 'em back there. You shore was slick, foolin' McVey into tellin' you where Clements was hidin', and foolin' that whole Ridgeway gang into thinkin' you aimed to rob Clements! Too bad you didn't know we was officers, so we could of worked together. But I gotta laugh when I think how McVey thought he was gyppin' you into stealin' for him, and all the time you was jest studyin' how to rescue Clements and bust up Ridgeway's gang! Haw! Haw! Haw!"

"But I didn't—" I begun dizzily, because my head was swimming.

"You jest made one mistake," says Kirby, "and that was when you let slip where Clements was hidin'."

"But I never told nobody but Sue Pritchard!" I says wildly.

"Many a good man has been euchered by a woman," says Kirby tolerantly. "We got the whole yarn from Montgomery. The minute you told her, she snuck out and called in two of Ridgeway's men and sent one of 'em foggin' it to tell Buck where to find Clements, and she sent the other'n, which was Montgomery, to go along with you and lay you out before you could git there. She lit for the hills when we come into Red Cougar and I bet her and Ridgeway are streakin' it over the mountains together right now. But that ain't yore fault. You didn't know she was Buck's gal."

The perfidity of wimmen!

"Gimme my hoss," I said groggily. "I been scorched and shot and cut and fell on by a avalanche, and my honest love has been betrayed. You sees before you the singed, skint and blood-soaked result of female treachery. Fate has dealt me the joker. My heart is busted and the seat is tore outa my pants. Git outa the way. I'm ridin'."

"Where to?" they ast, awed.

"Anywhere," I bellers, "jest so it's far away from Red Cougar."

HIGH HORSE RAMPAGE

I GOT A LETTER FROM Aunt Saragosa Grimes the other day which said:

Dear Breckinridge:

I believe time is softenin' yore Cousin Bearfield Buckner's feelings toward you. He was over here to supper the other night jest after he
shot the three Evans boys, and he was in the best humor I seen him in
since he got back from Colorado. So I jest kind of casually mentioned
you and he didn't turn near as purple as he used to every time he heered
yore name mentioned. He jest kind of got a little green around the
years, and that might of been on account of him chokin on the b'ar
meat he was eatin'. And all he said was he was going to beat yore brains
out with a post oak maul if he ever ketched up with you, which is the
mildest remark he's made about you since he got back to Texas. I believe
he's practically give up the idee of sculpin' you alive and leavin' you on
the prairie for the buzzards with both laigs broke like he used to swear
was his sole ambition. I believe in a year or so it would be safe for you
to meet dear Cousin Bearfield, and if you do have to shoot him, I hope

you'll be broad-minded and shoot him in some place which ain't vital because after all you know it was yore fault to begin with. We air all well and nothin's happened to speak of except Joe Allison got a arm broke argyin' politics with Cousin Bearfield. Hopin' you air the same, I begs to remane,

Yore lovin' Ant Saragosa.

It's heartening to know a man's kin is thinking kindly of him and forgetting petty grudges. But I can see that Bearfield is been misrepresenting things and pizening Aunt Saragosa's mind agen me, otherwise she wouldn't of made that there remark about it being my fault. All fair-minded men knows that what happened warn't my fault—that is all except Bearfield, and he's naturally prejudiced, because most of it happened to him.

I knowed Bearfield was somewheres in Colorado when I j'ined up with Old Man Brant Mulholland to make a cattle drive from the Pecos to the Platte, but that didn't have nothing to do with it. I expects to run into Bearfield almost any place where the licker is red and the shotguns is sawed-offs. He's a liar when he says I come into the High Horse country a-purpose to wreck his life and ruin his career.

Everything I done to him was in kindness and kindredly affection. But he ain't got no gratitude. When I think of the javelina meat I et and the bare-footed bandits I had to associate with whilst living in Old Mexico to avoid having to kill that wuthless critter, his present attitude embitters me.

I never had no notion of visiting High Horse in the first place. But we run out of grub a few miles north of there, so what does Old Man Mulholland do but rout me outa my blankets before daylight, and says, "I want you to take the chuck wagon to High Horse and buy some grub. Here's fifty bucks. If you spends a penny of that for anything but bacon, beans, flour, salt and coffee, I'll have yore life, big as you be."

"Why'n't you send the cook?" I demanded.

"He's layin' helpless in a chaparral thicket reekin' with the fumes of vaniller extract," says Old Man Mulholland. "Anyway, yo're responsible for this famine. But for yore inhuman appetite we'd of had enough grub to last the whole drive. Git goin'. Yo're the only man in the string I trust with money and I don't trust you no further'n I can heave a bull by the tail."

Us Elkinses is sensitive about sech remarks, but Old Man Mulholland was born with a conviction that everybody is out to swindle him, so I maintained a dignerfied silence outside of telling him to go to hell, and harnessed the mules to the chuck wagon and headed for Antioch. I led Cap'n Kidd behind the wagon because I knowed if I left him unguarded he'd kill every he-hoss in the camp before I got back.

Well, jest as I come to the forks where the trail to Gallego splits off of the

High Horse road, I heard somebody behind me thumping a banjer and singing, "Oh, Nora he did build the Ark!" So I pulled up and purty soon around the bend come the derndest looking rig I'd saw since the circus come to War Paint.

It was a buggy all painted red, white and blue and drawed by a couple of wall-eyed pintos. And they was a feller in it with a long-tailed coat and a plug hat and fancy checked vest, and a cross-eyed nigger playing a banjer, with a monkey setting on his shoulder.

The white man taken off his plug hat and made me a bow, and says, "Greetings, my mastodonic friend! Can you inform me which of these roads leads to the fair city of High Horse?"

"That's leadin' south," I says. "T'other'n goes east to Gallego. Air you all part of a circus?"

"I resents the implication," says he. "In me you behold the greatest friend to humanity since the inventor of corn licker. I am Professor Horace J. Lattimer, inventor and sole distributor of that boon to suffering humanity, Lattimer's Lenitive Loco Elixir, good for man or beast!"

He then h'isted a jug out from under the seat and showed it to me and a young feller which had jest rode up along the road from Gallego.

"A sure cure," says he. "Have you a hoss which has nibbled the seductive loco-weed? That huge brute you've got tied to the end-gate there looks remarkable wild in his eye, now—"

"He ain't loco," I says. "He's jest blood-thirsty."

"Then I bid you both a very good day, sirs," says he. "I must be on my way to allay the sufferings of mankind. I trust we shall meet in High Horse."

So he drove on, and I started to cluck to the mules, when the young feller from Gallego, which had been eying me very close, he says, "Ain't you Breckinridge Elkins?"

When I says I was, he says with some bitterness, "That there perfessor don't have to go to High Horse to find locoed critters. They's a man in Gallego right now, crazy as a bedbug—yore own cousin, Bearfield Buckner!"

"What?" says I with a vi'lent start, because they hadn't never been no insanity in the family before, only Bearfield's great-grand-uncle Esau who onst voted agen Hickory Jackson. But he recovered before the next election.

"It's the truth," says the young feller. "He's sufferin' from a hallucination that he's goin' to marry a gal over to High Horse by the name of Ann Wilkins. They ain't even no gal by that name there. He was havin' a fit in the saloon when I left, me not bearin' to look on the rooins of a onst noble character. I'm feared he'll do hisself a injury if he ain't restrained."

"Hell's fire!" I said in great agitation. "Is this the truth?"

"True as my name's Lem Campbell," he declared. "I thought bein' as how yo're a relation of his'n, if you could kinda git him out to my cabin a few miles south of Gallego, and keep him there a few days maybe he might git his mind back—"

"I'll do better'n that," I says, jumping out of the wagon and tying the mules. "Foller me," I says, forking Cap'n Kidd. The Perfessor's buggy was jest going out of sight around a bend, and I lit out after it. I was well ahead of Lem Campbell when I overtaken it. I pulled up beside it in a cloud of dust and demanded, "You say that stuff kyores man or beast?"

"Absolutely!" declared Lattimer.

"Well, turn around and head for Gallego," I said. "I got you a patient."

"But Gallego is but a small inland village" he demurs. "There is a railroad and many saloons at High Horse and—"

"With a human reason at stake you sets and maunders about railroads!" I roared, drawing a .45 and impulsively shooting a few buttons off of his coat. "I buys yore whole load of loco licker. Turn around and head for Gallego."

"I wouldn't think of argying," says he, turning pale. "Meshak, don't you hear the gentleman? Get out from under that seat and turn these hosses around."

"Yes suh!" says Meshak, and they swung around jest as Lem Campbell galloped up.

I hauled out the wad Old Man Mulholland gimme and says to him, "Take this dough on to High Horse and buy some grub and have it sent out to Old Man Mulholland's cow camp on the Little Yankton. I'm goin' to Gallego and I'll need the wagon to lug Cousin Bearfield in."

"I'll take the grub out myself," he declared, grabbing the wad. "I knowed I could depend on you as soon as I seen you."

So he told me how to get to his cabin, and then lit out for High Horse and I headed back up the trail. When I passed the buggy I hollered, "Foller me into Gallego. One of you drive the chuck wagon which is standin' at the forks. And don't try to shake me as soon as I git out of sight, neither!"

"I wouldn't think of such a thing," says Lattimer with a slight shudder. "Go ahead and fear not. We'll follow you as fast as we can."

So I dusted the trail for Gallego.

It warn't much of a town, with only jest one saloon, and as I rode in I heard a beller in the saloon and the door flew open and three or four fellows come sailing out on their heads and picked theirselves up and tore out up the street.

"Yes," I says to myself," Cousin Bearfield is in town, all right."

GALLEGO LOOKED ABOUT like any town does when Bearfield is celebrating. The stores had their doors locked and the shutters up, nobody was on the streets, and off down acrost the flat I seen a man which I taken to be the sheriff spurring his hoss for the hills. I tied Cap'n Kidd to the hitch-rail and as I approached the saloon I nearly fell over a feller which was crawling around on his all-fours with a bartender's apron on and both eyes swelled shet.

"Don't shoot!" says he. "I give up!"

"What happened?" I ast.

"The last thing I remember is tellin' a feller named Buckner that the Democratic platform was silly," says he. "Then I think the roof must of fell in or somethin'. Surely one man couldn't of did all this to me."

"You don't know my cousin Bearfield," I assured him as I stepped over him and went through the door which was tore off its hinges. I'd begun to think that maybe Lem Campbell had exaggerated about Bearfield; he seemed to be acting in jest his ordinary normal manner. But a instant later I changed my mind.

Bearfield was standing at the bar in solitary grandeur, pouring hisself a drink, and he was wearing the damnedest-looking red, yaller, green and purple shirt ever I seen in my life.

"What," I demanded in horror, "is that thing you got on?"

"If yo're referrin' to my shirt," he retorted with irritation, "it's the classiest piece of goods I could find in Denver. I bought it special for my weddin'."

"It's true!" I moaned. "He's crazy as hell."

I knowed no sane man would wear a shirt like that.

"What's crazy about gittin' married?" he snarled, biting the neck off of a bottle and taking a big snort. "Folks does it every day."

I walked around him cautious, sizing him up and down, which seemed to exasperate him considerable.

"What the hell's the matter with you?" he roared, hitching his harness for'ard. "I got a good mind to—"

"Be ca'm, Cousin Bearfield," I soothed him. "Who's this gal you imagine yo're goin' to marry?"

"I don't imagine nothin' about it, you ignorant ape," he retorts cantankerously. "Her name's Ann Wilkins and she lives in High Horse. I'm ridin' over there right away and we gits hitched today."

I shaken my head mournful and said, "You must of inherited this from yore great-grand-uncle Esau. Pap's always said Esau's insanity might crop out in the Buckners again some time. But don't worry. Esau was kyored and voted a straight Democratic ticket the rest of his life. You can be kyored too, Bearfield, and I'm here to do it. Come with me, Bearfield," I says, getting a good rassling grip on his neck.

"Consarn it!" says Cousin Bearfield, and went into action.

We went to the floor together and started rolling in the general direction of the back door and every time he come up on top he'd bang my head agen the floor which soon became very irksome. However, about the tenth revolution I come up on top and pried my thumb out of his teeth and said, "Bearfield, I don't want to have to use force with you, but—*ulp!*" That was account of him kicking me in the back of the neck.

My motives was of the loftiest, and they warn't no use in the saloon owner belly-aching the way he done afterwards. Was it my fault if Bearfield missed me with a five-gallon demijohn and busted the mirror behind the bar? Could I help it if Bearfield wrecked the billiard table when I knocked him through it? As for the stove which got busted, all I got to say is that self-preservation is the first law of nature. If I hadn't hit Bearfield with the stove he would of ondoubtedly scrambled my features with that busted beer mug he was trying to use like brass knucks.

I'VE HEARD MANIACS fight awful, but I dunno as Bearfield fit any different than usual. He hadn't forgot his old trick of hooking his spur in my neck whilst we was rolling around on the floor, and when he knocked me down with the roulette wheel and started jumping on me with both feet I thought for a minute I was going to weaken. But the shame of having a maniac in the family revived me and I throwed him off and riz and tore up a section of the brass foot-rail and wrapped it around his head. Cousin Bearfield dropped the bowie he'd jest drawed, and collapsed.

I wiped the blood off of my face and discovered I could still see outa one eye. I pried the brass rail off of Cousin Bearfield's head and dragged him out onto the porch by a hind laig, jest as Perfessor Lattimer drove up in his buggy. Meshak was behind him in the chuck wagon with the monkey, and his eyes was as big and white as saucers.

"Where's the patient?" ast Lattimer, and I said, "This here's him! Throw me a rope outa that wagon. We takes him to Lem Campbell's cabin where we can dose him till he recovers his reason."

Quite a crowd gathered whilst I was tying him up, and I don't believe Cousin Bearfield had many friends in Gallego by the remarks they made. When I lifted his limp carcass up into the wagon one of 'em ast me if I was a law. And when I said I warn't, purty short, he says to the crowd, "Why, hell, then, boys, what's to keep us from payin' Buckner back for all the lickin's he's give us? I tell you, it's our chance! He's unconscious and tied up, and this here feller ain't no sheriff."

"Git a rope!" howled somebody. "We'll hang 'em."

They begun to surge for'ards, and Lattimer and Meshak was so scairt they couldn't hardly hold the lines. But I mounted my hoss and pulled my pistols and says. "Meshak, swing that chuck wagon and head south. Perfessor, you foller him. Hey, you, git away from them mules!"

One of the crowd had tried to grab their bridles and stop 'em, so I shot a heel off'n his boot and he fell down hollering bloody murder.

"Git outa the way!" I bellered, swinging my pistols on the crowd, and they give back in a hurry. "Git goin'," I says, firing some shots under the mules' feet to encourage 'em, and the chuck wagon went out of Gallego jumping and bouncing with Meshak holding onto the seat and hollering blue ruin, and the Perfessor come right behind it in his buggy. I follered the Perfessor looking back to see nobody didn't shoot me in the back, because several men had drawed their pistols. But nobody fired till I was out of good pistol range. Then somebody let loose with a buffalo rifle, but he missed me by at least a foot, so I paid no attention to it, and we was soon out of sight of the town.

I was a feared Bearfield might come to and scare the mules with his bellering, but that brass rail must of been harder'n I thought. He was still unconscious when we pulled up to the cabin which stood in a little wooded cove amongst the hills a few miles south of Gallego. I told Meshak to onhitch the mules and turn 'em into the corral whilst I carried Bearfield into the cabin and laid him on a bunk. I told Lattimer to bring in all the elixir he had, and he brung ten gallons in one-gallon jugs. I give him all the money I had to pay for it.

Purty soon Bearfield come to and he raised his head and looked at Perfessor Lattimer setting on the bunk opposite him in his long tailed coat and plug hat, the cross-eyed nigger and the monkey setting beside him. Bearfield batted his eyes and says, "My God, I must be crazy. That can't be real!"

"Sure, yo're crazy, Cousin Bearfield," I soothed him. "But don't worry. We're goin' to kyore you—"

Bearfield here interrupted me with a yell that turned Meshak the color of a fish's belly.

"Untie me, you son of Perdition!" he roared, heaving and flopping on the bunk like a python with the belly-ache, straining agen his ropes till the veins knotted blue on his temples. "I oughta be in High Horse right now gittin' married—"

"See there?" I sighed to Lattimer. "It's a sad case. We better start dosin' him right away. Git a drenchin' horn. What size dose do you give?"

"A quart at a shot for a hoss," he says doubtfully. "But—"

"We'll start out with that," I says. "We can increase the size of the dose if we need to."

IGNORING BEARFIELD'S terrible remarks I was jest twisting the cork out of a jug when I heard somebody say, "What the hell air you doin' in my shack?"

I turned around and seen a bow-legged critter with drooping whiskers glaring at me kinda pop-eyed from the door.

"What you mean, yore shack?" I demanded, irritated at the interruption. "This shack belongs to a friend of mine which has lent it to us."

"Yo're drunk or crazy," says he, clutching at his whiskers convulsively. "Will you git out peaceable or does I have to git vi'lent?"

"Oh, a cussed claim-jumper, hey?" I snorted, taken his gun away from him when he drawed it. But he pulled a bowie so I throwed him out of the shack and shot into the dust around him a few times jest for warning.

"I'll git even with you, you big lummox!" he howled, as he ran for a scrawny looking sorrel he had tied to the fence. "I'll fix you yet," he promised blood-thirstily as he galloped off, shaking his fist at me.

"Who do you suppose he was?" wondered Lattimer, kinda shaky, and I says, "What the hell does it matter? Forgit the incident and help me give Cousin Bearfield his medicine."

That was easier said than did. Tied up as he was, it was all we could do to get that there elixir down him. I thought I never would get his jaws pried open, using the poker for a lever, but when he opened his mouth to cuss me, we jammed the horn in before he could close it. He left the marks of his teeth so deep on that horn it looked like it'd been in a b'ar-trap.

He kept on heaving and kicking till we'd poured a full dose down him and then he kinda stiffened out and his eyes went glassy. When we taken the horn out his jaws worked but didn't make no sound. But the Perfessor said hosses always acted like that when they'd had a good healthy shot of the remedy, so we left Meshak to watch him, and me and Lattimer went out and sot down on the stoop to rest and cool off.

"Why ain't Meshak onhitched yore buggy?" I ast.

"You mean you expect us to stay here overnight?" says he, aghast.

"Over night, hell!" says I. "You stays till he's kyored, if it takes a year. You may have to make up some more medicine if this ain't enough."

"You mean to say we got to rassle with that maniac three times a day like we just did?" squawked Lattimer.

"Maybe he won't be so vi'lent when the remedy takes holt," I encouraged him. Lattimer looked like he was going to choke, but jest then inside the cabin sounds a yell that even made my hair stand up. Cousin Bearfield had found his voice again.

We jumped up and Meshak come out of the cabin so fast he knocked Lattimer out into the yard and fell over him. The monkey was right behind him streaking it like his tail was on fire.

"Oh, lawdy!" yelled Meshak, heading for the tall timber. "Dat crazy man am bustin' dem ropes like dey was twine. He gwine kill us all, sho'!"

I run into the shack and seen Cousin Bearfield rolling around on the floor and cussing amazing, even for him. And to my horror I seen he'd busted some of the ropes so his left arm was free. I pounced on it, but for a few minutes all I was able to do was jest to hold onto it whilst he throwed me hither and thither around the room with freedom and abandon. At last I kind of wore him down and got his arm tied again jest as Lattimer run in and done a snake dance all over the floor.

"Meshak's gone," he howled. "He was so scared he run off with the monkey and my buggy and team. It's all your fault."

Being too winded to argy I jest heaved Bearfield up on the bunk and staggered over and sot down on the other'n, whilst the Perfessor pranced and whooped and swore I owed him for his buggy and team.

"Listen," I said when I'd got my wind back. "I spent all my money for that elixir, but when Bearfield recovers his reason he'll be so grateful he'll be glad to pay you hisself. Now forgit sech sordid trash as money and devote yore scientific knowledge to gittin' Bearfield sane."

"Sane!" howls Bearfield. "Is that what yo're doin'—tyin' me up and pizenin' me? I've tasted some awful muck in my life, but I never drempt nothin' could taste as bad as that stuff you poured down me. It plumb paralyzes a man. Lemme loose, dammit."

"Will you be ca'm if I onties you?" I ast.

"I will," he promised heartily, "jest as soon as I've festooned the surroundin' forest with yore entrails!"

"Still vi'lent," I said sadly. "We better keep him tied, Perfessor."

"But I'm due to git married in High Horse right now!" Bearfield yelled, giving sech a convulsive heave that he throwed hisself clean offa the bunk. It was his own fault, and they warn't no use in him later blaming me because he hit his head on the floor and knocked hisself stiff.

"Well," I said, "at least we'll have a few minutes of peace and quiet around here. Help me lift him back on his bunk."

"What's that?" yelped the Perfessor, jumping convulsively as a rifle cracked out in the bresh and a bullet whined through the cabin.

"That's probably Droopin' Whiskers," I says, lifting Cousin Bearfield. "I thought I seen a Winchester on his saddle. Say, it's gittin' late. See if you cain't find some grub in the kitchen. I'm hungry."

Well, the Perfessor had an awful case of the willies, but we found some bacon and beans in the shack and cooked 'em and et 'em, and fed Bearfield, which had come to when he smelt the grub cooking. I don't think Lattimer enjoyed his meal much because every time a bullet hit the shack he jumped and choked on his grub.

Drooping Whiskers was purty persistent, but he was so far back in the bresh he wasn't doing no damage. He was a rotten shot anyhow. All of his bullets was away too high, as I p'inted out to Lattimer, but the Perfessor warn't happy.

I didn't dare untie Bearfield to let him eat, so I made Lattimer set by him and feed him with a knife, and he was scairt and shook so he kept spilling hot beans down Bearfield's collar, and Bearfield's langwidge was awful to hear.

Time we got through it was long past dark, and Drooping Whiskers had quit shooting at us. As it later appeared, he'd run out of ammunition and gone to borrow some ca'tridges from a ranch house some miles away. Bearfield had quit cussing us, he jest laid there and glared at us with the most horrible expression I ever seen on a human being. It made Lattimer's hair stand up.

But Bearfield kept working at his ropes and I had to examine 'em every little while and now and then put some new ones on him. So I told Lattimer we better give him another dose, and when we finally got it down him, Lattimer staggered into the kitchen and collapsed under the table and I was as near wore out myself as a Elkins can get.

But I didn't dare sleep for fear Cousin Bearfield would get loose and kill me before I could wake up. I sot down on the other bunk and watched him and after while he went to sleep and I could hear the Perfessor snoring out in the kitchen.

About midnight I lit a candle and Bearfield woke up and said, "Blast yore soul, you done woke me up out of the sweetest dream I ever had. I drempt I was fishin' for sharks off Mustang Island."

"What's sweet about that?" I ast.

"I was usin' you for bait," he said. "Hey, what you doin'?"

"It's time for yore dose," I said, and then the battle started. This time he got my thumb in his mouth and would ondoubtedly have chawed it off if I hadn't kind of stunned him with the iron skillet. Before he could recover hisself I had the elixir down him with the aid of Lattimer which had been woke up by the racket.

"How long is this going on?" Lattimer ast despairingly. "*Ow!*"

It was Drooping Whiskers again. This time he'd crawled up purty clost to the house and his first slug combed the Perfessor's hair.

"I'm a patient man but I've reached my limit," I snarled, blowing out the candle and grabbing a shotgun off the wall. "Stay here and watch Bearfield whilst I go out and hang Droopin' Whiskers' hide to the nearest tree."

I snuck out of the cabin on the opposite side from where the shot come from, and begun to sneak around in a circle through the bresh. The moon was coming up, and I knowed I could out-Injun Drooping Whiskers. Any Bear Creek man could. Sure enough, purty soon I slid around a clump of bushes and seen him bending over behind a thicket whilst he took aim at the cabin with a Winchester.

So I emptied both barrels into the seat of his britches and he give a most amazing howl and jumped higher'n I ever seen a bow-legged feller jump, and dropped his Winchester and taken out up the trail toward the north.

I was determined to run him clean off the range this time, so I pursued him and shot at him every now and then, but the dern gun was loaded with bird-shot and all the shells I'd grabbed along with it was the same. I never seen a white man run like he did. I never got clost enough to do no real damage to him, and after I'd chased him a mile or so he turned off into the bresh, and I soon lost him.

Well, I made my way back to the road again, and was jest fixing to step out of the bresh and start down the road toward the cabin, when I heard hosses coming from the north. So I stayed behind a bush, and purty soon a gang of men come around the bend, walking their hosses, with the moonlight glinting on Winchesters in their hands.

"Easy now," says one. "The cabin ain't far down the road. We'll ease up and surround it before they know what's happenin'."

"I wonder what that shootin' was we heered a while back?" says another'n kind of nervous.

"Maybe they was fightin' amongst theirselves," says yet another'n. "No matter. We'll rush in and settle the big feller's hash before he knows what's happenin'. Then we'll string Buckner up."

"What you reckon they kidnaped Buckner for?" some feller begun, but I waited for no more. I riz up from behind the bushes and the hosses snorted and reared.

"Hang a helpless man because he licked you in a fair fight, hey?" I bellowed, and let go both barrels amongst 'em.

THEY WAS RIDING SO clost-grouped don't think I missed any of 'em. The way they hollered was disgusting to hear. The hosses was scairt at the flash and roar right in their faces and they wheeled and bolted, and the whole gang went thundering up the road a dern sight faster than they'd come. I sent a few shots after 'em with my pistols, but they didn't shoot back, and purty soon the weeping and wailing died away in the distance. A fine mob *they* turned out to be!

But I thought they might come back, so I sot down behind a bush where I could watch the road from Gallego. And the first thing I knowed I went to sleep in spite of myself.

When I woke up it was jest coming daylight. I jumped up and grabbed my guns, but nobody was in sight. I guess them Gallego gents had got a bellyful. So I headed back for the cabin and when I got there the corral was empty and the chuck wagon was gone!

I started on a run for the shack and then I seen a note stuck on the corral fence. I grabbed it. It said—

> Dear Elkins:
>   This strain is too much for me. I'm getting white-haired sitting and watching this devil laying there glaring at me, and wondering all the time how soon he'll bust loose. I'm pulling out. I'm taking the chuck wagon and team in payment for my rig that Meshak ran off with. I'm leaving the elixir but I doubt if it'll do Buckner any good. It's for locoed critters, not homicidal maniacs.
>   Respectfully yours,
>   Horace J. Lattimer, Esquire.

"Hell's fire," I said wrathfully, starting for the shack.

I dunno how long it had took Bearfield to wriggle out of his ropes. Anyway he was laying for me behind the door with the iron skillet and if the handle hadn't broke off when he lammed me over the head with it he might of did me a injury.

I dunno how I ever managed to throw him, because he fit like a frothing maniac, and every time he managed to break loose from me he grabbed a jug of Lattimer's Loco Elixir and busted it over my head. By the time I managed to stun him with a table laig he'd busted every jug on the place, the floor was swimming in elixir, and my clothes was soaked in it. Where they wasn't soaked with blood.

I fell on him and tied him up again and then sot on a bunk and tried to get my breath back and wondered what in hell to do. Because here the elixir was all gone and I didn't have no way of treating Bearfield and the Perfessor had run off with the chuck wagon so I hadn't no way to get him back to civilization.

Then all at onst I heard a train whistle, away off to the west, and remembered that the track passed through jest a few miles to the south. I'd did all I could for Bearfield, only thing I could do now was to get him back to his folks where they could take care of him.

I run out and whistled for Cap'n Kidd and he busted out from around the corner of the house where he'd been laying for me, and tried to kick me in the belly before I could get ready for him, but I warn't fooled. He's tried that trick too many times. I dodged and give him a good bust in the nose, and then I throwed the bridle and saddle on him, and brung Cousin Bearfield out and throwed him acrost the saddle and headed south.

That must of been the road both Meshak and Lattimer taken when they run off. It crossed the railroad track about three miles from the shack. The train had been whistling for High Horse when I first heard it. I got to the track before it come into sight. I flagged it and it pulled up and the train crew jumped down and wanted to know what the hell I was stopping them for.

"I got a man here which needs medical attention," I says. "It's a case of temporary insanity. I'm sendin' him back to Texas."

"Hell," says they, "this train don't go nowheres near Texas."

"Well," I says, "you unload him at Dodge City. He's got plenty of friends there which will see that he gits took care of. I'll send word from High Horse to his folks in Texas tellin' 'em to go after him."

So they loaded Cousin Bearfield on, him being still unconscious, and I give the conductor his watch and chain and pistol to pay for his fare. Then I headed along the track for High Horse.

When I got to High Horse I tied Cap'n Kidd nigh the track and started for the depot when who should I run smack into but Old Man Mulholland who immejitly give a howl like a hungry timber wolf.

"Whar's the grub, you hoss-thief?" he yelled before I could say nothing.

"Why, didn't Lem Campbell bring it out to you?" I ast.

"I never seen a man by that name," he bellered. "Whar's my fifty bucks?"

"Heck," I says, "he looked honest."

"Who?" yowled Old Man Mulholland. "Who, you polecat?"

"Lem Campbell, the man I give the dough to for him to buy the grub," I says. "Oh, well, never mind. I'll work out the fifty."

The Old Man looked like he was fixing to choke. He gurgled, "Where's my chuck wagon?"

"A feller stole it," I said. "But I'll work that out too."

"You won't work for me," foamed the Old Man, pulling a gun. "Yo're fired. And as for the dough and the wagon, I takes them out of yore hide here and now."

Well, I taken the gun away from him, of course, and tried to reason with him, but he jest hollered that much louder, and got his knife out and made a pass at me. Now it always did irritate me for somebody to stick a knife in me, so I taken it away from him and throwed him into a nearby hoss trough. It was one of these here V-shaped troughs which narrers together at the bottom, and somehow his fool head got wedged and he was about to drown.

Quite a crowd had gathered and they tried pulling him out by the hind laigs but his feet was waving around in the air so wild that every time anybody tried to grab him they got spurred in the face. So I went over to the trough and taken hold of the sides and tore it apart. He fell out and spit up maybe a gallon of water. And the first words he was able to say he accused me of trying to drownd him on purpose, which shows how much gratitude people has got.

But a man spoke up and said, "Hell, the big feller didn't do it on purpose. I was right here and I seen it all."

And another'n said, "I seen it as good as you did, and the big feller did try to drownd him, too!"

"Air you callin' me a liar?" said the first feller, reaching for his gun.

But jest then another man chipped in and said, "I dunno what the argyment's about, but I bet a dollar you're both wrong!"

And then some more fellers butted in and everybody started cussing and hollering till it nigh deefened me. Someone else reaches for a gun and I seen that as soon as one feller shoots another there is bound to be trouble so I started to gentle the first feller by hitting him over the head. The next thing I know someone hollers at me, "You big hyener!", and tries to ruint me with a knife. Purty soon there is hitting and shooting all over the town. High Horse is sure on a rampage.

I jest had finished blunting my Colts on a varmit's haid when I thinks disgustedly, "Heck, Elkins, you came to this town on a mission of good will! You got business to do. You got yore poor family to think about."

I started to go on to the depot but I heard a familiar voice screech above the racket. "There he is, Sheriff! Arrest the dern' claim-jumper!"

I whirled around quick and there was Drooping Whiskers, a saddle blanket wropped around him like a Injun and walking purty spraddle-legged. He was p'inting at me and hollering like I'd did something to him.

Everybody else quieted down for a minute, and he hollered, "Arrest him, dern him. He throwed me out of my own cabin and ruint my best pants with my own shotgun. I been to Knife River and come back several days quicker'n I aimed to, and there this big hyener was in charge of my shack. He was too dern big for me to handle, so I come to High Horse after the sheriff—soon as I got three or four hundred bird-shot picked out my hide."

"What you got to say about this?" ast the sheriff, kinda uncertain, like he warn't enjoying his job for some reason or other.

"Why, hell," I says disgustedly. "I throwed this varmint out of a cabin, sure, and later peppered his anatomy with bird-shot. But I was in my rights. I was in a cabin which had been loaned me by a man named Lem Campbell—"

"Lem Campbell!" shrieked Drooping Whiskers, jumping up and down so hard he nigh lost the blanket he was wearing instead of britches. "That wuthless critter ain't got no cabin. He was workin' for me till I fired him jest before I started for Knife River, for bein' so triflin'."

"Hell's fire!" I says, shocked. "Ain't there no honesty any more? Shucks, stranger, it looks like the joke's on me."

At this Drooping Whiskers collapsed into the arms of his friends with a low moan, and the sheriff says to me uncomfortably, "Don't take this personal, but I'm afeared I'll have to arrest you, if you don't mind—"

Jest then a train whistled away off to the east, and somebody said, "What the hell, they ain't no train from the east this time of day!"

Then the depot agent run out of the depot waving his arms and yelling, "Git them cows off'n the track! I jest got a flash from Knife River, the train's comin' back. A maniac named Buckner busted loose and made the crew turn her around at the switch. Order's gone down the line to open the track all the way. She's comin' under full head of steam. Nobody knows where Buckner's takin' her. He's lookin' for some relative of his'n!"

There was a lot of noise comin' down that track and all of it waren't the noise that a steam-ingine makes by itself. No, that noise was a different noise all right. That noise was right familiar to me. It struck a chord in my mind and made me wonder kinda what happened to them trainmen.

"Can that be Bearfield Buckner?" wondered a woman. "It sounds like him. Well, if it is, he's too late to git Ann Wilkins."

"*What?*" I yelled. "Is they a gal in this town named Ann Wilkins?"

"They was," she snickered. "She was to marry this Buckner man yesterday, but he never showed up, and when her old beau, Lem Campbell, come along with fifty dollars he'd got some place, she up and married him and they lit out for San Francisco on their honeymoon—Why, what's the matter, young man? You look right green in the face. Maybe it's somethin' you et—"

It weren't nothin' I et. It was the thoughts I was thinkin'. Here I had gone an' ruint Cousin Bearfield's whole future. And outa kindness. Thet's what busted me wide open. I had ruint Cousin Bearfield's future out of kindness. My motives had been of the loftiest, I had tried to kyore an hombre what was loco from goin' locoer yet, and what was my reward? What was my reward? Jest thet moment I looks up and I seen a cloud of smoke a puffin' down the track and they is a roarin' like the roarin' of a herd of catamounts.

"Here she comes around the bend," yelled somebody. "She's burnin' up the track. Listen at that whistle. Jest bustin' it wide open."

But I was already astraddle of Cap'n Kidd and traveling. The man which says I'm scairt of Bearfield is a liar. A Elkins fears neither man, beast nor Buckner. But I seen that Lem Campbell had worked me into getting Bearfield out of his way, and if I waited till Bearfield got there, I'd have to kill him or get killed, and I didn't crave to do neither.

I headed south jest to save Cousin Bearfield's life, and I didn't stop till I was in Durango. Let me tell you the revolution I got mixed up in there was a plumb restful relief after my association with Cousin Bearfield.

"NO COWHERDERS WANTED"

I HEAR A GANG OF buffalo hunters got together recently in a saloon in Dodge City to discuss ways and means of keeping their sculps onto their heads whilst collecting pelts, and purty soon one of 'em riz and said, "You mavericks make me sick. For the last hour you been chawin' wind about the soldiers tryin' to keep us north of the Cimarron, and belly-achin' about the Comanches, Kiowas and Apaches which yearns for our hair. You've took up all that time jawin' about sech triflin' hazards, and plannin' steps to take agen 'em, but you ain't makin' no efforts whatsoever to pertect yoreselves agen the biggest menace they is to the entire buffalo-huntin' clan—which is Breckinridge Elkins!"

That jest show's how easy prejudiced folks is. You'd think I had a grudge agen buffalo hunters, the way they takes to the bresh whenever they sees me coming. And the way they misrepresents what happened at Cordova is plumb disgustful. To hear 'em talk you'd think I was the only man there which committed any vi'lence.

If that's so I'd like to know how all them bullet holes got in the Diamond Bar saloon which I was using for a fort. Who throwed the mayor through that board fence? Who sot fire to Joe Emerson's store, jest to smoke me out? Who started the row in the first place by sticking up insulting signs in public places? They ain't no use in them fellers trying to ack innercent. Any unbiased man which was there, and survived to tell the tale, knows I acted all the way through with as much dignity as a man can ack which is being shot at by forty or fifty wild-eyed buffalo skinners.

I had never even saw a buffalo hunter before, because it was the first time I'd ever been that far East. I was taking a pasear into New Mexico with a cowpoke by the name of Glaze Bannack which I'd met in Arizona. I stopped in Albuquerque and he went on, heading for Dodge City. Well, I warn't in Albuquerque as long as I'd aimed to be, account of going broke quicker'n I expected. I had jest one dollar left after payin' for having three fellers sewed up which had somehow got afoul of my bowie knife after criticizing the Democratic party. I ain't the man to leave my opponents on the public charge.

Well, I pulled out of town and headed for the cow camps on the Pecos, aiming to git me a job. But I hadn't went far till I met a waddy riding in, and he taken a good look at me and Cap'n Kidd, and says: "You must be him. Wouldn't no other man fit the description he gimme."

"Who?" I says.

"Glaze Bannack," says he. "He gimme a letter to give to Breckinridge Elkins."

So I says, "Well, all right, gimme it." So he did, and it read as follers:

Dere Breckinridge:
I am in jail in Panther Springs for nothin all I done was kind of push the deperty sheriff with a little piece of scrap iron could I help it if he fell down and fracktured his skull Breckinridge. But they say I got to pay $Ten dolars fine and I have not got no sech money Breckinridge. But old man Garnett over on Buck Creek owes me ten bucks so you colleck from him and come and pay me out of this hencoop. The food is terrible Breckinridge. Hustle.
Yore misjedged frend,
Glaze Bannack, Eskwire.

Glaze never could stay out of trouble, not being tactful like me, but he was a purty good sort of hombre. So I headed for Buck Creek and collected the money off of Old Man Garnett, which was somewhat reluctant to give up the dough. In fact he bit me severely in the hind laig whilst I was setting on him prying his fingers loose from that there ten spot, and when I rode off down the road with the dinero, he run into his shack and got his buffalo gun and shot at me till I was clean out of sight.

But I ignored his lack of hospitality. I knowed he was too dizzy to shoot straight account of him having accidentally banged his head on a fence post which I happened to have in my hand whilst we was rassling.

I left him waving his gun and howling damnation and destruction, and I was well on the road for Panther Springs before I discovered to my disgust that my shirt was a complete rooin. I considered going back and demanding that Old Man Garnett buy me a new one, account of him being the one which tore it. But he was sech a onreasonable old cuss I decided agen it and rode on to Panther Springs, arriving there shortly after noon.

The first critter I seen was the purtiest I gal I'd saw in a coon's age. She come out of a store and stopped to talk to a young cowpuncher she called Curly. I reined Cap'n Kidd around behind a corn crib so she wouldn't see me in my scare-crow condition. After a while she went on down the street and went into a cabin with a fence around it and a front porch, which showed her folks was wealthy, and I come out from behind the crib and says to the young buck which was smirking after her and combing his hair with the other hand, I says: "Who is that there gal? The one you was jest talkin' to."

"Judith Granger," says he. "Her folks lives over to Sheba, but her old man brung her over here account of all the fellers over there was about to cut each other's throats over her. He's makin' her stay a spell with her Aunt Henrietta, which is a war-hoss if I ever seen one. The boys is so scairt of her they don't dast try to spark Judith. Except me. I persuaded the old mudhen to let me call on Judith and I'm goin' over there for supper."

"That's what you think," I says gently. "Fact is, though, Miss Granger has got a date with me."

"She didn't tell me—" he begun scowling.

"She don't know it herself, yet," I says. "But I'll tell her you was sorry you couldn't show up."

"Why, you—" he says bloodthirsty, and started for his gun, when a feller who'd been watching us from the store door, he hollered: "By golly, if it ain't Breckinridge Elkins!"

"Breckinridge Elkins?" gasped Curly, and he dropped his gun and keeled over with a low gurgle.

"Has he got a weak heart?" I ast the feller which had recognized me, and he said, "Aw, he jest fainted when he realized how clost he come to throwin' a gun on the terror of the Humbolts. Drag him over to the hoss trough, boys, and throw some water on him. Breckinridge, I owns that grocery store there, and yore paw knows me right well. As a special favor to me will you refrain from killin' anybody in my store?"

So I said all right, and then I remembered my shirt was tore too bad to call on a young lady in. I generally has 'em made to order, but they warn't time for that if I was going to eat supper with Miss Judith, so I went into the general store and bought me one. I dunno why they don't make shirts big enough to fit reasonable sized men like me. You'd think nobody but midgets wore shirts. The biggest one in the store warn't only eighteen in the collar, but I didn't figger on buttoning the collar anyway. If I'd tried to button it it would of strangled me.

So I give the feller five dollars and put it on. It fit purty clost, but I believed I could wear it if I didn't have to expand my chest or something. Of course, I had to use some of Glaze's dough to pay for it with but I didn't reckon he'd mind, considering all the trouble I was going to gitting him out of jail.

I rode down the alley behind the jail and come to a barred winder, and said, "Hey!"

Glaze looked out, kinda peaked, like his grub warn't setting well with him, but he brightened up and says, "Hurray! I been on aidge expectin' you. Go on around to the front door, Breck, and pay them coyotes the ten spot and let's go. The grub I been gitten' here would turn a lobo's stummick!"

"Well," I says, "I ain't exactly got the ten bucks, Glaze. I had to have a shirt, because mine got tore, so—"

HE GIVE A YELP LIKE a stricken elk and grabbed the bars convulsively.

"Air you crazy?" he hollered. "You squanders my money on linens and fine raiment whilst I languishes in a prison dungeon?"

"Be ca'm," I advised. "I still got five bucks of yore'n, and one of mine. All I got to do is step down to a gamblin' hall and build it up."

"Build it up!" says he fiercely. "Lissen, blast your hide! Does you know what I've had for breakfast, dinner and supper, ever since I was throwed in here? Beans! Beans! Beans!"

Here he was so overcome by emotion that he choked on the word.

"And they ain't even first-class beans, neither," he said bitterly, when he could talk again. "They're full of grit and wormholes, and I think the Mex cook washes his feet in the pot he cooks 'em in."

"Well," I says, "sech cleanliness is to be encouraged, because I never heard of one before which washed his feet in anything. Don't worry. I'll git in a poker game and win enough to pay yore fine and plenty over."

"Well, git at it," he begged. "Git me out before supper time. I wants a steak with ernyuns so bad I can smell it."

So I headed for the Golden Steer saloon.

They warn't many men in there jest then, but they was a poker game going on, and when I told 'em I craved to set in they looked me over and made room for me. They was a black whiskered cuss which said he was from Cordova which was dealing, and the first thing I noticed, was he was dealing his own hand off of the bottom of the deck. The others didn't seem to see it, but us Bear Creek folks has got eyes like hawks, otherwise we'd never live to git grown.

So I says, "I dunno what the rules is in these parts, but where I come from we almost always deals off of the top of the deck."

"Air you accusin' me of cheatin'?" he demands passionately, fumbling for his weppins and in his agitation dropping three or four extra aces out of his sleeves.

"I wouldn't think of sech a thing," I says. "Probably them marked kyards I see stickin' out of yore boot-tops is merely soovernears."

For some reason this seemed to infuriate him to the p'int of drawing a bowie knife, so I hit him over the head with a brass cuspidor and he fell under the table with a holler groan.

Some fellers run in and looked at his boots sticking out from under the table, and one of 'em said, "Hey! I'm the Justice of the Peace. You can't do that. This is a orderly town."

And another'n said, "I'm the sheriff. If you cain't keep the peace I'll have to arrest you!"

This was too much even for a mild-mannered man like me.

"Shet yore fool heads!" I roared, brandishing my fists. "I come here to pay Glaze Bannack's fine, and git him outa jail, peaceable and orderly, and I'm tryin' to raise the dough like a #$%&*! gentleman! But by golly, if you hyenas pushes me beyond endurance, I'll tear down the cussed jail and snake him out without payin' no blasted fine."

The J.P. turnt white. He says to the sheriff: "Let him alone! I've already bought these here new boots on credit on the strength of them ten bucks we gits from Bannack."

"But—" says the sheriff dubiously, and the J.P. hissed fiercely, "Shet up, you blame fool. I jest now reckernized him. That's Breckinridge Elkins!"

The sheriff turnt pale and swallered his adam's apple and says feebly, "Excuse me—I—uh—I ain't feelin' so good. I guess it's somethin' I et. I think I better ride over to the next county and git me some pills."

But I don't think he was very sick from the way he run after he got outside the saloon. If they had been a jackrabbit ahead of him he would of trompled the gizzard out of it.

Well, they taken the black whiskered gent out from under the table and started pouring water on him, and I seen it was now about supper time so I went over to the cabin where Judith lived.

❖   ❖   ❖

I WAS MET AT THE DOOR by a iron-jawed female about the size of a ordinary barn, which give me a suspicious look and says "Well, what's *you* want?"

"I'm lookin' for yore sister, Miss Judith," I says, taking off my Stetson perlitely.

"What you mean, my sister?" says she with a scowl, but a much milder tone. "I'm her aunt."

"You don't mean to tell me!" I says looking plumb astonished. "Why, when I first seen you, I thought you was her herself, and couldn't figger out how nobody but a twin sister could have sech a resemblance. Well, I can see right off that youth and beauty is a family characteristic."

"Go 'long with you, you young scoundrel," says she, smirking, and giving me a nudge with her elbow which would have busted anybody's ribs but mine. "You cain't soft-soap me—come in! I'll call Judith. What's yore name?"

"Breckinridge Elkins, ma'am," I says.

"So!" says she, looking at me with new interest. "I've heard tell of you. But you got a lot more sense than they give you credit for. Oh, Judith!" she called, and the winders rattled when she let her voice go. "You got company."

Judith come in, looking purtier than ever, and when she seen me she batted her eyes and recoiled vi'lently.

"Who—who's that?" she demanded wildly.

"Mister Breckinridge Elkins, of Bear Creek, Nevader," says her aunt. "The only young man I've met in this whole dern town which has got any sense. Well, come on in and set. Supper's on the table. We was jest waitin' for Curly Jacobs," she says to me, "but if the varmint cain't git here on time, he can go hongry."

"He cain't come," I says. "He sent word by me he's sorry."

"Well, I ain't," snorted Judith's aunt. "I give him permission to jest because I figgered even a bodacious flirt like Judith wouldn't cotton to sech a sapsucker, but—"

"Aunt Henrietta!" protested Judith, blushing.

"I cain't abide the sight of sech weaklin's," says Aunt Henrietta, settling herself carefully into a rawhide-bottomed chair which groaned under her weight. "Drag up that bench, Breckinridge. It's the only thing in the house which has a chance of holdin' yore weight outside of the sofie in the front room. Don't argy with me, Judith! I says Curly Jacobs ain't no fit man for a gal like you. Didn't I see him strain his fool back tryin' to lift that there barrel of salt I wanted fotched to the smoke house? I finally had to tote it myself. What makes young men so blame spindlin' these days?"

"Pap blames the Republican party," I says.

"Haw! Haw! Haw!" says she in a guffaw which shook the doors on their hinges and scairt the cat into convulsions. "Young man, you got a great sense of humor. Ain't he, Judith?" says she, cracking a beef bone betwixt her teeth like it was a pecan.

Judith says yes kind of pallid, and all during the meal she eyed me kind of nervous like she was expecting me to go into a war-dance or something. Well, when we was through, and Aunt Henrietta had et enough to keep a tribe of Sioux through a hard winter, she riz up and says, "Now clear out of here whilst I washes the dishes."

"But I must help with 'em," says Judith.

Aunt Henrietta snorted. "What makes you so eager to work all of a sudden? You want yore guest to think you ain't eager for his company? Git out of here."

So she went, but I paused to say kind of doubtful to Aunt Henrietta, "I ain't shore Judith likes me much."

"Don't pay no attention to her whims," says Aunt Henrietta, picking up the water barrel to fill her dish pan. "She's a flirtatious minx. I've took a likin' to you, and if I decide yo're the right man for her, yo're as good as hitched. Nobody couldn't never do nothin' with her but me, but she's learnt who her boss is—after havin' to eat her meals off of the mantel-board a few times. Gwan in and court her and don't be backward!"

So I went on in the front room, and Judith seemed to kind of warm up to me, and ast me a lot of questions about Nevada, and finally she says she's heard me spoke of as a fighting man and hoped I ain't had no trouble in Panther Springs.

I told her no, only I had to hit one black whiskered thug from Cordova over the head with a cuspidor.

AT THAT SHE JUMPED UP like she'd sot on a pin.

"That was my uncle Jabez Granger!" she hollered. "How dast you, you big bully! You ought to be ashamed, a, great big man like you pickin' on a little feller like him which don't weigh a ounce over two hundred and fifteen pounds!"

"Aw, shucks," I said contritely. "I'm sorry Judith."

"Jest as I was beginnin' to like you," she mourned. "Now he'll write to pap and prejudice him agen you. You jest got to go and find him and apologize to him and make friends with him."

"Aw, heck," I said.

But she wouldn't listen to nothing else, so I went out and clumb onto Cap'n Kidd and went back to the Golden Steer, and when I come in everybody crawled under the tables.

"What's the matter with you all?" I says fretfully. "I'm lookin' for Jabez Granger."

"He's left for Cordova," says the barkeep, sticking his head up from behind the bar.

Well, they warn't nothing to do but foller him, so I rode by the jail and Glaze was at the winder, and he says eagerly, "Air you ready to pay me out?"

"Be patient, Glaze," I says. "I ain't got the dough yet, but I'll git it somehow as soon as I git back from Cordova."

"What?" he shrieked.

"Be ca'm like me," I advised. "You don't see *me* gittin' all het up, do you? I got to go catch Judith Granger's Uncle Jabez and apolergize to the old illegitimate for bustin' his conk with a spittoon. I be back tomorrer or the next day at the most."

Well, his langwidge was scandalous, considering all the trouble I was going to jest to git him out of jail, but I refused to take offense. I headed back for the Granger cabin and Judith was on the front porch.

I didn't see Aunt Henrietta, she was back in the kitchen washing dishes and singing: "They've laid Jesse James in his grave!" in a voice which loosened the shingles on the roof. So I told Judith where I was going and ast her to take some pies and cakes and things to the jail for Glaze, account of the beans was rooining his stummick, and she said she would. So I pulled stakes for Cordova.

It laid quite a ways to the east, and I figgered to catch up with Uncle Jabez before he got there, but he had a long start and was on a mighty good hoss, I reckon. Anyway, Cap'n Kidd got one of his hellfire streaks and insisted on stopping every few miles to buck all over the landscape, till I finally got sick of his muleishness and busted him over the head with my pistol. By this time we'd lost so much time I never overtaken Uncle Jabez at all and it was gitting daylight before I come in sight of Cordova.

Well, about sun-up I come onto a old feller and his wife in a ramshackle wagon drawed by a couple of skinny mules with a hound dawg. One wheel had run off into a sink hole and the mules so pore and good-for-nothing they couldn't pull it out, so I got off and laid hold on the wagon, and the old man said, "Wait a minute, young feller, whilst me and the old lady gits out to lighten the load."

"What for?" I ast. "Set still."

So I h'isted the wheel out, but if it had been stuck any tighter I might of had to use both hands.

"By golly!" says the old man. "I'd of swore nobody but Breckinridge Elkins could do that!"

"Well, I'm him," I says, and they both looked at me with reverence, and I ast 'em was they going to Panther Springs.

"We aim to," says the old woman, kind of hopeless. "One place is as good as another'n to old people which has been robbed out of their life's savin's."

"You all been robbed?" I ast, shocked.

"WELL," SAYS THE OLD man, "I ain't in the habit of burdenin' strangers with my woes, but as a matter of fact, we has. My name's Hopkins. I had a ranch down on the Pecos till the drouth wiped me out and we moved to Panther Springs with what little we saved from the wreck. In a ill-advised moment I started speculatin' on buffler-hides. I put in all my cash buyin' a load over on the Llano Estacado which I aimed to freight to Santa Fe and sell at a fat profit—I happen to know they're fetchin' a higher price there now than they air in Dodge City—and last night the whole blame cargo disappeared into thin air, as it were.

"We was stoppin' at Cordova for the night, and the old lady was sleepin' in the hotel and I was camped at the aidge of town with the wagon, and sometime durin' the night somebody snuck up and hit me over the head. When I come to this mornin' hides, wagon and team was all gone, and no trace. When I told the city marshal he jest laughed in my face and ast me how I'd expect him to track down a load of buffalo hides in a town which was full of 'em. Dang him! They was packed and corded neat with my old brand, the Circle A, marked on 'em in red paint.

"Joe Emerson, which owns the saloon and most all the town, taken a mortgage on our little shack in Panther Springs and loaned me enough money to buy this measly team and wagon. If we can git back to Panther Springs maybe I can git enough freightin' to do so we can kind of live, anyway."

"Well," I said, much moved by the story, "I'm goin' to Cordova, and I'll see if I cain't find yore hides."

"Thankee kindly, Breckinridge," says he. "But I got a idee them hides is already far on their way to Dodge City. Well, I hopes you has better luck in Cordova than we did."

So they driv on west and I rode east, and got to Cordova about a hour after sun-up. As I come into the aidge of town I seen a sign-board about the size of a door stuck up which says on it, in big letters, "No cowherders allowed in Cordova."

"What the hell does that mean?" I demanded wrathfully of a feller which had stopped by it to light him a cigaret. And he says, "Jest what it says! Cordova's full of buffler hunters in for a spree and they don't like cowboys. Big as you be, I'd advise you to light a shuck for somewhere else. Bull Croghan put that sign up, and you ought to seen what happened to the last puncher which ignored it!"

"#\$%&*¢!" I says in a voice which shook the beans out of the mesquite trees for miles around. And so saying I pulled up the sign and headed for main street with it in my hand. I am as peaceful and mild-mannered a critter as you could hope to meet, but even with me a man can go too damned far. This here's a free country and no derned hairy-necked buffalo-skinner can draw boundary lines for us cowpunchers and git away with it—not whilst I can pull a trigger.

They was very few people on the street and sech as was looked at me surprized-like.

"Where the hell is them fool buffalo hunters?" I roared, and a feller says, "They're all gone to the race track east of town to race hosses, except Bull Croghan, which is takin' hisself a dram in the Diamond Bar."

So I lit and stalked into the Diamond Bar with my spurs ajingling and my disposition gitting thornier every second. They was a big hairy critter in buckskins and moccasins standing at the bar drinking whiskey and talking to the bar-keep and a flashy-dressed gent with slick hair and a diamond hoss-shoe stickpin. They all turnt and gaped at me, and the hunter reched for his belt where he was wearing the longest knife I ever seen.

"Who air you?" he gasped.

"A cowman!" I roared, brandishing the sign. "Air you Bull Croghan?"

"Yes," says he. "What about it?"

So I busted the sign-board over his head and he fell onto the floor yelling bloody murder and trying to draw his knife. The board was splintered, but the stake it had been fastened to was a purty good-sized post, so I took and beat him over the head with it till the bartender tried to shoot me with a sawed-off shotgun.

I grabbed the barrel and the charge jest busted a shelf-load of whiskey bottles and I throwed the shotgun through a nearby winder. As I neglected to git the bartender loose from it first, it appears he went along with it. Anyway, he picked hisself up off of the ground, bleeding freely, and headed east down the street shrieking, "Help! Murder! A cowboy is killin' Croghan and Emerson!"

WHICH WAS A LIE, BECAUSE Croghan had crawled out the front door on his all-fours whilst I was tending to the bar-keep, and if Emerson had showed any jedgment he wouldn't of got his sculp laid open to the bone. How did I know he was jest trying to hide behind the bar? I thought he was going for a gun he had hid back there. As soon as I realized the truth I dropped what was left of the bung starter and commenced pouring water on Emerson, and purty soon he sot up and looked around wild-eyed with blood and water dripping off of his head.

"What happened?" he gurgled.

"Nothin' to git excited about," I assured him knocking the neck off of a bottle of whiskey. "I'm lookin' for a Gent named Jabez Granger."

It was at this moment that the city marshal opened fire on me through the back door. He grazed my neck with his first slug and would probably of hit me with the next if I hadn't shot the gun out of his hand. He then run off down the alley. I pursued him and catched him when he looked back over his shoulder and hit a garbage can.

"I'm a officer of the law!" he howled, trying to git his neck out from under my foot so as he could draw his bowie. "Don't you dast assault no officer of the law."

"I ain't," I snarled, kicking the knife out of his hand, and kind of casually swiping my spur acrost his whiskers. "But a officer which lets a old man git robbed of his buffalo hides, and then laughs in his face, ain't deservin' to be no officer. Gimme that badge! I demotes you to a private citizen!"

I then hung him onto a nearby hen-roost by the seat of his britches and went back up the alley, ignoring his impassioned profanity. I didn't go in at the back door of the saloon, because I figgered Joe Emerson might be laying to shoot me as I come in. So I went around the saloon to the front and run smack onto a mob of buffalo hunters which had evidently been summoned from the race track by the bar-keep. They had Bull Croghan at the hoss trough and was trying to wash the blood off of him, and they was all yelling and cussing so loud they didn't see me at first.

"Air we to be defied in our own lair by a #$%&*¢! cowsheperd?" howled Croghan. "Scatter and comb the town for him! He's hidin' down some back alley, like as not. We'll hang him in front of the Diamond Bar and stick his sculp onto a pole as a warnin' to all his breed! Jest lemme lay eyes onto him again—"

"Well, all you got to do is turn around," I says. And they all whirled so quick they dropped Croghan into the hoss trough. They gaped at me with their mouths open for a second. Croghan riz out of the water snorting and spluttering, and yelled, "Well, what you waitin' on? Grab him!"

It was in trying to obey his instructions that three of 'em got their skulls fractured, and whilst the others was stumbling and falling over 'em, I backed into the saloon and pulled my six-shooters and issued a defiance to the world at large and buffalo hunters in particular.

They run for cover behind hitch racks and troughs and porches and fences, and a feller in a plug hat come out and says, "Gentlemen! Le's don't have no bloodshed within the city limits! As mayor of this fair city, I—"

It was at this instant that Croghan picked him up and throwed him through a board fence into a cabbage patch where he lay till somebody revived him a few hours later.

The hunters then all started shooting at me with .50 caliber Sharps' buffalo rifles. Emerson, which was hiding behind a Schlitz sign-board, hollered something amazing account of the holes which was being knocked in the roof and walls. The big sign in front was shot to splinters, and the mirror behind the bar was riddled, and all the bottles on the shelves and the hanging lamps was busted. It's plumb astonishing the damage a bushel or so of them big slugs can do to a saloon.

They went right through the walls. If I hadn't kept moving all the time I'd of been shot to rags, and I did git several bullets through my clothes and three or four grazed some hide off. But even so I had the aidge, because they couldn't see me only for glimpses now and then through the winders and was shooting more or less blind because I had 'em all spotted and slung lead so fast and clost they didn't dast show theirselves long enough to take good aim.

BUT MY CA'TRIDGES BEGUN to run short so I made a sally out into the alley jest as one of 'em was trying to sneak in the back door. I hear tell he is very bitter toward me about his teeth, but I like to know how he expects to git kicked in the mouth without losing some fangs.

So I jumped over his writhing carcase and run down the alley, winging three or four as I went and collecting a pistol ball in my hind laig. They was hiding behind board fences on each side of the alley but them boards wouldn't stop a .45 slug. They all shot at me, but they misjedged my speed. I move a lot faster than most folks expect.

Anyway, I was out of the alley before they could git their wits back. And as I went past the hitch rack where Cap'n Kidd was champing and snorting to git into the fight, I grabbed my Winchester .45-90 off of the saddle, and run acrost the street. The hunters which was still shooting at the front of the Diamond Bar seen me and that's when I got my spurs shot off, but I ducked into Emerson's General Store whilst the clerks all run shrieking out the back way.

As for that misguided hunter which tried to confiscate Cap'n Kidd, I ain't to blame for what happened to him. They're going around now saying I trained Cap'n Kidd special to jump onto a buffalo hunter with all four feet after kicking him through a corral fence. That's a lie. I didn't have to train him. He thought of it hisself. The idjit which tried to take him ought to be thankful he was able to walk with crutches inside of ten months.

Well, I was now on the same side of the street as the hunters was, so as soon as I started shooting at 'em from the store winders they run acrost the street and taken refuge in a dance hall right acrost from the store and started shooting back at me, and Joe Emerson hollered louder'n ever, because he owned the dance hall too. All the citizens of the town had bolted into the hills long ago, and left us to fight it out.

Well, I piled sides of pork and barrels of pickles and bolts of calico in the winders, and shot over 'em, and I built my barricades so solid even them buffalo guns couldn't shoot through 'em. They was plenty of Colt and Winchester ammunition in the store, and whiskey, so I knowed I could hold the fort indefinite.

Them hunters could tell they warn't doing no damage so purty soon I heard Croghan bellering, "Go git that cannon the soldiers loaned the folks to fight the Apaches with. It's over behind the city hall. Bring it in at the back door. We'll blast him out of his fort, by golly!"

"You'll ruin my store!" screamed Emerson.

"I'll rooin' your face if you don't shet up," opined Croghan. "Gwan!"

Well, they kept shooting and so did I and I must of hit some of 'em, jedging from the blood-curdling yells that went up from time to time. Then a most remarkable racket of cussing busted out, and from the remarks passed, I gathered that they'd brung the cannon and somehow got it stuck in the back door of the dance hall. The shooting kind of died down whilst they rassled with it and in the lull I heard me a noise out behind the store.

THEY WARN'T NO WINDERS in the back, which is why they hadn't shot at me from that direction. I snuck back and looked through a crack in the door and I seen a feller in the dry gully which run along behind the store, and he had a can of kerosine and some matches and was setting the store on fire.

I jest started to shoot when I recognized Judith Granger's Uncle Jabez. I laid down my Winchester and opened the door soft and easy and pounced out on him, but he let out a squawk and dodged and run down the gully. The shooting acrost the street broke out again, but I give no heed, because I warn't going to let him git away from me again. I run him down the gully about a hundred yards and catched him, and taken his pistol away from him, but he got hold of a rock which he hammered me on the head with till I nigh lost patience with him.

But I didn't want to injure him account of Judith, so I merely kicked him in the belly and then throwed him before he could git his breath back, and sot on him, and says, "Blast yore hide, I apolergizes for lammin' you with that there cuspidor. Does you accept my apology, you pot-bellied hoss-thief?"

"Never!" says he rampacious. "A Granger never forgits!"

So I taken him by the ears and beat his head agen a rock till he gasps, "Let up! I accepts yore apology, you #$%&*¢!"

"All right." I says, arising and dusting my hands, "and if you ever goes back on yore word, I'll hang yore mangy hide to the—"

It was at that moment that Emerson's General Store blew up with a ear-splitting bang.

"What the hell?" shrieked Uncle Jabez, staggering, as the air was filled with fragments of groceries and pieces of flying timbers.

"Aw," I said disgustedly, "I reckon a stray bullet hit a barrel of gunpowder. I aimed to move them barrels out of the line of fire, but kind of forgot about it—"

But Uncle Jabez had bit the dust. I hear tell he claims I hit him onexpected with a wagon pole. I didn't do no sech thing. It was a section of the porch roof which fell on him, and if he'd been watching, and ducked like I did, it wouldn't of hit him.

I clumb out of the gully and found myself opposite from the Diamond Bar. Bull Croghan and the hunters was pouring out of the dance hall whooping and yelling, and Joe Emerson was tearing his hair and howling like a timber wolf with the belly ache because his store was blowed up and his saloon was shot all to pieces.

But nobody paid no attention to him. They went surging acrost the street and nobody seen me when I crossed it from the other side and went into the alley that run behind the saloon. I run on down it till I got to the dance hall, and sure enough, the cannon was stuck in the back door. It warn't wide enough for the wheels to git through.

I HEARD CROGHAN ROARING acrost the street, "Poke into the debray, boys! Elkins' remains must be here somewheres, unless he was plumb dissolved! That—!"

Crash!

They was a splintering of planks, and somebody yelled, "Hey! Croghan's fell into a well or somethin'!"

I heard Joe Emerson shriek, "Dammitt, stay away from there! Don't—"

I tore away a section of the wall and got the cannon loose and run it up to the front door of the dance hall and looked out. Them hunters was all ganged up with their backs to the dance hall, all bent over whilst they was apparently trying to pull Croghan out of some hole he'd fell into headfirst. His cussing sounded kinda muffled. Joe Emerson was having a fit at the aidge of the crowd.

Well, they'd loaded that there cannon with nails and spikes and lead slugs and carpet tacks and sech like, but I put in a double handful of beer bottle caps jest for good measure, and touched her off. It made a noise like a thunder clap and the recoil knocked me about seventeen foot, but you should of heard the yell them hunters let out when that hurricane of scrap iron hit 'em in the seat of the britches. It was amazing!

To my disgust, though, it didn't kill none of 'em. Seems like the charge was too heavy for the powder, so all it done was knock 'em off their feet and tear the britches off of 'em. However, it swept the ground clean of 'em like a broom, and left 'em all standing on their necks in the gully behind where the store had been, except Croghan whose feet I still perceived sticking up out of the ruins.

Before they could recover their wits, if they ever had any, I run acrost the street and started beating 'em over the head with a pillar I tore off of the saloon porch. Some sech as was able ariz and fled howling into the desert. I hear tell some of 'em didn't stop till they got to Dodge City, having run right through a Kiowa war-party and scairt them pore Injuns till they turnt white.

Well, I laid holt of Croghan's laigs and hauled him out of the place he had fell into, which seemed to be a kind of cellar which had been under the floor of the store. Croghan's conversation didn't noways make sense, and every time I let go of him he fell on his neck.

So I abandoned him in disgust and looked down into the cellar to see what was in it that Emerson should of took so much to keep it hid. Well, it was plumb full of buffalo hides, all corded into neat bundles! At that Emerson started to run, but I grabbed him, and reached down with the other hand and hauled a bundle out. It was marked with a red Circle A brand.

"So!" I says to Emerson, impulsively busting him in the snout. "You stole old man Hopkins' hides yoreself! Perjuice that mortgage! Where's the old man's wagon and team?"

"I got 'em hid in my livery stable," he moaned.

"Go hitch 'em up and bring 'em here," I says. "And if you tries to run off, I'll track you down and sculp you alive!"

I went and got Cap'n Kidd and watered him. When I got back, Emerson come up with the wagon and team, so I told him to load on them hides.

"I'm a ruined man!" sniveled he. "I ain't able to load no hides."

"The exercize'll do you good," I assured him, kicking the seat loose from his pants, so he give a harassed howl and went to work. About this time Croghan sot up and gaped at me weirdly.

"It all comes back to me!" he gurgled. "We was going to run Breckinridge Elkins out of town!"

He then fell back and went into shrieks of hysterical laughter which was most hair raising to hear.

"The wagon's loaded," panted Joe Emerson. "Take it and git out and be quick!"

"Well, let this be a lesson to you," I says, ignoring his hostile attitude. "Honesty's always the best policy!"

I then hit him over the head with a wagon spoke and clucked to the hosses and we headed for Panther Springs.

Old man Hopkins' mules had give out half way to Panther Springs. Him and the old lady was camped there when I drove up. I never seen folks so happy in my life as they was when I handed the team, wagon, hides and mortgage over to 'em. They both cried and the old lady kissed me, and the old man hugged me, and I thought I'd plumb die of embarrassment before I could git away. But I did finally, and headed for Panther Springs again, because I still had to raise the dough to git Glaze out of jail.

I GOT THERE ABOUT SUN-UP and headed straight for Judith's cabin to tell her I'd made friends with Uncle Jabez. Aunt Henrietta was cleaning a carpet on the front porch and looking mad. When I come up she stared at me and said, "Good land, Breckinridge, what happened to you?"

"Aw, nothin'," I says. "Jest a argument with them fool buffalo hunters over to Cordova. They'd cleaned a old gent and his old lady of their buffalo hides, to say nothin' of their hosses and wagon. So I rid on to see what I could do about it. Them hairy-necked hunters didn't believe me when I said I wanted them hides, so I had to persuade 'em a leetle. On'y thing is they is sayin' now that I was to blame fer the hull affair. I apologized to Judith's uncle, too. Had to chase him from here to Cordova. Where's Judith?"

"Gone!" she says, stabbing her broom at the floor so vicious she broke the handle off. "When she taken them pies and cakes to yore fool friend down to the jail house, she taken a shine to him at first sight. So she borrored the money from me to pay his fine—said she wanted a new dress to look nice in for you, the deceitful hussy! If I'd knowed what she wanted it for she wouldn't of got it—she'd of got somethin' acrost my knee! But she paid him out of the jug, and—"

"And what happened then?" I says wildly.

"She left me a note," snarled Aunt Henrietta, giving the carpet a whack that tore it into six pieces. "She said anyway she was afeared if she didn't marry him I'd make her marry you. She must of sent you off on that wild goose chase a purpose. Then she met him, and—well, they snuck out and got married and air now on their way to Denver for their honeymoon—Hey, what's the matter? Air you sick?"

"I be," I gurgled. "The ingratitude of mankind cuts me to the gizzard! After all I'd did for Glaze Bannack! Well, by golly, this is lesson to me! I bet I don't never work my fingers to the quick gittin' another ranny out of jail!"

THE CONQUERIN' HERO
OF THE HUMBOLDTS

I WAS IN SUNDANCE ENJOYING myself a little after a long trail-drive up from the Cimarron, when I got a letter from Abednego Raxton which said as follers:

Dear Breckinridge:

That time I paid yore fine down in Tucson for breaking the county clerk's laig you said you'd gimme a hand anytime I ever need help. Well Breckinridge I need yore assistance right now the rustlers is stealing me ragged it has got so I nail my bed-kivers to the bunk every night or they'd steal the blankets right offa me Breckinridge. More-over a stumbling block on the path of progress by the name of Ted Bissett is running sheep on the range next to me this is more'n a man can endure Breckinridge. So I want you to come up here right away and help me find out who is stealing my stock and bust Ted Bissett's

hed for him the low-minded scunk. Hoping you air the same I begs to
remane as usual,
      Yore abused frend,
        Raxton, Esq.

P. S. That sap-headed misfit Johnny Willoughby which used to work for
me down on Green River is sheriff here and he couldn't ketch flies if
they was bogged down in merlasses.

Well, I didn't feel it was none of my business to mix into any row Abednego
might be having with the sheepmen, so long as both sides fit fair, but rustlers was a
different matter. A Elkins detests a thief. So I mounted Cap'n Kidd, after the usual
battle, and headed for Lonesome Lizard, which was the nighest town to his ranch.

I found myself approaching this town a while before noon one blazing hot
day, and as I crossed a right thick timbered creek, shrieks for aid and assistance
suddenly bust the stillness. A hoss also neighed wildly, and Cap'n Kidd begun to
snort and champ like he always does when they is a b'ar or a cougar in the vicinity. I
got off and tied him, because if I was going to have to fight some critter like that, I
didn't want him mixing into the scrap; he was jest as likely to kick me as the varmint.
I then went on foot in the direction of the screams, which was growing more
desperate every minute, and I presently come to a thicket with a big tree in the
middle of it, and there they was. One of the purtiest gals I ever seen was roosting in
the tree and screeching blue murder, and they was a cougar climbing up after her.

"Help!" says she wildly. "Shoot him!"

"I jest wish some of them tender-foots which calls theirselves naturalists could
see this," I says, taking off my Stetson. A Elkins never forgits his manners. "Some of
'em has tried to tell me cougars never attacks human beings nor climbs trees, nor
prowls in the daytime. I betcha this would make 'em realize they don't know it all.
Jest like I said to that'n which I seen in War Paint, Nevada, last summer—"

"Will you stop talkin' and do somethin'?" she says fiercely. *"Ow!"*

Because he had reched up and made a pass at her foot with his left paw. I
seen this had went far enough, so I told him sternly to come down, but all he
done was look down at me and spit in a very insulting manner. So I reched up
and got him by the tail and yanked him down, and whapped him agen the
ground three or four times, and when I let go of him he run off a few yards, and
looked back at me in a most pecooliar manner. Then he shaken his head like he
couldn't believe it hisself, and lit a shuck as hard as he could peel it in the general
direction of the North Pole.

"Whyn't you shoot him?" demanded the gal, leaning as far out as she could
to watch him.

"Aw, he won't come back," I assured her. "Hey, look out! That limb's goin' to break—"

Which it did jest as I spoke and she come tumbling down with a shriek of despair. She still held onto the limb with a desperate grip, however, which is why it rapped me so severe on the head when I catched her.

"Oh!" says she, letting go of the limb and grabbing me. "Am I hurt?"

"I dunno," I says, "You better let me carry you to wherever you want to go."

"No," says she, gitting her breath back. "I'm all right. Lemme down."

So I done so, and she says: "I got a hoss tied over there behind that fir. I was ridin' home from Lonesome Lizard and stopped to poke a squirrel out of a holler tree. It warn't a squirrel, though. It was that dang lion. If you'll git my hoss for me, I'll be ridin' home. Pap's ranch is jest over that ridge to the west. I'm Margaret Brewster."

"I'm Breckinridge Elkins, of Bear Creek, Nevada," I says. "I'm headin' for Lonesome Lizard, but I'll be ridin' back this way before long. Can I call on you?"

"Well," she says, "I'm engaged to marry a feller, but it's conditional. I got a suspicion he's a spineless failure, and I told him flat if he didn't succeed at the job's he's workin' on now, not to come back. I detests a failure. That's why I likes yore looks," says she, giving me a admiring glance. "A man which can rassle a mountain lion with his b'ar hands is worth any gal's time. I'll send you word at Lonesome Lizard; if my fiansay flops like it looks he's goin' to do, I'd admire to have you call."

"I'll be awaitin' yore message with eager heart and honest devotion," I says, and she blushed daintily and clumb on her hoss and pulled her freight. I watched her till she was clean out of sight, and then hove a sigh that shook the acorns out of the surrounding oaks, and wended my way back to Cap'n Kidd in a sort of rose-colored haze. I was so entranced I started to git onto Cap'n Kidd on the wrong end and never noticed till he kicked me vi'lently in the belly.

"Love, Cap'n Kidd," I says to him dreamily, batting him between the eyes with my pistol butt, "is youth's sweet dream."

But he made no response, outside of stomping on my corns; Cap'n Kidd has got very little sentiment.

SO I MOUNTED AND PULLED for Lonesome Lizard, which I arriv at maybe a hour later. I put Cap'n Kidd in the strongest livery stable I could find and seen he was fed and watered, and warned the stable-hands not to antagonize him, and then I headed for the Red Warrior saloon. I needed a little refreshments before I started for Abednego's ranch.

I taken me a few drams and talked to the men which was foregathered there, being mainly cowmen. The sheepmen patronized the Bucking Ram, acrost the street. That was the first time I'd ever been in Montana, and them fellers warn't familiar with my repertation, as was showed by their manner.

Howthesomever, they was perlite enough, and after we'd downed a few fingers of corn scrapings, one of 'em ast me where I was from, proving they considered me a honest man with nothing to conceal. When I told 'em, one of 'em said: "By golly, they must grow big men in Nevada, if yo're a sample. Yo're the biggest critter I ever seen in the shape of a human."

"I bet he's as stout as Big Jon," says one, and another'n says: "That cain't be. This gent is human, after all. Big Jon ain't."

I was jest fixing to ast 'em who this Jon varmint was, when one of 'em cranes his neck toward the winder and says: "Speak of the devil and you gits a whiff of brimstone! Here comes Jon acrost the street now. He must of seen this gent comin' in, and is on his way to make his usual challenge. The sight of a man as big as him is like wavin' a red flag at a bull."

I looked out the winder and seen a critter about the size of a granary coming acrost the street from the Bucking Ram, follered by a gang of men which looked like him, but not nigh as big.

"What kind of folks air they?" I ast with interest. "They ain't neither Mexicans nor Injuns, but they sure ain't white men, neither."

"Aw, they're Hunkies," says a little sawed-off cowman. "Ted Bissett brung 'em in here to herd sheep for him. That big 'un's Jon. He ain't got no sense, but you never seen sech a hunk of muscle in yore life."

"Where they from?" I ast. "Canader?"

"Naw," says he. "They come originally from a place called Yurrop. I dunno where I it is, but I jedge it's somewhere's east of Chicago."

But I knowed them fellers never originated nowheres on this continent. They was rough-dressed and wild-looking, with knives in their belts, and they didn't look like no folks I'd ever saw before. They come into the barroom and the one called Jon bristled up to me very hostile with his little beady black eyes. He stuck out his chest about a foot and hit it with his fist which was about the size of a sledge hammer. It sounded like a man beating a bass drum.

"You strong man," says he. "I strong too. We rassle, eh?"

"Naw," I says, "I don't care nothin' about rasslin'."

He give a snort which blowed the foam off of every beer glass on the bar, and looked around till he seen a iron rod laying on the floor. It looked like the handle of a branding iron, and was purty thick. He grabbed this and bent it into a V, and throwed it down on the bar in front of me, and all the other Hunkies jabbered admiringly.

This childish display irritated me, but I controlled myself and drunk another finger of whiskey, and the bartender whispered to me: "Look out for him! He aims to prod you into a fight. He's nearly kilt nine or ten men with his b'ar hands. He's a mean 'un."

"Well," I says, tossing a dollar onto the bar and turning away, "I got more important things to do than rassle a outlandish foreigner in a barroom. I got to eat my dinner and git out to the Raxton ranch quick."

But at that moment Big Jon chose to open his bazoo. There are some folks which cain't never let well enough alone.

"'Fraid!" jeered he. "Yah, yah!"

The Hunkies all whooped and guffawed, and the cattlemen scowled.

"What you mean, afraid?" I gasped, more dumbfounded than mad. It'd been so long since anybody's made a remark like that to me. I was plumb flabbergasted. Then I remembered I was amongst strangers which didn't know my repertation, and I realized it was my duty to correct that there oversight before somebody got hurt on account of ignorance.

So I said, "All right, you dumb foreign muttonhead, I'll rassle you."

But as I went up to him, he doubled up his fist and hit me severely on the nose, and them Hunkies all bust into loud, rude laughter. That warn't wise. A man had better twist a striped thunderbolt's tail than hit a Elkins onexpected on the nose. I give a roar of irritation and grabbed Big Jon and started committing mayhem on him free and enthusiastic. I swept all the glasses and bottles off of the bar with him, and knocked down a hanging lamp with him, and fanned the floor with him till he was limp, and then I throwed him the full length of the barroom. His head went through the panels of the back door, and the other Hunkies, which had stood petrified, stampeded into the street with howls of horror. So I taken the branding iron handle and straightened it out and bent it around his neck, and twisted the ends together in a knot, so he had to get a blacksmith to file it off after he come to, which was several hours later.

All them cowmen was staring at me with their eyes popped out of their heads, and seemed plumb incapable of speech, so I give a snort of disgust at the whole incerdent, and strode off to git my dinner. As I left I heard one feller, which was holding onto the bar like he was too weak to stand alone, say feebly to the dumb-founded bartender: "Gimme a drink, quick! I never thunk I'd live to see somethin' I couldn't believe when I was lookin' right smack at it."

I COULDN'T MAKE NO sense out of this, so I headed for the dining room of the Montana Hotel and Bar. But my hopes of peace and quiet was a illusion. I'd jest started on my fourth beefsteak when a big maverick in Star-top boots and store-bought clothes come surging into the dining room and bellered: "Is your name Elkins?"

"Yes, it is," I says. "But I ain't deef. You don't have to yell."

"Well, what the hell do you mean by interferin' with my business?" he squalled, ignoring my reproof.

"I dunno what yo're talkin' about," I growled, emptying the sugar bowl into my coffee cup with some irritation. It looked like Lonesome Lizard was full of maneyacks which craved destruction. "Who air you, anyhow?"

"I'm Ted Bissett, that's who!" howled he, convulsively gesturing toward his six-shooter. "And I'm onto you! You're a damn Nevada gunman old Abed' Raxton's brought up here to run me off the range! He's been braggin' about it all over town! And you starts your work by runnin' off my sheepherders!"

"What you mean, I run yore sheepherders off?" I demanded, amazed.

"They ran off after you maltreated Big Jon," he gnashed, with his face convulsed. "They're so scared of you they won't come back without double pay! You can't do this to me, you #$%&*!"

The man don't live which can call me that name with impunity. I impulsively hit him in the face with my fried steak, and he give a impassioned shriek and pulled his gun. But some grease had got in his eyes, so all he done with his first shot was bust the syrup pitcher at my elbow, and before he could cock his gun again I shot him through the arm. He dropped his gun and grabbed the place with his other hand and made some remarks which ain't fitten for to repeat.

I yelled for another steak, and Bissett yelled for a doctor, and the manager yelled for the sheriff.

The last-named individual didn't git there till after the doctor and the steak had arrove and was setting Bissett's arm—the doctor, I mean, and not the steak, which a trembling waiter brung me. Quite a crowd had gathered by this time and was watching the doctor work with great interest, and offering advice which seemed to infuriate Bissett, jedging from his langwidge. He also discussed his busted arm with considerable passion, but the doctor warn't a bit worried. You never seen sech a cheerful gent. He was jovial and gay, no matter how loud Bissett yelled. You could tell right off he was a man which could take it.

But Bissett's friends was very mad, and Jack Campbell, his foreman, was muttering something about 'em taking the law into their own hands, when the sheriff come prancing in, waving a six-shooter and hollering: "Where is he? P'int out the scoundrel to me?"

"There he is!" everybody yelled, and ducked, like they expected gunplay, but I'd already recognized the sheriff, and when he seen me he recoiled and shoved his gun out of sight like it was red hot or something.

"Breckinridge Elkins!" says he. Then he stopped and studied a while, and then he told 'em to take Bissett out to the bar and pour some licker down him. When they'd went he sot down at the table, and says: "Breck, I want you to understand that they ain't nothin' personal about this, but I got to arrest you. It's agen the law to shoot a man inside of the city limits."

"I ain't got time to git arrested," I told him. "I got to git over to old Abed' Raxton's ranch."

"But lissen, Breck," argyed the sheriff—it was Johnny Willoughby, jest like old Abed' said—"what'll folks think if I don't jail you for shootin' a leadin' citizen? Election's comin' up and my hat's in the ring," says he, gulping my coffee.

"Bissett shot at me first," I said. "Whyn't you arrest him?"

"Well, he didn't hit you," says Johnny, absently cramming half a pie into his mouth and making a stab at my pertaters. "Anyway, he's got a busted arm and ain't able to go to jail jest now. Besides, I needs the sheepmen's votes."

"Aw, I don't like jails," I said irritably, and he begun to weep.

"If you was a friend to me," sobs he, "you'd be glad to spend a night in jail to help me git re-elected. I'd do as much for you! The whole county's givin' me hell anyway, because I ain't been able to catch none of them cattle rustlers, and if I don't arrest you I won't have a Chinaman's chance at the polls. How can you do me like this, after the times we had together in the old days—"

"Aw, stop blubberin'," I says. "You can arrest me, if you want to. What's the fine?"

"I don't want to collect no fine, Breck," says he, wiping his eyes on the oil-cloth table cover and filling his pockets with doughnuts. "I figgers a jail sentence will give me more prestige. I'll let you out first thing in the mornin'. You won't tear up the jail, will you, Breck?"

I promised I wouldn't, and then he wants me to give up my guns, and I refuses.

"But good gosh, Breck," he pleaded. "It'd look awful funny for a prisoner to keep on his shootin' irons."

So I give 'em to him, jest to shet him up, and then he wanted to put his hand-cuffs onto me, but they warn't big enough to fit my wrists. So he said if I'd lend him some money he could have the blacksmith to make me some laig-irons, but I refused profanely, so he said all right, it was jest a suggestion, and no offense intended, so we went down to the jail. The jailer was off sleeping off a drunk somewheres, but he'd left the key hanging on the door, so we went in. Purty soon along come Johnny's deperty, Bige Gantry, a long, loose-j'inted cuss with a dangerous eye, so Johnny sent him to the Red Warrior for a can of beer, and whilst he was gone Johnny bragged on him a heap.

"Why," says he, "Bige is the only man in the county which has ever got within' shootin' distance of them dern outlaws. He was by hisself, wuss luck. If I'd been along we'd of scuppered the whole gang."

I ast him if he had any idee who they was, and he said Bige believed they was a gang up from Wyoming. So I said well, then, in that case they got a hang-out in the hills somewhere, and ought to be easier to run down than men which scattered to their homes after each raid.

BIGE GOT BACK WITH THE beer about then, and Johnny told him that when I got out of jail he was going to depertize me and we'd all go after them outlaws together. So Bige said that was great, and looked me over purty sharp, and we sot down and started playing poker. Along about supper time the jailer come in, looking tolerable seedy, and Johnny made him cook us some supper. Whilst we was eating the jailer stuck his head into my cell and said: "A gent is out there cravin' audience with Mister Elkins."

"Tell him the prisoner's busy," says Johnny.

"I done so," says the jailer, "and he says if you don't let him in purty dern quick, he's goin' to bust in and cut *yore* throat."

"That must be old Abed' Raxton," says Johnny. "Better let him in—Breck," says he, "I looks to you to pertect me if the old cuss gits mean."

So old Abed' come walzing into the jail with fire in his eye and corn licker on his breath. At the sight of me he let out a squall which was painful to hear.

"A hell of a help you be, you big lummox!" he hollered. "I sends for you to help me bust up a gang of rustlers and sheepherders, and the first thing you does is to git in jail!"

"T'warn't my fault," I says. "Them sheepherders started pickin' on me."

"Well," he snarls, "whyn't you drill Bissett center when you was at it?"

"I come up here to shoot rustlers, not sheepherders," I says.

"What's the difference?" he snarled.

"Them sheepmen has probably got as much right on the range as you cowmen," I says.

"Cease sech outrageous blasphermy," says he, shocked. "You've bungled things so far, but they's one good thing—Bissett had to hire back his derned Hunkie herders at double wages. He don't no more mind spendin' money than he does spillin' his own blood, the cussed tightwad. Well, what's yore fine?"

"Ain't no fine," I said. " Johnny wants me to stay in jail a while."

At this old Abed' convulsively went for his gun and Johnny got behind me and hollered: "Don't you dast shoot a ossifer of the law!"

"It's a spite trick!" gibbered old Abed'. "He's been mad at me ever since I fired him off'n my payroll. After I kicked him off'n my ranch he run for sheriff, and the night of the election everybody was so drunk they voted for him by mistake, or for a joke, or somethin', and since he's been in office he's been lettin' the sheepmen steal me right out of house and home."

"That's a lie," says Johnny heatedly. "I've give you as much pertection as anybody else, you old buzzard! I jest ain't been able to run any of them critters down, that's all. But you wait! Bige is on their trail, and we'll have 'em behind the bars before the snow falls."

"Before the snow falls in Guatemala, maybe," snorted old Abed'. "All right, blast you, I'm goin', but I'll have Breckinridge outa here if I have to burn the cussed jail! A Raxton never forgits!" So he stalked out sulphurously, only turning back to snort: "Sheriff! Bah! Seven murders in the county unsolved since you come into office! You'll let the sheepmen murder us all in our beds! We ain't had a hangin' since you was elected!"

After he'd left, Johnny brooded a while, and finally says: "The old lobo's right about them murders, only he neglected to mention that four of 'em was sheepmen. I know it's cattlemen and sheepmen killin' each other, each side accusin' the other'n of rustlin' stock, but I cain't prove nothin'. A hangin' *would* set me solid with the voters." Here he eyed me hungrily, and ventured: "If somebody'd jest up and confess to some of them murders—"

"You needn't to look at me like that," I says. "I never kilt nobody in Montana."

"Well," he argyed, "nobody could *prove* you never done 'em, and after you was hanged—"

"Lissen here, you," I says with some passion, "I'm willin' to help a friend git elected all I can, but they's a limit!"

"Oh, well, all right," he sighed. "I didn't much figger you'd be willin', anyway; folks is so dern selfish these days. All they thinks about is theirselves. But lissen here: if I was to bust up a lynchin' mob it'd be nigh as good a boost for my campaign as a legal hangin'. I tell you what—tonight I'll have some of my friends put on masks and come and take you out and pretend like they was goin' to hang you. Then when they got the rope around yore neck I'll run out and shoot in the air and they'll run off and I'll git credit for upholdin' law and order. Folks always disapproves of mobs, unless they happens to be in 'em."

So I said all right, and he urged me to be careful and not hurt none of 'em, because they was all his friends and would be mine. I ast him would they bust the door down, and he said they warn't no use in damaging property like that; they could hold up the jailer and take the key off'n him. So he went off to fix things, and after while Bige Gantry left and said he was on the trace of a clue to them cattle rustlers, and the jailer started drinking hair tonic mixed with tequila, and in about a hour he was stiffer'n a wet lariat.

WELL, I LAID DOWN ON the floor on a blanket to sleep, without taking my boots off, and about midnight a gang of men in masks come and they didn't have to hold up the jailer, because he was out cold. So they taken the key off'n him, and all the loose change and plug tobaccer out of his pockets too, and opened the door, and I ast: "Air you the gents which is goin' to hang me?" And they says: "We be!"

So I got up and ast them if they had any licker, and one of 'em gimme a good snort out of his hip flask, and I said: "All right, le's git it over with, so I can go back to sleep."

He was the only one which done any talking, and the rest didn't say a word. I figgered they was bashful. He said: "Le's tie yore hands behind you so's to make it look real," and I said all right, and they tied me with some rawhide thongs which I reckon would of held the average man all right.

So I went outside with 'em, and they was a oak tree right clost to the jail nigh some bushes. I figgered Johnny was hiding over behind them bushes.

They had a barrel for me to stand on, and I got onto it, and they throwed a rope over a big limb and put the noose around my neck, and the feller says: "Any last words?"

"Aw, hell," I says, "this is plumb silly. Ain't it about time for Johnny—"

At this moment they kicked the barrel out from under me.

Well, I was kind of surprized, but I tensed my neck muscles, and waited for Johnny to rush out and rescue me, but he didn't come, and the noose began to pinch the back of my neck, so I got disgusted and says: "Hey, lemme down!"

Then one of 'em which hadn't spoke before says: "By golly, I never heard a man talk after he'd been strung up before!"

I recognized that voice; it was Jack Campbell, Bissett's foreman! Well, I have got a quick mind, in spite of what my cousin Bearfield Buckner says, so I knowed right oif something was fishy about this business. So I snapped the thongs on my wrists and reched up and caught hold of the rope I was hung with by both hands and broke it. Them scoundrels was so surprized they didn't think to shoot at me till the rope was already broke, and then the bullets all went over me as I fell. When they started shooting I knowed they meant me no good, and acted according.

I dropped right in the midst of 'em, and brung three to the ground with me, and during the few seconds to taken me to choke and batter them unconscious the others was scairt to fire for fear of hitting their friends, we was so tangled up. So they clustered around and started beating me over the head with their gun butts, and I riz up like a b'ar amongst a pack of hounds and grabbed four more of 'em and hugged 'em till their ribs cracked. Their masks came off during the process, revealing the faces of Bissett's friends; I'd saw 'em in the hotel.

Somebody prodded me in the hind laig with a bowie at that moment, which infuriated me, so I throwed them four amongst the crowd and hit out right and left, knocking over a man or so at each lick, till I seen a wagon spoke on the ground and stooped over to pick it up. When I done that somebody throwed a coat over my head and blinded me, and six or seven men then jumped onto my back. About this time I stumbled over some feller which had been knocked down, and fell onto my belly, and they all started jumping up and down on me enthusiastically. I reched around and grabbed one and dragged him around to where I could rech his left ear with my teeth. I would of taken it clean off at the first snap, only I had to bite through the coat which was over my head, but as it was I done a good job, jedging from his awful shrieks.

He put forth a supreme effort and tore away, taking the coat with him, and I shaken off the others and riz up in spite of their puny efforts, with the wagon spoke in my hand.

A wagon spoke is a good, comforting implement to have in a melee, and very demoralizing to the enemy. This'n busted all to pieces about the fourth or fifth lick, but that was enough. Them which was able to run had all took to their heels, leaving the battlefield strewed with moaning and cussing figgers.

Their remarks was shocking to hear, but I give 'em no heed. I headed for the sheriff's office, mad clean through. It was a few hundred yards east of the jail, and jest as I rounded the jail house, I run smack into a dim figger which come sneaking through the bresh making a curious clanking noise. It hit me with what appeared to be a iron bar, so I went to the ground with it and choked it and beat its head agen the ground, till the moon come out from behind a cloud and revealed the bewhiskered features of old Abednego Raxton!

"What the hell?" I demanded of the universe at large. "Is everybody in Montaner crazy? Whar air *you* doin' tryin' to murder me in my sleep?"

"I warn't, you jack-eared lunkhead," snarled he, when he could talk.

"Then what'd you hit me with that there pinch bar for?" I demanded.

"I didn't know it was you," says he, gitting up and dusting his britches. "I thought it was a grizzly b'ar when you riz up out of the dark. Did you bust out?"

"Naw, I never," I said. "I told you I was stayin' in jail to do Johnny a favor. And you know what that son of Baliol done? He framed it up with Bissett's friends to git me hung. Come on. I'm goin' over and interview the dern skunk right now."

So we went over to Johnny's office, and the door was unlocked and a candle burning, but he warn't in sight.

*   *   *

THEY WAS A SMALL IRON safe there, which I figgered he had my guns locked up in, so I got a rock and busted it open, and sure enough there my shooting-irons was. They was also a gallon of corn licker there, and me and Abed' was discussing whether or not we had the moral right to drink it, when I heard somebody remark in a muffled voice: "Whumpff! Gfuph! *Oompg!*"

So we looked around and I seen a pair of spurs sticking out from under a camp cot over in the corner. I grabbed hold of the boots they was on, and pulled 'em out, and a human figger come with 'em. It was Johnny. He was tied hand and foot and gagged, and he had a lump onto his head about the size of a turkey aig.

I pulled off the gag, and the first thing he says was: "If you sons of Perdition drinks my private licker I'll have yore hearts' blood!"

"You better do some explainin'," I says resentfully. "What you mean, siccin' Bissett's friends onto me?"

"I never done no sech!" says he heatedly. "Right after I left the jail I come to the office here, and was jest fixin' to git hold of my friends to frame the fake necktie party, when somebody come in at the door and hit me over the head. I thought it was Bige comin' in and didn't look around, and then whoever it was clouted me. I jest while ago come to myself, and I was tied up like you see."

"If he's tellin' the truth," says old Abed' "—which he seems to be, much as I hates to admit it—it looks like some friend of Bissett's overheard you all talkin' about this thing, follered Johnny over and put him out of the way for the time bein', and then raised a mob of his own, knowin' Breck wouldn't put up no resistance, thinkin' they was friends. I told you—who's that?"

We all drawed our irons, and then put 'em up as Bige Gantry rushed in, holding onto the side of his head, which was all bloody.

"I jest had a bresh with the outlaws!" he hollered. "I been trailin' 'em all night! They waylaid me while ago, three miles out of town! They nearly shot my ear off! But if I didn't wing one of 'em, I'm a Dutchman!"

"Round up a posse!" howled Johnny, grabbing a Winchester and cartridge belt. "Take us back to where you had the scrape, Bige—"

"Wait a minute," I says, grabbing Bige. "Lemme see that ear!" I jerked his hand away, disregarding the spur he stuck into my laig, and bellered: "Shot, hell! That ear was chawed, and I'm the man which done it! You was one of them illegitimates which tried to hang me!"

He then whipped out his gun, but I knocked it out of his hand and hit him on the jaw and knocked him through the door. I then follered him outside and taken away the bowie he drawed as he rose groggily, and throwed him back into the office, and went in and throwed him out again, and went out and throwed him back in again.

"How long is this goin' on?" he ast.

"Probably all night," I assured him. "The way I feel right now I can keep heavin' you in and out of this office from now till noon tomorrer."

"Hold up!" gurgled he. "I'm a hard nut, but I know when I'm licked! I'll confess! I done it!"

"Done what?" I demanded.

"I hit Johnny on the head and tied him up!" he howled, grabbing wildly for the door jamb as he went past it. "I rigged the lynchin' party! I'm in with the rustlers!"

"Set him down!" hollered Abed', grabbing holt of my shirt. "Quick, Johnny! Help me hold Breckinridge before he kills a valurebull witness!"

But I shaken him off impatiently and sot Gantry onto his feet. He couldn't stand, so I helt him up by the collar and he gasped: "I lied about tradin' shots with the outlaws. I been foolin' Johnny all along. The rustlers ain't no Wyoming gang; they all live around here. Ted Bissett is the head chief of 'em—"

"Ted Bissett, hey?" whooped Abed', doing a war-dance and kicking my shins in his glee. "See there, you big lummox? What'd I tell you? What you think now, after showin' so dern much affection for them cussed sheepmen? Jest shootin' Bissett in the arm, like he was yore brother, or somethin'! S'wonder you didn't invite him out to dinner. You ain't got the—"

"Aw, shet up!" I said fretfully. "Go on, Gantry."

"He ain't a legitimate sheepman," says he. "That's jest a blind, him runnin' sheep. Ain't no real sheepmen mixed up with him. His gang is jest the scrapin's of the country, and they hide out on his ranch when things gits hot. Other times they scatters and goes home. They're the ones which has been killin' honest sheepman and cattlemen—tryin' to set the different factions agen each other, so as to make stealin' easier. The Hunkies ain't in on the deal. He jest brung 'em out to herd his sheep, because his own men wouldn't do it, and he was afeared if he hired local sheepherders, they'd ketch onto him. Naturally we wanted you outa the way, when we knowed you'd come up here to run down the rustlers, so tonight I seen my chance when Johnny started talkin' about stagin' that fake hangin'. I follered Johnny and tapped him on the head and tied him up and went and told Bissett about the business, and we got the boys together, and you know the rest. It was a peach of a frame-up, and it'd of worked, too, if we'd been dealing with a human bein'. Lock me up. All I want right now is a good, quiet penitentiary where I'll be safe."

"Well," I said to Johnny, after he'd locked Gantry up, "all you got to do is ride over to Bissett's ranch and arrest him. He's laid up with his arm, and most of his men is crippled. You'll find a number of 'em over by the jail. This oughta elect you."

"It will!" says he, doing a war-dance in his glee. "I'm as good as elected right now! And I tell you, Breck, t'ain't the job alone I'm thinkin' about. I'd of lost my gal if I'd lost the race. But she's promised to marry me if I ketched them rustlers and got re-elected. And she won't go back on her word, neither!"

"Yeah?" I says with idle interest, thinking of my own true love. "What's her name?"

"Margaret Brewster!" says he.

"What?" I yelled, in a voice which knocked old Abed' over on his back like he'd been hit by a cyclone. Them which accuses me of vi'lent and onusual conduck don't consider how my emotions was stirred up by the knowledge that I had went through all them humiliating experiences jest to help a rival take my gal away from me. Throwing Johnny through the office winder and kicking the walls out of the building was jest a mild expression of the way I felt about the whole dern affair, and instead of feeling resentful, he ought to have been thankful I was able to restrain my natural feelings as well as I done.

SHARP'S GUN SERENADE

I WAS HEADING FOR WAR Paint, jogging along easy and comfortable, when I seen a galoot coming up the trail in a cloud of dust, jest aburning the breeze. He didn't stop to pass the time of day. He went past me so fast Cap'n Kidd missed the snap he made at his hoss, which shows he was sure hightailing it. I recognized him as Jack Sprague, a young waddy which worked on a spread not far from War Paint. His face was pale and sot in a look of desprut resolution, like a man which has jest bet his pants on a pair of deuces, and he had a rope in his hand though I couldn't see nothing he might be aiming to lasso. He went fogging on up the trail into the mountains and I looked back to see if I could see the posse. Because about the only time a outlander ever heads for the high Humbolts is when he's about three jumps and a low whoop ahead of a necktie party.

I seen another cloud of dust, all right, but it warn't big enough for more'n one man, and purty soon I seen it was Bill Glanton of War Paint. But that was good enough reason for Sprague's haste, if Bill was on the prod. Glanton is from Texas, original, and whilst he is a sentimental cuss in repose he's a ring-tailed whizzer with star-spangled wheels when his feelings is ruffled. And his feelings is ruffled tolerable easy.

As soon as he seen me he yelled, "Where'd he go?"

"Who?" I says. Us Humbolt folks ain't overflowing with casual information.

"Jack Sprague!" says he. "You must of saw him. Where'd he go?"

"He didn't say," I says.

Glanton ground his teeth slightly and says, "Don't start yore derned hillbilly stallin' with me! I ain't got time to waste the week or so it takes to git information out of a Humbolt Mountain varmint. I ain't chasin' that misguided idjit to do him injury. I'm pursooin' him to save his life! A gal in War Paint has jilted him and he's so broke up about it he's threatened to ride right over the mortal ridge. Us boys has been watchin' him and follerin' him around and takin' pistols and rat-pizen and the like away from him, but this mornin' he give us the slip and taken to the hills. It was a waitress in the Bawlin' Heifer Restawrant which put me on his trail. He told her he was goin' up in the hills where he wouldn't be interfered with and hang hisself!"

"So that was why he had the rope," I says. "Well, it's his own business, ain't it?"

"No, it ain't," says Bill sternly. "When a man is in his state he ain't responsible and it's the duty of his friends to look after him. He'll thank us in the days to come. Anyway, he owes me six bucks and if he hangs hisself I'll never git paid. Come on, dang it! He'll lynch hisself whilst we stands here jawin'."

"Well, all right," I says. "After all, I got to think about the repertation of the Humbolts. They ain't never been a suicide committed up here before."

"Quite right," says Bill. "Nobody never got a chance to kill hisself up here, somebody else always done it for him."

BUT I IGNORED THIS SLANDER and reined Cap'n Kidd around jest as he was fixing to bite off Bill's hoss's ear. Jack had left the trail but he left sign a blind man could foller. He had a long start on us, but we both had better hosses than his'n and after awhile we come to where he'd tied his hoss amongst the bresh at the foot of Cougar Mountain. We tied our hosses too, and pushed through the bresh on foot, and right away we seen him. He was climbing up the slope toward a ledge which had a tree growing on it. One limb stuck out over the aidge and was jest right to make a swell gallows, as I told Bill.

But Bill was in a lather.

"He'll git to that ledge before we can ketch him!" says he. "What'll we do?"

"Shoot him in the laig," I suggested, but Bill says, "No, dern it! He'll bust hisself fallin' down the slope. And if we start after him he'll hustle up to that ledge and hang hisself before we can git to him. Look there, though—they's a thicket growin' up the slope west of the ledge. You circle around and crawl up through it whilst I git out in the open and attracts his attention. I'll try to keep him talkin' till you can git up there and grab him from behind."

So I ducked low in the bresh and ran around the foot of the slope till I come to the thicket. Jest before I div into the tangle I seen Jack had got to the ledge and was fastening his rope to the limb which stuck out over the aidge. Then I couldn't see him no more because that thicket was so dense and full of briars it was about like crawling through a pile of fighting bobcats. But as I wormed my way up through it I heard Bill yell, "Hey, Jack, don't do that, you dern fool!"

"Lemme alone!" Jack hollered. "Don't come no closer. This here is a free country! I got a right to hang myself if I wanta!"

"But it's a dam fool thing to do," wailed Bill.

"My life is rooint!" asserted Jack. "My true love has been betrayed. I'm a wilted tumble-bug—I mean tumble-weed—on the sands of Time! Destiny has slapped the Zero brand on my flank! I—"

I dunno what else he said because at that moment I stepped into something which let out a ear-splitting squall and attached itself vi'lently to my hind laig. That was jest my luck. With all the thickets they was in the Humbolts, a derned cougar had to be sleeping in that'n. And of course it had to be me which stepped on him.

Well, no cougar is a match for a Elkins in a stand-up fight, but the way to lick him (the cougar, I mean; they ain't *no* way to lick a Elkins) is to git yore lick in before he can clinch with you. But the bresh was so thick I didn't see him till he had holt of me and I was so stuck up with them derned briars I couldn't hardly move nohow. So before I had time to do anything about it he had sunk most of his tushes and claws into me and was reching for new holts as fast as he could rake. It was old Brigamer, too, the biggest, meanest and oldest cat in the Humbolts. Cougar Mountain is named for him and he's so dang tough he ain't even scairt of Cap'n Kidd, which is plumb pizen to all cat-animals.

Before I could git old Brigamer by the neck and haul him loose from me he had clawed my clothes all to pieces and likewise lacerated my hide free and generous. In fact he made me so mad that when I did git him loose I taken him by the tail and mowed down the bresh in a fifteen foot circle around me with him, till the hair wore off of his tail and it slipped out of my hands. Old Brigamer then laigged it off down the mountain squalling fit to bust yore ear-drums. He was the maddest cougar you ever seen, but not mad enough to renew the fray. He must of recognized me.

At that moment I heard Bill yelling for help up above me so I headed up the slope, swearing loudly and bleeding freely, and crashing through them bushes like a wild bull. Evidently the time for stealth and silence was past. I busted into the open and seen Bill hopping around on the aidge of the ledge trying to git holt of Jack which was kicking like a grasshopper on the end of the rope, jest out of rech.

"Whyn't you sneak up soft and easy like I said?" howled Bill. "I was jest about to argy him out of the notion. He'd tied the rope around his neck and was standin' on the aidge, when that racket bust loose in the bresh and scairt him so bad he fell offa the ledge! Do somethin'."

"Shoot the rope in two," I suggested, but Bill said, "No, you cussed fool! He'd fall down the cliff and break his neck!"

BUT I SEEN IT WARN'T a very big tree so I went and got my arms around it and give it a heave and loosened the roots, and then kinda twisted it around so the limb that Jack was hung to was over the ledge now. I reckon I busted most of the roots in the process, jedging from the noise. Bill's eyes popped out when he seen that, and he reched up kind of dazed like and cut the rope with his bowie. Only he forgot to grab Jack before he cut it, and Jack hit the ledge with a resounding thud.

"I believe he's dead," says Bill despairingful. "I'll never git that six bucks. Look how purple he is."

"Aw," says I, biting me off a chew of terbacker, "all men which has been hung looks that way. I remember onst the Vigilantes hung Uncle Jeppard Grimes, and it taken us three hours to bring him to after we cut him down. Of course, he'd been hangin' a hour before we found him."

"Shet up and help me revive him," snarled Bill, gitting the noose off of his neck. "You seleck the damndest times to converse about the sins of yore infernal relatives—look, he's comin' too!"

Because Jack had begun to gasp and kick around, so Bill brung out a bottle and poured a snort down his gullet, and pretty soon Jack sot up and felt of his neck. His jaws wagged but didn't make no sound.

Glanton now seemed to notice my disheveled condition for the first time. "What the hell happened to you?" he ast in amazement.

"Aw, I stepped on old Brigamer," I scowled.

"Well, whyn't you hang onto him?" he demanded. "Don't you know they's a big bounty on his pelt? We could of split the dough."

"I've had a bellyfull of old Brigamer," I replied irritably. "I don't care if I never see him again. Look what he done to my best britches! If you wants that bounty, you go after it yoreself."

"And let me alone!" onexpectedly spoke up Jack, eyeing us balefully. "I'm free, white and twenty-one. I hangs myself if I wants to."

"You won't neither," says Bill sternly. "Me and yore paw is old friends and I aim to save yore wuthless life if I have to kill you to do it."

"I defies you!" squawked Jack, making a sudden dive betwixt Bill's laigs and he would of got clean away if I hadn't snagged the seat of his britches with my spur. He then displayed startling ingratitude by hitting me with a rock and, whilst we was tying him up with the hanging rope, his langwidge was scandalous.

"Did you ever see sech a idjit?" demands Bill, setting on him and fanning hisself with his Stetson. "What we goin' to do with him? We cain't keep him tied up forever."

"We got to watch him clost till he gits out of the notion of killin' hisself," I says. "He can stay at our cabin for a spell."

"Ain't you got some sisters?" says Jack.

"A whole cabin-full," I says with feeling. "You cain't hardly walk without steppin' on one. Why?"

"I won't go," says he bitterly. "I don't never want to see no woman again, not even a mountain-woman. I'm a embittered man. The honey of love has turnt to tranchler pizen. Leave me to the buzzards and cougars."

"I got it," says Bill. "We'll take him on a huntin' trip way up in the high Humbolts. They's some of that country I'd like to see myself. Reckon yo're the only white man which has ever been up there, Breck—if we was to call you a white man."

"What you mean by that there remark?" I demanded heatedly. "You know damn well I h'ain't got nary a drop of Injun blood in me—hey, look out!"

I glimpsed a furry hide through the bresh, and thinking it was old Brigamer coming back, I pulled my pistols and started shooting at it, when a familiar voice yelled wrathfully, "Hey, you cut that out, dern it!"

THE NEXT INSTANT A pecooliar figger hove into view—a tall ga'nt old ranny with long hair and whiskers, with a club in his hand and a painter hide tied around his middle. Sprague's eyes bugged out and he says: "Who in the name uh God's that?"

"Another victim of feminine wiles," I says. "That's old Joshua Braxton, of Chawed Ear, the oldest and the toughest batchelor in South Nevada. I jedge that Miss Stark, the old maid schoolteacher, has renewed her matrimonical designs onto him. When she starts rollin' sheep's eyes at him he always dons that there grab and takes to the high *sierras.*"

"It's the only way to perteck myself," snarled Joshua. "She'd marry me by force if I didn't resort to strategy. Not many folks comes up here and sech as does don't recognize me in this rig. What you varmints disturbin' my solitude for? Yore racket woke me up, over in my cave. When I seen old Brigamer high tailin' it for distant parts I figgered Elkins was on the mountain."

"We're here to save this young idjit from his own folly," says Bill. "You come up here because a woman wants to marry you. Jack comes up here to decorate a oak limb with his own carcass because one wouldn't marry him."

"Some men never knows their luck," says old Joshua enviously. "Now me, I yearns to return to Chawed Ear which I've been away from for a month. But whilst that old mudhen of a Miss Stark is there I haunts the wilderness if it takes the rest of my life."

"Well, be at ease, Josh," says Bill. "Miss Stark ain't there no more. She pulled out for Arizona three weeks ago."

"Halleloojah!" says Joshua, throwing away his club. "Now I can return and take my place among men—Hold on!" says he, reching for his club again, "likely they'll be gittin' some other old harridan to take her place. That new-fangled schoolhouse they got at Chawed Ear is a curse and a blight. We'll never be shet of husband-huntin' 'rithmetic shooters. I better stay up here after all."

"Don't worry," says Bill. "I seen a pitcher of the gal that's comin' from the East to take Miss Stark's place and I can assure you that a gal as young and pretty as her wouldn't never try to slap her brand on no old buzzard like you."

"Young and purty you says?" I ast with sudden interest.

"As a racin' filly!" he declared. "First time I ever knowed a school-marm could be less'n forty and have a face that didn't look like the beginnin's of a long drouth. She's due into Chawed Ear on the evenin' stage, and the whole town turns out to welcome her. The mayor aims to make a speech if he's sober enough, and they've got up a band to play."

"Damn foolishness!" snorted Joshua. "I don't take no stock in eddication."

"I dunno," says I. That was before I got educated. "They's times when I wisht I could read and write. We ain't never had no school on Bear Creek."

"What would you read outside of the labels onto whiskey bottles?" snorted old Joshua.

"Funny how a purty face changes a man's viewp'int," remarked Bill. "I remember onst Miss Stark ast you how you folks up on Bear Creek would like for her to come up there and teach yore chillern, and you taken one look at her face and told her it was agen the principles of Bear Creek to have their peaceful innerence invaded by the corruptin' influences of education. You said the folks was all banded together to resist sech corruption to the last drop of blood."

"It's my duty to Bear Creek to pervide culture for the risin' generation," says I, ignoring them slanderous remarks. "I feels the urge for knowledge a-heavin' and a-surgin' in my boozum. We're goin' to have a school on Bear Creek, by golly, if I

have to lick every old mossback in the Humbolts. I'll build a cabin for the schoolhouse myself."

"Where'll you git a teacher?" ast Joshua. "Chawed Ear ain't goin' to let you
have their'n."

"Chawed Ear is, too," I says. "If they won't give her up peaceful I resorts to
force. Bear Creek is goin' to have culture if I have to wade fetlock deep in gore to
pervide it. Le's go! I'm r'arin' to open the ball for arts and letters. Air you-all with
me?"

"No!" says Jack, plenty emphatic.

"What we goin' to do with him?" demands Glanton.

"Aw," I said, "we'll tie him up some place along the road and pick him up as
we come back by."

"All right," says Bill, ignoring Jack's impassioned protests. "I jest as soon. My
nerves is frayed ridin' herd on this young idjit and I needs a little excitement to
quiet 'em. You can always be counted on for *that*. Anyway, I'd like to see that there
school-marm gal myself. How about you, Joshua?"

"YO'RE BOTH CRAZY," growls Joshua. "But I've lived up here on nuts and
jackrabbits till I ain't shore of my own sanity. Anyway, I know the only way to dis-
agree successfully with Elkins is to kill him, and I got strong doubts of bein' able to
do that. Lead on! I'll do anything within reason to help keep eddication out of
Chawed Ear. T'ain't only my personal feelin's regardin' schoolteachers. It's the
principle of the thing."

"Git yore clothes and le's hustle then," I says.

"This painter hide is all I got," says he.

"You cain't go down into the settlements in that rig," I says.

"I can and will," says he. "I look as civilized as you do, with yore clothes all
tore to rags account of old Brigamer. I got a hoss clost by. I'll git him if old
Brigamer ain't already."

So Joshua went to git his hoss and me and Bill toted Jack down the slope to
where our hosses was. His conversation was plentiful and heated, but we ignored it,
and was jest tying him onto his hoss when Joshua arrov with his critter. Then the
trouble started. Cap'n Kidd evidently thought Joshua was some kind of a varmint
because every time Joshua come nigh him he taken in after him and run him up a
tree. And every time Joshua tried to come down, Cap'n Kidd busted loose from me
and run him back up again.

I didn't git no help from Bill. All he done was laugh like a spotted hyener till
Cap'n Kidd got irritated at them guffaws and kicked him in the belly and knocked
him clean through a clump of spruces. Time I got him ontangled he looked about

as disreputable as what I did because most of his clothes was tore off of him. We couldn't find his hat, neither, so I tore up what was left of my shirt and he tied the pieces around his head, like a Apache. Exceptin' Jack, we was sure a wild-looking bunch.

But I was disgusted thinking about how much time we was wasting whilst all the time Bear Creek was wallering in ignorance, so the next time Cap'n Kidd went for Joshua I took and busted him betwixt the ears with my six-shooter and that had some effect onto him—a little.

So we sot out, with Jack tied onto his hoss and cussing something terrible, and Joshua on a ga'nt old nag he rode bareback with a hackamore. I had Bill to ride betwixt him and me so's to keep that painter hide as far away from Cap'n Kidd as possible, but every time the wind shifted and blowed the smell to him, Cap'n Kidd reched over and taken a bite at Joshua, and sometimes he bit Bill's hoss by accident, and sometimes he bit Bill, and the langwidge Bill directed at that pore animal was shocking to hear.

We was aiming for the trail that runs down from Bear Creek into the Chawed Ear road, and we hit it a mile west of Bowie Knife Pass. We left Jack tied to a nice shady oak tree in the pass and told him we'd be back for him in a few hours, but some folks is never satisfied. 'Stead of being grateful for all the trouble we'd went to for him, he acted right nasty and called us some names I wouldn't of endured if he'd been in his right mind.

But we tied his hoss to the same tree and hustled down the trail and presently come out onto the War Paint-Chawed Ear road, some miles west of Chawed Ear. And there we sighted our first human—a feller on a pinto mare and when he seen us he give a shriek and took out down the road toward Chawed Ear like the devil had him by the britches.

"Le's ast him if the teacher's got there yet," I suggested, so we taken out after him, yelling for him to wait a minute. But he jest spurred his hoss that much harder and before we'd gone any piece, Joshua's fool hoss jostled agen Cap'n Kidd, which smelt that painter skin and got the bit betwixt his teeth and run Joshua and his hoss three miles through the bresh before I could stop him. Bill follered us, and of course, time we got back to the road, the feller on the pinto mare was out of sight long ago.

SO WE HEADED FOR CHAWED Ear but everybody that lived along the road had run into their cabins and bolted the doors, and they shot at us through the winders as we rode by. Bill said irritably, after having his off-ear nicked by a buffalo rifle, he says, "Dern it, they must know we aim to steal their schoolteacher."

"Aw, they couldn't know that," I says. "I bet they is a war on betwixt Chawed

Ear and War Paint."

"Well, what they shootin' at *me* for, then?" demanded Joshua.

"How could they recognize you in that rig?" I ast. "What's that?"

Ahead of us, away down the road, we seen a cloud of dust, and here come a gang of men on hosses, waving guns and yelling.

"Well, whatever the reason is," says Bill, "we better not stop to find out! Them gents is out for blood, and," says he as the bullets begun to knock up the dust around us, "I jedge it's *our* blood!"

"Pull into the bresh," says I. "I goes to Chawed Ear in spite of hell, high water and all the gunmen they can raise."

So we taken to the bresh, and they lit in after us, about forty or fifty of 'em, but we dodged and circled and taken short cuts old Joshua knowed about, and when we emerged into the town of Chawed Ear, our pursewers warn't nowheres in sight. In fack, they warn't nobody in sight. All the doors was closed and the shutters up on the cabins and saloons and stores and everything. It was pecooliar.

As we rode into the clearing somebody let *bam* at us with a shotgun from the nearest cabin, and the load combed Joshua's whiskers. This made me mad, so I rode at the cabin and pulled my foot out'n the stirrup and kicked the door in, and whilst I was doing this, the feller inside hollered and jumped out the winder, and Bill grabbed him by the neck. It was Esau Barlow, one of Chawed Ear's confirmed citizens.

"What the hell's the matter with you buzzards?" roared Bill.

"Is that you, Glanton?" gasped Esau, blinking his eyes.

"A-course it's me!" roared Bill. "Do I look like a Injun?"

"Yes?*ow*! I mean, I didn't know you in that there turban," says Esau. "Am I dreamin' or is that Josh Braxton and Breck Elkins?"

"Shore it's us," snorted Joshua. "Who you think?"

"Well," says Esau, rubbing his neck and looking sidewise at Joshua's painter skin. "I didn't know!"

"Where is everybody?" Joshua demanded.

"Well," says Esau, "a little while ago Dick Lynch rode into town with his hoss all of a lather and swore he'd jest outrun the wildest war-party that ever come down from the hills!"

"'Boys,' says Dick, 'they ain't neither Injuns nor white men! They're wild men, that's what! One of 'em's big as a grizzly b'ar, with no shirt on, and he's ridin' a hoss bigger'n a bull moose! One of the others is as ragged and ugly as him, but not so big, and wearin' a Apache headdress. T'other'n's got nothin' on but a painter's hide and a club and his hair and whiskers falls to his shoulders. When they seen me,' says Dick, 'they sot up awful yells and come for me like a gang of man-eatin' cannibals. I fogged it for town,' says Dick, warnin' everybody along the road to fort theirselves in their cabins."

"Well," says Esau, "when he says that, sech men as was left in town got their hosses and guns and they taken out up the road to meet the war-party before it got into town."

"Well, of all the fools!" I says. " Say, where's the new teacher?"

"The stage ain't arriv yet," says he. "The mayor and the band rode out to meet it at the Yaller Creek crossin' and escort her in to town in honor. They'd left before Dick brung news of the war-party."

"Come on!" I says to my warriors. "We likewise meets that stage!"

So we fogged it on through the town and down the road, and purty soon we heard music blaring ahead of us, and men yipping and shooting off their pistols like they does when they're celebrating, so we jedged they'd met the stage and was escorting it in.

"What you goin' to do now?" ast Bill, and about that time a noise bust out behind us and we looked back and seen that gang of Chawed Ear maniacs which had been chasing us dusting down the road after us, waving their Winchesters. I knowed they warn't no use to try to explain to them that we warn't no war-party of cannibals. They'd salivate us before we could git clost enough to make 'em hear what we was saying. So I yelled: "Come on. If they git her into town they'll fort theirselves agen us. We takes her now! Foller me!"

SO WE SWEPT DOWN THE road and around the bend and there was the stage coach coming up the road with the mayor riding alongside with his hat in his hand, and a whiskey bottle sticking out of each saddle bag and his hip pocket. He was orating at the top of his voice to make hisself heard above the racket the band was making. They was blowing horns and banging drums and twanging on Jews harps, and the hosses was skittish and shying and jumping. But we heard the mayor say, "—And so we welcomes you, Miss Devon, to our peaceful little community where life runs smooth and tranquil and men's souls is overflowin' with milk and honey—" And jest then we stormed around the bend and come tearing down on 'em with the mob right behind us yelling and cussing and shooting free and fervent.

The next minute they was the damndest mix-up you ever seen, what with the hosses bucking their riders off, and men yelling and cussing, and the hosses hitched to the stage running away and knocking the mayor off'n his hoss. We hit 'em like a cyclone and they shot at us and hit us over the head with their music horns, and right in the middle of the fray the mob behind us rounded the bend and piled up amongst us before they could check their hosses, and everybody was so confused they started fighting everybody else. Nobody knowed what it was all about but me and my warriors. But Chawed Ear's motto is: "When in doubt, shoot!"

So they laid into us and into each other free and hearty. And we was far from idle. Old Joshua was laying out his feller-townsmen right and left with his ellum club, saving Chawed Ear from education in spite of itself, and Glanton was beating the band over their heads with his six-shooter, and I was trompling folks in my rush for the stage.

The fool hosses had whirled around and started in the general direction of the Atlantic Ocean, and the driver and the shotgun guard couldn't stop 'em. But Cap'n Kidd overtook it in maybe a dozen strides and I left the saddle in a flying leap and landed on it. The guard tried to shoot me with his shotgun so I throwed it into a alder clump and he didn't let go of it quick enough so he went along with it.

I then grabbed the ribbons out of the driver's hands and swung them fool hosses around on their hind laigs, and the stage kind of revolved on one wheel for a dizzy instant, and then settled down again and we headed back up the road lickety-split and in a instant was right amongst the fracas that was going on around Bill and Joshua.

About that time I noticed that the driver was trying to stab me with a butcher knife so I kind of tossed him off the stage and there ain't no sense in him going around threatening to have me arrested account of him landing headfirst in the bass horn so it taken seven men to pull him out. He ought to watch where he falls when he gits throwed off of a stage going at a high run.

I also feels that the mayor is prone to carry petty grudges or he wouldn't be so bitter about me accidentally running over him with all four wheels. And it ain't my fault he was stepped on by Cap'n Kidd, neither. Cap'n Kidd was jest follering the stage because he knowed I was on it. And it naturally irritates him to stumble over somebody and that's why he chawed the mayor's ear.

As for them other fellers which happened to git knocked down and run over by the stage, I didn't have nothing personal agen 'em. I was jest rescuing Joshua and Bill which was outnumbered about twenty to one. I was doing them Chawed Ear idjits a favor, if they only knowed it, because in about another minute Bill would of started using the front ends of his six-shooters instead of the butts and the fight would of turnt into a massacre. Bill has got a awful temper.

Him and Joshua had did the enemy considerable damage but the battle was going agen 'em when I arriv on the field of carnage. As the stage crashed through the mob I reched down and got Joshua by the neck and pulled him out from under about fifteen men which was beating him to death with their gun butts and pulling out his whiskers by the handfulls and I slung him up on top of the other luggage. About that time we was rushing past the dogpile which Bill was the center of and I reched down and snared him as we went by, but three of the men which had holt of him wouldn't let go, so I hauled all four of 'em up onto the stage. I then handled the team with one hand and used the other'n to pull them idjits loose from Bill like pulling ticks off'n a cow's hide, and then throwed 'em at the mob which was chasing us.

MEN AND HOSSES PILED up in a stack on the road which was further messed up by Cap'n Kidd plowing through it as he come busting along after the stage, and by the time we sighted Chawed Ear again, our enemies was far behind us, though still rambunctious.

We tore through Chawed Ear in a fog of dust and the women and chillern which had ventured out of their shacks squalled and run back again, though they warn't in no danger. But Chawed Ear folks is pecooliar that way.

When we was out of sight of Chawed Ear I give the lines to Bill and swung down on the side of the stage and stuck my head in. They was one of the purtiest gals I ever seen in there, all huddled up in a corner and looking so pale and scairt I was afraid she was going to faint, which I'd heard Eastern gals has a habit of doing.

"Oh, spare me!" she begged. "Please don't scalp me!"

"Be at ease, Miss Devon," I reassured her. "I ain't no Injun, nor no wild man neither. Neither is my friends here. We wouldn't none of us hurt a flea. We're that refined and soft-hearted you wouldn't believe it—" At that instant a wheel hit a stump and the stage jumped into the air and I bit my tongue and roared in some irritation, "Bill, you condemned son of a striped polecat, stop this stage before I comes up there and breaks yore cussed neck!"

"Try, you beef headed lummox," he invites, but he pulled up the hosses and I taken off my hat and opened the door. Bill and Joshua clumb down and peered over my shoulder. Miss Devon looked tolerable sick. Maybe it was something she et.

"Miss Devon," I says, "I begs yore pardon for this here informal welcome. But you sees before you a man whose heart bleeds for the benighted state of his native community. I'm Breckinridge Elkins, of Bear Creek, where hearts is pure and motives is lofty, but culture is weak.

"You sees before you," says I, growing more enthusiastic about education the longer I looked at them big brown eyes of her'n, "a man which has growed up in ignorance. I cain't neither read nor write. Joshua here, in the painter skin, he cain't neither, and neither can Bill"

"That's a lie," says Bill. "I can read and—*ooomp!*" I'd kind of stuck my elbow in his stummick. I didn't want him to spile the effeck of my speech. Miss Devon was gitting some of her color back.

"Miss Devon," I says, "will you please ma'm come up to Bear Creek and be our schoolteacher?"

"Why," says she bewilderedly, "I came West expecting to teach at Chawed Ear, but I haven't signed any contract, and—"

"How much was them snake-hunters goin' to pay you?" I ast.

"Ninety dollars a month," says she.

"We pays you a hundred," I says. "Board and lodgin' free."

"Hell's fire," says Bill. "They never was that much hard cash money on Bear Creek."

"We all donates coon hides and corn licker," I snapped. "I sells the stuff in War Paint and hands the dough to Miss Devon. Will you keep yore snout out of my business."

"But what will the people of Chawed Ear say?" she wonders.

"Nothin'," I told her heartily. "I'll tend to *them!*"

"It seems so strange and irregular," says she weakly. "I don't know."

"Then it's all settled!" I says. "Great! Le's go!"

"Where?" she gasped, grabbing holt of the stage as I clumb onto the seat.

"Bear Creek!" I says. "Varmints and hoss-thieves, hunt the bresh! Culture is on her way to Bear Creek!" And we went fogging it down the road as fast as the hosses could hump it. Onst I looked back at Miss Devon and seen her getting pale again, so I yelled above the clatter of the wheels, "Don't be scairt, Miss Devon! Ain't nothin' goin' to hurt you. B. Elkins is on the job to perteck you, and I aim to be at yore side from now on!"

At this she said something I didn't understand. In fack, it sounded like a low moan. And then I heard Joshua say to Bill, hollering to make hisself heard, "Eddication my eye! The big chump's lookin' for a wife, that's what! Ten to one she gives him the mitten!"

"I takes that," bawled Bill, and I bellered, "Shet up that noise! Quit discussin' my private business so dern public! I—what's that?"

It sounded like firecrackers popping back down the road. Bill yelled, "Holy smoke, it's them Chawed Ear maniacs! They're still on our trail and they're gainin' on us!"

CUSSING HEARTILY I poured leather into them fool hosses, and jest then we hit the mouth of the Bear Creek trail and I swung into it. They'd never been a wheel on that trail before, and the going was tolerable rough. It was all Bill and Joshua could do to keep from gitting throwed off, and they was seldom more'n one wheel on the ground at a time. Naturally the mob gained on us and when we roared up into Bowie Knife Pass they warn't more'n a quarter mile behind us, whooping bodacious.

I pulled up the hosses beside the tree where Jack Sprague was still tied up to. He gawped at Miss Devon and she gawped back at him.

"Listen," I says, "here's a lady in distress which we're rescuin' from teachin' school in Chawed Ear. A mob's right behind us. This ain't no time to think about yoreself. Will you postpone yore sooicide if I turn you loose, and git onto this stage and take the young lady up the trail whilst the rest of us turns back the mob?"

"I will!" says he with more enthusiasm than he'd showed since we stopped him from hanging hisself. So I cut him loose and he clumb onto the stage.

"Drive on to Kiowa Canyon," I told him as he picked up the lines. "Wait for us there. Don't be scairt, Miss Devon! I'll soon be with you! B. Elkins never fails a lady fair!"

"Gup!" says Jack, and the stage went clattering and banging up the trail and me and Joshua and Bill taken cover amongst the big rocks that was on each side of the trail. The pass was jest a narrer gorge, and a lovely place for a ambush as I remarked.

Well, here they come howling up the steep slope yelling and spurring and shooting wild, and me and Bill give 'em a salute with our pistols. The charge halted plumb sudden. They knowed they was licked. They couldn't git at us because they couldn't climb the cliffs. So after firing a volley which damaged nothing but the atmosphere, they turnt around and hightailed it back towards Chawed Ear.

"I hope that's a lesson to 'em," says I as I riz. "Come! I cain't wait to git culture started on Bear Creek!"

"You cain't wait to git to sparkin' that gal," snorted Joshua. But I ignored him and forked Cap'n Kidd and headed up the trail, and him and Bill follered, riding double on Jack Sprague's hoss.

"Why should I deny my honorable intentions?" I says presently. "Anybody can see Miss Devon is already learnin' to love me! If Jack had *my* attraction for the fair sex, he wouldn't be luggin' around a ruint life. Hey, where's the stage?" Because we'd reched Kiowa Canyon and they warn't no stage.

"Here's a note stuck on a tree," says Bill. "I'll read it—well, for Lord's sake!" he yelped, "*Lissen to this*:

"'Dere boys: I've desided I ain't going to hang myself, and Miss Devon has desided she don't want to teach school at Bear Creek. Breck gives her the willies. She ain't altogther shore he's human. With me it's love at first site and she's scairt if she don't marry somebody Breck will marry her, and she says I'm the best looking prospeck she's saw so far. So we're heading for War Paint to git married.

Yores trooly, Jack Sprague.'"

"Aw, don't take it like that," says Bill as I give a maddened howl and impulsively commenced to rip up all the saplings in rech. "You've saved his life and brung him happiness!"

"And what have I brung me?" I yelled, tearing the limbs off a oak in a effort to relieve my feelings. "Culture on Bear Creek is shot to hell and my honest love has been betrayed! Bill Glanton, the next ranny you chase up into the Humbolts to commit sooicide he don't have to worry about gittin bumped off—I attends to it myself, personal!"

ABOUT THE ARTWORK

THE ARTWORK THAT appears at the start of each story is the art that appeared at the start of the story in its original appearance. Artists are as follows:

Frank McAleer - "The TNT Punch."

Amos Sewell - "The Sign of the Snake," "Blow the Chinks Down!," "Breed of Battle," "Dark Shanghai."

Rudolph Belarski - "Guns of the Mountain," "The Scalp Hunter," "A Gent from Bear Creek," "Cupid from Bear Creek," "The Riot at Cougar Paw," "The Apache Mountain War," "Pilgrims to the Pecos," "Pistol Politics," "Evil Deeds at Red Cougar," "High Horse Rampage."

L. Bjorklond - "Road to Bear Creek," "The Haunted Mountain."

Leslie Ross - "War on Bear Creek," "The Feud Buster," "'No Cowherders Wanted'," "Conquerin' Hero of the Humbolts," "Sharp's Gun Serenade."

Unknown - "Mountain Man."

CPSIA information can be obtained at www.ICGtesting.com
Printed in the USA
LVOW12*1743301014

411275LV00012B/503/A